PRAISE FOR

GIRL IN A BOX

"... The comprehensive yet expressive text is interspersed with the author's original translations of the poet's work ... Kocienda's work is buttressed by extensive proof of the clearly enormous amount of research underlying it, including photos, references, a family tree, a guide to Japanese naming conventions, a glossary, and a bibliography. A detailed work that effectively conveys the truths of an extraordinary life."

—Kirkus Reviews

"Jean vividly describes the literary circles of Japan in the early years of the 20th century and their bohemian and unconventional, even rebellious way of life. This book is a page-turner—it was pure delight to absorb myself in the life of this extraordinary woman and poet."

—Mia Kankimäki, bestselling author of *The Women I Think About at Night*

"In a series of sharply observed scenes, Jean Gordon Kocienda gives us Yosano Akiko whole: girl, woman, writer, wife, mother, widow. Fully imagined and emotionally true. A convincing and compulsively readable portrait."

—Gaye Rowley, author of *Yosano Akiko and The Tale of Genji*

"*Girl in a Box* is a huge accomplishment, and a pleasure to read. Kocienda—with her deep knowledge and poetic sensibility–brings this prickly, stubborn, passionate poet to life. Well done!"

—Katherine Govier, award-winning novelist and author of *The Printmaker's Daughter*

"… The author vividly captures this poet's ever-evolving quest to find her place during monumental historical shifts. Yosano's poetry is a prominent strand in the tapestry of this novel, with Gordon Kocienda proving especially adept at portraying the exchanges of verse between Yosano, her husband-to-be, and her rivals in a manner that evokes the poetic jousting found in the early 11th-century *Tale of Genji*, a classic that haunted Yosano for much of her life. *Girl in a Box* is a magical tale of a life lived in and for poetry."

—James Dorsey, Associate Professor of Japanese and Comparative Literature, Dartmouth College

"Magnificently researched, *Girl in a Box* recounts the story of a budding poet who defied convention charting her path to become an artist. Lyrical prose and scrupulous detail make Jean Gordon Kocienda's debut novel a winning read.

—Joan Gelfand, author of the award-winning *Outside Voices, a Memoir of the Berkeley Revolution*

"Graceful and delicately crafted, the historical novel *Girl in a Box* creates an ambiance and delicacy about a Japan I was unaware of. A culture and an era reveal an unfamiliar world, a world carved by the artistic talent of Jean Gordon Kocienda…"

—Linda Joy Myers, Ph.D., founder of the National Association of Memoir Writers, and author of the prize-winning historical novel *The Forger of Marseille*

"Akiko Yosano lived her life as a representative female poet and artist since the Meiji era in Japan. I sincerely hope and believe that the charm of Akiko will resonate with readers not only in English-speaking countries but also all over the world."

—Noboru Ota, Chairman, Yosano Akiko Club of Japan and Emeritus Professor, Tenri University

"*Girl in a Box* speaks directly to contemporary conversations about women's labor, care work, and the myth of balance."

—Margaret Dilloway, author of How to Be an American Housewife and *Tale of the Warrior Geisha*

"This biographical novel paints a lyrical and passionate picture of a gifted poet breaking free of everything that holds her back."

—Jonelle Patrick, author of *The Last Tea Bowl Thief*

"[A] beautifully written novel that is equally fascinating as character study of a complicated woman and artist, a love story, and an exploration of women in Japanese society during a turbulent time of change."

—Sheri T. Joseph, author of *Edge of the Known World,* winner Best New Voice in Fiction by the Independent Book Publishers Association and the American Fiction Awards

"Kocienda's lyrical prose is captivating … *Girl in a Box: A Novel* is a stunning debut!"

—Lora J. Chilton, author of *1666: A Novel*

"If you enjoy historical fiction based on real people, you'll love this tale of passion, poetry, and the power of words."

—Kate Shanahan, author of *Tangled Spirits* and *The Iron Palace*

GIRL IN A BOX

THE TANGLED LIFE OF JAPANESE POET, YOSANO AKIKO

A Novel

JEAN GORDON KOCIENDA

Sibylline
Press

Sibylline Press

Copyright © 2026 by Jean Gordon Kocienda
All Rights Reserved.

Published in the United States by Sibylline Press,
an imprint of All Things Book LLC, California.

Sibylline Press is dedicated to publishing the
brilliant work of women authors ages 50 and older.
www.sibyllinepress.com

ISBN Trade: 9798897400126
eBook ISBN: 9798897400133
Library of Congress Control Number: 2025940868

Cover Design: Alicia Feltman
Book Production: Aaron Laughlin

This is a work of historical fiction based on a real life. Descriptions, settings, dialogue, and some characters are products of the author's imagination and should not be taken as fact.

Sibylline
Press

GIRL
IN A
BOX

THE TANGLED LIFE
OF JAPANESE POET,
YOSANO AKIKO

A Novel

JEAN GORDON
KOCIENDA

Hako-Iri Musume (箱入り娘): (Late nineteenth – early twentieth century Japan) Literally, "daughter (or girl) in a box"; a sheltered daughter, protected from the outside world like a fragile doll until old enough to marry.

On Names and Translations

In this book, Japanese names are presented family name first, according to convention: ("Yosano" is a family name, "Akiko" is a given name).

Pen names were common in Akiko's day, but pose challenges for storytellers. Yosano Akiko's given name at birth was Sho; she assumed the name Akiko when she was about twenty-two. Though Tekkan reverted to his birth name Hiroshi around that time, the name Tekkan is used throughout this book for the sake of clarity. Kōno's pen name was Tetsunan, but the family name Kōno is used to differentiate him from other characters with similar names in this book.

The suffixes -*san* and -*sama* are polite titles; -*chan* is familiar. In the Kansai region where Akiko grew up, -*han* is another informal alternative, so Akiko's family sometimes called her "Shoko-han."

There is a glossary of Japanese words at the end of this book.

See the Bibliography for translation sources and recommendations for further reading. Unless otherwise indicated or implied through context, all poems are Akiko's and all translations are the author's.

CONTENTS

I: FIREBIRD

1900, Sho is twenty-two years old
Sakai, Japan

消えむものか歌よむ人の夢とそはそは夢ならむさて消えむものか

Will it all disappear?

Was it just a poet's dream, nothing more?

One January evening in 1900, as the wind from the ocean made people on the train platform dance to keep warm and the conductor turn up his collar and blow into his hands, a well-dressed woman of about twenty stepped off the train. Her given name was Sho, but the world would come to know her as Akiko. She was not beautiful in the classic sense—her chin was too square, her thick hair resisted being pulled back in an orderly bun, and the corners of her mouth turned down—but her eyes were dark and thoughtful.

Her little brother Chūsaburo had talked her into coming to a New Year party hosted by the Kansai Young Men's Literary Society, but he was running late, and now she was, apart from the maid, quite on her own.

Dusk was settling over the busy street in front of the train station. Red paper lanterns swayed from noodle stands and a group of men in long coats and fedoras passed by on their way to toast the New Year with clients, their breath misting the cold air. Ladies in fur stoles and red and white holiday kimonos glimmered like dashes of bright paint in the fading light. Despite her worries, Sho caught her breath.

She imagined the scene as the beginning of a great novel, or the first line of a poem. This sort of imagining was more than a habit; it was compulsive, like chanting a sutra to keep evil spirits away. She had never known a time in her life when she had not done this, but she told no one about it. She didn't have any friends to speak of, and even if she had, she preferred to keep it to herself.

With her maid trailing behind her, she made for the Inn of Long Life, an old hotel on the sand at the beachfront Hamadera Park. Rickshaw drivers called out to her as she passed, but she didn't want a ride. She was in no hurry to face a roomful of writers—in fact, her stomach was churning.

She *was* curious, though, and Chūsaburo, who was a member of the Literary Society, had said they were curious about her. Her poems were appearing in literary magazines, and the community was small enough that the family name Hō had brought inquiries his way.

"I'll introduce you around," her brother had said. "We won't stay long." Anything seemed possible to him, but Sho had been sure their parents wouldn't allow it. Unmarried daughters of merchants in this traditional town did not socialize with men, and she was accustomed to being locked in her room at night once her chores were finished. *Girl-in-a-Box*, they called it.

Years ago, when Sho was small, a girl in her neighborhood had been trapped in her own "box" when the family brewery caught fire. Sho sometimes imagined the girl hammering on the locked bedroom door with her fists, begging for help, until heat and smoke choked her life away.

To Sho, the world was an unsympathetic place. She was a third daughter, born into a family that needed a second son. The situation had been urgent enough that as a newborn she was secreted off to an aunt's house, to be kept out of her mother's arms until Chūsaburo arrived three years later.

Sho sometimes wondered if her ill-timed entrance into the world explained her parents' odd treatment of her. They had dressed her in boyish clothes when she was small, and kept her hair short and cropped close to her head. Standing at the edge of the girls' schoolyard, she had watched jealously as her classmates ran about in pretty kimonos, flower combs holding up their long hair. Her quilted *hanten* jacket was brown and drab, like a grandfather in a school play, while her classmates' hantens were bright red or blue. This is how she knew, without anyone having to tell her, and without knowing her crime, that she was guilty.

Yet there was something else she knew. This knowledge had been nudging at her since she was very small, insistent as a cat, until she accepted it as her own: she was intelligent. Gifted, even. She was faster and more accurate with the abacus than her classmates; she could sew faster; she had a facility with the written word, and a boundless imagination. She had to fight not to sigh audibly when her classmates faltered in their recitations. While they struggled to learn elementary *kanji* characters, she was teaching herself to read classical literature and memorizing large sections of important works. No wonder the corners of her mouth turned down in a frown while her eyes grew dark and deep. She was solemn and her mouth was shut, but in her mind, the lights were shining bright.

Crossing the threshold into the inn, Sho tensed at the sound of clattering dishes and loud voices. Servers carrying trays of drinks and finger foods brushed past her, greeting her with a hurried "*Irasshaimase!*" as she slipped out of her *zori* sandals and stepped up onto the raised floor. She hesitated, and might have turned on her heel and fled, if a young man had not come forward.

"Hello! Are you here for the party?" With his Western suit coat and bowtie, he looked ready for a wedding. For a moment, Sho wondered if she had come to the wrong place.

"I—the Kansai Young Men's Literary—" she faltered.

"The same!" beamed the man, bowing deeply. "Taku Gangetsu at your service. Well, that is my pen name."

Sho knew she should introduce herself, but she hesitated. Her family name Hō, or "Firebird," was unusual—some neighbors even whispered that her ancestors came from Korea—and the oddness was compounded by her one-syllable first name, which had no music or feminine softness. She drew a breath. "My name is Hō Sho. I am—"

"Ah, Hō-san, wonderful! I thought perhaps you might be!" Gangetsu rocked back and forth on his heels happily, hands clasped behind his back. "I am a friend of Chūsaburo. Delighted! Allow me to introduce you around."

He escorted her into a room where several groups of young men stood on the *tatami* rice mats around a long, low table lined with bottles of *saké*, beer, and finger foods. There were no familiar faces, and no women. As he introduced her to two men near the doorway, Sho's knees trembled.

The first man was thin, with wire-rimmed glasses, a boyish face, and coarse clothes. "Kōno Tetsunan is my pen name," he said. "My father oversees Kakuōji Temple."

"Ah, yes, I know it," Sho managed. Kakuōji was not far from her family's confectionery business. "By the way," she added, "does everyone use a pen name?" Maybe she could use one, too.

Kōno and his companion glanced at each other, suppressing smiles. Perhaps that was rude.

"Not everyone uses a pen name," the other man said. "But it is the fashion. And it offers a modicum of discretion for our families."

He bowed, the expensive silk of his robe reflecting the electric lights. "You're from Surugaya Confectionery? My mother has been going there for years; she loves *yōkan* sweets. My father owns the kimono shop down the street."

"We're neighbors!" said Kōno warmly, crossing his arms and sliding his hands into his wide sleeves. "I know your brother Chūsaburo," he said. "Where is he?"

Of course, everyone knows Chu. "I think he is coming later. I came only to say hello. I must go soon." She took a step backward, swaying slightly.

"Please, don't hurry away," said Kōno, looking alarmed. "We've read your poems. We're impressed."

"I'd like some for our literary magazine," the other man agreed. "I'm the editor. We want more female contributors, especially talented ones like you."

"Oh, they're nothing," said Sho, and then, desperate to change the subject, she looked at Kōno. "Are you a poet?"

He looked simultaneously smug and embarrassed. "I'm an old friend of the poet Yosano Tekkan. Perhaps you have heard of him?"

She had. He was making a splash with his swashbuckling, romantic poetry.

"He lives in Tokyo now, but we went to temple school together in Kyoto as kids."

"Will you be staying with the temple?" Sho asked.

A shadow flitted across Kōno's face. "I am the eldest son, so I must enter the priesthood soon." Then he shrugged. "The temple life does give one plenty of ideas for poetry."

Sho imagined him in a great hall before a carved Buddha. Asking for wisdom and guidance, perhaps. Lighting a candle and ringing a bell, then bowing his head in prayer. *The gods would like such a man,* she thought. *They would listen to him.*

"We spend many hours in contemplation, of course, and in the winter, I think of anything to take my mind off the cold."

"I always wondered how monks can sit still for so long," said Sho, feeling suddenly reckless. "I would expect your legs to fall off after kneeling for two hours."

"Yes, that used to bother me, but I hardly notice anymore." He grimaced. "In the summer, it's worse, of course. Mosquitoes!"

At that moment, Gangetsu approached them with a gangly, nervous-looking man with a mustache and glasses, whose name Sho immediately forgot.

"This is Hō Sho, Chūsaburo's sister," said Gangetsu.

The man bowed nervously. "It's nice to meet you. Your brother is a good friend."

"Are you in school?" asked Sho, shy again.

"Yes, I'm studying medicine," he cleared his throat.

"How interesting," said Sho. She didn't know what else to say.

"Well!" said Kōno. "Let's get something to drink, shall we?"

But Sho was exhausted. "I should be going," she said, starting for the door. The others bowed, looking surprised.

"You're not leaving already, are you?" Gangetsu chased after her, stockinged feet slipping on the gleaming wood floors, as she hopped into her *zori* sandals in the entryway and murmured an apology. The maid, who had taken a seat, leapt up to get her shawl.

"Well, we'll be looking for your poems, then!" he called behind her as she fled into the darkness.

Once she had left the lights of the inn behind her, Sho paused for the maid to catch up. Her heart was pounding. *A room full of poets! And Kōno!* She tested saying his name aloud into the night. Earnest, handsome, and spiritual, he was like a character from her beloved *Tale of Genji*, the meandering classical novel. The roar of the ocean behind her filled her head, thunderous as spirit voices. *Kōno!*

"Miss! Do you think it was rude to leave so quickly?" asked the maid, trotting beside her.

"Probably," Sho said. But she was thinking, *what a glorious night!*

Back home, safely locked in her room, Sho bent over a stack of poetry magazines, looking for poems by Kōno.

She found one—it seemed lovely now, though she hadn't thought much of it when she read it the other day. It was one thing to read a poem in a magazine by a stranger and another thing to meet him, and to find that he is handsome, warm, and kind. She wondered what he was doing right now. Perhaps he was kneeling in the chilly hall at Kakuōji, composing verses with brush and ink. Perhaps incense was rising around his head in shimmering silver threads. She imagined taking his calloused hands in hers and kissing them.

She went to her desk and drew out a few sheets of writing paper, ground some ink, and dipped her brush. Since she was old enough to read, she had been filling her head with old stories. She had read everything in her father's library, including all his Japanese and Chinese classical texts. She favored court intrigue, romance, and princely poetry over military history. Her favorite was the great *Tale of Genji*, written by a court woman, Lady Murasaki Shikibu, during the Heian Period more than eight hundred years ago. It was customary for new lovers in that golden age to exchange letters, so Sho decided to compose a letter to Kōno now. Her frame of reference was more fairytale than modern world, so the letter she wrote to him was very odd indeed.

> *I count it an immense delight, one not to be forgotten, to have had the honor of finding myself in the presence of your tender and most solicitous voice and treated without the reserve that my gender might normally provoke—you, whose name alone was known to me until this day, and before whose poems I had long trembled, sensing therefrom how great must be your manly powers ...*

She addressed the letter to Kōno and asked one of the maids to deliver it. Then she went back to her place at the counter in Surugaya to stuff *mochi* balls with red *adzuki* bean paste, roll them in powdered sugar or sesame, wrap them in bamboo leaves, and daydream.

When Kōno did not answer her letter immediately, she began to fret. She had no experience with men. *Am I a fool? I barely say a word out loud, but when I write, I say too much.*

Chūsaburo had first goaded Sho into writing poetry six years earlier, when she was sixteen. She was a hungry reader, so he brought her literary magazines to keep her occupied when business was slow. Accustomed to the classical literature of her father's library, she had found popular poetry almost laughable. *I could write better than that,* she thought, tossing one issue after another onto a pile.

She was absorbed in such a magazine one day when she realized that Chūsaburo was standing before her. She looked up.

"You should submit something," he said. At thirteen, he was starting to get the stretched look of a budding adolescent, as if he slept on a rack at night, pulled from both ends, so each day his legs were a bit longer, his cheekbones sharper.

Sho shook her head. "I couldn't. Mother would never let me."

"Why does she have to know? *Literary Club* prints poems that people send them. Look," he said, pulling the magazine from her hand. "In the back, there's a writing prompt. Every month there's a new one."

"I know *that*," Sho said, affecting indifference, but her eyes went to where he pointed.

"This month it's *koto*."

That was easy enough. Along with dance and tea ceremony, Sho had been plucking away at the classical zither-style instrument for the past year as part of her finishing school requirements. She could write a poem about a koto. But submit it for publication? "I don't think so, Chu. Thanks."

He shrugged, gave her an easygoing shove, and walked to the back of the shop, where a sliding door led to the inner house.

Later that afternoon when she closed the ledger, Sho paused, listening. Apart from kitchen noises, it was quiet. She pulled a scrap of paper toward her, pursed her lips thoughtfully, then dipped her brush:

露しけき葎か宿の琴の音に秋を添へたる鈴むしのこゑ

To dew-wet grass and koto music at an inn
Add the bell-voices of crickets in autumn

She scrutinized her work. Not bad: it had thirty-one syllables as required in the classical *tanka* form, it used a seasonal reference, and it included the prompt word. Satisfied, she invented an excuse to go to the post office the next day. Her heart thumped as she counted out coins for the clerk. When she confided in Chūsaburo that night, he was delighted.

One afternoon a few weeks later, he exploded into the shop. His school hat was sitting back on his head and his rucksack thumped against his back as he ran, sending the cat skittering. "Big Sister, look!" He was waving a magazine. "Look! They published your poem!"

"What?!" Sho jumped from her seat and grabbed at the September 1895 issue of *Literary Club*, but he whirled away and rifled through the pages.

"Wait—look—here!" he said breathlessly. Sho snatched it from him. Her chest heaved as she read: "... *the bell-voices of crickets in autumn*," followed by her name: *Hō Shoko* (she had daringly added "*ko*" to her name), *Sakai City*. She looked up at Chūsaburo, eyes shining. *Amazing! I'm published! Mother will be furious!*

Eventually, Sho's secret leaked, but her poems were already published in two or three magazines by the time a neighbor innocently asked her mother Tsuné about it. Tsuné had been upset, of course, but Sho's father, who fancied himself an intellectual, couldn't hide his pleasure. She was twenty-two years old now, after all. When called to atone for her sins, Chūsaburo had insisted that the idea was his. And now, in 1900, he had even talked them into letting her attend the Literary Society's New Year Party. *Good old Chu.*

One day, while Sho was folding mochi into bamboo leaf wrappers, someone ducked under the shop curtain. Silhouetted against the street, it was Kōno, tall and straight in his monk's robe. With a sharp intake of breath, Sho put a hand to her hair and wiped sesame powder from her arms and face.

"Good afternoon, Hō-san," he said.

As she greeted him from the counter, she thought, *did you receive my letters? Why didn't you respond?*

He hesitated. "I—uh—have an order to place for a temple event next week. My mother sent me."

"Of course," Sho said, pulling an order form from under the counter. *A true poet would have answered my letters. He would have sent me poems.* She couldn't help but think it.

He cleared his throat as she calculated the order, flicking abacus beads with an efficient index finger and thumb: click, click, click. Her mother, helping another customer, glanced in their direction as Sho handed a copy of the order to Kōno. As soon as she looked away, he leaned forward and began to speak quietly.

"I mentioned my friend Tekkan, the poet, at the party, remember? I got a letter from him. He wants you to submit one of your poems to his magazine." He pulled a crumpled piece of paper from the bag at his waist and handed it to her. "Look, he wrote a poem just for you."

いまだ見ぬ君にはあれど名のゆかし晶子のおもと歌送れかし
Though I have never met you, your name is known to me
Lady Shoko, send me a poem!

The hairs on Sho's arms stood on end. She tried to picture Tekkan Sensei. His patriotic, romantic poetry had earned him the nickname *Tiger Tekkan*, so the image she conjured was of a battle-worn samurai standing on a hilltop at twilight, hair falling from its binding, one hand on his sword. She tucked the letter into her bosom and turned away, too distracted to remember her manners.

That night, locked in her room, she rushed to her writing pile. She must not disappoint Tekkan Sensei, she thought, but her frown deepened as she searched through her papers. *Nothing is good enough.* She had until midnight, when the electricity went off, to write more. She would send her best to him in the morning. She opened her notebook.

With practice, her writing had become better and faster. She could work herself into a state of intense concentration, almost a trance. It was like pushing a boat from shore to the middle of a stream where the current ran fast. In that slightly dangerous, out-of-control place, she could hear the music more clearly, the music of words.

Tanka poems were like *haiku*, but with thirty-one syllables instead of seventeen, arranged in syllable groups of five-seven-five-seven-seven. Tanka was older than haiku, and more beautiful, she thought. She collected ideas as she went about her day like threads of silk: the coolness of mochi in her hands, dust on the street, a woman's hair comb, the temple bell at dusk. At night she laid them on her loom and wove them together, bits of gold and silver glinting in the light as she counted out syllables on her fingers. When the electricity went off with a clank that night, she sat for a moment, mid-line, and in the darkness saw sparks on her hands.

She was standing in the Surugaya Confectionery kitchen a month later, hair pulled back in a kerchief, apron covering her skirt front, when she learned that Tekkan Sensei had chosen two of her poems for his *Myōjo* magazine. She read her name twice to be sure, and confidence began to glow inside her. She had a voice. A way with words. Others recognized it in her. She may be an unwanted daughter; she may not be beautiful; but she *had* something. *She could write.*

II: GIRL-IN-A-BOX

1889, Sho is twelve

いさめますか道ときますかさとしますか宿世のよそに血を召し
ませな

Are you so wise, so holy?

Come stay in this transient world,

Taste its blood

She might not have questioned her fate if she hadn't just watched her half-sister Hana die. A doctor had given Hana a "wasting" diagnosis when, stuck in an unhappy arranged marriage, she fell ill. She had asked to be brought home to Surugaya, where she died, barely thirty years old. Sho still didn't really understand what had happened.

The trouble with Hana had started when Sho was twelve. She remembered standing at the work counter after school one afternoon, a bar of yōkan jelly in one hand and a bamboo leaf wrapper in the other, when she noticed that Hana was missing. *Come to think of it, she's been missing a lot recently.* She rubbed her neck with the back of an arm as she puzzled.

As Hana's absences became more frequent, Sho formed a theory. There was a certain cousin—an apprentice blacksmith with strong arms and broad shoulders—who had been visiting the shop frequently of late. Whenever he appeared, Hana flushed pink. He would hover politely, talking about the weather or the latest gossip, until the confectionery apprentice Sadashichi looked away. Then, he would make a face at Hana or lunge for something off the counter, and she would giggle and swat him with her towel.

Are they in love? Sho wondered. She had read about forbidden romance in *The Tale of Genji*, and though she was murky about the details, she knew that love had something to do with poetry, stealthy night visits, and the pathos of being apart. Now Sho imagined her half-sister in her cousin's arms, leaning against a wall in an alley as cherry petals floated around them.

Hana deserved happiness. Her life had not been easy. She had been born in secret to her father Sōshichi's first wife not long after their divorce. Because children were the property of their fathers, Hana's mother did not tell him about the baby. Instead, in a futile effort to keep her hidden, she shuttled the baby between family and friends. By the time Sōshichi discovered and brought Hana to Surugaya, it was her fourth home, and Tsuné was her third stepmother.

She had been a pretty girl, "a peony behind the shop curtain," Tsuné had called her, so she was kept at the front of the store. Tsuné sometimes even made her stand out on the street, luring potential customers inside with yōkan samples and her sweet smile.

Plain-faced, quiet Sho stayed in back. She was better at math, so when Tsuné became sickly, Sho—even at twelve—was entrusted with Surugaya bookkeeping. After school, and on days when shop duties required her to stay home from school altogether, she sat at the ledger, adding columns and chasing down missing *sen*. A mess accumulated around her: a pile of literary magazines appeared alongside the ink well and electric lamp, receipts and bills stacked up next to a box of official stamps and vermillion ink, and a newspaper saturated with ink splotches was left on a bundle of extra bamboo wrappers. There were trays and wooden boxes on the floor around and behind the desk. Sho floated in the middle on a cushion like a fisherman in a crowded harbor.

She was sitting like that one day, imagining the riverlike silk of Heian court ladies' kimonos and tilting her abacus back and forth dreamily, when Sadashichi poked his head out from the kitchen. The aroma of rice and adzuki beans simmering over *kamado* stoves filled the air.

"Where is Hana?" he asked.

She jumped. "I don't know."

"Do you think she—?" he began.

"I don't know," Sho repeated, a little crossly. She got up, went to the front of the store, and stuck her head under the curtain to look up and down the street. When she ducked back in, Sadashichi was looking at her, twisting a towel around one hand. She stomped past him to the desk.

"How are the accounts looking this month?" he ventured, a tuft of hair standing at an angle from his head. The flesh of his face was like steamed mochi, and there was a spot of powdered sugar on his forehead.

"They're all right," Sho said. Her father spent too much on evening entertainment and art, but he didn't need to know that.

"You don't mind? Doing the books, I mean?"

"No, I like numbers," she said. It wasn't numbers she minded but being forced to skip school. She had just graduated from elementary school and had been allowed to attend the well-thought-of Sakai Girls' Middle School, whose curriculum focused on sewing and home economics. She preferred history, literature, and mathematics, but girls had few options, and she had little hope of attending high school.

"Poor Sho," he said. "You drew the short straw, didn't you?"

Her frown deepened. "What do you mean?"

"Well, it's rude of me to say, but you are doing a lot of the Surugaya work these days."

She held his gaze for a moment, then looked down at the ledger. Being alone with Sadashichi was getting uncomfortable. Her monthly bleeding had begun, so Tsuné had given her permission to grow out her hair and wear more girlish clothes. Now he looked at her in a different way. He might be sizing her up as a wife; he may even have spoken to her father about it already. She was too young to marry, but she was not too young for plans to be made. Some of Sho's classmates were already spoken for. The apprentice was fifteen years older than her, and she had always thought of him as an uncle. She could not imagine marrying him. The prospect of a life rolling mochi balls as Sadashichi's wife filled her with despair.

Sho's theory about Hana had proved correct. The romance was discovered in due time and a more suitable marriage partner—a widowed shopkeeper—was found.

The night before the engagement ceremony, Hana wept like a child. Moonlight slanted through the window, frosting her head as Sho lay next to her. Hana's unbound hair tumbled around her, making Sho think of the long hair of court ladies. Never cut, their tresses flowed to the floor like heavy, black waterfalls. Sho's own hair was getting longer, and it was even thicker than Hana's. Someday, it might be pretty.

"I cannot, I *cannot* marry that man!" Hana wailed. "He's old and disgusting! Does Papa have no *feelings*?"

Sho touched her shoulder, but Hana knocked her hand away, crouching on the mattress like a dog. "I'll run away. I'll go tonight. Don't tell them where I am."

"Where will you go?"

"I'll go to Auntie in Kobe."

"She can't hide you," Sho said. "She couldn't lie to Mother."

The fire in Hana's eyes flickered; she knew it was true. "I'll go to an inn," she said defiantly. "I have money saved."

"Hana ..." It was impossible. Someone would recognize her wherever she ran. Secrets didn't last long around here. The husband Sōshichi had chosen was kind, even if he was old for her. He would take care of her, and she would adjust—or so he must think.

Tsuné had arranged for a hairdresser and makeup specialist to come in the morning before the engagement ceremony. *It will not help much*, Sho thought: her sister's face would be as swollen as if she had been in a fistfight.

"Poor Hana, it's not fair, is it?" Sho whispered. "Luck has never shined on you."

Nor on me, she thought. *I'm the one with the short straw, am I not?* At least Hana had been happy for a while. At least she was getting out of Surugaya.

That's when a thought pushed its way to the front of her mind for the first time: *I could say no.* It had been as clear as though someone had spoken it aloud. She didn't have to marry. There was honor in being a spinster daughter. She could care for her parents and keep the store without marrying Sadashichi or anyone else. Her parents would value that. With no husband or children, maybe she could even continue school.

She looked down again at Hana's dark head, sunken back against her pillow, face turned away. She was hiccoughing and moaning; the storm had passed for now.

At least I would own my own body and soul.

III: THE BUTTERFLY

1900, Sho is twenty-two

うすものの二尺のたもとすべりおちて 蛍ながるる夜風の青き

Sliding down the long silk sleeve of her summer kimono
The firefly floats into the blue night

S ummer was the season of festivals. For three days at the end of
July, everything in town shut down as teams of men, sweaty legs
and arms shining in the sun, transported the Sumiyoshi gods in
gold-covered shrines five miles from their home temple in Osaka to
Shukuin Temple in Sakai. Brightly painted wagons festooned with lanterns, vermillion weavings, bells, and carvings carried the gods down the
crowded street. A golden phoenix rode on top of one, outspread wings
and tail lurching drunkenly from side to side as it was borne along like
a barge on a swollen river.

The wagon pullers wore headbands emblazoned with their shrine
affiliations: Daikai-hama, Shukuin-hama, Kumano-hama. Criers with
fans stood on wagon fronts, chanting *Oissha! Oissha!* in time with the

drums to keep the pullers in sync. The excitement brought waves of exultant, sweaty customers to Surugaya in search of shaved ice, sweets, and shade.

These were some of the busiest days of the year, and everyone pitched in. Sadashichi never seemed to sleep; when Sho shuffled yawning into the kitchen around dawn, he was already pounding steaming mortars of rice with a heavy wooden mallet into glossy mochi. Even Sōshichi helped hang fresh curtains, unfurl long straw mats across the flagstones, and spread brightly colored felt on benches.

After a long day of work, when the shadows lengthened and the heat began to ease, Sho escaped into the courtyard with a cup of cool barley tea, a letter from Kōno, and the new issue of *Myōjo*. She dangled her sore legs over the porch edge and let her wooden *geta* sandals fall onto the hard-packed ground. First, she read Kōno's letter. Their correspondence had achieved an awkward cadence. Sho sent him poetry, and Kōno responded conversationally. Her ardor for him had cooled; his writing failed to inspire her, but he was an amiable source of gossip about other poets in their community. She turned to the magazine. Last month, *Myōjo* had called out Sho and another girl, Yamakawa Tomiko of Kyoto, as "promising new female poets." In this month's issue, beneath two of Sho's tanka, was one by Tomiko:

君よ手をあてても見ませこの胸に奇しきひびきのあるは何なる
Oh, touch me
What is this strange feeling in my chest?

Flirtatious, Sho thought. She made a mental note to send Tomiko a postcard introducing herself. Just then, her mother called her for her turn in the bath, her last chance before the busy night ahead.

The approaching drums resonated in her bones as she washed herself next to the wooden tub and tossed buckets of water over her head. In the steaming bath a few minutes later, she watched the surface ripple

in time with the drums. She closed her eyes and sank down into the water, but only for a moment, as the procession was drawing close. She jumped out, twisting her long, wet hair in a bun on top of her head and folding her cotton *yukata* summer kimono over her still-wet body. She grabbed her apron and ran to the front of the store, just in time to see the procession pass.

About two weeks later, a young woman walked into Surugaya, dressed in the white top and rust-colored *hakama* skirt of an expensive Kyoto girls' school.

"My name is Yamakawa ... Yamakawa Tomiko," the girl said, gripping her bag.

"Ah! You are—"

"Are you Hō-san?"

They both broke into smiles. Tomiko bowed low.

"I wasn't expecting you!" Sho jumped up. A fellow writer—and a girl her age—what a thrill!

"I got your postcard. School break started today. I'm sorry, dropping in unannounced like this, but I wanted to meet you," Tomiko began.

"I'm so happy you came!" Sho led her into the parlor in the back of the shop.

Her mother seemed pleased that she had made such a well-heeled friend. "Sho says you are a schoolteacher, how admirable," Tsuné said as the maid poured tea and set out a dish of chestnut yōkan.

"Oh, no." Tomiko lowered her eyes. "I'm just helping. My parents want me to return home now that I've graduated." She placed the teacup in her left palm, turned it twice, and raised it to her mouth delicately. Clearly, she had been trained in tea ceremony. Sho raised an eyebrow.

Left alone to talk, Tomiko dropped her guard. The two compared notes on writing, books, and gossip about the Kansai writers' group. Tomiko told Sho about her hometown, north over the mountains on the Japan Sea. In summer it was unbearably hot, and in winter, the snow was heavy and wet. It was little more than a fishing village on an estuary, "a briny *swamp*," she sighed. "Rice paddies surrounded by rotting seaweed and smelly *washi* paper factories."

They lived in a villa with many servants, she explained, and as an unmarried daughter, she had no freedom. She had escaped to her married sister's house in Kyoto to attend school, and after graduating had devised an excuse to stay a few months more.

"You'll go home at the end of summer, then?"

"Not if I can help it." Tomiko's shoulders sagged. "But I don't know how much longer I can stall." She lowered her voice. "I wanted to ask you something."

Sho glanced over her shoulder to make sure they were alone, then leaned in.

"I heard from Kōno that the teacher from Tokyo is coming to Osaka for a speaking engagement."

"The teacher from Tokyo ... you mean Tekkan Sensei? Oh!" Sho felt her face go pink.

"There's a get-together next week at the Hirai Inn in Osaka with some local writers. I don't want to be the only girl there. Please say you'll come."

It was already hot when Sho and her maid arrived at the Hirai Inn in Osaka's busy riverside Kitahama District. The window in the stuffy hotel room was open, and guests fanned themselves as they sat around a low table crowded with dictionaries, literary magazines, ashtrays, and teacups. Tomiko was absent. Seated next to Kōno, reclined against a pillar like a Buddha, was a handsome man with high cheekbones and a cleft chin. Tekkan Sensei, surely.

He was so charismatic, it was hard to look away. He had the air of a man who has made his fortune and solved life's challenges. But Sho knew his life was complicated. According to Kōno, he and his pregnant fiancée were arguing over money. He had been taking loans from his future father-in-law to fund *Myōjo*. He insisted on printing his magazine on high-quality paper and commissioning art nouveau cover illustrations. He took out expensive advertisements in newspapers. This trip to Kansai to build his community of followers was yet another expense.

"Miss Hō!" called Tekkan as she came in, "I was hoping to meet you! Do sit down." He motioned to an empty spot next to him; but she shook her head shyly and sat close to the door instead. He leaned forward to pick up his fan, the V of his collar opening at his throat to reveal warm brown skin.

Kōno introduced Sho to the people around the table. She remembered the medical student from the New Year party; his name was Kyōan. There was a new woman named Masako, and another face she recognized from the party: a well-coiffed man named Tenmin, the one whose father owned the kimono store.

"Tenmin has been immensely helpful in promoting *Myōjo*," Tekkan said. "He has the local connections. He is from Sakai, too."

Tenmin, his manicured hands folded, lowered his head. "I've just moved to Osaka," he clarified. "Last year I started a business selling blankets and futons. My father is helping me. I want to write professionally, but ..." He picked up his empty teacup and set it down again. "Well, I have bills to pay."

Masako poured him fresh tea as Kyōan nodded. "Not many of us have the luxury to be a full-time poet."

Sho was thinking the same thing.

Kōno laughed. "Unless you're already poor. No wonder so many monks are poets!"

"Anyone can write poetry, just for joy or understanding," said Tekkan. "We live, we write." Then he returned to his lecture.

"Traditional poetry, especially tanka, is in danger of being overwhelmed by Western culture," he told the group gravely. "It must be protected, but persisting with the old tropes dooms it to irrelevancy. The best of Western ideas: individuality, romanticism, impressionism, democracy"—he tapped his fan on the table as he said each word—"these must be adapted, used to *invigorate* tanka, not replace it. Instead of cherry blossoms and tea ceremony, we should write about what we *feel*. We should dare to write about modern things: streetcars, telegraph wires. Or modern love, children, politics, even *sex*. We must say something new. Saving tanka is nothing short of a patriotic duty," he said, and he met the eyes of each of his followers in turn. They nodded solemnly as fans swayed and cigarette smoke curled toward the ceiling.

As he spoke, Tekkan's eyes kept coming back to Sho. Perhaps it was her tight *obi* sash, or the smothering heat of the room, but she felt short of breath. She fanned herself weakly.

Another guest arrived, obliging Sho to scoot closer to him, so she angled her knees away as she resettled.

"Hō-san," he said, taking the opportunity to address her directly, "I hear you've made quite a study of the classics." With his fan, he gestured toward Kōno to indicate the source of his information.

Sho looked down and nodded. "I just read what we have at home lying about. I haven't had any formal education in the classics. And I didn't read them in order ..."

She wanted to tell him that she loved the Shining Genji, favorite son of the emperor, from *The Tale of Genji*. The prince spent his life in amorous affairs, poetry writing, and court intrigue. She adored the sweet sadness of his many lovers, each one beautiful but flawed. His stepmother Fujitsubo, consumed by guilt after bearing Genji's son, had withdrawn from public life. His legitimate wife was aloof and cold. The girl Murasaki, the embodiment of feminine virtues, suffered from sorrow and jealousy. The lonely Yugao died young. What a flawed, believable world. Each of these women was trapped in some way, and Sho felt for them, as she was trapped, too. She wondered if Tekkan knew these stories.

"If you read what you love just for the joy of it, so much the better. Is it true that you memorized the entire *Shin Kokinshu?*" he asked, referring to a work compiled in the 1200s which, with its older siblings, the *Kokinshu* and the *Manyōshu*, constituted the most influential anthologies of Japanese poetry.

He knew the classics! "Oh, well, I read it many times over, and before I knew it ..."

"You accidentally memorized it? That's an incredible thing. I'm glad it was the *Shin Kokinshū*. It's a lot better than the *Kokinshū*," he said, eyes twinkling. "When did you start writing?"

There were spots swimming before Sho's eyes. "My brother talked me into it when I was sixteen. But I was just imitating real poets," she added, drawing the deepest breath she could under her tight obi, and, for the first time that day, letting her mouth curve into a smile. *Actually, I'm good at it.* She risked a look straight into his eyes.

"Everyone is so, at first," Tekkan continued unaware. "When I was a boy, I used to pretend I was one of the old poet heroes. I used to say, 'If you can't afford paper on which to write, you can stand in the middle of the river and sing.' Kōno would remember those days." He looked over at his friend, who nodded. "We spent many afternoons after school plotting our escape."

Another guest arrived, so Tekkan turned back to introductions, allowing Sho to catch her breath. She moved her fan back and forth slowly as she studied the others. Mostly in their teens or early twenties, they wore jackets with college insignia or the uniforms of young workers.

The futon salesman Tenmin took advantage of the interruption and announced, "I'm afraid I need to get going." He got to his feet and bent to pick up the silk jacket he had placed on the floor. "I'll look forward to seeing you all tomorrow at the presentation. If Ms. Yamakawa comes, tell her I'm sorry I missed her."

As the others rose to see him off, Sho and Tekkan were left momentarily alone. He regarded her with a quiet smile.

"You know, I studied in Sakai when I was a teenager," he said. "I used to pass Surugaya on the way to school. I remember seeing a girl in there; it must have been you."

"Oh, I don't think—" Sho began. She liked the idea that she might have been that girl, but it had probably been Hana.

"Give me your fan," he said.

White with a five-colored cloud pattern, it was faded in spots where her fingers had held it over the years. Blushing, Sho placed it on the table before him. With his right hand, he reached for his brush and opened the fan in his left, looking at it closely.

"This is nice. It's from the Minoya store, isn't it?" He ran his thumb over the dangling silk tassel. "May I?"

Sho nodded.

He dipped his brush and held it motionless for a moment, thinking. Then he wrote a tanka poem in a strong, fluid hand, his brush scratching faintly on the *washi* paper. Suddenly the door slid open and a woman entered. It was Tomiko, apologizing for her lateness.

Tekkan set down his brush and rose to greet her. Sho retrieved the fan, holding it open carefully to let the ink dry. She scooted backward toward the threshold again, smiling up at Tomiko and yielding the seat closest to Tekkan. Safely out of the spotlight, she looked at what he had written.

髪さげしむかしの君よ十年経て相見るえにし浅しと思ふな

Ten years since I saw you, long-haired;
Think it no coincidence that we meet again

Her face reddened. Even if it had really been Hana, he seemed to sense something about her that others hadn't. It was as if he meant that destiny connected them. And more than that, he might think of her not *just* as a woman—which would be wonderful—but as more than that: a voice, a whole person, almost like a man.

The idea shivered in her spine, then evaporated when she heard Tomiko say she would attend Tekkan's presentation at the Osaka Publishers' Guild tomorrow. Sho would surely not be allowed to go.

IV: THE INN OF LONG LIFE

August 1900, Sho is twenty-two

わが恋をみちびく星とゆびさして君ささやきし寺の夕

Temple at night

You point and whisper,

'There is the star that shows our love the way'

Tomiko appeared at Surugaya two days later, her pretty face flushed from summer heat and conspiratorial glee. She leaned over the rice crackers and yōkan bars on the shop counter and whispered, "Tekkan Sensei is doing another event. He's leading a poetry workshop tonight in Osaka. Can you come?"

Sho had missed the Publisher's Guild event. She couldn't bear to miss another one. Jealousy, like poison, would consume her if she did. She hesitated, then put a finger to her lips, leading her new friend toward the back of the shop. "If Father gives permission first, Mother won't be able to object," she whispered.

Tomiko slipped out of her geta and followed Sho wordlessly down the narrow hallway, past a bowing servant, to the door of the study.

"Father?" Sho called softly, then slid the door open. She had always loved this room, which smelled of tobacco, wood polish, and old books. Here Sōshichi kept many of his classical texts, and a favorite folding screen with Western lithographs. A glass-fronted case contained boards of pinned insects and butterflies and volumes of pressed mosses, leaves, and flowers. Above them, in the doorway transom, imported stained glass sent shafts of red and yellow light onto the floor. Sōshichi was kneeling before his reading table in the dim light, magnifying glass in one hand.

"This is Yamakawa Tomiko," Sho said.

Tomiko knelt before him, placing her palms on the tatami and lowering her head to the floor, her forehead touching the backs of her hands. Raising her eyes, she said, "It is an honor to meet you." Sho smirked—her friend was quite the aristocrat.

"Ah, Ms. Yamakawa," he said, with an inquisitive side glance at his daughter, "we are fortunate to have you as a guest, and it is nice of you to befriend Sho."

Sho told him about the poetry workshop.

He frowned. "You understand that there is little meaning in girls writing poetry. These men don't care what you have to say, they just want to toy with you," he said, setting down his magnifying glass. That stung, but Sho knew better than to argue.

"Perhaps I erred in letting you read so much as a child. You've spent too much time with your nose in poetry magazines rather than focused on work in the shop. And you know what your mother will think."

She did, but she thought he might still be inclined to let her go. Despite her parents' odd treatment of her, he had let her read more than some fathers might have. As a follower of the Western pseudoscience of eugenics, he watched closely for intelligence in his children. She had once overheard him say that her high forehead was an indicator of a large brain.

He seemed to be considering. "You'll go together? And leave together?" They nodded, and though he drew his brows into a stern line, Sho thought he looked pleased. "I'll expect you to work extra hard this coming week. Be back by eight o'clock." He picked up his magnifying glass again and went back to his work.

"Thank you, Father!" Sho said breathlessly.

On their way to the Nankai Railway station, Sho and Tomiko laughed like schoolgirls. Their wooden geta clopped happily on the dusty street as they twirled their parasols.

"I'm so glad you could come," Tomiko sang. "I feel like you're my big sister now."

"That's nice of you. I hardly know anything about the world myself. You have more freedom than I do."

"Right now, I do," said Tomiko, "but it is coming to an end. When this summer is over, I really do have to go home. It is time to get married."

"Oh, I'm—that's too bad," Sho stuttered, not knowing whether to congratulate or commiserate.

Tomiko shrugged. "It's all right. I'm enjoying being independent for now. By the way," she said, brightening her tone as they entered the train station, "you didn't miss a thing at the Publishers' Guild. It was crowded and *so hot*. Mostly it was old professors and miserly booksellers, hardly any young people."

They counted out coins at the ticket window and climbed to the platform for the Hamadera-bound train. They were going to the Inn of Long Life, Tomiko said, the same establishment where the New Year party had taken place earlier that year. A warm ocean breeze was blowing, but the conductor's black hat stayed clamped to his head thanks to a cord that drew a line under his sweaty double chin. A small flag in his hand fluttered.

"There was a professor at the presentation," Tomiko continued as she lowered her parasol to protect it from the wind. "He was trying to make Tekkan Sensei feel bad about his poor education. He kept asking Sensei questions about the classics, trying to trip him up."

Tomiko screwed her face into a sour expression, imitating the professor: "*Yosano-san, what do you think about the phonetic transcriptions of the Kojiki and Nihon Shoki texts and their influence on the early conception of the tanka form?*"

Sho widened her eyes. "What did Sensei say?"

"He had to treat the professor respectfully, of course. You should have seen it—the professor wore a plum-colored beret, like he was French or something. He thought he was so important."

Sho laughed.

"*Really.* It's true. And you know what?" Tomiko asked, touching Sho's arm with her small hand. "He couldn't catch Sensei. He knew everything the professor asked about."

"He is amazing," Sho admitted.

The conductor blew his whistle as the train arrived at the platform, black smoke pouring from its stack. "Stand back! Stand back!" he called.

Tomiko handed her ticket to the conductor, whose eyes followed her appreciatively as she stepped onto the train. *No one looks at me that way,* Sho thought, stepping in behind her.

Tomiko leaned her head close and spoke softly so that the other passengers couldn't hear. "What did you think of him? Of Sensei, I mean."

Sho was guarded. "He's brilliant. Inspiring. It's easy to write poetry when he talks about it."

Tomiko nodded impatiently. "Yes. But I mean, don't you think he's—" she gestured with her hands.

Sho thought she knew what Tomiko meant, but she resisted. "What? What do you mean?"

"Oh," Tomiko said, exasperated. *"Really,* don't pretend you don't know. He's so *attractive.* So wise, so—" Her hands dropped helplessly to her lap.

Sho playfully elbowed Tomiko in the ribs and admitted, "Yes, I noticed. But he's older. Engaged. About to become a father! And if he notices anyone," she added, "it's you, not me."

"Oh no! How can you say that?" Tomiko said, her cheeks turning pink.

They looked out the window as the shops and houses trundled by. *I should be grateful that Tomiko invited me,* Sho thought, but she was already thinking ahead to the workshop. It was a poetry writing competition. She could write better than Tomiko—and she would make Tekkan Sensei notice.

The Inn of Long Life stood among battered beach pines, its wood face grey from years of pounding by briny wind, but the rice paper on the windows was new. It had been dark when Sho visited last January, so she hadn't appreciated its venerable presence. Now she gazed up at the heavy tile roof that curved outward, inviting beachgoers to shelter in the shadows under its eaves, and gathered poetic ideas like logs for a fire.

They found Kōno sliding open the shutters in a spacious sitting room on the second floor. The roar of the ocean and the tinkle of a wind chime came to them through the open windows. Cool tea, writing paper, brushes, and ink waited on a table.

Tekkan Sensei and three or four others were seated, heads bent together in discussion. Kōno, eyes bright through wire spectacles, beckoned to them from the veranda. "Ah, Hō-san, Yamakawa-san, you made it!"

"How beautiful!" Tomiko said, as they came to marvel at the view.

Kōno agreed. "It's a wonderful old place. It has been here since before my grandfather was born, but I hear there are plans to chop down the pines and build stores."

What a terrible idea, Sho thought as she admired the gnarled trees below.

"Come join us!" Tekkan called. He got to his feet, and his guests—the medical student Kyōan, the gregarious Gangetsu, and Tenmin—followed.

"Sorry we kept you waiting," said Tomiko.

"Think nothing of it! We were composing poems about the lateness of trains and the joys of waiting for friends," Tekkan said, eyes twinkling. "Hō-san, you had no trouble getting permission to come today?"

Sho smiled shyly and shook her head.

"I don't know if it's proper for girls to intrude on a poetry party; will the gods be angry?" Tomiko asked.

Standing at Tekkan's elbow, Kyōan laughed.

"Oh, undoubtedly," said Tekkan. "They'll be jealous."

"Just for today, Yamakawa-san, don't worry about being a girl," Kyōan offered. "You can make poems to curse men if you like!"

Tekkan grinned. "That's right; don't worry about being a girl. Kyōan here doesn't mind."

Kyōan turned apple red.

Before starting their poetry session, they headed to the baths to wash the day's dust from their bodies and prepare their minds. Sho and Tomiko entered the women's dressing room, leaving their clothes in wicker baskets and padding naked across the sweet-smelling mats to slide open a glass partition.

On one side of the steamy room, a line of water spigots was equipped with ground-level mirrors, wooden buckets, and low stools. Steam rose to the rafters and the sound of water and boisterous male voices from the other side of the partition echoed off the tiled walls. Before them, a pool looked out onto a tiny, walled garden.

Sho and Tomiko each chose a stool and set to the task of washing themselves. For a few minutes they said nothing, absorbed in the process of lathering, shampooing, massaging dusty feet, and rinsing themselves clean. As they tossed buckets of water over their heads, Sho stole a sideways glance at Tomiko. She was bent over, wringing out her washcloth, long legs bent up around her naked torso. Glistening black hair lay plastered on her thin back. She looked like a wood nymph in a mountain pool.

When they rose and went together to the bath, skin pink with heat, hair twisted up and piled on their heads with hand towels, she felt Tomiko's eyes on her—no wood nymph, Sho's body was strong, with ample breasts and hips. *She envies me, I envy her.*

その子二十櫛にながるる黒髪のおごりの春のうつくしきかな
A girl of twenty, combing her waterfall hair
Ah, the beauty of youth!

They sank down in the water up to their shoulders and reclined with sighs, looking out at the garden. A single pine tree bent over mossy rocks, surrounded by sand and late summer grass.

"Have you ever been in love?" Tomiko asked, closing her eyes.

Sho had not been expecting this. She considered for a moment. She had been in love with characters in her stories; in her mind she had felt the warmth of hands on her skin, but her infatuated letters to Kōno were as close as she had gotten in real life. "No," Sho said, pulling her knees up to her chin. "Have you?"

"No, but I want to. I wish I could be in love with my future husband," Tomiko said, running her hands across the rippling surface.

"Have you met him? Is he kind?" Sho thought of Hana's ill-fated marriage. "Maybe you will fall in love with him."

"Yes, I've met him. He seems nice." She paused. "I wish he could marry me because he wanted to, not because he had to." Tomiko shifted in the water, and perspiration glistened on her forehead. "I hope he will be a gentle lover."

Sho touched the unruly coil of hair on top of her head, then let her hand run down her neck. "I would like to be in love, but I don't think it will happen." She massaged her shoulder thoughtfully. "I think love should be so intense, you could die. It should be like fire. I don't think anything like that was meant for me."

"I know what you mean," Tomiko said softly. "Not in this life." Suddenly, peals of laughter from next door made them both jump, and Sho reflexively folded her arms in front of her chest.

"It's strange to be the only women here," Tomiko said. "Do you think they feel the same way we do? Do they think about love?"

Sho tilted her head to one side. "I suppose they do. I think they are in love with you."

"What do you mean?" Tomiko sat up. "Who?"

"Kyōan can't keep his eyes off you."

"Oh, him." Tomiko sat back. "He's very sweet, but he's not my type."

"He looked so embarrassed when Sensei teased him."

Tomiko sighed. "I'm not sure what to do about that."

"Sensei can't take his eyes off you, either."

Tomiko sat back up again. "Do you think so?"

"I do."

"He's looking at you, too! He loves when you talk; he loves what you write!" Tomiko babbled.

"I don't think so. And it doesn't matter either way," said Sho, rising out of the bath. "He's not available."

Tomiko rose slowly to follow her.

Later, dressed in their yukata, they rejoined the men in the second-floor room. Clean and refreshed, they leaned together over their lunch trays, dipping cool buckwheat noodles in a vinegared broth spiked with *wasabi* and washing it down with cold tea. The wood table felt smooth and cool on her forearms and the space underneath was crowded with long, brown legs pointed in every direction. She had never been so close to freshly bathed young men, bent on making beautiful verses. It tossed extra kindling on her fire.

Once the meal had been cleared away, they got to work. Tekkan, skin glowing, damp hair recklessly disheveled, kicked off the competition by writing out several themes with an ink brush: *pine, pluck, friend, fan, star*, and *robes*. He handed them around.

"In old-fashioned poetry competitions there were many rules," he explained, "but we are modern writers. We are free. Use the theme words anywhere in your poem, in whatever way you like. Make them your own." Periodically, he would call them back to share their compositions.

"Sensei," Sho asked timidly, "we won't be working in teams to make poems as in a *uta awase* game, is that right?"

Tekkan's face was serious. "Write whatever you like. Surprise me. But if you write a tanka, I will try to write an answer to it." He paused. "And please, don't call me Sensei. Call me Tekkan. I'm not above you. We are all friends, teaching each other."

Sho certainly thought of him as her sensei, and she doubted that she could ever call him just "Tekkan," but it was appealingly modern of him to say. In fact, she thought, he might be the first truly modern man she had ever met.

They spread out around the room, which smelled pleasantly of soap, ink, and the ocean. Some sat with their backs against the wall, some stood; others went to the veranda, each with paper and pencil or brush. Sho chose a spot just inside, her face toward the salt air. The roar of the surf and the wind in the pines drowned out almost all the sounds of the city. She closed her eyes. She was a disciplined writer by now; in the time that the others managed one or two poems, she had written a dozen. She circled the ones she liked best and looked up. *I'm faster than anyone. I'll show them I'm better, too.*

When Tekkan called them back, the men shook their heads, theatrically mopping their foreheads. He stroked his chin with amusement as he looked over their work. Once or twice, he sent a pointed glance that made Sho wonder whether that person had written something quite clever. Everyone in the room was quiet. He looked at Tomiko, and a moment later, at Sho.

"I believe this one is by Ms. Yamakawa," he said finally.

筆あらひ硯きよめて星の子のくだりきますと人へ書くふみ
I wash my brush and clean my inkstone,
Having written of a Star Child
Come down from heaven

Tomiko blushed and nodded as the others murmured praise.

"Very nice. Now, give me a moment ..." He looked up at the ceiling. *He's composing a reply on the spot*, Sho realized. He wrote something in quick script underneath Tomiko's poem, and handed it to Kōno to read aloud:

やさぶみに添へたる紅のひと花も花と思はず唯君と思ふ
Don't think this red flower poem
Is about anything but you

This was met by wide eyes and silence; these poets knew what a red flower symbolized. Tekkan was smug, though, and proceeded to compose replies for all the others with a facility that—Sho had to admit—rivalled hers. When it was her turn, she suddenly could not bear for him to read her poem aloud. For an instant, she considered snatching the paper from his hand, but too late:

師とよぶをゆるしたまへな紅させる口にていかで友といわれん
Please, let me call you Teacher
With these reddened lips, I cannot call you friend

Tekkan's poem for Tomiko had been bold, but this was bolder. He paused a half second too long, then chuckled. "Yes, you can, Miss Hō. Now, let me think ..."

He tapped his brush on his forehead, eyes closed, still shaking his head. Kōno and Tenmin whispered, Sho's heart thumped. *Have I embarrassed him? Are they laughing at me? A plain girl like me should not write so boldly. I have gone too far.*

Finally, Tekkan opened his eyes and wrote his reply, handing it to Kōno, who took one look, then handed it back to his friend with a shake of his head. "You read it."

Tekkan grunted in protest, but read aloud:

京の紅は君にふさはず我が嚙みし小指の血をばいざ口にせよ
Kyoto lipstick does not suit you.
Here, I have bitten my little finger,
Smear this blood on your lips

Sho flushed, but she didn't look down. She looked right back at him. "My, this is a hot August!" Tenmin said, and the others laughed.

"Is there any more beer?" someone else said to more laughter.

Tekkan seemed to be enjoying himself. "All right," he said, "time for new themes." He wrote several more characters on paper cards and handed them out. "Let's go another round!"

Sho was already formulating her response. She no longer cared about being too bold; she had Tekkan's attention and wanted to keep it. She wrote another dozen poems, choosing this one:

もゆる口に何を含まむといひし人のをゆびの血は涸れはてぬ

What shall we put on my burning lips?
Let us redden them, you say,
But there is not enough blood in your finger

But maybe she *had* gone too far, because his response felt like a step back:

夕潮に磯の松が根あともなしいづこぞ君とふたり立ちたる

Evening tide pounding the rocky shore leaves only
The rooted pines and we two

Which two? Sho wondered, *Tomiko or me? Or someone else—his fiancée?* Her tanka had been red; this one was blue and green.

Tomiko, sitting on the floor with her back against a wall, asked Tekkan Sensei if she could read her own poem this time. It used the old name for Hamadera Beach:

松多き高師の浜のまさご路にわが歌反古を埋めて去なむ

Along the sandy road from Takashi Beach, thick with pines,
I bury my poems and go

The others sighed appreciatively. "Don't go yet, Tomiko!" said Kyōan, and Tekkan smirked.

The shadows were lengthening; the heat was beginning to ease. As she waited for the others to finish the next round, Sho's mind drifted. She imagined Heian era aristocrats facing off in a poetry competition, with judge and scribe presiding. She might be one of them, perhaps the beautiful and talented Ono no Komachi. Like other female poets, Ono no Komachi might have sat modestly hidden from view by a screen.

Sho wondered if being hidden had empowered women writers back then, giving them courage to show off their intellectual gifts. In her mind, musicians plucked koto and played flutes near a whispering river while she laced her poems with fire. She imagined peeking from behind her screen to seek out the most handsome among them, Tekkan Sensei, resplendent in his Heian silks, looking back at her.

V: POETS ON THE BEACH

August 1900, Sho becomes Akiko

肩おちて経にゆらぎのそぞろ髪をとめ有心者春の雲こき

Hair, spilling from her shoulders,

Dangles over the open sutra

Under spring rain clouds

The girl's thoughts are on her teacher

S everal hours and more than forty tanka later, the poets began to
tire. The light on the veranda deepened to orange, and the sun slid
like a golden egg yolk from pink-orange clouds into the pines. They
leaned against the railing, and the cool waves called them down to the
sand, some of them with paper and pencil.

Their bellies were full of saké and hearts with the thrill of youth
and freedom. Tenmin swung from a lantern pole up to the eaves of the
inn, climbing to the roof's peak to look at the stars through a pocket

telescope. Kyōan suggested a swim under the moon. Tekkan knelt where the waves washed the sand and wrote lines with a finger, then watched as they were carried away.

Some of the poets called goodnight to their friends, while the rest sat on the sand where their bare feet could be kissed by the waves.

"How did you come to be a writer, Sensei?" asked Tomiko.

"Not 'Sensei,' please." He sat back on his hands with the posture of a storyteller. "I've wanted to write as long as I can remember. My father wanted me to follow him into the priesthood, but my mother—her father was a merchant, I think they were wealthy—she wanted more for me. I had older brothers, though, and I was an extra expense. They couldn't afford to educate me, so they sent me away."

The surf roared as Tomiko tucked her bit of paper into the front of her kimono and pierced the dark hair over her ear with her pencil. Tenmin lay back, hands clasped behind his head, and looked at the sky.

"They sent me to a big temple nearby—it might as well have been a hundred miles away. I didn't see my family much after that."

"How old were you?" Sho asked, thinking of her own experience of being sent away as a baby.

"Eleven or twelve. I didn't mind at first. I thought I would get a good education there. People said I was intelligent, and this was a great opportunity. It didn't work out that way."

"Why not?"

"Well, those temple schools are big business, you know. It didn't take long for my foster parents to figure out that they could put me to work as a teacher. I was only a little older than my students, but I was teaching them, rather than studying myself. A lot of them were rich kids, and they laughed at my coarse clothes. I didn't have a hat, or real shoes, just straw sandals I made myself. I studied at night so I could teach others during the day. It made me angry because I felt I could do better if—"

Suddenly, they were scrambling in a jumble of hands, knees, sand, and saltwater as a rogue wave crashed over them. Tomiko let out a happy scream while Kyōan, on his knees, wrung out a panel of his yukata with mock drama. Sho tried to shake her paper dry and Tekkan took two giant steps up the beach, motioning for the others to join him.

When they were seated once more, Tomiko had claimed the spot next to Tekkan, yet when Sho stretched out her legs on the warm sand, his eyes lingered on her strong calves. Her mother had always complained that they were thick as giant radishes, but against the sun-warm sand her skin was the color of eggshells.

He cleared his throat. "I started reading the classics, and I found a good teacher. It wasn't a formal arrangement, but one of the priests took me under his wing. He saw I was hungry to learn. We started with sutras, but soon we were reading the classics. Then we found our way to other things, like the *Manyōshu* collection. It was so beautiful, it made me want to write beautiful things, too." He took a breath:

"Waiting for you,
My heart is filled with longing.
The autumn wind blows
As if it were you
Swaying the bamboo blinds of my door."

Sho let out an appreciative breath. She liked that one, too.

"That's when I started to write. It's also when I decided to leave the temple. I was not meant to be a priest. I like women and saké too much," he said to laughter.

Tomiko trickled sand onto his feet, and he flexed his toes to let the tiny grains slide away. She countered with a heavy handful, burying one foot entirely, as Sho's heart sank.

"I didn't have many options," Tekkan went on after a pause. "I wrote to my brother, who was working at a girls' school in Yamaguchi Prefecture. He got me a teaching position. I'll admit," he said, wiggling his toes thoughtfully, "I didn't want to teach. But if I wasn't going to get an education, I needed a way out."

Tomiko was now trickling sand onto her own feet.

"How did you get the pen name Tekkan?" asked Tenmin, watching her.

Tekkan looked embarrassed. "My birth name was Hiroshi, but I needed a strong name as a writer. So, I chose Tekkan. The first character is '*Tetsu*'—'iron,' and '*Kan*' is 'tree trunk.'"

Tenmin smirked. "'The Iron Trunk?'"

"I have always loved plum trees. Tough little heralds of spring, you know, blossoming in February, my birth month." Tekkan shrugged. "So yes, I chose 'Iron Trunk' for my pen name. It had to be masculine. Strong. Tanka poetry had gotten too soft."

"Did anyone think it was a little *too* strong?" Tenmin teased.

"I've never been guilty of false humility. It's hard to be humble when you have something to say, isn't that right, Miss Hō? Or is it Shoko now?" He leaned forward, looking past Tomiko to her.

"I never liked my name," Sho said, suddenly defensive. "Since many of you use pen names, I thought I would try it."

"It's good," said Tekkan. He wasn't making fun of her.

"I like it, too," said Tenmin.

"... but it's not different enough if you don't like being Sho," Tekkan continued. "The character for *Sho* is also read *Aki*. Have you thought of 'Akiko'?"

"Akiko," she repeated, testing it. It felt daring to take a new name, like her modern, intellectual friends had done. The girl Sho was trapped in a box; perhaps Akiko was not.

Tekkan returned to his story. "Later, when my poetry began to draw attention, someone nicknamed me Tiger-and-Sword-Tekkan. I didn't argue! If you're going to be a poet, you must be bold. Take risks." Then he made a sound, an intake of breath, as though a part of him wanted to stop talking. "Speaking of risks, I suppose I was having too much fun with the students in Yamaguchi. I got into trouble."

Sho thought she knew what he was talking about. After his 1894 *Sounds of a Dying Nation* launched his reputation as a romantic writer, gossip columnists had floated rumors about him. Sho had read that Tekkan had been fired after getting a student pregnant. *Was it true after all?* She became suddenly intent on folding her paper into an origami crane.

"I decided it was time to make my way as a real poet and writer. I went back home, and my mother told me I should apprentice myself to an established poet in Tokyo. She didn't have any money to give me, so I went up to the city with just the clothes I was wearing. I didn't have much of a plan. I hoped Ochiai Naobumi might take me in."

Naobumi was well known in the literary community. He and another poet, the army surgeon Mori Ōgai, had formed a literary society in Tokyo. Like Tekkan, Naobumi wanted to revitalize tanka, to save it from what he saw as the disruptive forces of European culture. It made sense that Tekkan would look to him.

"Well, I went to Tokyo and knocked on his door. It was winter and I didn't have a decent coat, just my hanten, no hat. Wooden geta on my feet.

"The servant told me that the Sensei wasn't home, and anyway, he only took meetings with his students. He wouldn't talk to a beggar." Tekkan looked pained.

"So, I found his school. Stood in back of the classroom. He was a small man with wire glasses, a little mustache, and hair that stood on end. I was taller than him, and not much younger. I didn't see what there was to be afraid of. When the lecture was over, I introduced myself."

He paused. "Naobumi wasn't impressed. He was busy, and there were other students who needed to talk to him—real students, not just a man in rags off the street. He told me he was not taking in apprentices and wished me luck."

A wave washed up and kissed the bottoms of her bare feet, so Sho drew her knees up to her chin and leaned her head on them as the last light in the sky set the hairs on Tekkan's arm ablaze.

"That was a bad day," he said. "I didn't have another plan. I was eighteen years old; I had no money, no job, and nowhere to stay. It was cold, and I was hungry. How long was I like that? I don't know, probably not long, a week maybe, but it aged me. I slept on the ground. Covered myself with anything I could find to keep warm—rice sacks, wooden boards. I slept with a stray dog. And I stole food a few times."

Sho felt that she could not blame him.

"Then I had a bit of luck. I ran into an old friend from Osaka. He didn't have anything either, but sharing misery was better than bearing it alone. He had a plan to rent an empty hut at a temple nearby with some students. They would pay my rent if I would cook for them."

He shook his head. "The hut was cold and leaky, with a dirt floor, but it kept the snow out. The priest gave us potatoes and barley. Some days, that's all we had to eat." Tomiko had stopped playing with Tekkan's feet and was staring at the water.

"Have you ever been hungry?" he asked. "It's something you won't soon forget."

Sho had never been hungry, not that way, and she hoped she never would.

"Then, another bit of luck. It was February or March, and I was sitting under a leafless tree at the temple, wrapped in a blanket. I was so hungry I couldn't think straight. A man came up to me; it was the Sensei, it was Naobumi!

"'Are you Yosano?' he said. 'I saw you sleeping in that hut last week, through the torn paper door. You had only that one blanket. It's cold for that,' he said, and then, 'You're a poet, aren't you? I've seen your work. It'd be a shame if a talented man like you died of exposure.'

"He invited me to dinner at his house that night. I couldn't believe my luck. I scrubbed my face and hands and combed my hair, but I had no decent clothes to wear.

"Dinner was *so good*. I hadn't had a real meal in so long, it was hard not to just scoop everything up with my hands and swallow it whole." His face lit up, reliving the moment. "But I had to make a good impression on Naobumi; it was my only chance. And I'll be honest, it wasn't hard. We saw things the same way. We talked until two or three in the morning.

"After that, Naobumi found me a job. The military was hiring Japanese teachers in Korea, so that's where I went. But that's another story!"

Dusk had deepened as they talked, and the lights from the inn glowed behind them. The steady movement of the waves was like breath, in and out, in and out.

When they made their way back to the inn, the pines loomed like dark figures against the light. Tekkan and Tomiko walked together. The air was cooler now, and Sho held her hem shut so gusts of wind didn't open her yukata to the thigh. She watched Tomiko hold back a stray lock of hair with a slender hand as her sleeves fluttered. Tekkan helped her step over a log.

They were obviously attracted to each other. But Tekkan had noticed her, too. He had listened to her poetry, and looked at her in the way a man looks at a woman.

A gust of wind suddenly whipped the origami crane out of her hand. "Oh!" she said as it cartwheeled down the beach into the gloom. Tenmin scrambled after it, but it was gone.

He turned back, "I'm sorry, Miss Hō!" he said, but she waved her hand.

"Let it go," and then, "Please, call me Akiko."

VI: STAR CHILDREN

August 1900, Akiko is twenty-two

この歌の一つ缺けなば空にてもくしき光の星ひとつきえむ

If one of these poems disappeared

A shining star would go out

—Tekkan

The Taiko Bridge at Osaka's Sumiyoshi Shrine arched over a koi pond like a full moon on the calm surface. The pond also reflected the figure of Kyōan, carrying skewers of grilled mochi for Tomiko, Akiko, and Tekkan, who awaited him on a bench.

"Here, one for each of us," Kyōan said as he handed them out, dripping with sweet bean sauce. He sat down next to Tomiko. She twirled her skewer in her fingertips, holding it out to keep it from dripping on her yukata.

"Sorry, it's messy. Good, though!" Kyōan said cheerfully, but when he looked at Tomiko, his face fell. "Don't you like *yakimochi*, Ms. Yamakawa?"

"I like it well enough," she said, looking down at her sticky fingers.

The weather seemed to sympathize with Kyōan. It had been drizzling all day and the tree branches above them, strung with lanterns, swayed and dripped on their heads.

Nearby, food vendors hawked barbecued corn on the cob, grilled octopus and mochi, and sweet shaved ice. A fortune teller sat at a lamplit table and young people lined up to climb over the half-moon bridge. Some of the girls had flowers in their hair.

After a while, Kyōan sighed. "I need to be in the clinic early tomorrow. Perhaps you ladies must also get home? May I escort you to the train station?" He looked at Tomiko, and Tomiko looked at Tekkan.

"I can stay a bit longer," Tekkan said—rather smugly, Akiko thought. His confidence was charming, but not his vanity.

"I live close by," Akiko said. "I don't need to leave just yet." *Not that anyone cares.* Then it occurred to her that Tomiko lived farther away and might need an alibi, so she added, "And Tomiko is staying with me tonight at Surugaya."

Tomiko looked grateful as Kyoan disappeared a few minutes later into the shimmering crowd.

"Shall we walk over the bridge?" Tomiko suggested.

"More like *crawl*," said Akiko, gauging the steep incline.

"It's supposed to cleanse your sins if you go over it," said Tekkan.

"We must do it, then!" said Tomiko, clapping her hands.

Standing next to Tekkan as they waited their turn, Akiko wondered if the vermillion bridge could cleanse her mind of sinful thoughts. When her feet slipped on the wet boards, Tekkan steadied her with one firm hand on her elbow. At the top, where the air was thick with rain, incense, and pond algae, they lingered for a moment under the stars that shined through the ragged clouds.

"Let's make a promise," Tomiko said breathlessly.

"Like what?" Tekkan's head was thrown back, smiling at the sky.

"I don't know! Something we'll always remember!"

"Well—let us always be friends."

"Let us be children of the stars," Akiko said softly. Her heart was galloping. "Like you said in your poem, Tomiko."

"Star Children," Tekkan echoed. Then they scrambled down the other side.

"Those lotus paddies are so big and flat," Tomiko pointed. "They look like they were meant to be written on."

They were lingering beside the pond, unwilling to let the evening end.

"Why don't you try it, Tomiko? I have my brush in my bag," Tekkan said, and Akiko noticed that he used her first name.

Tomiko noticed, too. "Really?" She walked up to the water's edge, doubtful. The wet grass brushed her hem, so she pulled it up with one hand and squatted, her calves white in the lantern light. She reached for a lotus paddy as Tekkan, hair hanging in his face, took the inkstone from his bag. The air smelled of oncoming rain and lightning.

She imagined touching the cleft in his chin, his whiskers, the warmth of his neck—then stopped herself. "Here, use this," she said quickly, offering Tomiko a stick to distract from her thoughts.

Tomiko hooked it under the lotus stem and pulled, as thunder rumbled above them. She pulled again, harder, but it held firm. She pulled still harder. "Oh!" she fell backward.

Chuckling, Tekkan found a knife in his bag. "Use this," he said, and Tomiko slit the fibrous stem with the blade.

He dried the leaf with his sleeve and laid it flat on a tree stump while Tomiko dipped the brush in ink:

歌かくと蓮の葉をれば藕糸の中に小さきこゑする何のささやき
As I write, from inside the lotus leaf's silk threads
Comes a thin voice; what is it trying to say?

Tekkan wrote next:

神もなほ知らじとおもふなさけをは蓮のうき葉の裏に書くかな
I will write on the back of that lotus leaf
Of feelings even the gods do not know

Akiko wondered what those feelings were as she knelt before the stump. The gods were whispering to her, she thought, telling her what he wanted from her. When the breeze blew a lock of hair into her mouth, she bit down on it, her mouth forming a determined line.

荷葉なかば誰にゆるすの上の御句ぞ御袖片取る若き師の君
Young teacher pulls back his sleeve to write;
To whom will he give the lotus leaf, to finish for him?

Tekkan was about to answer when a harder gust of wind brought a few drops of rain, then a few more, then the sky collapsed onto them in a glorious downpour.

They ran for cover, Tekkan snatching his writing set with one hand and his book bag with the other. Under the eaves of a gardener's shack, they shuddered, hair standing on end from the lightning's proximity. Akiko was glad he hadn't had the chance to answer her question. She was afraid to know.

"Wait here," he said then, and dashed back out into the whirlwind. A moment later he was back with two waxed paper umbrellas. "The attendants said we can use these." Face wet and kimono plastered to his chest, he looked radiant.

As they started for home, leaning together under the umbrellas, a memory came to Akiko of a time when, as a little girl, she had summited a pile of wooden crates in her father's storehouse. Her big brother Hidetaro had dared her to jump, but from there, the hard earth floor looked a long way down. Still, she idolized him and wanted to prove that she was not afraid. When he egged her on, she leaned forward to the tipping point, then past it.

When she hit the ground, she lay still for a second, thinking about how cold it felt, and how her forehead and arms burned. When Hidetaro laughed, she melted into tears.

The same feeling of recklessness filled her now. A threesome, she knew, was inherently unstable. She also knew that she must lean forward until the balance tipped, even if she toppled headlong into shame.

VII: THREE POETS

Fall 1900, Akiko is twenty-two

秋かぜにふさはしき名をまゐらせむ「そぞろ心のみだれ髪の君」

You in the autumn wind I will call
"Girl of Tangled Hair and Wandering Heart"

—*Tekkan*

Autumn came, and with it, more rain—but unlike the showers that had washed through the happiest summer of Akiko's life, this rain was cold. It beat like fists on the roofs of Sakai and ran in rivulets along roof tiles. It collected faster than gutters could swallow it, spilling over the side onto the muddy street below, splattering everywhere. A sheet of water cascaded over Surugaya's entrance, splashing on the stone threshold and puddling in the doorway.

Tsuné hovered in the entrance; at the accounting desk in back, Akiko switched on the electric lamp. She fingered the smooth beads of her abacus and brooded. Summer seemed a long time ago, and the merciless rain made the walls of Surugaya feel close.

A sudden gust of wind sent curtains flapping and paper wrappers flying. Akiko jumped up to help her mother pull back bins of candies and *o-senbei* crackers from the entrance. They pulled down the flapping *noren* curtains, threw them over piles of boxes to dry, and slid shut the doors with a bang.

"Turn around," said the old woman. Wisps of grey hair stood on end around her face, giving her a crazed look. "There's mud on your back. Hold still."

Akiko turned and Tsuné beat at her kimono with one hand. "There."

Akiko turned round to assess her mother's mud-spattered front. "You'll need to wash this out." As she headed back to the desk, she said over her shoulder, "Do you want to close early? I don't think anyone will come by in this weather."

"No," said her mother flatly. "We close at nine." Thunder rumbled outside, and Akiko watched gloomily as her mother put the bins and displays back in order, arranging the o-senbei crackers in neat rows and lining up packages of candies with maddening precision: *crack, crack, crack.*

Akiko was itching to get back to the privacy of her room. Tucked flat and safe against her bosom, waiting deep inside her kimono front, was a letter that had come in the day's mail. It was from Tekkan.

He corresponded with all his *Myōjo* contributors, but the tone of Tekkan's letters to Akiko was changing. After their first meeting, he had written:

> *I trust you are well. I am afraid I caught a bad cold on the way back to Tokyo and have been lying on my pallet staring at the ceiling most of the day. I am of no use like this, but I feel better when I remember seeing you.*

Thank you for your submissions. I will include the following poem in the next issue of Myōjo:

かたみぞと風なつかしむ小扇のかなめあやふくなりにける
かな

*I love this old fan
And the sentimental breeze it makes,
But alas, it is falling apart*

You are a bright light among writers. White Clover, I look forward to more in the future.

Tekkan Sensei had given flower names to the three women in his poetry group—Akiko was "White Clover," Tomiko was "White Lily," and Masako, the woman they had met at the Hirai Inn, was "White Plum."

Tonight's letter struck an even warmer tone:

Autumn has come to Dogen Hill. The night air smells of sweet potatoes and smoke. I hope you are staying healthy and keeping out of the rain. I like your latest submissions very much and I will use this one for Myōjo:

月の夜の蓮のおばしま君うつくしうら葉の御歌わすれはせ
ずよ

*Moonlit night above lotuses, and you at the railing so beautiful,
I'll not forget the poem you wrote on the back of the leaf*

I feel I should have written it myself. I will always remember that night at Sumiyoshi Shrine. By the way, I know now how I would answer your question.

I will be in Kansai in mid-November to meet with the Poetry Society in Osaka and to visit my parents' grave in Kyoto. The autumn foliage is wonderful at that time of year, so I am asking some friends to meet me. Do you think you can get permission? I'll send an exact date as soon as I can.

Please send more poems, White Clover. It makes me so happy to see your handwriting.

Akiko smoothed the letter on her writing desk and read it again. *Oh, Tekkan Sensei,* she thought, *if my handwriting makes you happy, how much happier yours makes me!*

As for the invitation, she felt sure her parents would not let her go. She had been in considerable trouble after the August poetry meetings, particularly the one on the beach, when she hadn't gotten home until quite late. For that, she had been locked in her room early every night without dinner for a week.

Now, for the first time, she considered lying. She wanted out of her box.

Tomiko helped her a few days later. Knowing Tekkan's plans, she wrote to Akiko, *Would you like to stay at my sister's house in Kyoto for a weekend in mid-November? We can see the foliage near Nanzenji Temple.*

They were purposely vague in their letters in case one was intercepted, but Akiko knew her friend was offering an alibi, just as she had given Tomiko one a few months earlier at Sumiyoshi Shrine. She accepted the invitation quickly, even as she pondered why Tomiko was willing to share Tekkan with her. Perhaps it was because Tomiko was getting married anyway. Perhaps she was simply a kinder person. If their places were reversed, Akiko would not be so generous.

"I have run out of time," Tomiko declared when the November weekend finally arrived. She and Akiko were standing on a streetcar platform, headed for Tekkan Sensei's hotel. Her wedding date was set, she said, and she had been ordered back home to prepare.

Akiko felt a mix of sadness and excitement. She had been looking forward to this day for weeks, but now it was meaningful in another way. She might never see Tomiko again.

"I have always understood my role in my family, my destiny," Tomiko said as the streetcar rattled past a construction site where workers crawled on bamboo scaffolding like ants on a half-eaten apple. Even in the chilly air they were half-dressed, muscular buttocks cinched with sturdy loincloths, tattooed arms and legs free for climbing.

"My father spoiled me. Is it horrible to say that I am his favorite? Don't tell my sister," Tomiko smiled as Akiko gave her a look of mock approbation.

"It's true. He wasn't home very often, but when he was, I used to follow him around like a puppy." Tomiko smiled up at the hand straps swaying overhead, her slender neck long and smooth.

A memory came unbidden to Akiko then. Her mother's brother was a fishmonger, and she had watched him butcher fish many times as a child. With horror and admiration, she had watched him grasp a live mackerel from a bin of icy water and slap it onto a cutting board. The pretty thing flopped desperately for a second or two, flashing silver, until he drove a spike through its head. As he sliced the body open, she wondered what the fish had thought in its last moments. It had wanted to live, certainly; to swim freely in the ocean. Now, as she looked at Tomiko's white throat, the memory made her shudder.

"I had no brothers, only one sister," Tomiko went on. "My father told me when I was twelve that he had agreed on my husband. He will take the Yamakawa name and inherit our assets." Tomiko looked down again, splaying her fingers on her lap.

Akiko said nothing.

"I must bear a son, so that the Yamakawa bloodline continues, and my father has a grandson to inherit his title." She looked at Akiko imploringly. "I want to write, I do, but this is my duty."

"Of course, Tomiko-san. You must do what your family asks of you." She leaned into her friend's shoulder comfortingly and wondered what it would be like to have an important role like that. Even if it were to marry an appointed heir and bear his child, wouldn't that be better than being extraneous, as she was? They were both inconvenient daughters, but Tomiko had value, because there *were* no Yamakawa sons. Akiko had two brothers, as well as more marriageable sisters. If Akiko disappeared, it would not matter.

Obligation and love were locks on the box that trapped Tomiko, she realized then, locks that for Akiko were rattling loose.

They found Tekkan at the Hirai Inn, several cigarettes deep into conversation with a gaunt-looking man with a furry upper lip. He looked like a skinny dog that had been left on a chain outside all winter. The man glanced up at them warily, and Akiko wondered if he had been telling Tekkan something private that would now go unsaid. Tekkan leaned back, though, and welcomed the newcomers with a hand behind his neck.

"Ah, Miss Akiko, Miss Tomiko, this is Susukida Kyūkin. Perhaps you have heard his name? He is contributing now to *Myōjo*."

Tomiko bubbled. "Oh, I have read your poetry! It feels European. *Flute in the Dark* was so sad."

Kyūkin smiled and tilted his head politely. He reached for a cigarette, and when Akiko saw that his hand was shaking, she said, "We should not have intruded. Tomiko and I can go for a walk while you two finish your conversation."

"No, no, please sit down!" Tekkan moved to make room at the table.

"Yes, come sit," said Kyūkin—half-heartedly, Akiko thought—so she brought out a gift box of Surugaya yōkan and Tomiko put fresh tea leaves in the teapot. In a few moments, they had relaxed into a discussion of European long form poetry, the angst of John Keats, and the love affairs of Lord Byron.

When their discussion slowed and their backs grew tired from sitting on the floor, Tekkan turned to Tomiko and Akiko and slapped the tabletop with his palm. "I'm afraid we're on our own today. Kyōan and Tenmin are working, and Kōno is sick, so no one else can come with us to Kyoto."

Turning back to Kyūkin, he said, "It would not be appropriate for me to accompany two single ladies to Kyoto alone. Would you like to come? It would be a favor to me." He winked at Akiko, and her heart thumped.

But Kyūkin could not be persuaded; he had things to do, he said nervously, so they walked him to the streetcar, and before they knew it, they were three. A mixture of panic and elation snaked through Akiko's veins as she realized that the day was young, and her parents didn't expect her home until tomorrow.

"Well, what are we to do, then?" Tekkan asked as they followed him across the streetcar tracks toward the side of the road. "Will you come to Kyoto with me, after all?" A flicker of doubt showed in his handsome face as he stamped his feet to keep warm. "I must visit my parents' grave while I'm here. If anyone asks why we're together, can we say we ran into each other on the train?"

Tomiko's face lit up. "We were on our way to Kyoto to see the foliage anyway. It was just a coincidence that we ran into you!"

An hour later, the three poets were bound for Kyoto. Like a boat on a rain-heavy river, it swept them away.

Rusty red, orange, and gold leaves swirled out of the Kyoto sky, pulling them down the street in a windy river from the train station toward the Otani Honbyō graveyard where Tekkan's ancestors were buried. The autumn gods seemed to urge them on, deeper and further from reason. Red paper lanterns hung in shop doorways, vats of simmering pork, eggs, and vegetables filled the air with tempting smells, and red-orange persimmons dangled from the trees like festival orbs.

Carrying a wooden bucket of water and a brush, Tekkan led them up a hill studded with old trees and gravestones. Roots grasped at their feet, tripping them up, while branches crowded over their heads as though craning to see. Tekkan came to stand before a plot of marker stones bearing the name YOSANO. He scrubbed off the grime, doused the stones with clean water, then lit a stick of incense and knelt on the ground, bowing his head. Akiko and Tomiko stood back, and Akiko imagined the boy he had been once, with that same head of hair, and those same big feet sticking out of his hakama trousers.

After a while, they wandered north toward the Nanzenji Temple grounds. There, the massive wooden Sanmon Gate nested like a great eagle over the entrance steps, resting its wings on time-blackened pillars hewn from ancient trees.

Akiko had picked up a brochure at the entrance. "It says that Nanzenji is the head of the Rinzai sect of Zen Buddhism. The original gate dates to around 1295. This one was built in 1628!"

Tomiko looked up at the heavy columns that held the gate over her head. "Why do I always feel like I should whisper here?"

Indeed, other visitors around them dropped their voices as they approached.

"It feels like it's alive," said Akiko. "Like it couldn't have been built by humans; it had to be flung out of the heavens by the gods, to land here with a crash!"

This elicited glances from Tekkan and Tomiko.

"You have an amazing way of saying things," Tekkan said. "You should talk more."

As they stepped through the gate, Akiko was seized by the idea that it was a charmed portal and that passing through would change them. She thought of the night they became Star Children at Sumiyoshi Shrine. Perhaps fate had brought them here, too.

Three people walking abreast on the narrow, tree-lined path felt crowded, so she lagged behind Tekkan and Tomiko. Garden walls and houses skirted the road, their mud and straw walls topped with slate-grey tiles, their gates guarded by gargoyles. She wondered if Prince Genji had walked along this very path, dreaming of the beautiful Lady Fujitsubo and regretting his doomed infatuation with her.

"Where are we going?" Tomiko asked, a little breathless as the path steepened.

"Eikando Temple. Have you been? Beautiful this time of year. And when we're tired, there's an inn nearby. It's better than having to go all the way back into town tonight, don't you think?"

Akiko and Tomiko exchanged looks but neither objected, and Tekkan kept talking. "There are legends about this place. Nanzenji was founded by a Zen priest who was supposed to rid the emperor of the spirits that taunted him. They say there are many ghosts here."

"I believe it," said Tomiko as they skirted a temple wall.

"If I were a ghost, I would come here," said Akiko, stopping to admire the green pond that opened before them. The water rippled with the spine of a carp in the shadows under the old stone bridge. A line of heavy temple roofs pressed their backs against the dark mountain, and everywhere she looked, rust-colored leaves shimmered. *If there are gardens in heaven*, Akiko thought, *they look like this.*

秋を三人椎の実なげし鯉やいづこ池の朝かぜ手と手つ めたき
Autumn finds we three throwing nuts for koi in a pond
In the morning breeze, your hands are cold on mine

They wandered along the mossy paths flecked with golden light until a breeze made Akiko shiver. Tekkan looked up at the sun and said, "It's getting on. The inn is just ahead."

They followed him without comment, Tomiko stumbling wearily in her geta. Akiko took her arm, wondering whether they would go to hell for what they were about to do.

VIII: FORGET-ME-NOTS

November 1900, Akiko is twenty-two

それとなく紅き花みな友にゆずりそむきて泣て忘れ草つむ

I turned my back like it was nothing,
Leaving the red blooms all to my friend,
And weeping, plucked the forget-me-nots

—*Tomiko*

"You should come to Tokyo, both of you," Tekkan said as they made their way to the inn. He stooped to pick a handful of late wildflowers and tucked a few stems into Tomiko's hair, then Akiko's. "There is a women's college starting up in Tokyo," he said, positioning the blossoms over Akiko's forehead as she held her breath. "You could study literature."

Tomiko adjusted one of the blossoms over her ear. "That would be wonderful, Sensei. It's like a dream, being here with you both, but …" She let her arms fall to her sides. "I must wake up soon. My wedding is in the spring. I'll be going back home before the New Year."

"It will be lovely, I'm sure," Akiko said. "In your wedding kimono, you will be like one of the ladies in *The Tale of Genji*."

Tekkan looked up at Tomiko with surprise and—was it dismay? Perhaps he hadn't known about her betrothal. Akiko kept talking, hoping to dispel the shadow that had passed between them. She wanted the balance to tip, but not for that reason. She didn't want to be a second choice. "Tell us about him—Tomeshichiro, was that his name? Do you like him?"

Tomiko tilted her head, considering. "I don't really know him. We've only met once or twice." She shrugged. "He's very polite."

"Does he work?" asked Akiko, thinking about the apprentice Sadashichi, who would always pound mochi for a living.

"He works for the Foreign Office. He wants to be a diplomat. But after we're married, he will have to spend more time on the estate with my father."

"You can keep writing, of course," said Tekkan, suddenly serious. "We need your poems for *Myōjo*; I won't take no for an answer."

"You may have to," she said, breathing in to adjust the tight obi around her middle. "My parents don't think it's proper for me to write, particularly after I'm married. They are being tolerant now, but a married woman in my station must think of the family name and reputation."

"Your reputation?" Perhaps Tomiko's family background was also news to Tekkan.

"My grandfather was a senior samurai in the Obama Domain. My father is a banker." That was an understatement, thought Akiko. Tomiko's father Teizo was President of the National 25th Bank of Japan.

"They can't have the Yamakawa name showing up in cheap romantic magazines," Tomiko said, and then turned pink. "I'm sorry, that was rude."

"No, of course not," said Tekkan, but he rubbed his chin, frowning. "Can they really keep you from writing?" he asked.

"They can keep me from publishing," she said. "I will always write. I can't help myself." She stopped, looking at something on the ground at her feet. "Oh look." She knelt. A butterfly, with blue and black wings, lay on the path. As Tekkan and Akiko looked at the motionless form, a puff of wind rolled it over.

"Get me something to pick it up with," said Tomiko. "We can't leave it here where it will get stepped on."

"It's dead, Tomiko-san," said Akiko simply, thinking again about the busy household in which she had grown up, in which animals and humans were born and died. Tomiko must have been sheltered from kitchens and livestock at her family's estate.

"I know," said Tomiko, motioning impatiently toward the debris at the side of the path. Tekkan brought her a leaf, and she used it to scoop up the butterfly. She made a small indentation in a patch of moss and set it down carefully. "Maybe it knew it was dying," she said, standing up, "and tried to find a quiet place, but the wind picked it up and tossed it onto the path, and it didn't have the strength to move anymore."

Looking at the butterfly, Akiko thought of Hana. When her sister stopped eating, she had asked to be brought home to Surugaya. Akiko had stayed with her that final week, sponging her forehead and dry lips and helping her to roll over onto her side. Relatives had come to visit, and a monk had said prayers at the foot of her mattress.

They had talked quietly while Hana was still able, but she didn't, or couldn't, say what Akiko wanted to hear. She had wanted Hana to make her promise to marry for love. Perhaps it would have given meaning to Hana's short life.

Now, Akiko regretted feeling that way. It had not been Hana's job, in her final days and hours, to turn Akiko's personal desire into a deathbed promise, knowing it would be against their parents' wishes. *It was selfish and prideful of me*, she thought. *If I want to marry for love, I must do it for myself.*

Akiko saw some mushrooms growing from a fallen tree limb. "I think these are edible," she said, crouching to pull a few out of the wet earth by the stems to examine them.

"Let's ask the cook at the inn to prepare them for breakfast!" Tekkan said, reaching for them.

"Oh no, Sensei. I could be wrong. They could be poisonous." She dropped the mushrooms to the ground, but he picked them up.

"And if they are? We'll die together," he said with a reckless grin, pocketing them. Akiko didn't know if he was joking; she glanced at Tomiko, whose pink mouth had dropped open.

The sunlight had gone weak and the shadows at the base of the Higashiyama Mountains were long by the time they arrived at Tsujino Inn.

"Hello?" Tekkan called as they hesitated in the stone-floored entry. A row of slippers and a ceramic umbrella holder stood against the raised wooden platform, but it was quiet as a temple hall. It was only slightly warmer than outdoors, and it smelled of incense, old tatami, and roasting fish. The one electric light on the ceiling could not dispel the gloom.

"*Hai!*" sang a voice, and a moment later a woman of about sixty with dyed-black hair emerged from the back. She appraised the three travelers as she knelt on the floor before them. Behind her, a steep stairway rose next to a faded screen and a vase of dusty silk flowers. A calendar on the wall, open to April, displayed advertisements for a men's clothier.

"*Oideyasu*," said the matron, bowing her head to the floor. "Welcome." Her eyes rested on Tekkan for a half-second too long, making Akiko wonder if she recognized him. If so, she was too discreet to let on, or to ask why he was accompanied by young women with wildflowers in their hair. She casually inquired how many rooms they needed, lipstick feathering her wrinkled lips.

It was agreed that the women would share an eight-mat tatami room. Tekkan would take the adjoining smaller room. Tomiko insisted on paying and, using the telephone in the parlor, called her sister to say where she and Akiko were spending the night. She did not mention the third guest.

They took their dinner in their room next to the glowing *hibachi,* the table quilt pulled over their knees. Tekkan wolfed down the grilled mackerel, stopping only to comment that Kyoto had the best radish pickles.

"I'm sorry to hear about your engagement, if it's not what you want," he said to Tomiko later, picking at a tooth thoughtfully. The smell of *miso* lingered and bits of seaweed stuck to the bottom of their lacquered soup bowls. "I will miss you. But things are changing for women, aren't they?"

"Not soon enough for me," sighed Tomiko, touching her teacup with a finger. "To be fair, I don't suppose this would be Tomeshichiro's choice either." She shrugged. "For some men, things are almost as bad as for women." She swirled the leaves in her cup, but the tea had gone cold. "It never bothered me until recently. Maybe the wedding date makes it real. And because I've been away at school. And met you. It's changed how I think."

Heaped with glowing coals, the hibachi smoked softly. In the dimming light, Akiko's gaze wandered to the sliding *fusuma* door that led to Tekkan's room. There was no hibachi in there; it would be quite cold tonight.

"My parents want me to marry the apprentice," Akiko said suddenly. "I won't."

Tomiko looked up. "What do you mean, 'you won't'? What can you do?"

"I can refuse. My father can't make me. If I don't marry—with no husband or children to take care of—I'll have more time to write and read." She realized how that might make Tomiko feel, so she clarified. "It's different for me. Our family name is not important, and I have two brothers. My older brother has gone to Tokyo, so Chūsaburo will inherit Surugaya."

"Things *are* changing," mused Tekkan. He uncrossed his legs and extended them under the table, bumping Akiko's leg. They both pulled back quickly.

"What about you, Sensei? You have marriage plans, too?" Tomiko asked.

"Oh," his face clouded. "My fiancée and I ... it's difficult right now. My son Atsumu was born in September. We don't agree about his family name—or mine."

He had mentioned Atsumu in letters, and they knew of Hayashi Takino, his fiancée.

"You see, the Hayashis don't have a son, so I agreed to become their heir, but I can't bear to change my name. My name is Yosano. I've built my reputation as Tiger Tekkan. These are the names I'm known by. 'Tiger Hayashi'?" he grunted bitterly. "Impossible. I can't go through with it. I told Takino's father that two weeks ago."

Akiko tried not to visibly start. *Go through with what, changing his name, or getting married, or both?* A possibility shimmered somewhere in the darkness behind him. He was glaring at his saké glass; he didn't seem predisposed to say more.

"I guess we are all running away from something," said Tomiko quietly.

"The same thing!" Akiko said. "Marriage!"

"There are things to run toward," said Tekkan, as though trying to convince himself.

"Like what?" With a burst of restless frustration, Akiko got to her feet. They looked up at her, surprised. The hem of her gown rode up on one leg, so she batted it down. Her eyes were defiant.

"Freedom. Truth. Love." Tekkan answered softly, looking up at her. "I won't be trapped, either."

"I want those things," said Tomiko. "But I can't have them. I *am* trapped."

"You aren't!" Akiko said, a lump rising in her throat.

"What do you know of freedom, Lady Akiko?" asked Tekkan, and there was pity in his voice. "What do you know of love?" He held out a hand to her, so she took it. Feeling at once deflated and comforted, she sat back down.

That night, Akiko lay in her futon next to Tomiko. Outside, an owl called, woody and sonorous, like a *shaku-hachi* flute. She felt far from home, tucked away in a mountain hideaway, like Genji's mysterious lover Yugao. Her hair, still damp from the bath, lay in a long plait by her side, tickling her elbow. She strained to hear over Tomiko's even breathing any sound from the room next door. Was he asleep? Was he wide awake like her? As she thought of his body lying strong and thin so near, she let one hand wander up to her breast. The other hand strayed to her warm belly.

Only a few minutes later, she thought she heard a movement. She wasn't sure at first, but then she heard it again—a creak of floorboards. She turned her head slightly to look up at the fusuma door in the darkness. It might have been her imagination, but it seemed that it slid open a crack. She held her breath and didn't move, fighting the urge to sit up. After a moment, the door slid quietly shut.

くろ髪の千すぢの髪のみだれ髪かつおもひみだれおもひみだ
るる
Black hair, a thousand strands of hair,
Tangled hair and tangled heart, my tangled heart

On Akiko's breakfast tray the next morning, next to her soup, rice, and fish, was a dish of something black and glossy. She gasped. "Are those the mushrooms from yesterday?"

She and Tomiko had woken early, whispering for almost an hour before Tekkan called to them through the door. The hibachi had long since burned down to ash, and the morning was so cold, their breath plumed as they talked. Wearing the inn's quilted hanten jackets, they went downstairs to the chilly parlor for breakfast. The only other guest was a man sitting by himself in a corner, staring at a newssheet, smoking. The three sat on flat cushions as close as they could to the stove.

Tekkan was eyeing the mushrooms, his hair disheveled from sleep. *Will you do it for me?* he seemed to be daring.

He doesn't know me very well, Akiko thought. She speared a mushroom with her chopsticks and popped it in her mouth. It was slippery and pungent. She chewed and swallowed, glaring at him triumphantly as she washed it down with a scalding mouthful of tea.

He arched an eyebrow and sat back, impressed. "This child is qualified to talk of love."

Tomiko took up her chopsticks then, not wanting to be outdone. She watched Akiko's face for signs of distress and then said, "All right," and swallowed a mushroom whole. She made a face as she washed it down.

"I don't care," Tomiko said hotly, as her friends stared at her in equal surprise. She swallowed hard again. "I'm dying inside anyway."

"This is a breakfast I will not soon forget," said Tekkan, grinning, but he left his mushroom untouched.

いはず聴かずただうなづきて別れけりその日は六日二人と一人

Without asking or saying, but just a nod,
They parted on the sixth:
Two people
And one

As Tomiko and Akiko waved goodbye to Tekkan from their rickshaw later that morning, Akiko felt his eyes on her, as though he wanted to tell her something. *It must be my imagination*, she thought, and didn't dare look up.

The rickshaw descended the quiet hillside and turned onto the wide Higashiyama boulevard, moving into the stream of pedestrians, pull-carts, and wagons. Tomiko dabbed her face with her sleeve. She was quiet.

"What's wrong?" Akiko asked after a while, offering a handkerchief from her bag.

Tomiko pushed it away. "I want you to be happy, to write poetry, to do what I can't do."

"What?" Akiko asked. "What do you mean?"

"We can't both have him," said Tomiko.

"Neither of us can!"

Tomiko sighed. "You heard him. He's going to leave his fiancée."

"He didn't say that."

Tomiko raised her eyebrows, then looked away, one hand shielding her face. They were silent again.

Akiko thought about it. She had been quick enough to pop wild mushrooms into her mouth for this penniless, vain man. Would she betray her family for him?

Even as the question formed in her mind, she knew the answer: She had never belonged with her own family; she wanted out of the box they had put her in. If Tekkan wanted her—if she weren't a second choice—if they could be partners, and choose their paths together, yes, she would.

IX: TWO POETS

January 1901, Akiko is twenty-three

鶯に朝寒からぬ京の山おち椿ふむ人むつまじき

Cold morning in the Kyoto hills

The call of a warbler and

Lovers treading on fallen camellias

The mistress of Tsujino Inn in Kyoto looked up from her mending as the front door slid open. "*Hai!*" she sang, glancing at her ledger for the day's reservations.

Akiko was shaking out her umbrella. "Is there a reservation for Mr. Yosano?" she asked in a low voice. Barely two months had gone by since she had stood in this same entry with Tekkan and Tomiko. Now she was alone.

"Yes, yes," said the matron.

"Is he here yet?" Akiko asked. She felt the woman's eyes on her. *Judging her.*

"No, but we'll get you settled with a cup of tea while you wait," the old lady said, leading her upstairs, past the room where they had stayed last time, to the last room on the end.

As the matron busied herself with the hibachi and hot water kettle, Akiko looked out the window, trying to steady her nerves. She set down her bag, opened and closed her fingers several times; her hand ached from her crazed grip.

"When would you like dinner?" asked the matron, and Akiko fought the urge to laugh. *Dinner? Should I be hungry?* It seemed an alien thought. She was like a bird, teetering on a telegraph wire in a storm. Food was far from her mind.

The matron waited in the doorway for Akiko's answer.

She did not know when Tekkan would come, or even *if* he would come. *I must see you again*, he had written to her after the November outing with Tomiko.

Only you this time. I will be in Kansai in January. I will speak in Kobe on the sixth and will go to Kyoto on the ninth. Can you meet me at Tsujino Inn, the same place as before? Please mention it to no one.

The letter had been tucked into a *Myōjo* editorial mailing.

"Dinner? Ask Mr. Yosano when he arrives," Akiko said to the matron, drawing herself up with as much confidence as she could muster.

"The kitchen closes at eight," the old woman said stiffly, and left.

Akiko waited. She drank tea, looked out the window, and fretted. She looked in the dressing mirror, smoothed her hair, reapplied her makeup. She pulled his letters from her bag to look at them again.

I must see you, White Clover. Since I saw you last, I can think of nothing else. I have something to say.

She thought she knew what it was. She looked again in the mirror, at her mouth with its turned-down corners, her full eyebrows and pale skin. She was terrified of misunderstanding, of being a fool. Her face looked calm in the mirror, but under the surface, a river was rushing.

I think of you day and night. When I cut my finger, the blood makes me think of you. When I read your words, I weep. I am a tormented man.

She went to the window again and looked down at the gate. The sun was sinking. Why wasn't he here? Had he meant for her to meet him at the train station? No, he had specified the Tsujino Inn. He was keen to avoid being seen. Perhaps he had been waylaid. Or changed his mind.

If so, it was just as well. Already, she had broken rules, and he hadn't even arrived yet. She had lied to her parents, fabricating a story about visiting an aunt, a Buddhist nun at a convent in Kyoto.

It was dark when Akiko, looking down from her window, saw movement outside. She strained to see the silhouette at the gate, breath misting in the cold air. Wrapped in a dark coat, hat shining wet in the lamplight, it was Tekkan. Despite the chill, she felt suddenly warm.

うき人のかどにたつ梅夕さめのそぼふるなかにほの白かりし

In the quietly falling evening rain
A dim figure stood by the gate
The plum tree glooming softly white

In a moment he was with her. Smiling and radiant with rain on his coat, he was as real as the ground under her feet.

"It's cold," he said. "And I made you wait. I'm sorry."

"Come warm yourself," she said, extending a hand. They met in the middle of the room by the glowing hibachi. Her heart hammered as she watched him press his hands against the rough, warm surface.

"You must be tired," she said.

"I am. It was a long day."

"Would you like some tea?" Akiko's cheeks reddened. *Playing wife?* an inner voice chided her.

He smiled, deepening the lovely cleft in his chin. He glanced at the ceramic decanter and cups that waited on the table next to a cold *bentō* box. "Tea is good, but if that's saké, I'll take it," he said.

He held a cup as she poured, and she flushed again at this traditional gesture between a husband and wife. *Am I a fool? Or a harlot?*

He downed it in one go and held out his cup for more, his hand red from cold. "Have some?"

"Oh, no, I don't drink," Akiko answered, pouring.

"Today you will drink," he said, and taking the decanter from her, filled the second cup. She hesitated, then took it.

"I guess I'm going to hell," she said, taking a tentative sip. It felt sweet and warm in her throat. "Ahh." She closed her eyes. "That's nice." *Who am I? Drinking saké in a hotel room with an almost-married man?* "All right, then," she said, steadying herself. "Why was your day so long?"

Tekkan still had his coat on, but he was warming up, so he undid a few buttons. "I was followed to Kyoto. Did you know that poets have no privacy once they say something controversial?"

"You were *followed*?" Akiko looked past him at the door, as though someone might burst through it. "Why?"

"You probably heard about the November issue of *Myōjo*," he said. Akiko nodded. It had been banned for its nude illustrations, including an art deco-style drawing of a topless nymph on the cover. "I received a letter from the Ministry of Home Affairs saying that Narumi's illustrations were offensive. The magazine has been pulled from stores, and one of my backers dropped me as well."

"I heard about the censors," Akiko said. "That's terrible. And poor Narumi, I wonder what it means for him."

"It could be good or bad for him in the long run, depending on whether being banned promotes interest in his work," Tekkan said, running a worried hand through his hair. "He hasn't answered my letters; he is probably lying low. No more *Myōjo* covers, I expect."

"You both must have known—"

"Oh, we knew it was a possibility, but can we be cowed so easily?" He scowled. "We must be bold, that's the only way things will change!"

"I didn't mean that, it's just—"

"No, I'm not angry with you, but people act as though they don't know what a woman looks like under her clothes. They pretend to be scandalized. Hypocrites! In Europe, nudity in art is normal!" He held out his cup for a refill, and Akiko obliged, thinking of her father's collection of erotic *ukiyo-e* prints.

"So naturally, everyone wants a copy of *Myōjo*. And I can't sell it to them." He was sitting with one arm on the hibachi. He tilted his head thoughtfully. "But I *can* fill a lecture hall. My presentation in Kobe on Tuesday was standing room only. I gave my lecture about *The Dying Country*, you know. I told them our culture is in decline, and they agreed with me." He shrugged and tossed back the saké. "But now they're following me around. Journalists got on the train with me at Osaka. I wasn't sure at first until two of them started asking me questions."

Downstairs, Akiko could hear the matron's voice welcoming another guest.

"At Kyoto Station, I tried to outpace them on the train platform, but they wouldn't let me out of their sight." He shook his head. "So, I ran! Out of the station, down side streets. I went into a toy store on Shichijo Street because it was crowded. I put my coat over my head and went out the side exit." He reached for the bentō box. "Can't a man meet a woman without it being reported in the newspaper?"

She blushed and cast her eyes down. "Do you think you will be found out?"

At that moment there was a knock at the door, and they both jumped. A woman's voice said, "May I lay out your futon?"

"Yes, yes," said Tekkan, and the door slid open to reveal a young woman about Akiko's age. As they watched, she pushed the table to one side and pulled two futon rolls from the closet. She laid them out next to each other on the tatami, arranging everything carefully. After an excruciating few minutes, she bowed silently out of the room.

A chill was creeping up Akiko's spine.

"Are you all right? You look pale."

"I—I'm fine," she said.

Tekkan wasn't convinced. "Please don't be afraid. I'm so glad you came all this way. I wanted to meet you in private. But that doesn't mean—" He looked at the futons and then back at her. "You must think poorly of me."

Akiko shook her head. "I'm just hungry and cold. Maybe I should go take my bath."

As she stood and gathered her things, her feet wobbled. The saké and hours of anxiety had worn on her.

In the downstairs washroom, she took deep breaths to slow her galloping pulse. She lathered her body, poured hot water over her head, then lowered herself into the bath up to her shoulders. The water closed around her like an embrace.

Naked, her knees pulled up to her chin, the girl struggled with the woman. She looked down at her body wavering in the steaming water: hips, belly, legs. *Am I beautiful? Can he love me first, not second?*

She put her face in her hot, wet hands and tried to think rationally. At this moment, she still had a choice. She could rise from the bath, make her apologies, and leave. But if she went to him now, if she laid with him, the choice was made. *Because that's what this is about; I mustn't lie to myself. He didn't meet me here for conversation.* Her parents betrayed, her future ruined, she would never be a good daughter. Was she sure it was what she wanted?

She stood up from the water and, dripping and warm, stepped out. *If he will have me, yes, it is what I want. But I do not know what to do. I do not know how to please a man.*

春みじかし何に不滅の命ぞとちからある乳を手にさぐらせぬ
Spring is short, nothing lasts, I said,
And brought his hand
To my powerful breast

Their nerves kept them talking another two hours, wrapped in blankets by the hibachi and refilling each other's saké cups until Akiko felt woozy. He was telling her about his time teaching in Korea, when a distant, metallic clank plunged them into darkness.

"Midnight," Akiko whispered. The only light now came from the window. As her eyes adjusted, she could see the outline of Tekkan's face.

"What's wrong? You look unhappy," he said.

She looked down, face hot, pulse throbbing in her ears. "Why are we here?"

"Don't you know?" He cocked his head to one side. "Silly girl."

"Don't laugh at me. You asked me to come. Tell me why."

He drew up his knees and rested his arms on them. "Let me see if I can say it right." He took a breath. "It starts with your poetry. It's new. Strong. Almost—if you'll forgive me—like a man's. The first time I read one of your poems, I thought, *I want to meet this woman!*

"Then when you came to that first meeting in Osaka, I ..." he swallowed. "I felt a connection. Did you feel it? I loved what you wrote, but I loved something else, too. I started to imagine—" He shook his head. "We poets, we imagine too much. You understand that."

She nodded.

"You know the story of Yokihi?"

"Of course." The tragic love story from Tang Dynasty China was everywhere in classical literature, including *The Tale of Genji*. Lady Yokihi was so beautiful, and the Emperor Genso loved her so much, that he neglected his duties. Their love affair ended when his advisors, worried about her power over him, forced him to have her strangled. "They were destined for each other, Yokihi and the Emperor."

His expression suggested that this was explanation enough, but she pressed for more. "I don't understand. Do you mean we are destined to be each other's downfall? Will you kill me?"

"Akiko," Tekkan laughed, shaking his head. "I don't want to kill you. I want to kiss you." He bent toward her, but she pulled away, heart hammering.

"You have a wife, or almost. And a son," she accused, tears stinging her eyes.

"The engagement is off. Takino knows it won't work."

He was so close to her, she could feel his breath, sweet with saké.

He whispered, "When we were here in November—"

Akiko tensed as she thought of Tomiko. Was he going to bring her up now? Despite her efforts to hold her tears back, they came.

"Oh, no, please don't cry. I'm not explaining myself well." The shadows on his face deepened. "Forgive me. I should go."

"No, no," Akiko said, raking an arm across her face, angry at her tears. "I want to be here. I want to be with you. I'm just confused. I can't believe ..." She couldn't say it out loud: *I can't believe you want me.*

"When we were here in November, I saw how strong you were, how clever, how brave. That's what I meant to say."

"I don't feel brave," she said.

He sat back while she found a handkerchief and wiped her eyes and nose.

"I didn't mean to frighten you," he said. "I won't touch you if you don't want me to."

"I do," she said, her voice thick. "I do want it."

Slowly, he put out his hand to touch the cord that held her hair in a damp coil behind her head. With one hand she reached up and released it for him. Her hair came spilling down over her shoulders, thick and dark. He took a heavy handful and arranged it tenderly on her shoulder. Then he ran the back of his hand along it, starting at her ear and moving down to where it ended at her elbow.

She took a ragged breath, and the tears felt cool on her face. Then, in a moment of daring, she took his hand and brought it to her breast. He ran his hand slowly over it, feeling it under her thick robe.

"You're trembling. Are you cold?" he whispered, and when he bent to kiss her, she didn't pull away. He wrapped them in the futon blanket and pulled her down next to him.

After a while, as she let her hand touch his collarbone, his cheek, as she traced the curves in his ear, her tears slowed. He waited, letting her touch him first, and as she began to warm under the blanket, she said, "I'll be alright," and knew it was true. She felt the stubble on his chin as he kissed her. She had wanted to do that for so long. She breathed in the scent of soap and saké. She kissed him back; it was her first kiss, her first embrace.

"Teach me what to do," she whispered.

"Oh, strong girl, I don't need to teach you anything. You know more than you think you do."

And she did.

人の世の掟の上のよきこともはたそれならぬよきこともせん
I want to do things that are said to be good,
But also, good things that are said to be bad

They bade a polite greeting to the matron the next morning, barely making it outside before Akiko's careful expression broke. "What must she *think*?"

"I don't care, as long as she doesn't say anything." Still skittish from the chase the night before, he looked around as though expecting to see eyes in the bushes.

Their feet took them through the red-light district of Gion, shuttered and sleeping, where crows picked at bits of leftover garbage in the empty streets. They turned south, passing through the temple grounds of Chion-in and strolling along the newly built canal, trying to walk off the awkwardness they felt.

She talked more that day than she had ever done in her life. For her, it was a release of nervous energy, but Tekkan encouraged her, saying he wanted to know everything about her.

"It keeps me from thinking about my troubles," he said. "Tell me about your family. You have brothers and sisters?"

"Yes, my elder brother Hidetaro is at Tokyo University studying engineering. Father thinks he has been away from home long enough. Hidetaro doesn't agree; he doesn't want to come home," she said, out of breath as they climbed the steep shop-lined path toward Kiyomizu Temple. They passed a line of stores that were just pushing open their doors; one of them sold ceramic pots, another sold tea. "He also doesn't think I should have my poetry published; he says it's not right for a girl."

"I see," said Tekkan quietly.

"I don't see why I must obey him. Times are changing, like you said. Women can make their own decisions." She shot a sideways look at him, hoping he would agree, but he pressed on.

"I know about your younger brother; he belongs to the Kansai Young Men's Literary Society. I'm glad he convinced you to join. I don't know if I've met him."

"That's Chūsaburo. You'd like him. Well, everybody likes him."

"What are his plans?" Tekkan asked, gesturing to a bench for them to rest. The first tourists plodded uphill past them, and shop ladies in kerchiefs and quilted hantens took their places in store fronts, like spiders at their webs. Tiny wind chimes tinkled in the chilly air. Sitting next to Tekkan, Akiko felt a shimmer of excitement, as though she had fallen asleep reading *Genji*, and woken to find the Prince with her. Their intimacy was still new, though; he seemed self-conscious, too.

"He's still in school. He must take over the shop after he graduates, so I think he's trying to enjoy himself now as much as he can."

"And what about your sisters?" Tekkan asked. She gazed at him, momentarily distracted by the shadow under his Adam's apple. She had kissed it just hours ago.

"Uh—well, my sister Hana—" She took a breath. "I didn't want to mention this to Tomiko when we were with her before, but she died last year. My—my father arranged a marriage for her, someone she didn't care for. She was so sad. I guess it broke her heart."

"That's terrible," said Tekkan.

"I guess it can't be helped. My other older sister Teru is married, too; they were my half-sisters. And then there's my little sister Sato." She put her hands on her cold cheeks. "This must be awfully boring for you!"

"No, I want to know everything about you."

"Well ..." Akiko dropped her hands to her lap and touched a pro-truding root with her toe. "I wanted my sister Sato to go to school as long as she could. It's too late for me, I'll never get past middle school, but I talked Father into letting her go to Kyoto City Girls High School. I promised him that I wouldn't marry until Chū was ready to take over the shop." Her father had looked over his glasses with a silent *I'll hold you to it.* That troubled her. She had never broken a promise like that. At least, before now.

Tekkan nodded. "And then, what of you? What will you do if your parents tell you to marry the apprentice?"

"I won't marry Sadashichi. But they need me in the shop since my mother got sick. She had a stroke a few years ago. She's never been strong since. So, I'm trapped." She looked down at her hands. "What do you think?"

"I think you'll break Sadashichi's heart," Tekkan said with a laugh. Then he became serious. "Come to Tokyo with me."

Part of her had been waiting for him to say it, but it made her tremble anyway. Loved or not, a man could be a doorway to a different fate. "Don't say that unless you mean it." She could not bear for him to tease her, to say it now and later change his mind. She had already made her decision, even if he had not. She could no longer bear to be parted from him.

われと歌をわれといのちを忌むに似たり恋の小車絲さらに巻け
Forsaking poetry and life
Like a thread on a spindle
Love reels us in

Lying together again that night, Tekkan played with the strands of hair that lay tangled on her pillow. "You know something ...?" he mused.

"Mmm?"

"When I was lecturing in Kobe, in front of all those people, I felt like a fraud."

"Why? They came to hear what you had to say."

He seemed to be weighing whether to tell her something. "I ... I never went to college. Or even high school."

"I know. Neither did I."

"But you're a woman," he said, and when she stiffened, he added, "You know what I mean. Most girls don't go to high school, but I might have."

Akiko nodded. It was frustrating, but true.

"I'm afraid of being exposed as an uneducated fool."

"You should have gone to college."

"My mother had hopes for me, but my father—well, I was one of five children. Four sons. He didn't have the money, and he only cared about my elder brothers."

Akiko understood this, too. "My mother doesn't care for me," she said.

Tekkan rolled onto his stomach and raised himself on his elbows to get a better look at her. Stringy muscles cut deep shadows along his forearms, and his eyes were earnest.

"Why?"

"Oh, you know how it is."

"No, really, how could your mother not like you?"

"I was supposed to be a son. I'm not graceful. I don't smile. And I read too much. She says that men don't like women who are scholarly."

"Hah!" Tekkan grasped her hip with his hand and pulled her toward him. "Just my kind of woman."

"Do you know what I think?" she asked.

"What?" His voice was muffled, kissing her neck.

She had to catch her breath before she could speak again. "We are like flowers or baby chicks: beautiful and young, but in a moment, we will be gone. The Lady Yokihi and the Emperor, does anyone care whether they followed the rules?"

"Not a bit. In fact, it's better that they didn't." His lips were moving down to the deep valley between her breasts.

"We don't care whether they were married," Akiko said, threading her fingers through his hair, "what rules they broke, or what plans they wrecked. We only care that they loved truly, if only for a short time."

She looked up at the boards lining the ceiling. A few of them were darkened with old water stains. An electric light dangled from the center, a black wire snaking across the ceiling and down one wall. "Beauty is more important than purity," she said. His mouth was moving back up again, to her neck, her ear lobes, her jaw. She loved how it felt to say scandalous things.

Tekkan raised his head. Apparently, she had got him thinking. "I never had a reputation to protect." He turned onto his back, so they were both looking up, like children watching clouds on a grassy hillside. He fit his arm under her shoulders and pulled her close. "I've never felt safe. I want to think about poetry but sometimes all I can think about is my empty stomach."

It felt strange to be in the company of someone in this way: relaxed, thoughtful, physically close. From the corner of her eye, she watched his hand move to his torso, where a tuft of hair grew just under his navel.

"With other women, I always felt alone." His voice was soft now. "It feels different with you. I've never met anyone like you."

She had imagined moments like this in her *Tale of Genji* fantasies, set against a backdrop of hyacinth and wind chimes. But not in this world, not for her. Tomorrow, she would remand herself to her parents' custody, and none of his promises might come to pass. It all might be pillow talk or lies. Like Yokihi and the Emperor Gensō, perhaps it wasn't meant to last. It was ridiculous anyway, that he should love the brooding, bookish third Surugaya daughter.

For now, though, it was real enough. She rolled toward him. If he was serious about bringing her to Tokyo, she thought, letting her hands move down past the small of his back, she would not turn him down. She wondered if he knew what he had found in her. She was no ordinary person. She would bind them together, weld them, even if his vanity and weakness weighed them down. If he sank into the waves, she would sink with him. Whatever happened, she could not go back to her old life. Everything was different now.

X: THE SECRET

Spring 1901, Akiko is twenty-three

Thinking of you
I fell asleep and saw you
If I had known it was a dream
I would not have opened my eyes

—Ono no Komachi (825-900 AD)

"I am sorry, Mrs. Otani, we don't have any *usukawa manju*," Akiko said. She had told Mrs. Otani the same thing just a few days earlier, but the old lady was forgetful. "We do have sweet potato yōkan, though; I think you'll like it." A loyal Surugaya customer as far back as Akiko could remember, Mrs. Otani repeatedly asked for an adzuki bean confection that Surugaya didn't carry. Luckily, she could usually be talked into yōkan, which Surugaya had in abundance.

"Sadashichi made it up this morning, and we always sell out," Akiko said, wrapping a yōkan bar while Mrs. Otani, who had the stance of an old crow, rummaged with arthritic fingers in her change purse.

Akiko suppressed the urge to wrench the purse from the old lady's hands and count out the money herself. She closed her eyes for a moment to quiet her nerves. Before parting, Tekkan had promised to send for her, to bring her to Tokyo to be his wife and business partner. It wouldn't be long, he had said, but he needed time to deal with issues related to his fiancée Takino and *Myōjo*—not the least of which was that Takino's father had stopped lending him money, but she was still Editor-in-Chief.

Akiko was no stranger to suppressing internal storms, but in her twenty-three short years she had never carried such a burden. She thought she might suddenly split in half or dissolve into hysterical laughter at the shop counter. She could feel her pulse thrumming in her ears whenever she stood still, so she distracted herself by studying her customers with the nostalgic eye of a departing traveler.

In addition to the corvine Mrs. Otani, there were the Nakazawa sisters, who had always been old as far as Akiko could remember. They came for the o-senbei rice crackers, the round ones wrapped in seaweed. Inoue-san, a widower in his thirties, came with his red-cheeked son, Shōta, who had grown from a toddler into a lanky lad. Shōta liked cherry-blossom candies, and, in summer, shaved ice.

The administrators at Aguchi Shrine regularly ordered yōkan for tea ceremony events, and in early spring the shrine's traditional dances and musical performances necessitated large orders as well. The priest Okawa-san, round and jolly with eyes that disappeared into his cheeks when he smiled, would come to pick them up, accompanied by young priests-in-training with shaved heads to carry the heavy trays.

These regular customers would be scandalized when the truth about her liaison became known. Some of them would stop patronizing Surugaya altogether. Sakai was a proud city, stubbornly un-modern.

Its elders dreamed of the days when samurai walked the streets with swords at their sides, or further back still, to the time when it was a wealthy trading port. Nonconformists were not indulged.

As the days ran into weeks, Akiko confided in no one. She balanced the books, filled orders, and saw customers to the door, bowing and thanking them as they went on their way. A picture of decorum, inside she was a girl on fire.

狂ひの子われに焔の翅かろき百三十里あわただしの旅
Like a crazed thing,
Three hundred miles I would fly,
On wings of fire

Her mother's eyes followed her around the shop so insistently it made her itch. Akiko avoided returning her gaze, fearful that the truth was written on her face. They said little to each other as they went about their days, helping themselves to rice, miso soup, and pickles by the *irori* floor hearth in the morning and fish and vegetables in the evening. Akiko was mostly silent—nothing unusual about *that*, she thought.

At night, unable to throttle back her emotions after long days of suppressing them, she wrote frenzied letters to Tekkan, detailing the depths of her love, lamenting her sins against Takino and her family, even threatening to take her own life. She wrote poems late into the night, lighting a gas lamp after the electricity went off. As the snows of February melted into the wet streets of March, she waited for a response, but his letters were few. Increasingly anxious, she wrote that he should forget her and move on; and every day, she waited in fear of a letter saying that he had done just that.

When Tekkan did write, he echoed her feelings but mentioned Takino casually, as though she and Akiko might someday be friends. Was he unwilling to consider marriage again so soon? If Akiko could be content with something less, would he prefer it? *If he thinks I will run away from home to be his mistress, he is mistaken.* At the same time, she feared she did not have the strength to turn him down, whatever he offered.

山ごもりかくてあれなのみをしへよ紅つくるころ桃の花さ
かむ

When the peach trees bloom, I will be out of rouge,
But you say I must stay hidden in the mountains

Better news came in April in a letter tucked into a thick *Myōjo* editorial mailing—at least, from her perspective it was better: *I never thought love could drive me mad like this,* he wrote. *You have broken me.*
Good, she thought.

He apologized for the delay, but new problems had arisen. In addition to his troubles with Takino, a libelous pamphlet was circulating. Titled *Yosano Tekkan: Portrait of a Demon of the Literary World,* it had appeared in the mailboxes of scores of literary scholars and booksellers. The anonymous booklet accused him of everything from infidelity and financial irresponsibility to rape, robbery, and arson. Tekkan suspected the author was a competitor who wanted to spoil *Myōjo*'s success. The allegations were fabricated, he assured her, but the timing was terrible, coming just as the magazine's sales were taking off.

Then, as April brought longer days and cherry blossoms, a letter addressed in a woman's hand arrived for Akiko. The return address read HAYASHI. *Takino,* thought Akiko breathlessly as she tore open the envelope. She scanned the graceful script, turning the tissue-thin pages with trembling hands:

> *By now, you will know my name and I know yours, so no introduction is necessary. I want you to know that I have broken off my engagement with Mr. Yosano. You may have him. Do not feel guilty; this is not your fault.*

Akiko wondered why this woman needed to unburden herself to her husband's mistress, but it did not matter as much as the news it brought:

You may think me a fool, but I suspected he was having an affair last fall. Perhaps you do not know that, as editor of Myōjo, I open the mail every day. I have read your poems, and those of other women like you.

Takino had confronted Tekkan about the flirtatious submissions, and he had not denied improprieties, arguing instead that romantic affairs were "essential inspiration" for an artist.

Bear that in mind. I write this so that you understand what kind of man he is before you make a decision that cannot be undone.

You should also know I am not the first woman to have borne a child by him. She was only a girl, really, a student, but she went back to her family after the baby died. I feel sorry for her. You are at least the third woman, Mistress Akiko.

My father lent him money repeatedly over the past two years and has gotten none of it back. Myōjo is a well-intentioned project, but it is destined to fail.

I had already made up my mind to leave him, but that horrid 'Demon' pamphlet settled it. Those stories are exaggerated but there is some truth to them, and now it is generally known.

When I told Tekkan that I was leaving, he followed me around the house like a child and begged me to stay. He says he still loves me. I canceled the lease on our rental house and used the proceeds to buy our son Atsumu and myself train tickets home. I have no idea where Tekkan is now, but you may find him sleeping on the ground outdoors. He has not a penny to his name. I leave him to you and wish you happiness.

Akiko read the letter twice. The allegations did not concern her, nor did news of another baby, although Takino's mention of poems from "other women like you" made her stiffen. Above all, she was relieved to hear that the engagement was truly over. In her deranged state of mind, she would have forgiven Tekkan anything, happily slept on the ground, or begged for food with him. It was better than living in a cage, never in control, smarter than most, yet condemned for it. The girl with the plain face and the ugly brown hanten jacket would always lurk inside her, but she would steer her own life, with him as partner, even if her family disowned her and no one in Sakai ever spoke to her again.

Akiko was tense as a koto string by early May. She went about her duties, jaw clenched, hands balled into fists. Those around her seemed maddeningly unaware of her torment. Perhaps they feigned innocence. She wondered if she was losing her mind.

A letter from Tekkan arrived one day as the wisteria vines of late spring curled up the courtyard wall and opened their blooms to the sky. Takino, after briefly enduring curious stares and tacit disapproval in her conservative hometown, was returning to Tokyo with baby Atsumu, he wrote. She would study for a teaching certificate at the new Japan Women's University. She would stay with him for a few weeks until she found a permanent place to stay. He wrote this casually, as though a mere acquaintance were coming to visit. Akiko threw down the letter, trying not to retch.

Then, three weeks later, in early June, the long-awaited letter finally arrived.

I am ready. Come to me and be my wife. He had moved to a flat on the outskirts of Tokyo to save money and leave behind gossiping neighbors.

He wanted to escort her to Tokyo, but she replied that she preferred to travel by herself, to preempt speculation about why she was leaving home. She was not being kidnapped or hoodwinked; she was not pregnant; this was her choice.

Next, she dashed off telegrams to Sato and Tomiko:

MEET ME KYOTO STATION MONDAY NOON.
AM EN ROUTE TO TOKYO. NO RETURN PLANNED.

With that, her future flipped like a switch from right to left, safe to perilous, and clear to chaos.

For her, Surugaya would become a memory, with its noisy streetfront, starlike points of dust suspended in the slant of morning light, and books in her father's library. Her mother's voice, her father's mouth pulling on his pipe, his *Tale of Genji* volumes: these no longer belonged to her. Akiko wished she could explain or apologize, but she held her tongue.

> *It floats in my memory,*
> *The house on the corner in my hometown of Sakai*
> *With the shop counter, the water-blue glow of*
> *an electric light,*
> *And in the store, two or three workers slumbering*
> *in the shadows of boxes.*
> *Suddenly, from under the black curtain*
> *Walking quietly, without a rustle of clothing,*
> *Looking in and then turning round to go back inside,*
> *With an obi the pink of nadeshiko flowers*
> *That young silhouette, disappearing as quietly as it appeared,*
> *Is me.*

"Shoko-han, your futon is laid out for you," the maid called from upstairs. If Akiko had been leaving home for a proper marriage, the maid would have accompanied her. What would become of her now? This girl, hardly older than her, had cared for her these last ten years. Now, she would probably be let go. Perhaps her mother would write her a recommendation for a new engagement. Layers of guilt accumulated like unpaid accounts in the Surugaya ledger.

Before turning out her light, she had one more task.

Mother,

When you read this letter, I will be on my way to Tokyo and my new life.

She tapped her ink pen and looked at her writing hand, with its blue veins branching from fingers to forearm. Her mother's arms had looked like these once. Strong and pale, they had washed floors and hung out mattresses to air.

Long ago, her mother and father had done the *mochizuki*, the pounding of rice into mochi, together. Akiko remembered how Tsuné would tie back her kimono sleeves with cords and cover her front with an apron that reached from her neck to her knees. Sōshichi would fill a massive mortar with steaming rice and pound it into a sticky mash with his heavy wooden mallet. To keep the mash consistent, Tsuné would reach in between blows to turn the heavy mass over. It was hard, physical work for them both. Lean in, turn, lean out, *whomp*. Lean in, turn, lean out, *whomp*. She was in no condition to do such work anymore, and Sōshichi preferred attending *Noh* plays, shopping for ukiyo-e prints, and reading, so Sadashichi and the servants had taken over.

But bookkeeping was critical, too. No one knew the books like Akiko, nor the ordering of supplies, the planning, the administrative maintenance. Sadashichi would handle it until Chūsaburo finished college. She had written a long note to him and tucked it into the ledger, explaining that he must place rice orders with the vendor Suzuki at least two months in advance; only Suzuki would deliver the highest quality local rice.

In time, Chū would get married; there would be a bride to help. Still, Akiko's gut was full of rocks and her temples throbbed. *I promised Father I would stay. What if they order Sato home from school? My mother was right. I am prideful and selfish. And now, I am betraying them all.*

The worst part for her mother would be the public humiliation. Very soon, everyone in town would know that Sho the Surugaya girl had run off with a married man and was publishing sexy poetry. Would the Nakazawa sisters buy their mochi elsewhere? What about Mrs. Otani? The smiling priest Okawa would avoid them, and when others called at the New Year—Suzuki the rice vendor, the adzuki bean wholesaler, the sugar salesman, the printer, the banker, and all their neighbors and friends—their visits would be clouded by knowing glances and veiled insinuations. They wouldn't even ask about Sho, as if she never existed.

For a moment, Akiko wavered. Except for the telegrams she had sent Tomiko and Sato, her secret was still safe, her world intact. She could choose to stay. That had been her original plan, after all.

She was leaning forward over the desk, the weight of her decision bending her like a sapling under ice. Then she looked at the door that locked her in, and her throat burned. Had Tsuné ever been in love? To Tsuné, cherry blossoms, roses, and persimmons signified mere shifts in Surugaya's seasonal offerings; they had no intrinsic music, no beauty. To her, daughters were commodities.

In her mind, she was back on the stack of boxes with her brother daring her to jump. *Why try to explain myself if she has no capacity to understand?* Fewer words were better.

I am going to marry the poet Yosano Tekkan. I have been a disappointment to you. Forgive me.

She had been a problem since the day of her birth, and now she added betrayal and dishonesty to her list of crimes. This would be her burden. Her mother would be proven right in the end.

Placing the letter on her table, Akiko went to bed for the last time at Surugaya.

母よびてあかつき問ひし君といはれそむくる片頬柳にふれぬ
"You're up early," Mother calls after me,
As I lower my head and brush past the willow tree

Akiko hoisted an overnight bag and a *furoshiki* scarf containing a writing tablet and a few precious books on her arm. She had told her mother she planned to meet Sato in Kyoto, where they would attend the rice planting festival at Fushimi Inari Shrine.

"When will you be back?" asked Tsuné. Her voice was cross. "You are always going away. Sadashichi can barely manage without you."

"Tomorrow afternoon," Akiko lied. Her heart was thumping; her cheeks blazed. The maid offered to walk her to the station, but Akiko waved her off and stepped out the door.

"Oh, my parasol ..." She reached back in the door to take it from the hook. "All right, then, see you. *Itte kimasu,*" she said, as she had said ten thousand times on the way out the door. *I go but I will come back.* The words sat black as crows on the threshold.

"*Itte irasshai,*" Tsuné said. *Go but come back.*

Akiko bowed, avoiding her eyes. She tried not to vomit on her shoes as she turned away. It took every bit of restraint she could muster not to break into a run. Excitement, guilt, and fear rose like a flood on the main street of Sakai, sweeping her off her feet and carrying her away as the maid and her mother returned to their morning chores.

XI: ESCAPE

June 1901, Akiko is twenty-three

Kyoto to Tokyo

来世とや捨てて来し日の母の泣く夢を見る子の何おののかむ

Haunted by dreams of my weeping mother,
This daughter fears no punishment in the afterlife

"Being married isn't so bad," pink-cheeked Tomiko said as they sipped tea on a bench outside Kyoto Station a few hours later. Sparrows picked at crumbs around their feet. The smell of early summer was in the air, and it seemed that the entire local population had found an excuse to be outside. Tomiko and Akiko had to raise their voices to be heard above the creak of rickshaw suspensions, the scrape of cart wheels, train whistles, and the screams of exultant children.

"The wedding was beautiful," Tomiko said. At the private Shinto ceremony, she had worn the same bridal kimono that her mother and grandmother had worn before her, a snow-white silk robe embroidered with white lilies and ivy. Her hair had been pulled back in a formal *taka-shimada* bun and covered with a peaked white silk hood.

At the reception—which the whole town turned out for, she said—she had changed into a multicolored kimono belonging to the groom Tomeshichiro's mother, symbolizing her new life. It was festooned with embroidered cranes against a grove of bamboo in brilliant vermillion, green, gold, and silver. Tomiko's father had laid out enough saké to keep the town fathers drunk for a month and a generous banquet of local *sashimi*, sea bream, festive red rice, and special spring delicacies. Tomeshichiro had been ill, though, so they had not been able to travel as a couple yet. She looked forward to spending time alone with him soon.

When Akiko asked about her plans for writing, she admitted that she had not been able to do much. In fact, she said, Tomeshichiro was suspicious about her correspondence with Akiko. And there was gossip about Tekkan.

"I didn't tell anyone that I'm meeting you today," Tomiko said, looking at Akiko carefully. "Tell me, you're going to Tokyo? You're going to be with Sensei? You'll be his—" She trailed off.

Akiko had not told her about the weekend in January. She did not want to hurt Tomiko further, and it felt scandalous to talk about.

"I am going to help him edit *Myōjo*," Akiko said simply. "He says I can stay with him."

"Are you—?" Tomiko pressed, but Akiko shrugged.

"He has broken off his engagement with Takino. I suppose we'll see." Their eyes met, and there was a long silence.

"I love the color of June in Kyoto," Tomiko said then, breaking their gaze to look up at the sky. "The light is so different from November."

わが心君を恋ふると高ゆくや親もちいさし道もちいさし

Raising up my love for you
My parents diminish,
My path forward
Narrows

The overnight local train was scheduled to arrive at Tokyo's Shimbashi Station early the next morning. As Akiko waved goodbye to Sato on the train platform, for the first time in her life she wondered where she would sleep tomorrow, what she would eat, and how she would pay for it.

She passed a fitful night, dozing on the hard train seat. An old woman sat across from her, kimono collar pulled primly around her wattled neck. There was a package wrapped in an indigo furoshiki scarf on her lap and a suitcase on the floor next to her. As the train rocked, the lady looked steadily at her, her mouth gathered in a wrinkled line. Perhaps she wondered what a young woman like her was doing alone on an overnight train to Tokyo.

Something naughty inside her wanted to lean forward and whisper, *It's true, Grandmother, I'm running away from home. My lover is a rake and a scoundrel.* Instead, she looked out the window into the darkness, her pale reflection looking back, while her thoughts ran in tortured circles. Eventually she drifted off, head against the windowpane.

The voice of the conductor announcing their arrival at Shimbashi Station jerked her awake. She sat up and looked around. It was morning, and the train was pulling into a large station building with a high metal ceiling. The air was filled with coal smoke and the cacophony of brakes, whistles, and voices. She reached up to touch her hair. *I must look half-crazed*, she thought, and pulled a compact from her purse to dab makeup on her cheeks and lips.

Once on the train platform, she looked around anxiously. She had wired ahead with her arrival time, but she couldn't be sure Tekkan had received it. She did not want to be alone in this strange, sprawling city.

Then she saw him. He was standing several cars down, thin and tall in his threadbare kimono. His body was angled away from her, searching faces as passengers poured off the train. A conductor with a black cap was bellowing at him to move out of the way, and a group of men in Western suits shouldered by, followed by a man pushing a cart and a woman with a baby strapped to her back, holding a toddler's hand.

"Tekkan-san!" she called, self-consciously using his first name. He turned further away as she swam toward him, and for a second, she let herself marvel at the line of his cheekbone in silhouette, the graceful slope of his nose, the windy darkness of his hair. "Tekkan-san!"

Then he turned toward her, and his face flushed with pleasure. They bowed to each other—in public it wouldn't be appropriate to do more—"You came!" he said, and the contrast between his words and the enormity of the moment made them both laugh.

He took her bag and led her out of the station, explaining that they would catch a streetcar to Shibuya.

"We could walk, but it's far, and you must be tired from your trip," he said.

"Actually, I feel like I could do anything," she said, and meant it, though she was trembling from head to toe.

She took in her surroundings. For three hundred years, Japan's five main highways had converged here, at Nihombashi. The boulevard before her was packed with horse-drawn street cars, rickshaws, pedestrians, and carts, most of them making for the wide bridge. Shops were open, colorful signs competed for attention, and a tangle of electrical wires and telegraph poles filled the sky. The river below was clogged with pole boats and moorings. To her, Osaka had always been the "big city," but Tokyo's population was ten times greater, and everyone seemed to be crossing the bridge at this very moment.

"What are you thinking?" he asked.

"Oh, I'm just amazed," she said. But she was also thinking, *I do not know what the future holds, but I will be like the earth beneath his feet, the air that he breathes. I will be stronger than ten men. He will not want any other woman. I will make him love me.*

The maid met them wordlessly at the door of Tekkan's shabby flat in the rice paddy-dotted suburb of Dogen Hill, stomping off to the back of the house with Akiko's bag, muttering about her mistress Takino.

"Keep that to yourself, or you'll find yourself out on the street!" Tekkan barked after her. He looked apologetic as he showed Akiko into a small sitting room. She hesitated while he found a cushion for her to sit on.

"She's angry about Takino leaving," he explained, moving a pile of books to one side. He set the cushion on the floor and gestured for her to sit down. "She was quite fond of Atsumu."

Akiko nodded; surly maids were nothing new to her. She did wonder what it cost to keep a maid in Tokyo, however, and made a mental note to look at household finances soon. If they were going to live on the proceeds of *Myōjo* sales, some belt-tightening might be in order.

The clear voice of a monk calling for alms outside woke Akiko early the next morning. She lay still for a moment, remembering where she was. Then she thought about Tekkan lying next to her and all they had talked about the night before, their joyous lovemaking, and felt as happy in that moment as she had ever been.

They had pushed the low table into a corner to make room for blankets and sheets on the tatami floor. Tekkan was sleeping on his stomach in the middle of the tangle, his buttocks splendidly exposed. So *male* they were, in their compact shape and shadow, unlike the women's and children's bodies she knew. She sat up, folded her legs to one side, and pulled her long hair forward to cover her breasts. He was deeply asleep, so she pulled out her notebook and pencil. Her heart was full, and she needed to write.

ひとすじにあやなく君が指おちてみだれなむとす夜の黒髪
Reaching out a finger absently, you tangle
A strand of my night-black hair

After a while, Tekkan opened an eye, so she lifted one eyebrow and sent him her smile, the one that bent only the corners of her mouth. He stretched and raised himself onto his forearms, making a low, throaty sound that became a cough, then a laugh.

"I'm sore all over," he groaned.

She set down her notebook and leaned toward him, letting her dangling hair tickle his chest. "My last name is Hō, you know. The phoenix. The firebird."

He took a handful of hair and pulled her down on top of him.

"I feel so good," she murmured, as he kissed her. "I did it. I really did it! I've been trapped so long, and now I want to stretch my wings."

"Mmmm," he agreed. "My firebird, open wide."

They lingered late that morning, kissing and playing, lying on their backs or sitting up, standing naked or curling up together on the floor. Akiko had never felt so alive. Beautiful, even. When she went to fetch tea, she put a robe over her shoulders, but Tekkan pulled it off again as soon as she came back with a tray.

"It's too warm for clothes," he said. "And I like looking at you."

"I'm not used to being naked before anyone other than my sisters," Akiko said, but kept her robe off. At mid-morning it was already quite warm, and she could feel sweat around the halo of her face and between her legs. She reached back to lift her heavy hair with both hands, winding it into a thick knot behind her head and securing it with a wooden pin. Nothing could weigh on her spirits today, not even the heat. "*Winter is best when it's fearfully cold, but summer is most summerlike when it's impossibly hot,*" she said aloud to herself, and her heart surged when Tekkan recognized it from *The Pillow Book*, a classic written about the same time as *The Tale of Genji*.

Conversation soon turned to the editing, publishing, and marketing work that had to be done. Tekkan wanted to announce something special in the July issue of *Myōjo*.

"I've been thinking," he said, "you wrote so much this spring. Did you bring your poems with you?"

"Many of them," she answered. "And I sent many of them to you."

"I think we should publish a collection."

Akiko's eyes grew wide. "You mean a standalone book? Just mine?" She had enough solid work to fill a collection, but books by women were rare. "Are you sure?"

"Of course. You and I will be great partners," he said.

"All right." Her mind was racing. "Here's an idea, a theme for the book, what ties these poems together."

"Let me guess," he said. "The keeping of a secret. Hidden love. Springtime and youth."

"Not bad," Akiko said. "But more like this: passionate, youthful love. The tangle of hair. The waning of spring." She hesitated. "And, well, guilt. Or repudiation of guilt. If love is a sin, that it can be forgiven."

"Fantastic," Tekkan muttered. He pressed his face into her hair and took a deep breath.

"For once, I don't have to imagine what it feels like," she whispered, and a piece of her soul burst from her chest and penetrated his, a stronger wedding bond than any human rite.

雲ぞ青き来し夏姫が朝の髪うつくしいかな水に流るる
How blue the clouds
Comes the summer nymph
To wash her pretty hair in the stream

They got to work that very day. After the banning of the *Myōjo* November issue, government censors and prudish academics would be watching closely, so they would have to go carefully. No nude illustrations. Tekkan was confident that if they could elude the censors, young people would be hungry for her romantic, sexy poems.

They laid out 399 tanka on 138 pages. Tekkan commissioned art from Fujishima Takeji, an artist who had done illustrations for *Myōjo*. His art deco design of a woman with raven hair set inside an arrow-pierced heart seemed perfect for the cover. They priced the 8" X 4" paper pamphlet at thirty-five sen. This was not cheap for middle-class readers: it would buy a respectable dinner for two people in Tokyo, but it was the best they could do.

Tangled Hair was printed in August 1901, a modest first run of a few hundred copies. To save money, Akiko and Tekkan borrowed a wagon and personally delivered boxes of *Myōjo* magazines and copies of *Tangled Hair* to bookstores and newsstands around Tokyo. Tekkan pulled the wagon and Akiko pushed on hills. At each stop, they introduced themselves and thanked the proprietor.

Then they turned to the next project. There was no time to waste.

In September, Akiko let go of the maid. This saved them only the cost of her food, as she received no salary. For the first time in her life, Akiko did all the housework herself. She was no stranger to hard work, but any dream of free time to focus on writing went out with the chamber pot.

It was lucky that she could write fast—dashing off twenty tanka in a sitting—because Tekkan was a slow writer and not inclined to help with housework. She scrubbed, shopped, cooked, swept, washed clothes, and aired out bedding, day after day, in addition to writing and editing. With no money for coal, she gathered wood outdoors to feed the stove. She dried and reused tea leaves. Instead of going to the public bathhouse, they washed their hands and faces in a basin of cold water.

It was not the work but the lack of food that was hardest. She had been accustomed to food of high quality. Her uncle the fishmonger had often sent them gifts of the latest catch, and her father had insisted on the best ingredients. He even had a ten-compartment lacquered dinner box in which his dinner was served on special days.

Akiko was thinking about this one evening as she flipped a mackerel on the stove with cooking sticks. She sprinkled the blistering skin with sea salt and breathed in the lovely aroma. In Sakai she had rarely cooked, but she was a quick study and a prudent shopper. She thought her meals were not half bad.

Tekkan came into the kitchen sniffing hungrily.

"What have you got there?" he asked, looking over her shoulder.

"Salt mackerel, and there is fresh rice and miso soup," she said. "And I tried making some *takuan* pickles."

She divided the fish with her cooking chopsticks, transferring half onto a bowl of rice for him and half for her.

He grew suddenly brusque. "What's this?"

She looked at him with surprise. "You don't like mackerel?"

"You cooked the whole thing?" he seemed astonished, but Akiko was equally so. She stared at him, rice bowl in hand.

"You need to stop acting like a rich girl. This much fish should make three meals." He stood up and dumped his fish irritably back onto the paper in which it had been wrapped, then placed his bowl back on the table with a clunk.

"I'm sorry, I—"

"And now we have no way to keep this fresh, it's too hot out. We'll have to eat this half in the morning and go without tomorrow night." He slumped back onto his floor cushion, folding his arms and legs crossly.

"I didn't—" tears of hurt came to her eyes. *If you didn't spend every penny of our income on Myōjo and entertaining your New Poetry Society friends, we might not be dividing one mackerel into six portions.*

Tekkan's tone softened when he saw her tears. "I grew up eating temple food. Barley and beans. Dirt and leaves. I know what hunger is. You are too soft."

In October, they held a small wedding ceremony at a local shrine. Writer and translator Kimura Takatarō acted as official witness. Tekkan had wanted his mentor Ochiai Naobumi to stand in this role, but refrained from asking him out of fear his own damaged reputation would be embarrassing.

They met some of Tekkan's friends for saké and sat for a wedding photograph. Akiko sent a telegram to Sakai to notify her parents and officially registered her new name at the town hall. Then the Yosanos got back to work.

One afternoon, as Akiko was wringing out undergarments and hanging them on the back porch, she heard Tekkan calling for her.

"I'm here," she said, coming inside. Her hair was tied back and covered with a kerchief.

"Look at this," he said, and waited while she dried her hands on her apron before handing her a copy of *Critic* magazine. It was open to an article entitled, "New-Style Poets and '*Tangled Hair*'".

Akiko cringed. So far, reviews of *Tangled Hair* had been mixed— young people were, as Tekkan had predicted, buying it up hungrily. It had not been banned, but some literary magazines had dismissed it as the prattle of a love-drunk girl. Several had been horrified by the sexual innuendo and narcissism. But there had been positive reviews as well, including an anonymous essay which (they knew privately) had been written by the respected poet Ueda Bin.

As she skimmed the *Critic* review, a light grew on her face. She looked up from time to time at Tekkan as she read; he was smiling back. The author mocked prudish readers for flapping their hands over her sensual poetry, pointing out that men had always written about sex. He went on to analyze her poetry for its literary merits and proclaimed Yosano Akiko "a promising new woman writer."

"Well done," Tekkan said, but she detected a strain in his voice. Few people had bought his work since the scandalous pamphlet had hurt his reputation. She wanted to dance for joy, but now she sensed that success might bring its own challenges.

XII: THE VISITOR

1902, Akiko is twenty-four
Tokyo

母にいにし昨日の魂や闇にまどふしら梅ちさき戸はうすみぞれ

Missing her mother, her spirit wanders, lost in the dark,

And like a thin plum tree, shivers in the freezing rain

In spring 1902, almost a year after Akiko left home, a trunk arrived in Dogen Hill. It contained linens, a silk kimono, obi sashes, furoshiki scarves, and lacquered hairpins. Lying on top was an envelope, addressed in her mother's spidery handwriting. It was the first letter she had received from home. Steeling herself, she opened it.

I can only regret what has come to pass and feel responsible, her mother wrote, following a formal greeting and inquiries after her health. She suggested that Akiko's disastrous decision to leave home could be attributed to the inauspicious circumstances of her birth.

Your father wanted a son, so we had to send you away to stay with my sister in Yanagi-machi. I wonder if you can understand how hard this was for me. I wanted to throw us both in the river to drown. In some way, the person you are now goes back to those days.

It was hard for you? Akiko thought angrily. *What about me?* Still, she wished she had known this before. There was an old saying: *the toddler's ghosts linger one hundred years.* It meant that childhood trauma lingered into adulthood and passed from one generation to the next. Akiko knew almost nothing of her mother's childhood; she wondered for the first time whether something had hurt her long before Akiko was born.

Well, Akiko thought, frowning, *it will stop with me.* There was a new ghost whispering in her ear, a new secret: she had not bled last month. She would not tell her family just yet, but Tekkan knew.

She set the letter aside and lifted the pretty textiles one by one. The afternoon sun picked up the indigo, white, and gold-threaded *yuzen* flower patterns. She carefully refolded each, estimating its value. As much as she could use new things to wear, those textiles would fetch two months' food and rent.

The next week, a clerk from the publisher Ito Bunyūkan hoisted the trunk onto a cart and pulled it to a pawnshop, with Akiko walking alongside. It would not have been appropriate for a woman of good upbringing to patronize such a store alone, so the clerk had agreed to accompany her. As he stood nearby, she told the broker she wanted cash. When they left the store a few minutes later, she held her head high, eyes shining. The clerk followed silently behind.

今ここにかへりみすればわがなさけ　闇をおそれぬめしひに似たり
Looking back now I see
My love was like a blindness
I did not fear the dark

One day in late summer, there was a loud knock at the front door. Akiko was on her hands and knees cleaning coal dust from the stove, so Tekkan answered. Soon, she heard raised voices. She strained to hear what was being said, wondering if it was a debt collector. The voice was familiar, though. After a moment, Tekkan poked his head through the door.

"It's your brother," he said. "He has come for you."

Akiko brushed coal dust off her hands and the hem of her skirt and hurried past him to find her elder brother Hidetaro scowling in the entryway. He stood, hat in hand, shoes on. She invited him inside, but he was in no mood for it. A man had been sent to him by Takino's family, he said, to collect the money that Tekkan owed them. It was the first he had heard of Tekkan's debts.

"I knew you had run off with a poet," he said, crushing his hat with both hands. "I didn't know he was engaged and had a child. I didn't know he was taking loans for his ridiculous magazine," he said. "Did you ever think to ask my permission? Do you know what people say about him, and about you?"

"Those are lies," Akiko said as calmly as she could. *At least, most of them are.* She was sorry to hear that Takino's family had involved him, she said, ignoring his comment about asking permission. She promised that she and Tekkan would pay off the debts. "You needn't pay a sen," she said. "Come inside and have some tea."

"This is not a social visit, Shoko-han, and I am not leaving without you."

They faced off like cats in the narrow entry. Standing below her on the dirt foundation, his nose was almost even with hers. As a child she had looked up to him, but things were different now. When he reached for her arm, she pulled away.

"I am married, and I will not be taken anywhere against my will. I decide for myself where I go and what I do."

Hidetaro raised a finger. "Here's one thing you'll do: you'll stop publishing slutty poems that are an embarrassment to your family. Did you think about how it affects us?"

Akiko felt herself hardening into the obstinate little girl he used to call a *selfish know-it-all*. She put her hands on her hips and said nothing.

"And you will stop living with an irreputable man," he continued.

"We are married."

"Did you know he had a baby by another woman before Takino?"

"Yes," she said as her hand went unconsciously to her belly. Hidetaro did not seem to notice.

"That baby died, and the woman went back to her family." His face was growing redder, like a pot of stew on a stove. "He has been borrowing money from the Hayashi family for years. Do you know," he shifted his weight from one foot to the other and clasped his arms across his chest, "how Takino found out that her engagement was off?"

Akiko waited, her face hot.

"Yosano and her father agreed to break it off and didn't even bother telling her! She found out from a friend, who went to Tokyo to find her and bring her home. No one even told her that her marriage was over!"

Akiko did not know this. It must have been too humiliating for Takino to mention in her letter.

Hidetaro apparently didn't recognize the irony of his outrage over the men dictating Takino's life, but Akiko did. She was no longer her brother's, or her father's, property. Legally—and here she felt a mixture of anger and shame—she was Tekkan's property now. So was the baby. *Double irony*, she thought. *Is the joke on me after all?*

When Hidetaro left, she returned to the sitting room where Tekkan waited. He raised his eyebrows in question.

She smiled and shrugged.

"Why didn't you go with him?" he asked. "I can't give you anything."

"You are my husband," she said. She turned toward the stove and busied herself with the teapot. With her back to him she said, "It's my decision. No one will force me to do anything." She poured hot water into the pot.

"Did you tell him about the baby?"

She shook her head. She wanted to ask him about Takino but decided that question could wait. "I told him we would bring honor to the family."

"What did he say?"

Akiko shrugged again. "He told me—" now her voice broke, and she turned to face him. "—to consider myself no longer family," she sank down on a stool, "and to stay away from Sakai."

Tekkan knelt before her. "I'm sorry," he said.

Akiko nodded, her eyes full of tears. She smiled ruefully and dabbed at the corner of an eye with her apron. "He didn't even know who 'Akiko' was at first, when the debt collector visited him. They always called me Shoko-han at home."

He chuckled. Shoko-han was gone for good.

XIII: FIREFLIES

Fall 1903, Akiko is twenty-five
Sakai

父ぞ来ます御列むかふる秋の寺つめたき廊の敷瓦かな

Oh, Father

Autumn greets your funeral procession

With the cold slate of the temple floor

As the rickshaw from Sakai Station bumped around the corner onto her street, Akiko held her infant son tightly on her lap and craned to see around the driver's back. She had come from Tokyo as quickly as she could when she received the news from Chūsaburo that their father had collapsed.

The driver snaked through foot traffic, taking her past all the familiar sights: the old temple, the saké store, the rice vendor, the stationery store run by the widow Kawakita-san, and the corner tobacco vendors. The shops were crowded with afternoon customers; children, some with younger siblings strapped to their backs, chased each other under the telegraph poles. It all looked the same as she remembered, until Surugaya came into view. A small crowd obscured the corner storefront; a man was tottering on a step stool, hanging black and white buntings across the entrance.

Akiko could feel the blood drain from her face as she stepped from the rickshaw. She recognized some faces; neighbors looked at the baby in her arms, but did not acknowledge her. The muffled chant of a sutra from inside the shop met her ears, low and sad, punctuated by the bong of a wooden mallet on a bell. Incense smoke stung her brain as she thought, *my father is dead.*

A servant recognized her and ran into the shop, calling for Tsuné, who appeared a moment later in the white kimono Akiko remembered from Hana's funeral. Tsuné's eyes went to the baby in Akiko's arms.

"Mother—" Akiko began, trying to read the emotions in her face.

Sato, dressed in black, emerged behind Tsuné and stopped short, staring. Her mouth dropped open. It occurred to Akiko that she must look different. The last two years had been hard on her.

"I'm too late," Akiko said, moving toward the shop entrance. Inside, she glimpsed black cloth draped over the candy counters, and three cedar tables festooned with white flowers. Candles, bowls of fruit and rice, and jars of saké stood before a lacquered *butsudan* altar inlaid with gold leaf on a tatami platform.

A formal portrait of her father, draped with a black sash, sat in the butsudan. Akiko knew it well. He had commissioned it less than ten years ago, for his fiftieth birthday. In the photograph, he stood next to an arrangement of spring blossoms on an ornately carved side table. He wore the family crest on his kimono sleeve and a fan protruded jauntily from his sash.

Sato stopped her with a hand. "I'm sorry, Big Sister, it's—uh, don't go in there right now. Why don't you wait in the sitting room?" She gestured toward the side entrance.

Akiko followed, heat prickling her neck. *I'm not even allowed inside?* She threw a glance at her mother, who stood motionless and small.

For the rest of the afternoon, Akiko stayed out of sight. Sato came to check on her occasionally, bringing Tsuné with her once. Conversation was uncomfortable. No one wanted to talk about Akiko's sudden departure, marriage, and new life. Instead, they admired the baby and talked about changes at Surugaya since she had left. Akiko wanted to know what had happened to her father.

Two days earlier, Sato said, he had not answered when called to dinner. In the study, the maid had found him sitting up but unable to speak. The doctor, hastily summoned, pronounced it a stroke. It would follow its natural course, he had said; there was nothing to be done. Sōshichi died later that night. He was only fifty-six.

As was the custom, they had washed his body and dressed him in a white funeral kimono, then held an overnight vigil. Following the reception, a funeral wagon would bear his body to the crematorium.

"I want to see him," Akiko said.

"Of course you do."

"Why can't I?"

"Hidetaro—" Sato stopped.

They both looked at the baby, whom Akiko and Tekkan had named Hikaru, after the "Shining" Lord Genji. Hikaru surveyed the surroundings with curious eyes and a frown that suddenly reminded her of her father. "He's like that," Akiko said. "Always the frown."

Sato reached out to let him curl a fist around her finger. "Like his mama. He's thinking about everything."

"I wish Father had met him." Akiko touched his soft head. "He was born not even a year ago. And I thought we would lose him this spring when he had whooping cough. He couldn't breathe. It was terrible." She looked at her sister for understanding, but she was shaking Hikaru's hand playfully. She had no idea—how could she? —how terrifying it was to be responsible for a child's life.

"We had no way to pay for it, but I called a doctor anyway. What choice did I have? He's still recovering. Maybe that's why he's so serious."

Sato brightened. "He looks healthy now. And I'm an aunt!" Teru had two children, but they were both girls. "My first nephew," Sato sighed happily.

"It will be your turn soon, you know," Akiko said, and Sato shrugged. "Maybe," and then she leaned forward to whisper, "Did you hear? Chū has a girlfriend!"

"What?!"

Sato was digging into the details when Chūsaburo came to the door. He looked handsome in his black mourning kimono; he was a man now, about to assume responsibility for Surugaya despite his unfinished studies. He had decided to leave college, adding another stone to Akiko's heavy trunk of guilt.

"Thank you for sending the wire, Chū." Akiko stood up, forcing herself to look him in the eye. More than anyone else, he had been kind to her.

"I'm sorry it arrived too late," he said. "Honestly, none of us had a chance to say goodbye. It happened so quickly. I was in Osaka." There were voices in the hallway, and he looked over his shoulder. "Hidetaro wants to see you," he said.

"Shall I go out to him?"

"No, he's coming here."

A moment later, Hidetaro ducked his head in the low doorway, bringing the scent of incense and camphor with him. At her front door in Tokyo, she had faced him straight on, but now he loomed over everyone, half a head taller than Chūsaburo. Sato retreated to a corner with the baby, leaving Akiko to confront him. She drew herself up. Tsuné appeared behind Hidetaro, and suddenly the tiny parlor was crowded.

"Who told you to come?" Hidetaro had been seething when she last saw him, but now he kept his temper in check. This was his territory.

"I got a telegram from Chū," she said.

"He had no right."

"He had every right. I am family," Akiko said.

"Not anymore."

Hidetaro's words did not surprise her, but they hurt. As a child, she had idolized him. He had read books to her by the hibachi in winter and taken her with him up to the fire platform on the roof in summer. She remembered holding onto his yukata with one hand as he pointed out constellations in the sky. What did those memories mean to him now? What about the others, who looked on and said nothing?

"I want to see him," Akiko said.

"I am head of the household now, and I forbid it."

"Mother," she appealed to Tsuné cringing behind him. Tradition and law dictated that widows obey their sons, but Akiko suspected it wasn't just tradition that silenced her. It was cowardice.

At last, Chūsaburo spoke. "Let her see him. At least let her light incense and say a prayer."

Hidetaro growled. He had spent years building his reputation among Tokyo's academic and scientific community. His sister's poetry and elopement were a headache for him. If he couldn't stop her from doing it, at least he could make it clear that he wanted no part.

"All right," he grunted. "Go say goodbye. But you will not walk in the procession. I won't be mocked by everyone in town."

It was not until that evening, when the reception room had emptied and the procession was forming outside, that Akiko was allowed to kneel before her father's shrine. She looked long at his photograph. She would never see it again.

"Father," she whispered, "Forgive me. I was a daughter when you needed a son. I was not beautiful, nor graceful, nor sweet. And I broke my promises. I caused you nothing but grief."

As she pressed her head on the cold floor, a memory came to her, unbidden, as though her father had sent it to comfort her.

One summer afternoon when she was about twelve or thirteen, she had escaped to the gloom of the warehouse behind the shop. It was a place she often went when Tsuné wasn't looking, to read among the crates, trunks, rice bags, and *tansu* dressers. She had loved how the wood floor cooled her bare feet, even in summer, how the organic scent of wattle and daub walls mixed with old paper, and the way the street noises outside were muffled, making them feel far away. There was a large trunk in the corner on which a beam of light shone on summer afternoons. It was like a stage before the first act.

That day, she knelt before the trunk, reading from *The Tale of Genji*. The string-bound set had belonged to her grandmother. She read without looking up, shifting her position to follow the sun as it moved across the window. Words gone from the vernacular a thousand years danced on the page: a noblewoman, beautiful and sad, gazed at a garden as she wrote with a thin brush. Her kimono lay in graceful folds on the wood floor, and a ribbon cinched her waterfall of hair. Then she imagined Lord Genji, dressed in handsome burgundy and white silk, astride a white stallion. He guided the horse gracefully as he joked with his retainer.

"Shirking your duties again?"

The voice broke her trance. Her father had come up behind her. A murky light gleamed down on his shoulders from the air vents above. She jumped, and fearing reproval, moved to hide the book, but his smile stopped her.

"It's just as Sadashichi said. I asked him what we should name our new yōkan. He said that you suggested, 'Princess Bridge', or 'Village of Drifting Flower Petals.' He has a soft spot for you, you know."

He sat down on a crate and looked at the open book. "Reading *Genji* again?"

Although it irritated Tsuné, he hadn't seemed to mind her book-
ishness. When she was old enough, he had let her attend Chinese
classics lessons with Chūsaburo and allowed her to read in his study.
He had even permitted her to attend poetry sessions. Perhaps he had
come to regret it.

"Thank you, Father," she whispered.

Chūsaburo touched her shoulder. She motioned him away, but
he pulled her arm.

"It's time to go. I'm sorry."

Outside, monks, musicians, family, and friends gathered around
the funeral wagon in the fading light. Hikaru squirmed in her arms
as Akiko watched. Burdened with the double loss of father and family, and disallowed from taking part, guilt compounded her grief.
Neighbors she had known all her life could not acknowledge her loss.

The priest ushered participants to their spots. Family members
came first, behind the wagon. Tsuné, ghostly in her white kimono,
held her husband's framed photograph, flanked by her two sons. Sister
Teru stood with her husband and daughters next to Hana's widower.
Sato was there. Behind them were town leaders: men from the Sakai
Merchants' Association, along with the priest Okawa-san and Mrs.
Otani with her daughter. Kōno was there in his monk's robes, next to
his father, representing Kakuōji Temple. The music of flutes, drums,
and bells started up with drunken disorderliness before settling into a
mournful dirge. Torchlight reflected off the wooden casket, fashioned
to look like a tiny temple with curving roof, faux doorway and little
torii gates.

Finally, the wagon creaked into motion.

For all her sadness, the sight comforted her. Funerals are important, she thought, as she watched the crowd move down the street into
the dusk. They give people something to do; they accept and honor
grief; they distract from the physical manifestation of death; they

underscore community and family ties. To be left out of her father's funeral did as much to isolate her as her brother's words had done. Yet, she had chosen this path. As a poet, she was obliged to break the blinders of tradition, to speak aloud about anger, grief, and loss. To find words for unspoken things, whatever the cost.

It's like catching feelings in flight, she thought. Like a child, who shows her friend the firefly in her palm. *I never knew that's what a firefly looked like close up,* her friend might say, peering into her hand, and what she means is, *thank you, yes, that's exactly the way I feel.*

When the last straggling funeralgoer disappeared around the bend, Akiko collected her things, tied Hikaru snugly to her back, and left for the station on foot. With much of the neighborhood taking part, the street in front of Surugaya was quiet. As she shut the door behind her, it made a final *click. I will never be locked in again,* she thought, and walked away, pocketing the key. She imagined a firefly in her hand, and lifting her palm, set it free.

A letter was waiting for Akiko back in Tokyo. It was from Tomiko.

I hope you are staying well as the days grow shorter. Here in Obama, the ocean wind is cold, and the trees have shed their leaves. Perhaps they are mourning with me, as my husband Tomeshichiro is dead. He passed to the Next World a few weeks ago. Our hopes for his recovery were in vain.

I have moved back home for now, but I cannot remain like this, feeling sorry for myself. I have a dream of attending the new Japan Women's University. My father would like me to remarry, but he says I can go to Tokyo for a little while. I would like to study English and earn a teaching certificate. I would like to turn my bad luck into something positive. It would give me some freedom to write again.

Tekkan had already penned a reply urging her to come to Tokyo but had set it aside for Akiko. He bounced Hikaru on his knee with uncharacteristic vigor while she composed her response. The words came slowly; she did not quite share his enthusiasm about a freer Tomiko coming back into their lives.

XIV: BROTHER, DO NOT DIE

1904, Akiko is twenty-six
Tokyo

われを問ふやみづからおごる名を誇る二十四時を人をし恋ふる

Who am I, you ask?

I am three things:

I am prideful, I am ambitious, and I love all day

One afternoon about eighteen months later, Akiko was propped against a wall with her legs splayed out before her, dozing, when a knock on the door startled her awake. Her newborn son Shigeru had fallen asleep at her breast and was sliding down her slack arm.

She hastily laid the baby down, closed her kimono front, and rolled to all fours. She shook off a wave of dizziness as she lurched past two-year-old Hikaru, who sat in his diaper before a toppled tower of newspapers, ink streaked across his face and chest. Tekkan's ashtray, saké cup, and papers sat on the table, and a heap of clean diapers—cut from old kimono cloth—waited on the floor to be folded. Akiko pulled her hair into a ragged bun, smoothed her front, and opened the door.

"Hello, hello! We want to meet the new baby!" Tomiko and Masako, whom Akiko remembered from the Kansai poetry group, stood on the threshold fresh as springtime, holding cookies, flowers, and poetry notebooks.

Akiko welcomed them inside.

"You remember Masako, don't you?" Tomiko asked.

"Of course I do," Akiko said, searching the shoe rack for two pairs of clean slippers. "You were at Hamadera four years ago, weren't you?"

Masako nodded, her owl-like eyes taking in the cluttered entry. Like Tomiko, she had an aristocratic bearing, but her face was harder, as though she had lived with sadness longer.

Akiko showed them into the sitting room, shuttling aside clutter to make room. Masako said, "Yes, it seems longer ago than that, doesn't it? I remember you, Akiko-san. I'm honored to meet you again, and sorry to trouble you when you have a new baby."

Akiko brushed away her formality. "Think nothing of it, Masako; please make yourself at home."

There was an awkward silence as they took their seats on the shabby cushions.

"How lucky that you found each other as roommates!" Akiko summoned a smile. She brushed at a patch of dried baby spit on the front of her kimono, then prepared tea water as Tomiko unwrapped the sweets they had brought to share.

There were shadows under Tomiko's eyes, but her face was bright. "It's amazing, isn't it? We both decided to go to college at the same time! We've been writing letters to each other since ... when was it we started?"

Masako was cautious, glancing at Akiko. "Oh, it hasn't been that long ..."

Akiko poured tea into three mismatched cups, taking the chipped one for herself.

"Yes, it has! It was right around the time I got married. I don't know what I would have done without you while Tomeshichiro was ill."

Akiko set the teapot down stiffly. She missed her former closeness with Tomiko.

"It was comforting to me, too," Masako said. "We both needed a shoulder to cry on. You see," she said to Akiko, picking up her teacup in both hands. "I should be married by now. My father values me mostly for my marriage potential, and he—and my stepmother, who can't stand me—they always remind me that I'm not pretty enough for an advantageous match."

I can relate to that, Akiko thought.

"Our families want to squeeze the life from us just as we are beginning to live," Tomiko said.

"I won't agree to an arranged marriage," Masako declared. "I will marry for love, or not at all." She looked at her friend. "I've made Tomiko promise, too; martyring herself for her family one time is enough." A sense of common purpose warmed the room. *If women refused to go along with the old system*, Akiko thought, *things might change.*

"How horrible this must have been for you," she said to Tomiko, and she meant it. "It's sad about what happened, but perhaps this *is* a second chance. Who could blame you for wanting that?"

They were standing outside about an hour later saying good-bye—with Hikaru seated on the ground, playing with a bucket of water—when Tekkan returned home from an errand.

"Come back inside for a few minutes," he urged as Akiko went to check on the napping Shigeru, but they insisted they had to get back to their studies.

"Have you joined my New Poetry Society yet?" he asked them. He had founded the group as a talent pool for *Myōjo*. "We've started a monthly 'One Night One Hundred Poems' series. We get together here, have saké and snacks, and stay as long as it takes for us to write one hundred tanka." He was earnest as a monk. "You must join us. Our next one is coming up. When is it?" He turned to look at Akiko, who had just reemerged from the house.

"The eleventh," she said automatically, as though she had been standing with them the whole time.

Tomiko and Masako promised to join. They also praised *Tangled Hair*, whose success Akiko attributed to Tekkan's clever marketing. He dismissed her praise but planted his feet wide in the dust, folding his arms across his chest. "I have an idea," he said. "What would you three think about collaborating on a book of poetry?"

Tomiko clapped her hands together. "Oh!"

"I don't know if we belong in a book with Akiko-san," said Masako, and Akiko thought, *listen to her*.

"You already have a lot of great work here," he gestured to the notebooks in their hands, "and Akiko has so many ideas, I think we could publish a book with a few months of focused work."

"I don't like the idea," Akiko told Tekkan later that night. "They are too busy with their studies, and it would be hard for us to do the editing that would be needed."

Tekkan shook his head. "Don't be silly. You heard them, they were thrilled. What an opportunity!"

She looked at him, exasperated. She had followed the successful *Tangled Hair* with two more books of poetry, *Little Fan* and *Thistle Weeds*. Both books were selling well, and Akiko was on her way to becoming one of Japan's best-known women poets. By contrast, Tomiko and Masako had published a few poems each in *Myōjo*, and

Akiko frankly didn't feel they were in her league. She was insulted by Tekkan's presumption. Not to mention, he did not need an excuse to spend more time with attractive, single women.

He poured another cup of saké and offered some to her, but she shook her head, nodding at Hikaru, who was dropping rice grains one by one onto the tatami, and Shigeru, who was squirming in her arms. A mother shouldn't be drinking with little ones around.

"Listen, I have my reasons," he began, pointing his empty saké cup at her for emphasis, and she waited. Irritated as she was, she was learning to listen to him on matters of marketing. "We need to distract attention from your 'Brother, Do Not Die' poem. This might do it." He was referring to Akiko's poem about Chūsaburo, who had been conscripted into the army to fight in Manchuria:

Ah, Little Brother, I cry for you,
You must not die.
The baby of the family,
You have a special place in your parents' hearts.
Did they put a sword in your hands,
And teach you to kill?
Is this what you grew twenty-four years to do?

In February that year, the Japanese Navy had launched a surprise attack on the Russian fleet moored in Port Arthur. They had scored a decisive naval victory, but the Russians had fought on. By summer it had evolved into a siege, and commanding General Nogi Maresuke was encouraging soldiers to volunteer as "human missiles." The *bushidō* warrior ethic was strong among Japanese men, and Akiko worried that Chusaburō would be tempted.

Nationalist newspapers were calling her poem dangerous, an affront to the people of Japan, disrespectful to the military, even treasonous. Akiko answered her critics in *Myōjo*, arguing that "Brother, Do Not Die" was personal, not political. She was only putting into words what any woman would feel when seeing a family member off to war. She invited critics to visit Shimbashi Station, and watch as families bade farewell to their sons, brothers, and fathers as they left on military convoys for the front. Yet, what most incensed her critics was her direct criticism of the Emperor:

> *Brother, do not give your life.*
> *How could His Majesty,*
> *Who does not Himself go into battle,*
> *Ask others to spill their blood and die like animals?*
> *How could He, with His deep heart,*
> *Think it noble?*

People had gone to jail for less, and activists both for and against the war were using the poem as a rallying theme. One morning Akiko had found paint splashed on their front door; another day university students threw rocks at their house.

"A new book of love poems, co-authored with two respectable young ladies, would pull attention away from that," Tekkan argued.

Shigeru was still fussing, so Akiko pulled open her kimono to nurse him. As he quieted, she grew thoughtful, regarding Tekkan across the only piece of furniture in the room. A friend had given the old and pockmarked table to him when he moved into this equally old and pockmarked house. Even with three books selling well, *Myōjo* was still in the red, and household expenses were mounting as the family grew.

"Romantic poetry, no politics, written by three talented women, one of whom happens to be you," Tekkan urged, sensing that she was softening. "We'll put Tomiko's poems up front—they're lovely—followed by Masako's, and finish with yours. Your section will be largest; your work is the best."

Akiko looked hard at him. *Why does he really want this?* He looked suspiciously flushed. Against her gut, she agreed.

XV: LOVERS' CLOTHES

1904-05, Akiko is twenty-seven

君かへらぬこの家ひと夜に寺とせよ紅梅どもは根こじて放れ

If you don't come home tonight,

I will make this house my night temple,

And rip out your red plum trees by the roots

The clock in the hallway wheezed, then ground out three chimes. Akiko lay on her side, face hot against her pillow. The tatami floor smelled like grass and dust, and her mind was full. In addition to the new poetry book, she had taken on contract writing work, including advertising copy and newspaper articles. She had not yet started the essay that was due to the *Daily Shimpō* newspaper. *Myōjo's* publication date was two weeks away, but a shortage of paper stock meant that higher prices would cut into any profits.

Next to her, little Shigeru's snores sounded a quiet rhythm. Hikaru's ragged breathing was close by; his nose was snotty from another cold. But what really kept her from sleep was the breathing she didn't hear: Tekkan's.

He had been staying out late networking with publishers, writers, and financial supporters. She needn't come along, he had said. The children needed watching; a woman shouldn't socialize after dark; and she wouldn't enjoy herself, anyway. This was his strength, not hers.

All true, but she was not naïve. Takino's letter of warning replayed in her mind. He had betrayed women before. She sighed and turned onto her back. Did she no longer satisfy him? After two babies, perhaps her changing body no longer appealed to him.

Her accomplishments as a writer paid the bills but strained their marriage. Magazine editors asked her, not Tekkan, for contributions. It must be hard for him; he had been the heartthrob star poet once. His chief sources of joy now seemed to be the monthly New Poetry Society sessions, and the hours spent editing the new manuscript with Tomiko and Masako.

Particularly Tomiko.

Letting them into the house one afternoon, Akiko frowned at the late summer green of Tomiko's kimono and the soft orange of her obi as she slipped out of her zori sandals, steadying herself with a slender arm. Stepping up into the house, she smiled warmly. She had pulled back her hair into a thick, glossy bun and tucked a persimmon-colored comb into the back. Tendrils of hair lay on her long neck like strands of silk. She was a butterfly in a pool of sunshine, light sparkling off her wings.

Tomiko and Tekkan sat together with papers, books, and teacups spread on the table. Akiko could sense the electricity between them. If one hand rested, the other automatically went down next to it, never quite touching. When one breathed in, the other followed; when one moved, the other mirrored, like courting birds. She glanced at Masako; was it possible she didn't notice?

When they departed, Tomiko left a sheaf of poems with Tekkan for review. He held onto it protectively as he saw the women to the door. Later, as Akiko attended to the children's dinner, he opened it up. She watched as he put one hand behind his neck, feeling the hairline along his nape as he read.

"Are those Tomiko's newest?" Akiko asked. "May I see?"

He started. "Yes, of course," he said, ears turning red. He handed her the folder.

髪ながき少女とうまれしろ百合に額は伏せつつ君をこそ思へ
Born a long-haired girl
I bow my head against white lilies,
As my thoughts turn to you

Akiko frowned. *"You" could be anyone. Poems aren't always autobiographical.* She read on.

恋に病みけふしぬほどにいとあつきをとめにふらせ紅梅の露
Sick with love, I could die today;
Give me, I beg,
The red plum dew

Red plum was a symbol for Tekkan, just as white lily sometimes referred to Tomiko. Akiko thought of Takino again, and how she had once searched for hidden meaning in Akiko's poetry submissions. Now Akiko was reading into Tomiko's. She had been a fool, thinking she could hold Tekkan through sheer willpower. She wondered if any one woman was enough for him.

She had failed as a daughter; was she failing as a wife, too?

One autumn morning, Masako visited Dogen Hill by herself. Tomiko was in bed with the flu. Work on the book was almost finished, and Tekkan had secured a contract with the publisher Hongo Shoin. It had been his idea to call the collection *Lover's Clothes*, after a poem in the *Manyōshu* in which a lover dresses in "robes of love." Tekkan described his vision of luxurious silk robes held against naked skin, or even skin itself which, like true love, cannot be shed. Two of the authors listened raptly; the other examined her fingernails as he spoke.

Masako hurried into the sitting room from the cold hallway carrying a bag of books. She warmed herself by the hibachi and sang, "Hey, Big Brother!" as Hikaru ran to her, waving the sleeves of his thick red hanten. "How is my big boy today?" She set her bag on the floor and picked him up. Akiko came in behind her and slid the fusuma door shut to keep the heat in the room.

"How are you?" Akiko asked.

"Not so good," Masako sighed, setting down Hikaru. She handed Akiko a letter printed on Japan Women's University letterhead. "I wanted you and Sensei to see this."

Masuda-sama,

It has come to the attention of university administrators that you and your classmate, Yamakawa Tomiko, are involved in the publication of a book of indecent poems.

After reviewing poems attributed to you in recent issues of the magazine Myōjo, and with the understanding that the book is to be titled Lovers' Clothes, the university has determined that the proposed book contravenes the government's stated ideal of educating women to be 'Good Wives and Wise Mothers.' Moreover, the sexual innuendo in these poems runs the risk of arousing young men and misrepresenting this institution of which you are a part. The University Fathers, dedicated to their mission of preparing women for lives as useful citizens through exemplary education and inculcation of morals, and in compliance with relevant laws, hereby require you to cease the project immediately, or face expulsion from the University and revocation of your names from alumni records and academic transcripts. Please acknowledge your understanding at your earliest convenience.

Copies of this letter will be sent to your parents.

"Tomiko got one just like it," said Masako. "Can they expel us just for writing poems? It's not pornography, it's not even close!" She crossed her arms over her chest irritably.

Akiko nodded, looking up from the letter. "Men can write about love and sex, but not us." She did not want her co-authors to back out of the book project at the last minute. "I'll speak to Tekkan tonight. He's good at handling this sort of thing."

"When do you expect him back?"

Akiko studied Masako's face for any sign that she was withholding information about her roommate, who was supposedly ill. "He left this afternoon on an errand. I expect him home in time for dinner." She paused, waiting for a reaction, but Masako was looking at the toddler.

"Well then," Masako gathered her things, "I should go. I just wanted to show you the letter. Shall I leave it with you so Sensei can see it?"

"You'd better," Akiko said, seeing Masako out. *Unless he sees Tomiko's copy first.*

Tekkan called on Hiraide Shū, a New Poetry Society member and lawyer, for help. He had handled legal problems related to Akiko's

"Brother, Do Not Die" poem. Arriving at the Yosano house with his leather attaché case and Western bowler hat, he suggested they start by writing to Tomiko and Masako's fathers for support.

"I expect the administrators will not want to make enemies of these wealthy donors," Hiraide said, patting his plump sides confidently.

As he suspected, Tomiko's father obliged, telling the university administration in strict language that his daughter did not deserve such treatment. A few days later, they toasted Hiraide and Tomiko's father when the university dropped the charges.

Lover's Clothes went on sale in January 1905. They charged 40 sen, more than for *Tangled Hair*, in part because Akiko's name was now known, but also because rumors about university and romantic entanglements raised interest in the book. Tekkan may not have been Machiavellian enough to encourage such rumors, but he did nothing to dispel them. The book was a financial and critical success.

むつれつつ菫のいひぬ蝶のいひぬ風はねがはじ雨に幸あらむ
Happily snuggling, the violet and butterfly say,
We don't like the wind, but oh
How wonderful the rain!
—*Masako*

おもひ出づな恨に死なむ鞭の傷秘めよと袖の女に長き
With her long sleeves, she hides her regret like a whip, a fatal wound
—*Tomiko*

わが恋は虹にもまして美しきいなづまとこそ似むと願ひぬ
My love will be
Beautiful as a rainbow
But like lightning too
—*Akiko*

Tomiko's flu lingered, and in February 1906, she spent two weeks in Tokyo University Hospital with pneumonia. She frequently missed classes and poetry sessions. By early spring, as ice turned to slush and plum blossoms swelled, as noses in Tokyo breathed in the heady promise of spring, Tomiko seemed to wilt.

"She's always out of breath," Masako confided to Akiko; often, on the way to classes, they had to stop halfway while Tomiko leaned on a post and fought for air.

Tomiko insisted it was nothing, but at poetry gatherings she held a handkerchief over her face while she coughed. Her poet friends winced as she fled into the hallway. Eyes met other eyes; *poor thing*, someone whispered.

Akiko found no joy in Tomiko's suffering, notwithstanding the suspicious ache in her heart. At night as she lay awake alone, staring into the darkness, she couldn't silence the voice that said, *you did this to her; you cursed her, and now your dark thoughts are coming to pass.*

XVI: BITTER WEEDS

Summer 1906, Akiko is twenty-eight

難破船二人の中にながめつつ君も救わずわれも救わず

Our ship is sinking as we watch
I don't save you, you don't save me

Akiko rested her forehead on the kitchen bucket. The smell of stale cooking oil, urine, and vomit filled her nostrils, and her arms and legs trembled as she wiped a thread of spit from her mouth.

In the next room, the voices of guests continued uninterrupted; she hoped they hadn't overheard. It was late and the poetry meeting was wrapping up with words of thanks and questions about the next get-together. The new maid—whom they could finally afford—brought Akiko a wet cloth to the muggy pantry where she crouched.

"Are you all right, madam?"

"Oh, I'm fine, I'm fine," Akiko said, leaning back on her heels and wiping her face. "I feel better. I'm sorry. That's not very pleasant, is it?"

"Are you ill?"

"I hope so," Akiko murmured, thinking, *not again, so soon.* She tried to remember when she last menstruated as she straightened her hair in the mirror and reemerged to bid the guests good night.

Tekkan, Masako, Tomiko, and a man named Chino lingered in the sitting room. With leftover writing paper, Chino was folding origami animals and setting them in a zoo line before Masako. A scholar of German literature, he had a big heart and an academic bearing, the sort of man who would gladly argue all night about love, art, or philosophy. On this night, he asserted that Japanese poetry left too much unsaid; it shied away from affairs of the heart. "Follow the European romantics," he said.

"I talked to Mori Ōgai about this only a few days ago," Tekkan said from the doorway where he held a guest's bag.

Chino sat up straight upon hearing the name, as though the respected Sensei had entered the room.

"Ōgai is my inspiration," he said, with saké-aided passion. "I've attended his lectures, but never spoken to him directly." An army doctor, Captain Mori Ōgai had encountered Western literature and philosophy while studying medicine in Germany. He called on fellow writers to consider whether Japanese literature must be protected from foreign influences, or whether it might evolve, using them as inspiration.

Tekkan tented his fingers. "Then we must take you next time we visit him. Won't we, Akiko?"

She nodded. "He's a good man. I'm sure he'd be happy to speak with you."

"Ōgai says we should study in France," Tekkan continued. "The Germans have made their mark in medicine, science, and literature; the place to be now is Paris." He looked up at the ceiling, as though imagining the City of Light. As Akiko watched him, her eyes suddenly met Tomiko's. They both looked away. "I want to study French," Tekkan went on. "I want to go to Paris one day, but even if I never do, at least I want to read the language, so I can understand the French sensibility."

Chino's attention had drifted back to Masako. He was trying to attach an origami monkey to the comb in her hair, but it found no purchase there. She laughed and batted his hands away.

Tomiko knelt to refill Tekkan's cup, then pitched off-balance into him. Saké tumbled from the bottle as she steadied herself with a hand on the table's edge. "Oh!" she set the bottle down awkwardly. "I'm sorry. I guess this is what it feels like!"

"This is what *what* feels like?" Tekkan blotted amiably at the spill with his dish towel.

"Being drunk!" She let out a happy sigh. "It's *won*-derful!"

"Yes, yes, it is," Tekkan agreed. "Have you not been drunk before?" Tomiko put a hand to her face. "No! Never a swallow of saké ever!"

Chino looked across the old wooden table at her, origami mid-fold in his hands. Next to him, Masako was folding a crane. "Saké is good for writers," Chino observed. "We stop worrying what others think. It's freeing."

"I don't like the way it tastes, but I like the way I feel," Tomiko sighed. "I'm tired of feeling sad. This is how an unhappy wife survives the night, isn't it? She doesn't care what anyone thinks, she just wants to feel good for a while."

Tekkan reached across the table to the line of origami animals and picked up an elephant. "Hold still," he said, and tried to perch it on Tomiko's nose.

She tilted her head back, allowing it to settle between her eyes. "There! Now I'll just walk home this way!" She laughed, but the laugh turned into a cough, and the elephant tumbled to the tabletop. She groped for her handkerchief. "Sorry! Sorry!" she gasped. "I'm all right!" but her eyes were shining with tears.

Tekkan's unpredictable schedule left Akiko with no sense of where he was or how long he would be gone. Once, he didn't come home for almost thirty-six hours. When he finally slid open the door, in high spirits, he explained that he had stayed over at a "writer friend's house." She stuffed flyers into a stack of new *Myōjo* magazines as he described where he had been, mopping his ruddy face, and she debated whether to believe him.

He had attended a poetry event in Kobe, he said, dropping his jacket to the floor, after which he and some friends had gone drinking. When the bar closed, they walked to the beach, singing military songs with arms slung around each other. Bottles of saké were concealed in their bags. They regaled each other with heroic lies, lying on their backs under the stars. Someone brought out a bag of oranges, which they ate, spitting out the seeds. Around dawn they made their way to a friend's house and slept off the day on his floor.

It sounded plausible, but when he went to the bathhouse down the street, Akiko picked up his jacket and sniffed it. It smelled of woman. She dropped it like a snake.

She wouldn't speak to him when he got home, sweet-smelling and relaxed, but he pushed her into a back room and closed the door behind them. He kissed her, one hand on her neck, the other on the small of her back, pulling her close. In a moment, they were on the floor in a twist of arms and legs. He was heavy on her and she gasped for breath. He whispered that he dreamed about her. What was she to think? How many women did he need? As he made love to her, tears slid down her face and pooled in her ears.

It was late and Tekkan was gone again. Akiko sat up, drawing her blanket around her shoulders. The moon seeped through the rice paper window, white as mother's milk. Outside, the sharp clack of wood blocks accompanied the neighborhood crier's nightly reminder to extinguish gas lights and cooking stoves: *"Hi no yō-jin!"* It was a comforting sound. *Prevent fires!* Clack! *"Hi-no-yoooooo-jin!"*

Her boys lay like puppies in a puddle of cream, Shigeru on his side with an arm thrown over Hikaru's neck and his nose on Hikaru's shoulder. She hitched the blanket up his arm and wished she could sleep as soundly. The baby in her belly was moving, more active than her first two. At four months she was already showing.

On her writing table, a pile of unfinished work awaited her attention. A promotional pamphlet for a local hatchery sat on top. She could dash off a draft in a half-hour. She crawled on her hands and knees to the table, lit her lamp, and ground some ink. *Farm fresh eggs delivered weekly!* she began. *Highest quality!* She kept thinking of Tekkan in Tomiko's feverish arms. *Eggs!* She wrote, but her mind said, *Tomiko!*

Eventually she gave up, closed the ink bottle, and turned down the lamp. To settle her nerves, she summoned a scene from *The Tale of Genji*, calling on it like an old friend. The tenseness in her shoulders eased as Lord Genji rode into her mind astride his white stallion, its saddle and harness festooned with adornments and bells.

She imagined him dressed now in silk robes of blue and gold, hair cinched back and covered with a tall black *eboshi* hat. Three of his retinue rode up behind him as he reined in his horse before a shabby country house. It was partially obscured by a wood-and-thatch fence covered in climbing vines, blossoms peeking out from every crack like voluptuous weeds. The high-peaked roof was dotted with grasses and moss; heavy eaves rested comfortably on wooden pillars.

> *"I wonder what those flowers are?"* Genji mused.
> *An attendant came up, bowing deeply. "The white flowers far off yonder are known as Evening Faces," he said. "A very human sort of name, and what a shabby place they have picked to bloom in."*

> *It was as the man said. The neighborhood was a poor one, chiefly of small houses. Some were leaning precariously, and there were Evening Faces at the sagging eaves.*
>
> *"A hapless sort of flower. Pick one off for me, would you?"*
>
> *The man went inside the raised gate and broke off a flower. A pretty girl in long, unlined yellow trousers of raw silk came out through a sliding door that seemed too good for the surroundings. Beckoning to the man, she handed him a heavily scented white fan.*
>
> *"Put it on this. It isn't much of a fan, but then it isn't much of a flower, either."*

Akiko knew this story by heart. On the fan, the girl had written a poem so hauntingly beautiful that Genji became obsessed with her. But *Evening Face,* or *Yugao* as she is called, dies suddenly, murdered by the jealous ghost of Genji's former mistress. Like Yokihi and the Emperor Genso, like a flower, the budding love between Genji and Yugao couldn't last.

As far back as she could remember, Akiko had been waiting for a translation of *The Tale of Genji* into modern Japanese. In its original form, only academics trained in the classics and a handful of devoted enthusiasts could decipher it. It was a shame. The people of Japan should know their proud heritage. They should know that a Japanese woman wrote the world's first novel, and they should be able to read it.

Kanao Tanejiro, an old friend from the Hamadera poetry group days, had urged Akiko to attempt the translation herself. As a publisher, he was always on the lookout for promising projects.

Impossible, she had said. It would take a group of scholars a lifetime to do it justice. She was not a scholar, nor did she have leisure time, unlike *Genji*'s author, the noblewoman and widow Lady Murasaki. No, she was a busy wife and working mother with a middle-school education. Moreover, notwithstanding Genji's feminine authorship, women were not taken seriously on literary subjects.

Now, though, she found herself thinking it over again. Perhaps Kanao was right. She knew the text intimately—after all, she'd been lecturing on it for years and reading it since childhood.

Tekkan recently had made the painful decision to discontinue *Myōjo*, and in its place they had launched an at-home lecture series for extra income. He led poetry seminars, and she spoke on classical literature.

A *Genji* translation could serve two purposes—in the short term, it could provide material for her lectures. Eventually, if she managed to complete it, it could be published. It would be an enormous undertaking, but if she paced herself, it might be possible. Her pulse quickened as she turned the idea over in her mind: *The Tale of Genji* interpreted in modern Japanese, by Yosano Akiko!

Just then, the front door downstairs rattled as a key slid into the lock. She couldn't make out the time on the wall clock, but from the slant of the moon it must be three or four o'clock in the morning. Would Tekkan smell of alcohol and smoke tonight? Or lilies?

In late 1906, Tekkan was hospitalized with high fever and migraine headaches. Heavily pregnant now, Akiko visited him nearly every day during his six-week stay while caring for the children, running the household, and writing.

Walking into the lobby of the high-ceilinged, gleaming Keio University Hospital one morning, with Shigeru strapped to her back and Hikaru trotting alongside, she passed a thin woman with a bag of medicines in one hand and an umbrella in the other. The woman recognized Akiko first.

"Oh! Good morning!" It was Tomiko. She looked quickly from Akiko's swelling belly to Hikaru at her side. "Big Brother," she said, with a smile, "you're getting so tall!"

"Tomiko-san!" *I almost didn't recognize you*, Akiko stopped herself from saying, just in time. Tomiko's cheekbones jutted sharply from her face; her hair was wispy and lifeless. "We were on our way to see Sensei."

"Yes, how is he doing?" Tomiko asked. There was makeup dabbed under her eyes—to hide the shadows, Akiko surmised.

"Oh, did you hear he had been admitted?"

"Masako told me. Meningitis, is it? Terrible. Is he feeling better?"

"I think so. He's had terrible head and neck aches, but the doctor said it's not as bad as it could be. The virus may have been dormant in his body since his time in Korea."

They stood at the hospital entrance, and freezing rain spattered them whenever someone brushed past. Akiko gently swayed back and forth as she talked, to keep Shigeru on her back quiet. "What about you, how are you?"

"Oh, I'll be better once the weather improves. The doctor says it's nephritis. It isn't infectious, so I can go back to class if I'm feeling up to it."

"Well, that's good news, isn't it?" Akiko was suspicious. Doctors were sometimes reluctant to tell patients the truth when the prognosis was grim.

"Yes, he thinks vitamins and more rest will help."

A few minutes later, sitting on a stool next to Tekkan's bed in the Men's Internal Medicine Ward, Akiko mentioned seeing Tomiko. The morning's cold rain permitted only a dull light through the tall windows, and anemic shadows fell across the dozen or so occupied beds. A low murmur of voices echoed off the walls and the smell of alcohol stung Akiko's nose. She leaned forward on her stool to better bear Shigeru's weight on her back while Hikaru crawled on the floor under the hospital beds.

"Yes, she stopped by to say hello this morning," Tekkan said. "She's looking better, don't you think?"

Oh, did she? Akiko paused a moment to study his face before answering. His eyes were half-obscured by the cloth on his forehead, so she couldn't read them. "She didn't mention that."

"Well, she is in and out of the hospital a lot these days. She must have been surprised to see you."

"I don't know why, I'm here a lot, too," Akiko answered pointedly. "It's more surprising that we haven't run into each other yet." She looked at him steadily, one hand on her big belly. *Don't lie to me, old man.*

"Don't you think she looks better?" he asked again.

Akiko raised her eyebrows. "Not really. Nephritis, she said. I don't even know what that is, but it seems risky to send her back to class if it could be infectious."

"If you think it's tuberculosis," Tekkan said defensively, "it's not. The doctors would know." He shot a glance at Hikaru, who was playing with a lever on the side of the bed. "Big Brother, stop that!"

"I suppose." She *did* suspect tuberculosis, given that Tomiko's husband had died of it just eighteen months earlier. Did it occur to Tekkan that he, too, could pay for his indiscretions with his life, if she had passed it to him?

Tekkan—thinner and weaker—was given a clean bill of health and released from the hospital before the New Year, but Tomiko could not seem to shake what ailed her. By February, she had missed so much coursework that she was suspended from school. Her parents begged her to come home, arguing that the ocean air and country lifestyle would do her good.

She resisted. "I've only started my life here," she complained over dinner at the Yosano house, picking at her rice. "I just want to enjoy myself for a while." She set her chopsticks down with a sigh. "It isn't fair."

"No, you're right, it isn't," said Tekkan.

"I'm not leaving." She straightened. "I'll take off the spring quarter and start classes again in the summer. I'll stay in Tokyo and keep writing."

Akiko nodded, looking at Tomiko's picked-over dinner. She searched for something encouraging to say. "Good sleep and good food will help," she offered.

It didn't help, though, and ten days later, after another stint in the hospital, Tomiko admitted defeat. Instead of going home to live with her parents, though, she opted for her sister's house in Kyoto. There were good doctors at Kyoto University; maybe there was a cure.

Tekkan did not hide his sadness at her departure and Akiko, out of sympathy, held her tongue. He went about the house glumly; his bravado flattened like leaves under frost. At night, when she crawled under his comforter, he pulled her close, but his lovemaking was sad.

One night, she reached for his hand and placed it on her enormous belly. She felt like an over-ripe watermelon, her belly so tight she thought she might split in two.

"The midwife says it might be twins," she whispered. The prospect filled her with dread; childbirth was dangerous enough with one baby.

Tekkan inhaled sharply, but after a moment he began to move his hand around, as though trying to determine where one baby ended and the other began. He kissed her cheek, then moved his head downward to put his ear to her abdomen, and murmured, "Are you one big heart? Or two small ones?"

Akiko's breath plumed in the chilly air the next morning. Shigeru was fussing, and the hibachi was cold. She poked Tekkan, dozing next to her, then rolled onto her knees with a groan. As she summoned the energy to stand, she could hear a monk call for alms out on the street, a wavering, wistful sound.

Tekkan shivered in his underclothes as he pulled down his kimono from a peg on the wall. He was still thin from his illness. She was tying her obi high over the mound of her abdomen when she looked up and saw him staring at her. His eyes were pleading.

"What?" she asked. *Was he going to confess?* She waited, wanting and not wanting it. A dog barked and a broom seller sang, the wheels of his cart grinding slowly past their window. He opened his mouth as if to speak, but no sound came.

ゆるしたまへ二人を恋ふと君泣くや聖母にあらぬおのれの前に
Forgive me, I love two women, you cry,
But I am not the Holy Mother, standing before you

Akiko's water broke one cold day in March. Instead of giving birth at home as she had done before, she had arranged to deliver at a newly built birthing clinic nearby. Staffed by midwives rather than doctors, it provided no specialized medical care, but it did offer privacy from her noisy household. Tekkan offered to call a rickshaw, but she preferred to walk the half mile. She was enormous, her back was aching, and the road was icy, but she hoped it would speed her labor. She put a cloth between her legs to catch the seeping clear fluid and he carried her overnight bag. They walked slowly, and he steadied her as they picked their way around piles of snow and patches of ice.

At the birthing center, he gave her shoulder a squeeze and left. He was not welcome here; this was the domain of women.

Her companions now were midwives and assistants. They tended to her in shifts as day changed to night, and night changed back to day. They gave her tea, rubbed her back, and helped her walk, but by morning, sleepless, she was no further along. Contractions rolled over her in miserable waves, straining but somehow always failing and falling back. She stared grimly at the white kerchiefs wrapped around the women's heads and their cold, strong, white arms.

Sometimes she was wakeful; sometimes she drifted. When starched cotton sleeve guards grazed her legs, arms, and torso, she shivered. One woman with a mole on her face bent over her. The mole lodged in the crease where her nose met her cheek. Akiko watched it crawl up her face like a bug, and marveled that it never reached her eye.

Another midwife, sturdy as a stockhorse, pushed at Akiko's abdomen ruthlessly, trying to get a sense for how the babies were positioned and asking her about her previous births. *Don't interrogate me*, Akiko groaned, *just deliver me of these fiends.*

Later, Akiko would say that the first baby gripped her so tightly that tiny fistfuls of innards must have been delivered with her. With the way apparently cleared, the second baby slid out within a few minutes. The midwife's assistant massaged the two blue and purple babies until their gurgles turned to screams. As they turned a bright, miraculous, screaming red, Akiko lay back, allowing herself a moment of euphoria. Two girls to join her two boys.

Now, back to work.

Two letters arrived from Sakai in one envelope, both from Tsuné. One was addressed to Akiko and the other to Tekkan.

Sho,

I received the telegram announcing your daughters' birth. Please accept my congratulations. For the sake of Hikaru and Shigeru, I pray for your quick recovery.

In a few days you should receive a package. It contains baby clothes and other trifles.

This morning it snowed, a heavy fall for this time of year, and several inches accumulated. As for names for the girls, what about 'Ōyuki' (Big Snow) and 'Koyuki' (Little Snow)?

I apologize for my poor handwriting. My hands are weak.

In the letter to Tekkan, she wrote more frankly:

It will be exceedingly difficult to take care of both girls at home; it is not good for the parents. Girls are not much use once they become adults, and without sufficient help, I fear they will only be a problem for you.

I feel they should be sent away to be cared for elsewhere at least for the first two or three months, and if they seem likely to survive, you may choose to send them to foster homes or perhaps bring them home to raise. My reasoning is that your effort may yield nothing. I have seen twins before, and they generally do not do well. You must take care of yourselves first.

Two days later, more news arrived from Sakai—this time it was a telegram from Chūsaburo. Tsuné was dead. She had passed away in her sleep.

Tekkan kept the news from Akiko for several days. Upon hearing, she crawled off into a corner with the tiny twins and pulled a blanket over their heads. She hoped to nap; instead, she stared blindly into the stifling darkness under the blanket and listened to her babies breathe. She didn't miss her mother; she missed ever having felt loved by her. She did not remember her exile as an infant, but she remembered her boyish kimono, her ugly brown hanten jacket, and her close-cropped hair. She remembered her mother saying she was too plain and bookish to make a good bride, too full of selfish pride. Yet for all of that, if Tsuné had valued her as Tomiko had been valued, perhaps she would not have run away. Now her mother's death ended any chance for redemption. The opportunity for apologies or understanding was dead—*that* was why she grieved.

The names Ōyuki and Koyuki were too confusing, Akiko felt. Tekkan suggested the name Tsuné, but she vetoed that too. Then a letter arrived from Capt. Mori Ōgai. The proud godfather had composed a poem for them:

むこ来ませ一人は山の八峰こえ一人は川の七瀬わたりて
Their husbands will come:
One will climb eight mountains,
The other will ford seven rivers.
—Mori Ōgai

Tekkan and Akiko named the girls Yatsuo ('Eight Mountains') and Nanasé ('Seven Rivers').

XVII: TOMIKO'S JOURNEY

1908-09, Akiko is thirty

冬の夜の星君なりき一つをば云ふにはあらずことごとく君

Winter evening

I see a star that must be you –

But no, not just one,

All of them are you

The winter of 1908 came early, and November snowstorms dropped heavy, wet snow across the main island of Honshu as far south as Kyoto where Tomiko was convalescing. She wrote frequently to say that she was feeling better. As the weather got colder, she wrote, she and her sister wrapped themselves in blankets and sat with their legs under the coal-heated *kotatsu* table. She looked forward to resuming her studies in Tokyo soon.

Envelopes of her haunting poetry arrived in Dogen Hill for Tekkan's review. Consumed with her own work, including her *Tale of Genji* translation, Akiko often saw only the ones he chose for publication.

おとしませ億劫さむき幽界の底そのいつはりの恋を守らむ
Drop me to the bottom of the eternal spirit world
Where I keep this false love alive
—Tomiko

虹もまた消えゆくものか我ためにこの地この空恋は残るに
Does the rainbow fade again?
For me, there is still this earth and this sky
Love remains
—Tomiko

Whether the love object of these poems was Tekkan, Tomiko's late husband, or some imagined lover, Akiko didn't know, and if Tomiko and Tekkan kept up a personal correspondence, Akiko never found a letter.

In December, Tomiko wrote to say that her father was on his deathbed.

I am filled with regret. I ignored his pleas for so long, playing my selfish games and lying to myself about my own health and his. Now time has run out, and the weather is too treacherous for travel. I will arrange with my brother, who is coming down from Tokyo today, to take me home as soon as the roads are passable. I'll write more soon.

A month passed before another letter came from Tomiko; this time it was postmarked from her hometown.

I apologize for my lateness. I have been ill, and we have been busy with the funeral and other preparations.

My father Teizo is dead, and I will follow him, and my husband, soon.

The trip north in December was difficult. The roads over the Hira Mountains were impassable from snow, and my brother and cousin were forced to stay in Kyoto for two nights before we could attempt the trip. They said I would not survive it, and tried to persuade me to stay behind, but I threatened to take my own life if they did not bring me. I could not bear it if my father had been waiting for me and I had not come.

The snow was so deep that our carriage had to stop many times. My brother and cousin helped pull it out of drifts and push it through freezing mud. The horses were exhausted by the time we got to Otsu, so we spent the night there. I did not want to stop, but they threatened to tie me to my bed if necessary. I am ashamed to say I cried like a child, but it was because I could hear Father's voice in my head, calling me.

We made better time the next day, taking the Kosei Road along the western shore of Lake Biwa. It was very cold, and even with many layers of blankets, I could not sleep with the bumping and my coughing. I know that I caused everyone to worry.

I don't remember the last part of the trip, but I am told it was easier on the horses because the snow and mud had frozen solid.

By the time we arrived, Father was no longer able to speak, but I believe he could hear me. I begged his forgiveness and thanked him. It was not long until he passed. You see, he had been waiting for me.

My fever and coughing hardly let up anymore. I must make peace with my fate.

In his life, Father allowed me to do more than other men in his position might have. I am sad to think that you all will soon forget me, but I am filled with joy to know that I will be reunited with him soon.

April 15, 1909, was a warm day. Cherry flower petals dropped from trees, sparrows flew about with sticks and fluff for nests, and Tomiko got her wish. She was just twenty-nine.

花かをる常世の島に船浮かべ笑む日あれかし君を待つかな
I will float in my boat to the next world
To an island, fragrant with flowers
Those will be smiling days
And I will wait for you

XVIII: TO BE LOVED

1909-1911, Akiko is in her early thirties

亡き人を悲しねたしと並べ云ふこのわろものを友とゆるせし

I grieve for the dead one, but I'm jealous of her, too–

Forgive me, I am a wretched friend

The twin girls Yatsuo and Nanasé were toddlers pulling on their mother's skirts, competing to get a look at their new brother Rin, when Akiko received the news of Tomiko's death. She stood in the doorway with the yellow telegram in her hand, wordlessly rocking month-old Rin on her back. Rain overnight had lifted into glorious morning, and the spring sun reflected off the wet streets. The scent of mud and flowering trees filled the air, but another birth had left her hollow as the gutters through which rainwater was noisily gushing.

She thought about the day Tomiko had first visited Surugaya, pretty and smart in her student uniform. So effortlessly kind. How could a person have nothing but good qualities? They had stood together on the bridge in Osaka with Tekkan and pledged to be forever friends—star children—and Tomiko had wept as they left him behind in their rickshaw under the falling red leaves, knowing he could never be hers.

"Why are you crying, Mama?" asked Shigeru, coming to the door.

"It's nothing. Go play with your sisters," Akiko said, wiping her eyes and turning to go inside. Death and birth, death and birth. Who was next?

Against Tsuné's advice, they raised the twins at home, and almost immediately Akiko was pregnant again. She suffered from persistent headaches, back pain, and numbness in her left arm and side that her doctor said might be permanent. She supplemented breast milk with costly cow's milk for baby Rin and hired a nanny, a skinny girl of twelve from a rural village, who was hardly old enough to care for herself, let alone infants.

"You're a famous lady, why don't you have any furniture?" asked the girl one day, bouncing Rin in her arms, a bottle of cow's milk in one hand. "I thought you were rich!"

Akiko prickled. "Young ladies should keep their thoughts to themselves," she said. She hardly set down her pen, it seemed, but money was tight. She had followed *Lover's Clothes* with *Dancing Girl* and *Flower Dreams* in 1906, *Mid-Summer* in 1908, and *Sun Goddess* in 1909. She wrote for newspapers *Daily Manchō*, *Two-Six News*, *Hometown News*, *Osaka Daily* and *Tokyo Daily*, and magazines such as *Middle School World* and *Women's Literary*. She was making steady progress on her *Tale of Genji* translation.

With no money for toys, she sewed dolls from leftover material and made building blocks with bits of discarded wood. Sometimes she brought home scrap paper and unused ink from the printing shop for the children. She took up writing children's stories. She tried them on her own children, then lined up publishing contracts for the best ones.

A mouse lives in my ceiling.
At night he makes a sound
like a sculptor who can't sleep,
tap-tapping with his chisel.
He also dances with his wife,
'Round and 'round,
With the energy of racehorses,
Unbeknownst to them
Raining dust from the ceiling
On top of my papers.

And yet, I think,
I can live with this mouse.
He has a bit of food,
And a warm little nest,
And sometimes he peeks
Through the hole in the ceiling
To check on me.

Expenses stubbornly outpaced income. Taxes on printed goods were unpredictable, and paper costs were rising. With their household now numbering nine—five children, two servants, Tekkan, and Akiko—they moved to a larger house and rented out an extra room.

Tekkan helped with copy editing and publicity, but Tomiko's death and the shutdown of *Myōjo* had left him emotionally adrift. He had few engagements with newspapers or magazines, and his New Poetry Society had disbanded. Busy with jobs and families, longtime members were no longer free to amuse themselves with poetry parties.

Akiko's writing was changing. Its edges were getting sharper. Her popular romantic poetry gave way to essays about childbirth, motherhood, and equal treatment for women.

I understand that men cannot fully comprehend the inconveniences of pregnancy or the pain of childbirth. A woman puts her life at risk when she loves someone, but that's not the case for a man. A man may love a woman to the point of personal peril, but he has no stake in giving birth, and he is of no help, either ...

Long ago, women were made into liabilities rather than assets, and even as they carried out their critical role, it was by the hand of man that the scriptures, ethics, and national laws were achieved. How is it that women came to be treated as sinners, as inferior and weak?

... You may think there is no better example of desperation than the last five minutes of life for a man facing a death sentence, but really, childbirth is not so different. The ones who are climbing up onto that cross and dying so others may live, these are women ...

I don't want to draw a sharp distinction between men and women or suggest that women are somehow intimidatingly superior. We are all human beings. Merely, we should be able to live in cooperation and fulfill the roles that are suitable for us. No one should be thought of as unclean because they give birth to children or deserve veneration because they go to war.

Such outspokenness, especially for a woman, carried a public cost. Once again, she became the subject of sneers and adulation. The attention kept new work coming in, but it was exhausting. She responded with as much grace as she could muster, but when her interviews were done for the day, she closed the door of her study and did not emerge again, often for many hours. She moved about the house like a shadow.

Eight-year-old Hikaru tried to keep his brothers and sisters from disturbing her at such times. Akiko was aware of his efforts and quietly loved him for it.

Meanwhile, the solitary *Tale of Genji* work continued. While the rest of the house slept, she sat in a circle of lamplight, reference books stacked around her like fortress walls. Dawn often surprised her, arriving quietly while she worked.

The last ten chapters of *Genji*, known as the "Uji Chapters," centered on Lord Genji's relative Kaoru. Less-committed readers might never read that far, having run out of stamina hundreds of pages earlier, but these were some of her favorites. Something about her translation was bothering her, though, creating friction, like a hole in a scratchy sock. Finally, she realized what it was: She had always imagined Tekkan as a modern Lord Genji—swashbuckling, confident, sexy—but now, she recognized another side of him in the hapless Kaoru.

In the Uji chapters, Kaoru realizes his love for the beautiful Oigimi as she lay dying. In her final hours, Oigimi grieves for her father, guilt-ridden over the trouble she had caused him, and content to follow him to the next world. Kaoru, left behind, is inconsolable. *Good heavens*, she thought, *Oigimi is Tomiko*:

> *Kaoru was in tears. Oigimi only wanted to die, at the thought of the burden of sin she must bear for her father's troubles. She longed to be with her father wherever he was, to join him before his soul had come to its final rest ...*

> *What store of sins had he brought with him from previous lives, [Kaoru] wondered, that, loving her so, he had been rewarded with sorrow and sorrow only, and that he now must say goodbye? If he could find a flaw in her, he might resign himself to what must be. She became the more sadly beautiful the longer he gazed at her, and the more difficult to relinquish ...*

Why did Akiko go on living in this gritty, unsympathetic world, ravaged by time, while Tomiko remained young and unsullied? Akiko's belly and breasts sagged from bearing Tekkan's children, and the years had rounded her face. He still whispered his love for her when he took her into his arms, but she could not stop thinking about that part of his heart that would never belong to her.

み心の半ばをわれにかへせよと云ふに過ぎざるさもしき妬み
If I were to say, 'Give me back half your heart,'
Would it be nothing more than ugly envy?

At least her children followed her about like ducklings. No one else adored her the way they did. Motherhood, fraught with peril and rich with rewards, was addictive.

楽しげに子らに交じりてくだものの紅き皮むく世のつねの妻
Just a wife
Happily peeling red apple skins
With my children

Daughter Sahoko was born in early 1910. Six months later, Akiko was pregnant again. However much she dreaded childbirth, she had always felt joy when the first symptoms of pregnancy came upon her. This time, however, she was filled with dark premonitions. This time, she sensed, she would be lucky to survive.

XIX: TALES FROM THE DELIVERY ROOM

1911, Akiko is thirty-three

生きてまた帰らじとするわが車刑場に似る病院の門

Riding through the hospital gate
Prison wagon takes me to my death

Akiko's bed in the south-facing maternity ward was warm and comfortable. A window filled the room with light. On her nightstand sat a vase of heliotrope blossoms and a neat pile of magazines. Around her, nurses and attendants spoke in whispers, and the ward was quiet, organized, and clean.

At the far end of the room, pages crinkled as a nurse looked through a pamphlet. A teapot hummed on a brazier. The muffled groans of a laboring woman could be heard through the wall, and the quiet whoosh and bang of a sliding door announced visitors down the hall. A hushed exchange of greetings floated up to Akiko's ears, along with the rustling of coats, hats, and boots. Slippered feet whispered up the hallway, along with the nurse's firm step.

Most of her visitors—friends from the New Poetry Society, publishing colleagues, neighbors, Chūsaburo and his wife, and Tekkan's sister—greeted her quietly and didn't ask questions. Akiko was grateful. Everyone knew she had given birth to twins again, but one of them had died. She didn't want to talk about it. No one even asked about the baby who did survive. Perhaps it was too awkward to ask about one but not the other. Instead, they talked about the latest show at the Imperial Theater or the miserable weather. After a few minutes, they left their gifts and were on their way, leaving the wounded mother behind them. She was beyond their ability to heal.

蛇の子に胎を裂かるる蛇の母そを冷くも「時」の見詰むる
Baby Snake rips Mother Snake's womb
Coldly, mother stares down time itself

On that longest of days in 1911, Akiko remembered hearing the midwife tell Tekkan that only medical intervention could save her and her babies. She would need to be taken to hospital immediately. Yes, it was twins again.

The baby sitting higher had turned sideways, causing Akiko almost unbearable pain. It felt like wings or a mechanical spreader against her ribs, like an airplane wedged inside her.

Akiko was dimly aware of the rickshaw that carried her to the hospital, and she had a memory of Tekkan's grim face. She screamed when the rickshaw jolted on the road, breaking one of her ribs. She remembered hospital orderlies lowering her into a wheelchair, and Tekkan telling the doctor, *whatever happens, save my wife.*

The hospital corridor looked like an execution chamber, the sort of place that mothers come to die. She panted like a dog.

I do not fear death, but I do fear suffering.

She prayed, not to Buddha, nor to Christ. She called on the Holy Mother, the Earth Mother, for strength.

"It will be over by and by, Mrs. Yosano," the doctor said. He looked barely old enough to shave. "Think of the miracle of birth. What a joy it must be."

What does he know about it? I know more than he. He does me no good right now. He might as well leave; they could all just leave. I am alone, facing death. They will not accompany me there, and I don't think they can save me from it.

She felt the nearness of other mothers, lifting her. She thought she might go with them. She was grateful to these sacred women who suffered to give life, who held her as she cried. She wondered if they had died in a pool of blood, if that would be her fate, too.

Look at me. In her dreamlike state she stood on a mountaintop and faced the rising sun. *I am Mother and Poet. With what I create, I give myself eternal life.*

Yet she was not ready to die.

The first baby was delivered: small but alive, a girl. The doctor pushed hard on Akiko's abdomen to turn the second, "airplane baby" around. She shrieked, surprising herself with her energy in reserve. Eventually, the doctor brought out forceps. Grimly, he dragged the baby out; he ripped and wrenched, and with it, half of what remained inside her. The second baby girl was lifeless and blue, and although the doctor cleared her windpipe and breathed into her tiny mouth, she took no breaths of her own.

This mother's bones are crushed. The baby inside my womb bit me, wordlessly waving its arms until even the demons fell silent. The weaker child died helpless inside me. She fought her mother, she fought her sister. Now, the healthy baby screams, and the dead baby lies next to its half-dead mother.

Akiko listened as her visitors retreated down the hallway and dressed themselves again in the trappings of the world. She tried to imagine what they wore or carried—a fedora, a lawyer's folded bar exam notes pushed into a pocket, a neighbor's padded hanten—as they left her with her demons in the whisper-quiet hospital ward.

Several times a day, the nurses brought newborns in a pushcart to the recovery ward and distributed them like mochi balls at a festival. Tucked in a tight swaddle, Baby Uchiko was collicky and weak. Nurses hitched Akiko into a sitting position; she grimaced as they propped pillows behind her. Uchiko wailed, unable to latch onto Akiko's breast. After a while, the nurse took the baby away. "Don't worry, we'll try again later," she said brightly, but Akiko neither smiled nor spoke.

She looked forward every day to nine-year-old Hikaru's after-school visit. When she heard his step in the hallway, her heart skipped. He would come to her bedside with a rush of outside air, his cheeks red, fingers chilly. She would remind him not to run in the hospital as he, out of breath, launched into a story in a loud whisper. Of her children, only Hikaru was allowed to visit; the others were too young (something Hikaru must be proud of, though he did not say so). Tekkan came by each evening as well, entering the room so quietly that sometimes he even slipped past the nurse.

Time in the maternity hospital gave Akiko's body needed rest, but she found no peace. She wished for noise. She missed her children. The doctor would not grant her release though: days after the delivery, she was still dizzy and could not stand for long. Her broken rib was bound and her head throbbed. She was still bleeding and had barely slept in a week. Whenever she drifted off, talons of physical and mental pain yanked her groaning back to remind her that one baby was alive and one was dead.

The doctor told Akiko that her pain was a good sign: it meant that her uterus was shrinking, but she was not comforted. She could not scream anymore; her throat was dry; nor could she weep; her heart was broken. Even when the sun shone brightly, she lay in darkness, wondering how to love her live baby while grieving for her dead one. In the end, all she felt was emptiness and a shredded, shrinking womb.

母なるが枕経よむかたはらのちひさき足をうつくしと見き
New mother chants a prayer through the night for the dead one
Tiny feet beside her, so beautiful

In the room next door, Akiko heard Tekkan's brother and Mr. Wagai, a friend from Subaru Publishing, speaking quietly and moving something around. Banging. *They are driving nails*, she realized.

Building a coffin. To take the dead baby away.

Tekkan came in softly. "Do you want to see her? She's beautiful," he said. "I have never seen a more beautiful baby." She could hear the pain in his voice, but she felt numb. She looked away and shook her head.

虚無を生む、死を生む、斯かる大事をも夢と現の境にて聞く
Lying on the border between dream and wakefulness,
I hear that I gave birth to emptiness, I gave birth to death

They wrapped the baby in a blanket and placed her tenderly into the tiny wooden box, and Chūsaburo took it to the crematorium in Kirigaya. When he returned that evening, he looked tired and cold. In the dim light, he looked like their father Sōshichi. He sat by her, and neither of them spoke. On the night table, the heliotrope blossoms were beginning to wilt. The hospital ward was quiet, but voices and the sounds of traffic outside could be heard through the cold windowpane. "It seems like ..." he started finally, looking at his hands. "It seems like a terrible thing to do to such a beautiful baby." He almost whispered the last words, and there were tears in his eyes. She felt a twinge of grief. It was detached and distant, like a voice from the next room, but it was reassuring to feel anything at all. This first grief was for her brother, not yet for herself, nor for the baby she lost, nor for the one who survived.

My exhausted body desperately needs sleep, but when I try to sleep, the dead child appears before me and peels back my eyelids with tiny fingers. It kept me awake for another day and night. I have never been tormented by such dreams. I have never been so exhausted.

Finally, she was allowed to go home. Balancing on spindly legs, ghost-like, she tottered into the waiting wheelchair. The nurse wrapped little Uchiko in a blanket and placed her in Akiko's arms. Then the nurse gathered Akiko's belongings. She picked up a little red blanket and a tiny shirt Akiko had made for Uchiko's sister. The nurse folded them and put them in Akiko's bag. As she chatted, she took the remaining heliotrope blossom from the vase and threw it away.

XX: ONE LONG DAY AND TWO DECISIONS

February 1911, Akiko is thirty-three

母として女人の身をば裂ける血に清まらぬ世はあらじとぞ思ふ

As a mother I think it not impossible
That the blood of women's bodies torn in birth
Might cleanse this world

One long day, not long after newborn Uchiko came home without her twin sister, Akiko made two big decisions. Problems had been chasing around in her head like *tanuki* dogs in an attic. On this day, they finally came crashing down through the ceiling to demand her attention. She would later say that one of them, at least, saved her life.

Four-year-old Nanasé had woken up that morning with a fever. Akiko summoned the nanny for help, but her heart sank when the girl appeared in her study, looking even more pitiful than Nanasé. Her face was swollen from chin to eye, and her jaw was bound with a jute cloth knotted on top of her head. She was sucking forlornly on a wad of Chinese herbs. She had a toothache, she croaked; clearly, she was in no shape to take care of anyone but herself today. Akiko sent her off to the dentist with a note promising to pay for the cost of pulling her tooth. She wondered—not for the first time—how different her life might be if she had her Sakai family to support her.

By the sound of Yatsuo and two-year-old Rin's whining, they were coming down with Nanasé's virus, but she had errands that would not wait. Leaving newborn Uchiko with Hikaru, she strapped Rin to her back and limped off to the *Mainichi News* office. Her left leg had been partially numb since the traumatic birth three weeks earlier, and a thick cloth between her legs soaked up the blood that was still coming. Rin's fever kept her back warm, but everything else was soon freezing—her fingers, her ears, even her knees. The streets were choked with ice and mud, and the socks under her geta sandals were soon soaked through to her toes. Walking through the street market, her numb feet almost tripped her twice.

Shivering and dripping in the entry back home, bags of *daikon* radishes, fish, scallions, and miso paste in bags dangling from her arms, she found a representative from *Chuo News* waiting in the parlor. She had forgotten about her appointment with him. She set down her bags with a sigh and bowed low. Would he mind coming back tomorrow afternoon? She had a houseful of sick children and hadn't begun to prepare a lecture scheduled for the next morning.

I used to put enormous effort into a single poem because my mood or imagination or feelings inspired me. These days, if I were to do that, we would all starve to death in short order.

It was almost six o'clock before she finally sat down to her writing table. She was deep in thought and Uchiko at her breast had finally dozed off when Tekkan came home with an unplanned overnight guest. She set down her pen to join them for dinner; she prepared the guest room and served the men drinks before returning to her desk at around ten o'clock. She lit a cigarette, hoping the nicotine would soothe her throbbing head.

As she stared at her lecture notes—the Young Murasaki chapters in *The Tale of Genji*—her mind kept wandering off course. Tekkan unfailingly sang her praises before others, but she knew her success as a writer rankled with him. The wall between them was growing thicker. Just the week before, a group of journalists had come asking for *Yosano-san*, and when the maid mistakenly introduced them to Tekkan rather than showing them to Akiko's study, he had scolded the poor girl in front of them all.

Akiko's cigarette had burned down to a stump. She made a small sound of disgust as she flicked it into the hibachi and pulled a new one from her box of Shikishima cigarettes. Lighting it, she took a slow draw and aimed a long plume of smoke toward the wall.

Tekkan had lured her into smoking, she mused, but he didn't need cigarettes the way she did. Once, when Hikaru complained about the smoke, Tekkan had sniped, "It can't be helped. Your mother is a man." It was not that women didn't work outside the home—that was common enough. But a woman outshining her husband in intellectual work was emasculating. That's what he meant.

She had tried everything. She had found him contract work and encouraged him to study French. To downplay the differences in their schedules, she tried waiting to eat breakfast with him in the mornings. He was a late riser, so she lingered over her hair, trying to stay calm as the minutes ticked by. Eventually, she gave up. In a letter to Sato she wrote:

> *Can you guess what my husband has been doing lately in the afternoons? He goes into the garden, and using a rusty knife, he kills ants coming out of the holes we dug for the dahlias.*

"You're at the ants again?" I say.

"Yes, I hate them."

And saying just that, 'I hate them, I hate them', he bangs away on the ground! What pitiful thing is this? What in the world am I supposed to do? My husband has unrealized skills—I suppose he has made many people angry—but here he is, not even forty years old, and he is practically a madman.

The howl and clatter of wind outside brought her back to the moment: a storm was blowing in, sending branches skittering across the roof and shaking the thin walls. Cold air pulsed through the room. She was so weary that she could barely sit up, let alone focus on her lecture. She closed her eyes and allowed the Shining Lord Genji to lead her on horseback through a mountain forest north of Kyoto and into the chapter about Young Murasaki.

In a lonely place, the prince comes upon a solitary but once-grand house. In the garden, he glimpses a beautiful girl, and upon inquiry learns that she is only ten years old. Her mother is dead, and her father is far away.

Genji is intrigued and asks to adopt her. Maids and attendants discourage his inquiries, but he insists, and they are afraid to offend a man of his status. One night, as a fierce wind blows, Genji creeps into the compound and, ignoring their protests, spends the night with the girl, reading and talking to her as the wind howls outside.

It was a stormy night. Sleet was pounding against the roof.

"How can she bear to live in such a lonely place? It must be awful for her." Tears came to his eyes. He could not leave her. *"I will be your watchman. You need one on a night like this."*

A sudden crash outside—a toppling of wooden crates, perhaps—caused Akiko to jump. The storm shutters rattled on their hinges, and baby Uchiko began to cry. Akiko picked her up, trying to soothe her, but she only cried harder. Tekkan, lying on a mattress across the room, groaned and rolled over, pulling the quilt over his head. Akiko wearily got to her feet and began to walk in circles, bouncing Uchiko and shushing her.

The baby's face was screwed into an angry mask in the faint light. She was a disagreeable little thing. Akiko wanted to love her, but her sister the "airplane baby" would not leave her mind. *They said she was beautiful.* Akiko imagined a tiny cherub with a pale face, eyes closed like she was only sleeping.

The long day—sick children, missed appointment, bad weather, unexpected guest—all of it bore down on Akiko with a sudden weight. She sank to her knees. Uchiko struggled as she bent forward. Rin began to cry in the next room, and their dual screams clawed at her brain.

Tekkan turned over. "Can't you quiet them? What will our guest think? That we live in a home for wayward urchins?"

I can't bear it anymore, Akiko thought. *I'm not strong enough.* They all deserved better. She had sent Uchiko's older sister Sahoko to live with a foster family soon after her birth. Wouldn't it be better if Uchiko went to live with a foster family, too? She had been thinking about it for a while, and now she made up her mind. She would find a family for Uchiko. She would talk to Tekkan in the morning.

But what about *him?* Tekkan was a drowning man. If nothing was done, he would end up dead, or worse.

Still on her knees, Akiko set Uchiko on the floor and curled up next to her, thinking hard. Tekkan had always wanted to see Europe, to walk on the Champs Élysées, to meet with the artists and writers in the City of Light, to drink from the fountain of Western culture. *What if I sent him to Paris? It would do him so much good.*

She would love to see Europe, too, but they couldn't afford to send one person, let alone two. She could not leave the children behind. Bringing them was out of the question. Perhaps she could borrow, or earn, enough for him to go for a few months. Maybe life would be easier without him around.

It was a mad idea. She could not fathom where the extra money would come from, and it might end a marriage already foundering, but inaction was no longer an option. By the time she laid Uchiko back in her nest of blankets and tiptoed back to her desk, she had made the second big decision of that very long day.

XXI: MAKING PLANS

March 1911, Akiko is thirty-three

かたちの子春の子血の子ほのほの子いまを自在の翅なからずや

Spring child, passionate child, fire child

I want to

Fly on my own wings

"Where are you going to get two thousand yen?" asked Kanao Tanejiro, offering Akiko a cigarette. Lace doilies on the Western-style chair backs and the faint smell of wood polish gave the Kanao Bunendo Publishing office a sophisticated feel.

She took a cigarette gratefully and let him light it, then waited as he lit his own. He tossed the spent match into an ashtray and sat back, regarding her with obvious affection. They were old friends by now and his financial support of her ongoing *Tale of Genji* translation work had been critical.

Kanao was one of those rare people who could turn a passion for art and literature into a successful business. Since taking over his father's modest Osaka-based publishing company specializing in Buddhist books, he had moved to Tokyo and shifted to poetry, classical literature, and large format, high-quality art books of woodblock prints and modern engravings. One of his more lucrative projects was a collection of poems by Susukida Kyūkin, the poet Akiko and Tomiko had found with Tekkan on the day they went to Kyoto.

After giving him an update on her Genji translation—she hoped to finish her primary draft within the year, so he could begin serial publication soon—Akiko explained her decision, no, her *need*, to send Tekkan to France. A second-class round-trip ocean berth ran about fifteen hundred yen. Adding expenses for up to a year of room and board in Paris, she reckoned Tekkan would need close to five thousand yen. It was an impossibly large sum. She had written to Sato asking for a loan, but no answer had come.

"My husband can find freelance jobs as a travel journalist, and those will begin to pay while he's there. We just need about two thousand yen to get him started. I don't know what I'll do if I can't find the money."

She held the tip of her cigarette over the ashtray, waiting for the ash to drop, afraid to look up at him.

"What does Sensei say?" he asked gently, meaning Tekkan.

"He doesn't really say anything, I think he just wants to get away."

"No, I mean what does he say about the money?"

"Well, he offered to ask his former fiancée Takino for the money, but—"

"Ah." Kanao nodded, rubbing his chin. "You know, if I had the money lying about, I would give it to you straightaway."

The ash fell in a clump. "Of course. I understand." When one is poor, anyone better off seems rich.

"I did have an idea ..." she said then. She pulled a newspaper advertisement out of her bag and unfolded it, smoothing it on the table.

"I can buy a plain paper screen for twenty yen. If I fill it with one hundred tanka, I think I could sell it for one hundred yen," she said, "but I need a loan to buy the screens, maybe three hundred, and I need help selling them. Can you advertise in your magazines?"

Kanao's face relaxed into a smile as he thought about it. "Screens with your tanka poems, written in your hand? That's not a bad idea! Why don't you make fans, as well? I'd be happy to run some ads. I don't know how many you'll sell, but it's worth a try." He tapped on the newspaper with his index finger. "Say, have you talked to Dr. Mori? I'm sure he would want to help, too."

"Mori Ōgai?" Akiko said. "Do you think so?"

"He thinks the world of you."

"He's been telling Tekkan to go to Europe for years. You're right, he might loan us some money, and newspapers might support us if he recommends it."

Kanao stubbed out his cigarette with a flourish. "There you are! Sensei will be in Paris before you know it." As he showed her to the door, he added, "Mrs. Yosano, if I may say so, I always knew you were gifted, but I did not know you would become a celebrity."

Akiko ducked her head, cheeks flushing. *Yet I still have to beg for money.*

Tekkan was elated. He began studying French in earnest and wrote letters to artists and writers in Europe requesting introductions and recommendations. He began composing poetry again. If he went out during the day, he returned in time for dinner, whistling in the doorway. One night, he even brought Akiko flowers.

She was torn. Part of her would be glad to be rid of him—things would be less complicated, though she would miss him terribly. She was also jealous that he would be living out his dream while she stayed home and faced the leaky roof, the deadlines, the sick children. Once she started to think about it, this thought began to burn a hole in her like a lit cigarette on newspaper. *Always the afterthought, Shoko-han. Never first in line.* She had escaped from one box only to find herself in a new one; one she had built around herself.

A knock downstairs interrupted Akiko's thoughts. She shifted uncomfortably on her cushion. Months after Uchiko's disastrous delivery, her leg still tingled if she sat too long. There was an insistent pressure on her lower spine, like a baby's foot pushing down, still waiting to be born.

She glanced at her appointment calendar: *April 10, 10:00 a.m., Miss Hiratsuka Haru.* She set down her brush as the maid showed in a young woman in fine silk kimono of pale spring pink cinched with a green *chirimen* obi. She wore crisp, formal white *tabi* socks, and her thick hair was pulled back into a rich knot. A young lady of means, clearly. Tucking an errant lock of hair behind her ear, Akiko frowned up at her visitor.

Hiratsuka was a former student, but Akiko did not know what brought her here today. It had been more than a year since they last met. Hiratsuka had been the object of salacious gossip in local papers recently for having an affair with her married teacher and attempting double suicide with him. What could Hiratsuka want from her? A recommendation, someone to defend her reputation? Perhaps she brought a writing contract. However busy she was, Akiko would not turn down paid work.

Hiratsuka pulled back the edge of her hem primly and knelt on a threadbare cushion. She bowed, placing her palms on the tatami as Tomiko might have done. "Pardon me for intruding, Sensei, I know you are very busy."

"Not at all, not at all, how are your studies?" Akiko asked as the maid set two steaming cups of tea before them. Akiko had worked with the teacher with whom Hiratsuka had fallen in love. He had seemed unremarkable, not the kind of man you'd expect to wander into the mountains in winter with a student, a knife, and a suicide note. If you believed the rumors, it was he who had lost his nerve, not her.

After the failed stunt, he had gone back to his wife and written a lucrative book about it. Hiratsuka, on the other hand, had been expelled from school, her reputation ruined. Akiko thought she had acted foolishly, but she also felt sorry for her. Men could have affairs and no one seemed to mind, but women became damaged merchandise.

"My studies are going well, thank you. I am focusing on European literature at Japan Women's University."

"How nice," Akiko murmured, thinking, *Japan Women's University must be crowded with rich girls studying literature.*

Akiko got to the point. "What can I do for you?"

"I would like to ask you for a writing contribution if you can spare the time. I want to start a literary magazine for women and by women," Hiratsuka said. "I want to call it *Bluestocking* after the 18th century British women's society."

No such magazine existed in Japan, and it was a daring undertaking in the current political environment. It was probably ill-fated. Women were perceived as a political threat in part because of their growing economic power. More than half of Japan's export workforce were women, and they were driven like cattle. She had seen it herself, particularly in textile factories in Sakai.

Government authorities were concerned as some women had led labor walkouts and boycotts. One young woman had been executed along with her male anarchist conspirators for her part in an assassination plot against the Emperor Meiji. Article Five of the new Police Security Regulation prohibited women from joining political organizations or even attending political meetings. In this environment, a magazine run by women might well be seen as a threat, and censors might make it their business to drag the magazine down.

There were other challenges. "Forgive me for asking, but where will you get the money for such an undertaking?" Akiko asked. "Magazines are expensive to produce and rarely profitable."

Hiratsuka looked at the floor. "My mother is helping me to pay for it. She had set aside money for my dowry, but now I will not make an advantageous marriage, so ..."

"I see."

"I want it to be a showcase for women's talent. I hope it will encourage their intellectual development," Hiratsuka went on, her hands pressing so hard on her knees that her knuckles turned white. "As you know, the lot of Japanese women is grim. Women in Europe and America are calling for change. We should do the same."

Hiratsuka was clearly intelligent. Passionate. But the word *volatile* also came to mind. An ambitious woman was a fast-burning firecracker, and it often ended with a *boom*. Akiko had some personal experience in this area. "You know, a women's magazine will be a difficult undertaking. I read creative submissions almost every day, from people across the country. I am always looking for new talent. But women are no good these days. The best writing comes from men."

Hiratsuka's jaw tightened. "Women are no good?"

"I am looking for bright lights, I *want* to see great writing from women. But I'll be honest, I don't see it."

"I don't mean to be rude," Hiratsuka said, flushing, "but women are writing great things, they just don't have the opportunity to publish."

I have obviously overcome this obstacle, Akiko thought, but she said, "Perhaps I've been unlucky in the submissions I've seen." She paused for a moment, thinking it over. "Actually, a women's magazine isn't a bad idea. A good way to cultivate talent. But you must not become conceited. Be humble. Be pragmatic. Give it your all."

Hiratsuka looked as though she did not know how to be humble and 'give it her all' at the same time. She bowed her head and said nothing.

"Now, what precisely did you need from me?" Akiko asked again, reaching for her cigarettes. She didn't want to let on, but she was interested.

"It is presumptuous to ask, but would you be willing to write something for our inaugural issue?" Hiratsuka said. "So many young women look up to you."

Akiko blew smoke toward the ceiling. "I am busy right now." She looked at her former student in her fine silk kimono. Hiratsuka had ruined her chances at a high-status marriage through her impulsive affair, but she would probably never go hungry. She would never have to work for a meal, so what business did she have, complaining about the treatment of women? Did she have any idea what it was like to feed a family of nine on a writer's income? "I'll see what I can do."

A few weeks later, ahead of the deadline and amid frantic preparations for Tekkan's departure, Akiko sent off a European-style poem to Hiratsuka. She did not know if a women's literary magazine could succeed, but maybe Hiratsuka could do it. She was pushy and self-important. Things would only change if annoying women pushed.

XXII: THE SECOND ESCAPE

November 1911, Akiko is thirty-three

海こえて君さびしくも遊ぶらん逐はるる如く逃るる如く

You cross the ocean

Alone on an adventure,

Half-running, half-chased

Tekkan left for France on November 8, 1911. Akiko accompanied him on the first leg of the trip, from Yokohama to the Port of Kobe, where she would visit with Chūsaburo in Sakai before returning home by train. The *Atsuta Maru*, a postal carrier that took on passengers, was bound for Marseille via the Strait of Malacca and the Suez Canal. The trip would take longer than the overland route across Siberia and was slightly more expensive, but it would give him better material for his writing and might be safer.

Gathered on the pier to wish them *bon voyage* were more than two dozen friends, supporters, and representatives of the newspapers and magazines that had commissioned his travel diaries. Akiko stood next to him on the deck and waved down to them. Tekkan, beaming in his new suit and bowler hat, looked as happy as she had seen him in years. She pushed away thoughts of the coming year without him. And his year without her, free to do as he pleased.

Three of the children—Hikaru, Shigeru, and Yatsuo—squirming in their best clothes and chaperoned by Tekkan's sister Shizuko, looked alarmed to see their parents already far away, high up on the mighty ship.

As the *Atsuta Maru* cast off, it let out a thunderous blast. Along with the other passengers, Akiko and Tekkan leaned over the railing, tossing streamers to create a last, fleeting bridge between ship and land. The children screamed and put their hands to their ears. Friends shouted last-minute exhortations from the pier. The streamer Tekkan threw to Shigeru went wide, and the children's voices were soon swallowed up in the noise. Akiko watched their small figures jumping up and down until they disappeared in the crush of bodies as the boat pulled away.

It was a strange sensation to leave off their everyday lives and set out to sea. She had been tethered to the children for so long that the relief was almost physical, as though she were setting down a burden to whose weight she had grown inured. For the moment, she and Tekkan were unreachable, surrounded by water and strangers, with no commitments for the rest of the day, at least.

It seemed a long time since they had simply enjoyed each other's company. The day was cool, and the wind blew sharp across the water, but the sun was warm on their faces. They strolled on the gently rolling deck and tried to identify landmarks as they came into view. Late autumn foliage of rust and yellow poked out between warehouses and buildings as their ship moved south along the coastline.

"Why don't you come with me to France?" Tekkan asked, as he had done several times before. Akiko had always rejected the idea, pointing out that they had seven children and barely enough money for him to make the trip alone. As it was, they would be paying down the debt for a year at least. She could scarcely spare the few days she was taking from her *Genji* translation. No, it made no sense.

But here on the deck, and as they lay together in his narrow berth that night, she wavered. She feared she would never see him again, that something horrible must happen to one of them. In the darkness, as the *Atsuta Maru* rocked like a cradle, she committed his scent and voice to memory. She had never been alone for more than a day or two in her life; now, the prospect of being without him unmoored her.

Neither of them could sleep, so they twined arms and legs together like the twisting roots of mated trees. He wound his hands through her hair and put a handful to his lips. "I will miss this," he breathed, and she leaned into him, feeling his chest rise and fall like the ship beneath them. She pressed her fingers against his neck to feel his pulse, and tears spilled from her eyes. She clung to him like a shipwrecked passenger to a piece of driftwood and wept like a child.

Two days later, she watched her husband's figure melt to a dot of color among hundreds of other dots at the ship's railing high above her. She wondered how he would change over the coming year, how she would change, and whether he would take a lover in Paris.

She summoned a smile for the group of friends who encircled her on the dock as the *Atsuta Maru* pulled away: Chūsaburo and his wife, newlyweds Masako and Chino, and loyal patrons Tenmin and Kanao.

Back in Tokyo, Masako and Chino stayed with her that first night on her own. Since the poetry party when he had made origami animals for Masako, Akiko had thought Chino was perfect for her. If Tekkan was a moody firecracker, he was a devoted companion.

Masako had been reluctant at first to accept his advances. He was from a poor family, and her parents did not approve. His loyalty and affection won her over, though. She had wanted to marry for love, and he did love her. They lived in a modest flat in Tokyo now and worked as teachers.

That night of Tomiko's first saké seemed a long time ago. None of them were strangers to saké anymore, nor sex, nor grief. Tomiko was gone. Even Tekkan was gone, on the open ocean somewhere.

Maybe they're together. Floating.

"You're white as a ghost," Masako said as they cleared the dinner dishes and tidied up while the maid put the children to bed.

"I feel old. I have many worries. I'm not well."

"You sent one of your daughters to a foster family?"

"Well, two. Sahoko is with a family in Tamagawa. I couldn't manage with her—Rin was barely a year old when she was born. I was so anemic; I could hardly stand. And then this year." She still could not talk about the loss of Uchiko's twin.

Masako busied herself stacking dishes.

"I found a family for Uchiko. Their name is Sakurai. They're good people."

"Will they bring her to visit sometimes?" Masako asked, as they returned to the sitting room where Chino sat crossed-legged under a quilt, bent over a newspaper.

Akiko sighed. "They did once, but when they left her with us overnight, she cried all night long. I had to call them first thing in the morning to come get her." She leaned over her tea, deflated. "My own child, but both of us were miserable."

"You poor thing," said Masako. "Of course, she's too young to know who her real mother is now." She shifted uneasily. "I mean, I'm sure you'll send for her when you're ready," she added, turning pink.

But Akiko wasn't listening. "I am in danger. I feel vulnerable. Fragile." She let her forehead fall into her palm.

"What do you mean?" Masako asked. "Are you ill?"

"Perhaps we should call for more hot water?" Chino looked up from his newspaper, alarmed. Masako slid open the shoji door to call for the maid, but Akiko shook her head.

"No, it's not that. What I mean is—sleeping alone, raising the children alone, taking breakfast alone—I'm like a rowboat, bobbing in the swells behind Tekkan's ship long after it's gone."

The maid appeared with a fresh kettle.

"I thought Tekkan would always be with me."

Steaming water was poured.

"He is with you, Akiko-san. You're so important to him."

You don't know how he feels, Akiko thought reflexively. *I don't even know how he feels.*

"You encouraged Tekkan to take this trip, remember?" Masako asked gently.

"What was I thinking? I feel like I've been asleep for ten years," Akiko groaned, "and I'm just waking up, trying to remember what I've done." She started. "Oh! I have something to show you."

From a stack of magazines and unopened mail on the tatami floor, she pulled out a magazine with a bright yellow and black cover. They leaned forward to see.

"*'Bluestocking',*" Chino read. The cover featured an illustration of what looked like a Greek goddess with a headdress and long, dangling braid. She stood with arms raised inside the silhouette of a kimono.

"It's a new women's literary magazine. First issue. One of my former students, Hiratsuka Haru, is doing it."

"Isn't she the one who tried to commit suicide with her teacher?" Masako was curious. She turned to the preface and read it aloud.

> *In the beginning, woman was the sun.*
> *An authentic person.*
> *Today, she is the moon, living through others,*
> *Reflecting the brilliance of others,*
> *Pale-faced and sickly, like the moon.*
>
> *What women do now invites only mockery ...*
> *But I am not in the least afraid.*
> *Are women simply valued for regurgitating things?*
> *No, no, we are authentic beings ...*
> *We must restore our inner sun that we have been hiding away.*

"It's signed 'Hiratsuka Raichō'. Is that her new pen name?"

Akiko clucked. "Apparently. Raichō means 'Thunderbird.' A little presumptuous, don't you think?"

"Does she know your maiden name was Hō, the Firebird?"

"Probably not." Akiko didn't like to think she had anything in common with this self-important young woman. "I warned her not to get too full of herself. What does *she* know about life? She has no children. No husband. Plenty of money. She is free."

Masako turned to the next page. "Oh look, here's a poem by you." She began to read:

> *The day the mountains move has come.*
> *I speak, but no one believes me.*
> *For a time the mountains have been asleep,*
> *But long ago, they danced with fire.*
> *It doesn't matter if you believe this, friends,*
> *As long as you believe:*
> *All the sleeping women*

Are now awake,
Are moving.

Chino shook his head, impressed. Masako read it a second time silently. "Powerful," she murmured. They could not know that both poems would live on as feminist anthems for women around the world.

Akiko was frowning. "What kind of fool am I, to write that women have been sleeping, and not recognize that I've been sleeping, too?" She stared at the table as she spoke. "Sleepwalking toward an empty future." She fingered the ashtray before her. "My life has gone grey, like ashes."

She closed her eyes and rested her chin on her hand with a sigh.

"Perhaps it's time for bed." said Masako. "It's late."

"Of course. I'm sorry, I've kept you up," Akiko said without opening her eyes. She sighed again, wiped her face with a cloth, and began pushing half-heartedly at the low table. Chino jumped up to help pull it to one side to make room for the futons. He and Masako would sleep here tonight; she would sleep with the children.

Chino excused himself while Akiko and Masako unrolled the bedding on the floor. There was just enough room to squeeze the mattresses between the table and a pile of screens leaning against the wall, some with poems already scrawled on them, ready for sale. At the foot of the mattresses were unsold *Myōjo* issues, a box of fans, and Akiko's ink and brush supplies, wrapped in newspaper.

"I had a dream the other night," Akiko said, unfolding a blanket while Masako fetched pillows from the closet. "It was a rose-colored dream."

"Rose-colored? I thought everything was grey," Masako smiled.

"You're right, I said that, didn't I? It's shifting, I guess. Like I said, I'm at a turning point."

"Tell me." Masako sat on the futon and folded her hands over her knees, prepared to listen.

"I drove my husband away," said Akiko. "It was a whim. I decided for my own sake that he had to leave."

Masako nodded.

"But," Akiko said, smoothing down the covers, "isn't it through whims that we live most fully? Perhaps I'm being selfish, but I neglected myself too long. They say that artists and writers live like hedonists, but if we don't tend to our hearts, if we just do the same thing over and over, a decade goes by, two decades, and soon we're ashes, with a stone over our heads."

Chino slid open the door, back from the washroom. He was wearing his undershirt and long underwear, freshly shaved, neck pink from scrubbing. Tekkan had a finer body, Akiko thought, but as he sat down next to Masako, he touched her shoulder with such tenderness she had to look away.

"I think I am in some danger," Akiko went on. I feel I must do something reckless if I am to save myself. Candidly, in my life, all my new energy has come from moments of recklessness—chasing crazy dreams."

Chino and Masako looked as though they wondered what she had in mind.

"It's like when I ran away from Sakai—it was reckless, and it has filled my life with misfortune, but it is mine, my authentic life. I did it for myself. Do you understand my meaning?"

Masako nodded, and now she was sitting up straighter. "I do. I left my family, the city I grew up in, to live my own life, too."

Akiko smiled softly. "My mother was—do I sound like an impetuous child if I say she was ignorant? I understand her better now that I have my own children, but I don't understand why she never considered my feelings."

"Never," Masako agreed. "Nor did my parents. They considered only the family inheritance. Having sons. I might have stayed, I might have gone forward with the marriage they had arranged, if they had been kinder."

Chino, who had been sitting quietly, chuckled. "I guess I should thank them."

Akiko was up early working on *Genji* when Masako came to her study holding a fan inscribed with poems in Akiko's *hiragana* calligraphy.

"This was in our room," Masako said, "with the screens. May I buy one? How much do you charge?"

"It's for the Paris trip," Akiko said. "Just take it. No need to pay."

"It's lovely. And I want to contribute." She held it up to the light.

"That's very kind, Masako, but we're doing all right. I managed to scrape together enough for Tekkan's outbound trip, and he has writing contracts with two newspapers once he gets there. I think he'll have enough. And anyway, you pay me by listening to my silly prattle." She patted the cushion next to her. "Can you bear to listen for a few more minutes before you go? I don't feel like I finished last night."

"Of course. Chino is still sleeping."

Akiko sighed. "I tired you both out. I'm sorry."

"No, that's why we came." She sat down and leaned an arm against Akiko's writing table. "Where were we? You were feeling reckless."

Akiko lit a fresh cigarette, studying her face. Could she trust her? Masako's loyalty had been first to Tomiko. She had also flirted with Tekkan back in the *Lover's Clothes* days, but her friendship felt sincere.

"You write. You understand. It takes so much out of me. To put emotions into words. Sometimes I don't *want* to write what I'm feeling because it's painful, but I have to." She breathed out a plume of smoke and laughed bitterly. "It's my job."

Masako nodded. The sounds of small feet, the maid's voice, and the smell of rice and miso soup floated up the stairs.

"But over the years, it took so much out of me. I poured out all the wine in my soul, bled out my body, and put nothing back in. I must have been a miserable person to be around. I understand better now why my husband was suffering. He was dying of thirst, and I gave him no water. How stupid I was."

"You are hard on yourself," Masako said. Her eyes went to the *Genji* translation on her desk—hundreds of dog-eared, handwritten pages—and the tipsy piles of dictionaries and reference books on the floor.

"I've done poorly," Akiko fretted, "as a wife, as a mother. But something has changed. I sent my husband away on a whim and it gave me a chance to think. I feel stronger now, like I'm twenty years old, and I want to run away from home all over again."

"This is a hard home to run from, Akiko-san. You have many responsibilities." Masako was starting to suspect what she was thinking.

But it was too late; Akiko had made up her mind. "Everyone needs to be alone sometimes," she said. "Especially women. The people who never have time to be alone are the ones who need it most. How can we know ourselves if we are never alone with ourselves?"

The sound of a crying child downstairs underscored her point. "We must live our lives as fully as we can. Poets need to replenish the wine in their souls. Women should be allowed to wander, too."

"You want to go to Paris," Masako said in a low voice.

Akiko looked at her, or just past her, and nodded. "I do."

"What about the children?"

Selfish, selfish. Neither of them said it, but Akiko saw it in her friend's eyes.

"I have some ideas. Tekkan's sister took care of them when I went to Kobe. She is single; she might be willing to stay with them."

"Even the little ones?"

Say it, Masako, I'm a monster. It's true. Well, Rin is almost four." *And the girls Sahoko and Uchiko are already gone.*

Her mind was far away now, across the ocean, in a land of flowers, cafés, and intellectual freedom. Space to breathe, time to write, time to fall in love again. She deserved her friend's approbation, and she didn't fear it. She had broken out of a box before and she would do it again or ruin herself in the effort. Masako must understand that. Poets run away sometimes to save themselves. And sometimes, mothers do, too.

XXIII: ACROSS THE STEPPE

May 1912, Akiko is thirty-four
Siberia

三千里わが恋人のかたはらに柳の絮の散る日に来る

Seven thousand miles to arrive this day at my lover's side

As white flowers fall from willow trees

The train heading west from Vladivostok consisted of an engine, freight car, dining car, and four passenger cars, the last reserved for women. Akiko placed one bag on the floor, and a porter helped her put another up in the shelving overhead. Tucked between her feet was a gift bag from Mr. Yaoshima, the Vladivostok-based *Tokyo Asahi Newspaper* correspondent. Before leaving, Akiko had secured two travelogue contracts: one from *Tokyo Asahi* and one with the affiliated *Ladies Picture Book* that would, if she was careful, pay for her expenses in Paris. Japanese were curious about Europe and the United

States. Literacy was high, and readers were hungry for information about foreign travel.

Yaoshima had seen her off at the platform, apologetically pressing into her hand a bag of sushi, fruit, a bottle of lemonade, and one hundred Russian-made cigarettes in a pink box. His colleague, Mr. Saito, would be on the train for the first two days, but after that she'd be on her own, he said.

I did want to be alone, Akiko thought grimly as she settled herself on the worn velvet seat. So far, traveling had not agreed with her. She had spent much of the choppy ocean trip from Yokohama vomiting over the side. The wind was frigid on the heaving deck, but below deck was nauseatingly stuffy, and for third-class passengers the only place to sleep was a wide expanse of threadbare carpet. It was crowded with people lying this way and that, crying children, heads propped on suitcases and trunks, coats for blankets.

Now she was aboard the train that would be her home for the next nine days. It would take her, with one change in Moscow, seven thousand three hundred miles across Siberia, crossing through Chinese territory, over the Ural Mountains, and into the heart of Europe. In her purse was three hundred yen, just enough to get her to Paris, the last of a gift from Mori Ōgai. There was nothing to spare; if there were unexpected expenses, if Tekkan were not there to meet her, she would be alone in a strange land without a sen to her name.

She cleared her throat and looked out the window at Mr. Yaoshima waiting on the platform. He gave her a reassuring smile as porters with military-style caps and passengers carrying leather suitcases and canvas bags swirled around him. European clothes were fashionable in Japan these days, but many of these Russian men wore strange clothes— long tunics belted at the waist, thick coats with fur collars, cylindrical hats, and knee-high leather boots. They had beards, many of them untrimmed, and they had high European noses like the ones Akiko had seen in books and magazines. Even women wore boots, and their heads were covered in colorful scarves, framing their chapped red faces and blue eyes. The sound of alien languages rose around her, mingling with the stench of coal smoke, body odor, and cabbage soup.

She stared down at her gloved hands folded on her European-style skirt as the train shuddered and jerked to a start, then looked up as great clouds of smoke rolled past Yaoshima, who waved one last time. For travel in the Western world, she had sewn a single ash-blue skirt, two blouses, and an overcoat. She had a navy blue felt hat and leather gloves to match. It was not her first attempt at Western-style sewing—in preparation for his trip, she had sewn Tekkan three shirts, two vests, and two pairs of trousers—but women's clothes were more complex. After consulting with a tailor in Tokyo, she had improvised—rather successfully, she thought.

The cost of new clothes had been added to the list of expenses for this ridiculous trip even as Tekkan had spent money on more frivolous things. Excited for his European adventure, he had argued that ten-year-old Hikaru should be enrolled in a French international school. *Impossible*, Akiko had said, looking over the fancy Gyōsei School flyer. In addition to tuition, there was a uniform. *We cannot even pay what we owe for the move to the new house and medical bills for Uchiko's birth*, she had argued. But Tekkan was so enamored of the idea that she dropped her objections, and off went Hikaru to private school.

He had been one of only two or three boys who wore kimono rather than the school uniform with its handsome hakama trousers. Remembering the ugly hanten coat of her childhood, Akiko had scrounged a few yen to buy the uniform hat, a little straw thing. It was all she could afford. The trousers would have to wait.

Now, as Akiko watched the grey buildings of Vladivostok give way to houses and farms, she thought of her son, setting off for school with his new hat, his sandals clacking like train wheels on tracks, his sturdy little body clad in his blue kimono.

"I will get you the trousers, Hikaru," she had promised, but he had said he didn't need them. In fact, none of her children seemed to mind the poverty that so humiliated her. Just weeks before, their nanny had commented that the children did not recognize a wooden tansu dresser in a picture book. "That's like not recognizing a chair!" the nanny had laughed, but Akiko had not thought it was funny.

わが子らは箪笥を知らず、不思議なる絵と思へる
My children do not know a tansu
They think it's just a funny picture

Not long after, with the pawn shop proceeds from two yuzen-woven textiles Teru had sent her after Tsuné died, she bought the trousers for Hikaru, unwrapping them for him the day before the school's first spring field trip.

"Mama!" he had said almost reprovingly, but he couldn't know what it meant to her.

No one will laugh at my son.

She opened her eyes. It was evening, and the sun was setting against the rolling hills. Though it was May, the ground was brown and white in the waning light, silver tips of brown grass catching the last rays of sun. Here and there, farmhouses dotted the horizon. The windowpane was cold.

Her stomach growled, and she realized she had not eaten since breakfast. She ignored it for a while, but hunger eventually drove her into the train corridor. She felt her way down to Mr. Saito's cabin, and tentatively peered in. He was reading a book but jumped up when he saw her and came out into the corridor.

"Have you eaten?" he asked, twisting his hands.

Akiko shook her head. "No, I—"

"Oh, heavens, I think the dining car closes soon, let's get you down there quickly." He pulled out his pocket watch.

Mr. Saito was a young man, not much taller than Akiko, with round spectacles and a nervous fidget. He looked like he did not want to be responsible for her, but Yaoshima had probably called in a favor. It was unusual for a woman to travel alone, and Yaoshima probably felt it was their responsibility to watch over her. She was—as Kanao had said—a bit of a celebrity.

Located directly behind the engine, the dining car was loud and smoky. Queasy from nerves, the smell of the food soured her stomach. They approached a buffet where an attendant in a white jacket stood, looking bored, his white apron spattered with gravy. There was only one choice for dinner—lamb stew, with sides of beer, bread, and tea. She took a bowl and followed Mr. Saito to a table by the darkening window. He looked out into the evening as though searching for something while Akiko stirred her stew listlessly. She could only manage a mouthful or two before telling Saito that she wasn't hungry after all. She apologized and fled, leaving him at the table.

Back in her cabin, she found her bedsheets had been pulled down and her bags set on the floor. The yellow glow of the gas lamp reflected off the black window pane, giving the tiny compartment a sickly cast. Pulling the curtains across the windows, she turned off the light and climbed into her bunk.

The train crawled across the Siberian steppe, one day much like the day before. It stopped occasionally to let passengers on and off and to reload the coal and water cars. At one point the engineer switched from coal to wood fuel, then back again at the next stop. Sometimes a woman shared Akiko's cabin for a few hours, then departed. With no language in common, they simply read books or stared out the window.

At station stops, Akiko sometimes got off the train to stretch her legs and take in the vast, empty country around her. The wind was always blowing, dirt roads stretched away into hills that were still winter-brown even in May, and far in the distance, mountains loomed. The dreary station buildings were brightened by the vendors gathered at them, some with pots of hot tea, others selling bread or crafts. Akiko looked wistfully at the bunches of fresh wildflowers for sale and thought that Yatsuo and Nanasé would have loved the little rag dolls.

Some stops were so brief that passengers were not allowed off, so villagers—just children, many of them—stood on wooden crates at the side of the train and held up handmade dolls, jewelry, scarves, boiled eggs, and bottles of milk. As windows slammed open and goods, coins and paper currency exchanged hands, the train corridors filled with smoke, food smells, and the sting of cold air.

Late on the third night, at the Chinese border, customs officials boarded the train, waking the passengers to check their luggage and tickets. The guards who came into Akiko's cabin looked barely old enough to shave. If they were embarrassed to intrude on a woman in her berth, they did not show it; they spoke brusquely to her in a language she did not understand. Trembling with cold and adrenalin, she leaned over to pull her travel papers out of her bag. If these swarthy men were to demand a bribe or arrest her, she would be helpless. As a woman, this thought filled her with dread.

With the help of two maids, Tekkan's sister Shizuko had agreed to stay with ten-year-old Hikaru, eight-year-old Shigeru, five-year-old twins Yatsuo and Nanasé, and three-year-old Rin. Shizuko had no children of her own and Akiko did not care for her, but she could not afford to be picky.

She thought about their chaotic home back in Tokyo, already forgetting how desperate she had been to escape from it. The corners of her mouth turned up as she remembered how, on the night before Tekkan's departure five months ago, he had pulled Yatsuo and Nanasé onto his lap.

"You're starting school next spring, aren't you?" he had asked.

They nodded. "I want you to be better students than your Papa was, do you understand?"

They nodded and grinned.

Akiko watched with fondness. He had not always been an attentive father, but that night he had wrapped one arm around each of the girls and squeezed them until they giggled.

"Do you want me to bring back a present for you?" he had asked. "What would you like?"

The girls agreed that ribbons and a doll would be good. Overhearing the discussion, the older boys came into the room.

"Are you talking about souvenirs, Papa?" Shigeru and Hikaru did not want to miss out.

"Yes, what would you like?"

Shigeru nudged his older brother, and when Hikaru hesitated, he delivered a sharp elbow in the ribs.

"We were thinking," Hikaru began, rubbing his side, "a watch would be swell, but ..." His confidence wavered. "There probably isn't money for that."

Shigeru made a perplexed sound.

Tekkan cocked his head to one side. "Maybe there is, maybe there isn't."

"Postcards are fine," Hikaru said quickly. Shigeru rolled his eyes, and Akiko felt her heart quiver. She gathered dinner dishes from the table and carried them into the kitchen. Rin was trying to climb into Tekkan's lap along with the girls.

"Rin, what do you want? Papa is going to France!" Hikaru said.

"How about a picture postcard?" prompted Yatsuo, making room for him.

"Yes, *you* don't need a watch, do you?" said Shigeru. With everyone looking at him, Rin was suddenly shy. Tekkan put his wide palm over Rin's close-trimmed hair and rubbed his head encouragingly.

In a tiny voice Rin faltered, "I want ... I want ..." They all waited. "I want an apple," he said, and Tekkan laughed out loud.

On the afternoon of the third day, Akiko entered the dining car to see its occupants crowded around the windows on one side. An enormous body of water spread before them. Lake Baikal!

Shimmering blue in the May sun, it was framed with melting ice close to shore, deepening in color further out. In places, the lake's fingers nudged against narrow peninsulas, and beyond that it stretched to the horizon, white, blue, and black, ice and water against the sky.

She glimpsed the roof of a hunter's cabin tucked among the trees, and once or twice she saw fishing boats dragging nets. It reminded her of a woodblock print by Hiroshige, a fishing trawler at Okitsu bobbing under the shadow of Mt. Fuji.

Someone entered her cabin at a train stop in the early hours. Akiko kept her blanket over her head and listened as a woman whispered to a coughing child. They settled into the berth across from her. The child's deep, reverberating cough reminded her of the whooping cough that had almost killed Hikaru. She fell asleep worrying about the child without even seeing him.

When she woke the next morning, she lay still for a while, not wanting to wake her bunkmates. She could see their faces reflected in the makeup mirror on the wall. Even in deep sleep the woman was beautiful, with one arm curved protectively around her child and long, golden hair tumbling across her face. Quietly, Akiko slipped out to visit the washroom. When she returned, closing the door with a soft click, they did not move, still deeply asleep. Outside, a river rushed alongside the train tracks. Mountains rose around them, and a light rain began to fall.

Akiko wrote in her notebook for hours as the train made its way across Siberia. It raced through forests of white birches that continued unbroken for miles, spaced in almost unnatural rows like a vast, pale army. Sometimes hours passed without a sign of human habitation, leaving the passengers alone with each other among mountains, grass, birds, and sky. In the evening, they passed through a vast wetland of brown reeds shining like golden spears in the setting sun. A group of water birds rose and curved gracefully like a grey curtain across the sky. They arched and bent as one, and the waning light lit the tips of their wings.

Akiko knew this was the time she had wished for, away from her responsibilities, but her mind, like the train, raced ahead, toward Moscow and beyond, a universe of unknowns.

Villages and towns became more frequent as they neared Moscow on the seventh day. Here Akiko would have to change trains. An expectant murmur and the sound of bags being pulled from shelves filled the corridors. The conductor, carrying a thick ticket book and bulging money bag, told her in French that second-class tickets for her connecting train were sold out. A first-class Nord ticket would cost an extra eighty yen. It was a major expense, but Akiko did not see what choice she had. She bought the ticket.

A carriage took her across town to her connecting train—she counted out the rubles she would need and held them tightly in her fist as the carriage clattered past buildings of stone and red brick with exotic spires and tall windows.

Before boarding the train, she wired Tekkan with her arrival information: Paris Gare du Nord at three o'clock on May 19th. The wire fee left her with only twenty-five yen. Her first-class ticket gave her a private berth, but she learned that she would need twenty-eight yen in customs fees before reaching Paris. And she still needed food for three days. She did not have enough.

She boarded the Nord in a panic, and as the train pulled out of Moscow Station, she considered her options. Mr. Saito had told her of a Japanese-owned inn in Berlin. They might be willing to defer payment. Maybe she could get off there and try to trade in her Nord ticket for a seat on the next available second-class train. She could wire Tekkan from there for money.

She approached the conductor, holding her French phrasebook in one hand, but he shook his head. "*Impossible*," he said, looking stern and uncompromising in his black uniform and gold braided shoulder cord. She clutched her bag to her chest as he launched into a rapid explanation in French. She shook her head, fighting tears. Would she be arrested? Thrown into debtor's prison, with no way to get a message to Tekkan?

She remembered a British gentleman who had introduced himself in the dining car a few days earlier. He had lived in Yokohama for many years and spoke Japanese. His name was Marius Russell. He had been on his way back to England with his daughters.

This train's terminus was Calais, on the English Channel, so perhaps he and his daughters had made the same connection in Moscow. Perhaps she could prevail upon him to speak to the conductor on her behalf. She hurried up the corridor looking for them. She passed through one car to the next at a half-run, searching in every cabin window. At last, she saw a gentleman sitting across from two young women. Her heart leapt: a bit of luck. She knocked and waved at him through the window.

When he came out with a smile and bow, she explained—trying not to sound like a panicked child—that she needed to get off the train at Berlin, but the conductor had said she could not, and she did not understand why. Would he be so kind as to speak to him? He could make himself understood, whereas she could not.

Russell assured her that he would try, and set off to find the conductor, with Akiko close behind.

The conductor explained something to Russell in French, looking sideways at Akiko and shaking his head.

"Ah, yes," Russell said solemnly, "yes, I see. I suppose it can't be helped then. Well, thank you very much," he said, and led Akiko away gently by the elbow.

There were customs requirements at the French border which made it impossible for her to get off the train, since she had already purchased a ticket to Paris, he said. Surely, she could send a telegram once she arrived, to whomever was expecting her in Berlin?

Her throat constricted.

"Please don't worry, Mrs. Yosano," he said, patting her hand. "Come with me, I want to introduce you to my daughters." He led her down the rocking train corridor, but as she followed him, lurching from side to side against the walls, she could no longer contain her emotions. Russell opened his cabin door and as the two young women stood up, she burst into tears. Mortified, she covered her face with her handkerchief.

"I'm just three yen short," she yammered at them in Japanese. "I didn't plan to take a first-class train, I had enough for the second-class train. How could I have known? And now I have no money for food, I will not eat for three days, I will only drink tea, I don't care about that, but what will become of me?"

Russell made a surprised sound. "My heavens, why didn't you say so?" he asked. "You didn't say that you didn't have the fare." He withdrew from his wallet the equivalent of thirty yen in French *francs* and handed it to her.

Akiko refused it at first, but he insisted. "I will not have a lady starving to death on this train."

What choice did she have? She took the money. Weak from hunger and hours of panic, she thanked him, fresh tears rolling down her cheeks.

She would make it to Paris, then, but what would be waiting for her?

XXIV: THE CITY OF LIGHT

May 1912, Akiko is thirty-four
Paris

ああ皐月仏蘭西の野は火の色す

君も雛罌粟われも雛罌粟

Ah, May in France,

The meadows are the color of fire

You are a coquelicot,

I am a coquelicot too

The train arrived at Paris Gare du Nord two hours behind schedule. As it came to an ear-splitting halt, puff-puffing copious clouds of coal smoke, Akiko searched the unfamiliar faces looking up at her.

Would Tekkan know her train was delayed? Would he be able to find her? What if he had come for her, and not finding her, already left? She had the address of his flat in Montmartre somewhere—she dug through her purse—but she had only a few francs left and did not know how far it was. She could not possibly find her way on foot, even if she did not have a heavy trunk. Not to mention, after two weeks on the road without a bath, she hardly felt presentable.

A white-gloved conductor helped her down the steps, and as she waited for her trunk, she looked around. Tekkan was nowhere to be seen. The glass-and-metal ceiling glared down on her like a storm front. She stood in a shifting sea of tall, smelly Europeans—mustachioed men, women in plumed hats and skirts, screeching children. They all seemed to be hugging and kissing. People lugging bags and pushing carts heavy with trunks called to each other, conductors blew ear-splitting whistles, and train brakes squealed.

She considered her options. Her train was already being readied to head back out, and new passengers were pushing onto it almost before it had emptied.

Tekkan might look for her at the station entrance, she decided, so she began to fight her way in that direction, dragging her heavy trunk behind her. Her heart was thumping, and she began to sweat. *No. No more tears.* She stopped to breathe.

An older woman stood alone by a sign post. She wore a felt hat with a brown feather and a conservative suit dress. She had a kind face and seemed unhurried, as though waiting for someone. Maybe she could help.

Akiko pulled out her phrase book and looked up the French words for "Where is?" and "Husband or Master": "*Où es le maitre.*" She repeated it a few times under her breath, then timidly approached the woman.

"Ahh—*Excusez-moi—Où es le maître?*" Akiko asked, trying to smile. She felt like an idiot as the woman turned to look at her with a mixture of curiosity and warmth.

"*Le maître? Le maître?*" asked the woman, confused but eager to help. She looked at Akiko in her travel clothes and shook her head. "*Je ne comprends pas. Est-ce que vous Chinoise?*"

Akiko shook her head. Chinese? Hardly. She was backing away when the woman seized her hand.

"*Le maître du gare? Venez avec moi.*"

She began to drag Akiko along, then saw her heavy trunk and dashed off. She was back a moment later with a porter. Perspiration coursed down Akiko's back as she shook her head vigorously. She could not pay for that!

Not knowing what else to do, she followed the woman to the station office, bumped and jostled by the throngs around her. She held her purse firmly against her chest—she had been warned about pickpockets.

The station master stepped out of his office as they approached, taking in the French woman, the porter, and the distraught Asian traveler in one glance. His mustache twitched. He gestured toward Akiko's purse, so she pulled out the Montmartre address and her passport with trembling hands. The woman and the station master looked them over, conferring. She waited for their adjudication, helpless as a lost child.

"Akiko!" The familiar voice behind her cut through the din of the station like a temple bell. She whirled about.

Tekkan was coming across the platform toward them. In his Western suit and hat, she might have mistaken him for a local, yet she knew every part of that face, the way he moved. Her heart leapt. Tekkan bowed to the station master and the woman and offered a few words in French as they handed back her papers. He brought a coin from his pocket for the porter.

"*Merci beaucoup,*" Akiko managed, bowing to the woman, who was looking back and forth between her and Tekkan with a relieved smile. *They must think me a fool, Akiko thought. Thank goodness for kind strangers.*

After they had backed away, Akiko and Tekkan looked each other over. Here in Paris, people embraced and kissed, but it would have been odd for them, so Tekkan touched her hand.

"I'm sorry," he said. "Your train was delayed, and the platform changed."

Akiko merely looked back at him, trying to master her emotions. She was still shaking from worry, fear, and relief. It seemed incredible that this handsome man had found her in this foreign place. Like a castaway bobbing in a stream, she held tight to his hand. Months of separation had made him more precious. They weren't star children anymore, but something else. Something more sea-worthy. At least, she felt that way, and to guess from the light in his eyes, perhaps—*perhaps*—he felt that way, too.

下に住む西班牙の子がピヤノを叩けば 起きてくろ髪を梳く

Woken by the Spanish child downstairs
Practicing piano
I rise and comb my dark hair

Two sounds tugged at Akiko's consciousness: the sound of a cuckoo, and the tinkling of piano keys. After two weeks on a train, she was accustomed to the creaking sway, the clacking tracks, and the puffing of engines; these sounds were new.

She opened her eyes. She was in a rented flat on the third floor of a walk-up boarding house at 21 Rue Victor Massé in Montmartre. Light streamed in the window at the far end of the high-ceilinged studio. A beam illuminated a threadbare red carpet in the middle of the studio and warmed the air. Besides the bed, there was a writing table with lamp, a bedstand, a standing mirror, a coal stove, a chamber pot behind a folding screen, and a few framed prints on the walls. Tekkan's lean body made a V in the center of the springy mattress, a gravity depression that pulled her toward him. A large red feather coverlet was pulled over them. She rolled into him, bedsprings complaining noisily, and let her unbound hair touch his face and chest. He was awake, staring up at the white plaster ceiling, one arm behind his head. He wore an expression of sleepy contentment—the afterglow of the night's lovemaking.

They listened to the plunking piano for a few minutes without speaking. With occasional stumbles and corrections, the notes repeated themselves from somewhere downstairs.

"I wonder what time it is," Akiko murmured, almost to herself.

"It's just after eight o'clock," Tekkan said with such certainty that she raised herself on an elbow to look at him, arching one eyebrow. He explained. "Every morning at eight, the Spanish girl downstairs starts her piano lesson."

"Ah." Another moment passed as the music continued. Then, "I heard a bird like a cuckoo just now, what was that?"

"The madame of this house told me it's a 'merle.' It's pretty, isn't it? It sounds like a Japanese warbler to me. So many things here remind me of home." Tekkan pulled Akiko close. They kissed for a long time, and her pulse quickened. It had been so long. They made love again to the novel sound of squeaking mattress springs, then dozed in each other's arms. By the time they were ready to get up, it was almost lunchtime. "What do you want to do today, *mon amour*?"

I want to stay right here, she thought. *I want to hear you say that again.* But she turned over, sat up, and reached for her cigarettes on the nightstand. Her hair cascaded down her naked back as she popped one in her mouth, lit a match, and said through her teeth, "Let's go for a walk!"

That first day, Tekkan led her down a cobblestone street lined with trees and teeming with horse-drawn coaches, wagons, and even a smoke-belching horseless carriage. They passed sidewalk cafés, vegetable and flower vendors, newsstands, and storefront windows stacked with bread, cheeses, and dried meats.

The people were even more curious. Men and women with tall noses walked arm in arm, many of them impeccably dressed. Nannies in white kerchiefs pushed prams, black-uniformed men in top hats drove coaches, ladies in plumed hats walked together, white-aproned waiters leaned in doorways, and old men, deep in conversation, gesticulated.

Tekkan sat her down at a café on the Promenade Coccinelle and proudly ordered lunch in French. On the table he set two guidebooks, one in French and one in Japanese, and placed a proprietary hand atop them as he told her about his new home. The circular street layout, electric streetlights, and architecture of Paris were the envy of the world, he said, sounding so much like a tour guide that Akiko suppressed a smile. The Tour Eiffel was a modern marvel of steel, and the Sacre Coeur Basilica, still under construction and enclosed in scaffolding, towered over the Paris skyline. He had even seen a dirigible the other day.

Together they marveled at the creative buzz that drew painters, writers, and dreamers like themselves to *La Ville Lumière*. It was more than great architecture and food, Tekkan said; it was the political tolerance and intellectual freedom of France's Third Republic that drew them here. The city's coffee houses and bars had been peopled by the likes of—here, Akiko contributed to Tekkan's list—Victor Hugo, Guy de Maupassant, Gauguin, Van Gogh, Matisse, Pisarro, Toulouse-Lautrec, Baudelaire, and Picasso.

"Everyone comes here because everyone is here," Akiko said.

Tekkan nodded. "Here we are." Tossing back the last of his seltzer water and lighting up, he leaned back, blowing out smoke slowly. He had enjoyed a warm welcome thus far, he told her. With letters of introduction from Tokyo friends and accompanied by expatriate Japanese such as the painter Matsuoka Shoson, he had met with French, German, British, and Dutch artists and writers who were as interested in Japan as he was in European literature and poetry.

He had been surprised at the enthusiasm for Japanese art. Oriental fans, silks, carvings, screens, and flower arrangements were all the rage. "These days, art dealers are making a fortune importing ukiyo-e woodblock prints by the crateful. They're everywhere! If I had known, I would have brought some with me. It would pay for this entire trip."

"What do they think of Chinese or Korean art?" Akiko asked.

"It's exotic to them," Tekkan said, leaning toward her. "but ukiyo-e is what most interests painters and collectors. The colors, the subjects, and the perspective—they are mad for it."

He paused as a coachman at the curb engaged in an expletive-laced discussion with a pushcart owner. They watched, amused, until eventually the coachman was sent off by the bearded pushcart man with a rude gesture.

"You see women modeling in front of Japanese screens for portraits sometimes," Tekkan continued. "That's an obvious influence, but it's more subtle elsewhere. It's the choice of color, flatness—they call it *cubisme*—and attention to seasons. You'll see what I mean."

Then he picked up the art guidebook and leafed through it. "Here, here's an example." He showed her a letter written by Vincent Van Gogh to his brother Theo in 1888. Tekkan translated:

If we study Japanese art, then we see a man, undoubtedly wise and a philosopher and intelligent, who spends his time—on what?—studying the distance from the earth to the moon?—no; studying Bismarck's politics?—no, he studies a single blade of grass.

But this blade of grass leads him to draw all the plants—then the seasons, the broad features of landscapes, finally animals, and then the human figure. He spends his life like that, and life is too short to do everything.

Just think of that; isn't it almost a new religion that these Japanese teach us, who are so simple and live in nature as if they themselves were flowers?

"What do you think of that? 'Simple as flowers'!" He tossed the book on the café table with a chuckle, but Akiko was staring at the women walking past: how they carried themselves, what they wore. From her train window, she had studied the practical clothes of peasant folk along the long Siberian line. The fashions she had seen during her dash across Moscow between train stations had given her a first taste of urban skirts, high-necked blouses, parasols, hats, and dainty button boots—even in her distressed state she had gawked—but Paris was something else entirely.

Passing before her now were two women with straw boater hats, ankle-length black skirts, and leather shoes with silver buckles. Earrings dangled from their ears. They walked arm in arm, confident, laughing freely, showing their teeth. Akiko was wearing her kimono that day, as her travel clothes desperately needed washing, so she must have been a curiosity even for Parisians, who were accustomed to curiosities. As they passed, one of the women turned inquisitive eyes on her, and she looked back, unabashed.

四つ辻の薔薇を積みたる車よりよき香ちるなり初夏の雨
Street wagons heaped with roses
Shed their perfume in the first showers of summer

Over the next few weeks, Tekkan showed Akiko around Paris and introduced her to his new coterie of friends and benefactors, including a few wealthy Japanese globetrotters, such as the architect Nishimura Isaku, who insisted on contributing financially to their literary mission.

Cautiously, she allowed herself to relax. Her heart quivered when Tekkan touched her arm or held a door for her in the European style. Each evening, restauranteurs threw open their doors and set out tables on the sidewalks. Local theaters—including the Moulin Rouge with its windmill façade—lit up with gay can-can cabarets and variety shows. Strolling through Montmartre, they watched the *nouveaux riches* drink and dance.

Back in their flat after dinners and drinks with generous friends on sidewalks strung with lights, they stripped off each other's clothes and embraced in the darkness, not caring when light through the open window cast diagonal shafts across bare white buttocks and heaps of clothes on the floor.

At Versailles, she listened to the soft scuffling of shoes on parquet floors in the ballroom. In cavernous churches, she lifted her eyes toward pillars of sunlight piercing stained windows. In Tours, she walked with Tekkan along country roads and picked wildflowers. She watched girls with Bibles in their hands run along the road as a church bell rang. She saw women wash clothes in the river, boats dotting the shores, and listened to the air hum, thick with thirsty bees.

In a prayer chapel in the transept of an old church, Akiko knelt with local women before a marble mausoleum bearing images of two sleeping children. In the half-light, she prayed for her own children.

Local Parisian newspapers and magazines wrote about her—"*Une Célèbre Poétesse Japonaise à Paris*"—and she in turn wrote about Parisian fashion for her mostly female audience back home. Traditional European women's clothes were as uncomfortable and constricting as kimonos, she wrote, but French designers were introducing liberating new forms with Asian influences. Fashion designer Paul Poiret—"Le Magnifique," as he was known among the Paris fashion set—was showcasing gorgeous new dresses that did not require corsets and petticoats. Pigeon-breasted, tiny-waisted dresses with hoops and bustles were out; harem pants and draping silk robes were in.

Akiko also wrote about what French fashion said about women, and what she had learned about Japanese women during her time away.

The woman in Europe is always active, but the woman in the Orient is quiet. The beauty of quiet grace is fine, but it is not suitable for modern times. I hope that Japanese women will become more active soon. To the extent possible, I realize I want to show off the beauty of Japanese women to the world.

Of course, Japanese women's tendency to be shy and a little too easily pushed around is not good; but I think with some education I wouldn't worry that they can't have an awakening.

Akiko was critical of her countrywomen, but she was blunt about French women, too. They were comparatively outspoken and socially daring, but she saw that they were also constrained. These women could not vote; they, too, lacked legal rights; they, too, struggled to seek higher education or careers outside home and childrearing. As in Tokyo, the streets of Paris teemed with girls pushed into prostitution by poverty. And like Japanese women, she believed, French women were partly responsible for their predicament.

Tekkan was enraptured by the fantastic new world around him, but Akiko was more circumspect. Behind the lights and music, she sensed, French women were trapped, too.

XXV: A NEW ERA

1912, Akiko is thirty-four
Vienna

生きて世にまた見んことの難からば 悲しからまし暮れゆく巴里

Night descends on Paris

I am sad to think

That what I saw today

I will not see again in this life

They were in a hotel room in Vienna when news reached them that the Emperor Meiji, who had led Japan since before they were born, was dead.

Akiko leaned an elbow on the windowsill and brooded. Rain coursed down the brick front of the building across the street, reflecting the grey morning light and the gloom in her heart. Puddles on the cobblestones below sparkled, and the sound of wheels and horse hooves on pavement cut the air. They had spent May and June in France, then, with a grant from the Ministry of Culture, joined two friends on a monthlong tour of the great northern European cities. With artists Ishii Hakutei and Kobayashi Mango, they visited London, Amsterdam, Antwerp, Brussels, and Munich, before reaching Vienna. With each stop, Akiko grew more unsettled. European food didn't agree with her, she missed the children, and she was intellectually saturated.

Now, the news of the Emperor. A gust of wind blew in her face, flapping the curtains and flecking the floor at her feet with raindrops. Tekkan, who was standing with his back to her at a writing desk, said over his shoulder, "Really, close the window. We can't afford fees for wet draperies."

A moment later he sighed heavily and turned to her. "Let's go out."

Akiko didn't move at first. When someone dies, she thought, you want to be with others who share your sadness. Japan felt far away, and Vienna was a lonely place to be.

With the handwritten announcement from the Embassy, they had received a black ribbon and a mourning band, so Akiko pinned the ribbon to her lapel and helped Tekkan attach the band to his forearm. Then they set off under his umbrella for the Kunsthistorisches Museum on Neue Burg Heldenplatz. On the way, a top-hatted gentleman stopped them to express his condolences. The story of the Emperor's death was in the newspaper, he explained, and he had noticed their mourning attire.

Tekkan bought a paper at a newsstand. The new emperor, they learned, was to be Meiji's oldest surviving son, Yoshihito. Very little was known about the thirty-three-year-old, who was sickly and stayed out of the public eye, effectively a stranger to the Japanese people. The year up to that day had been Meiji 45; henceforth it would be known as Taisho 1, according to the Japanese system of numbering years by imperial reigns. They had never known another emperor. What would this new era be like? He tucked the paper under his arm and they walked on.

Wet shoes on the marble floors of the museum made them slippery, and whispers echoed off the walls. Akiko had little appetite for art that day, but she looked at the paintings to humor Tekkan. In one room, a winged figure looked out from an oil painting, surrounded by skulls, a guttering candle, and an hourglass. *"Nil Omne"* was scratched on the wooden table: "All is Nothing."

Tekkan was looking at his guidebook. "Austrian art is so moralistic," he said. "No heart." He gestured at a Madonna nearby. "These were done *after* the Italian Renaissance; you would think there would be more passion."

Akiko shrugged; she wasn't sure if she agreed, and anyway, "All is Nothing" brought her children to mind. *My children are not "nothing." They are my future, my husband's, my country's.* More than anything in Europe, she was learning what it meant to be Japanese. She was proud of how far her countrymen had come, with the Emperor's guidance, after centuries of isolation. The grant money on which they were now traveling was part of his effort to encourage understanding of European thought and technology. As she stood in the drafty museum hall, this thought comforted her. In her short life, she had done her part. She had given her country poetry, Genji scholarship, and seven healthy children. However small, these were her contributions, her creative gifts.

They made their way to the Embassy for a memorial service. Secretary Ōno, dressed in black mourning coat and armband, greeted them breathlessly. He led them up a marble staircase covered in patterned carpet to the formal parlor. "The Ambassador is receiving guests now," he said over his shoulder.

Fewer than thirty people—mostly Japanese businessmen and military officers with their wives, by the look of them—were gathered in the richly decorated room. Several were queued to meet with the Ambassador. The tall windows were draped with black buntings, and a portrait of the Emperor, surrounded by white flowers and incense, sat on an easel before a group of folding chairs.

"I had thought more people would come," murmured Tekkan.

"Perhaps these are all the Japanese in Vienna," she whispered back as they joined the reception line.

Ambassador Satsuo Akizuki was a short, dignified man with a lambchop mustache. Secretary Ono stood next to him, introducing guests. "Ambassador, may I introduce Mr. Yosano Tekkan and Mrs. Yosano Akiko. They are poets and writers."

"Goodness, Mrs. Yosano! I heard that you were in Europe!" The Ambassador's round face lit up. "How nice to meet you, and your husband." He bowed toward Tekkan. "You're a poet as well, are you not?"

"Why yes," Tekkan said, stiffening. "I wrote *Sounds of a Dying Country*; you may be familiar."

The Ambassador nodded vaguely as his gaze returned to Akiko. "Mrs. Yosano, your *Tangled Hair* found its way to Vienna, did you know? Some of your poems have been translated into German and French. My wife—she'll be here soon—loved it. I must introduce you." He glanced around for her. "She has a copy. She would be delighted to—ah, but today is not a day for celebrating."

Akiko and Tekkan bowed and moved on, and as they took their seats, Tekkan looked cross. She didn't blame him. Women were accustomed to being overlooked, but it was harder for men.

As the memorial service got underway, she wrapped her arms around her middle, trying to contain the ache inside. Since leaving Tokyo, and particularly since embarking on this multi-city tour, she had been fighting a nagging worry, as though she had left behind a purse or a passport on a train seat. At first, she couldn't identify what it was, but gradually she had come to realize that the lost valuable was her children.

She saw them everywhere. In Montmartre, students wore straw hats with yellow ribbons, just like Hikaru's school uniform. At the zoo at Jardin des Plantes, she had watched the little humans, not the animals. Washing up before bed at night, she ached for small bodies to scrub. She wrote in her journal:

After joining my husband in Paris, the first month flew by. Compared to how busy I was in my last months before leaving home, to have so much free time was like a dream at first. Before, I could not imagine a day spent without a writing brush in my hand, but here, my lifestyle is completely different. It should be relaxing, but somehow, I am uneasy. I used to savor the aroma of fine tobacco that accompanied me as I worked, but now, with nothing to do, it turns my stomach.

She had sent her husband away and found she could not live without him. She had left her children behind to chase after him, and found she could not live without them, either. She no longer wished to be a curiosity in a foreign land. The emperor's death was a sign. It was time to go home.

The malaise was not confined to her heart; she was physically ill. The weather had been muggy, and the long train rides and sagging hotel bedsprings made her back ache. She missed sleeping on firm tatami. She missed real baths. Everything was filthy here. The food—fatty meats, boiled vegetables, breads, unfamiliar spices, heavy sauces—made her sick to her stomach. Rats lurked in piles of garbage in the alleys of these great cities, and the stench of urine, rotting food, and body odor was everywhere. Repeated surges of dread and panic left her with dull headaches. *I feel like a different person here. I wonder how I became so weak, when in Japan I was so strong.*

Eventually, Tekkan called in a doctor who confirmed what Akiko already knew. She was pregnant. Furthermore, the doctor told her with hands placed sagely in his lapels, she suffered from hysteria, a common female affliction.

After showing him out, Tekkan came back and sat down on the edge of the bed where Akiko lay sipping the brandy the doctor had given her. They exchanged tense smiles.

"Do you want a boy or a girl this time?" he asked, trying to sound light-hearted.

Akiko was having none of it. "I want a healthy baby. And I don't think I can survive twins again."

"What a big family we have made. Are you pleased?"

Akiko frowned. "Pleased to be pregnant again? No. It's exhausting. And it is a lottery with the devil." She paused; the brandy was warming her throat. The pride she had felt in the museum was creeping back. She hated childbirth but secretly loved the quickening inside her, the seed of life, a manifestation of her love for her husband. She looked at him with the smile that touched only the edges of her mouth, "I admit to feeling a bit smug. Children are like great works of art."

The worry lines in his forehead softened.

"Back home," she continued, "we hear about our duty to the Emperor and to the Japanese people. The Emperor called on women to bring children into the world and to raise them well. Men have important roles, but only women can create new life."

"Leave it to you, my dear, to be fertile not only in your writing but also in your womb."

Akiko sighed. She would be relieved if this were her last child— but if there were more to come, well, she would do her duty as long as she could. If she died in a puddle of blood, no one could accuse her of not being a good citizen. She might be a failure as a daughter, but not as a loyal subject of the Emperor.

"If it's a girl, there's a name I've been thinking about—" he offered.

"Oh?"

"I love French names. What do you think of 'Hélène'?"

"I think it's lovely," Akiko said. "I have an idea for a boy, if we can use French names?"

"Why not?" Tekkan looked alarmed. Giving a girl an unconventional name was one thing, but saddling a boy with one was a different matter.

"Auguste," Akiko said. "After Monsieur Rodin." They had visited the famous sculptor's country studio in Meudon and had tea with him in Paris. She and Rodin had felt an immediate connection. "I'll never forget him. So gracious. If we could raise such a man, I would be proud."

Tekkan gave her a smile that said, *I will not argue with you in your delicate condition.*

"The doctor's recommendation that you should return to Japan as soon as possible doesn't make sense to me. If you're pregnant, the last thing you should do is embark on a long international trip."

Akiko shook her head. "No, he's right. I want to go home. Childbirth is dangerous enough without facing it in a foreign country where I cannot make myself understood."

"But—" Tekkan stood up restlessly. He thrust his hands into his pockets like a sullen schoolboy. "*I* don't want to leave. I'm happy here." He looked at her, eyes pleading. "And you just got here."

"That's not true," Akiko said. "I've been here almost four months." She held out her hand to him. "You don't have to leave. You can stay."

He shook his head. "You can't make that trip by yourself. The journey here was hard on you."

"I am more accustomed to it now. I can manage. And besides," she lay her hand over her eyes, "I miss the children so much. What kind of mother leaves seven small children behind to travel the world?"

"The children are fine," Tekkan said, for the hundredth time. "Shizuko is taking good care of them. They love her, they all say so."

"What does Shizuko know about children?" Akiko said crossly, with her hand still over her eyes.

"Is it too bright for you?" He got up and closed the heavy drapes, plunging the room into darkness.

"Thank you," Akiko sighed, letting her hand fall back to her side. "You're the father. Don't you miss them? Don't you worry? Men can go away for months, even years, and no one says a thing. The mother goes away, and—" She shrugged. "'Hysterical.'"

"Of course, I miss them." He sat back on the bed, reaching for a lock of hair that had fallen in her face and brushing it away gently. "But they are all right. I would miss *you* if you left."

"I want to go home."

In the end, they agreed that Akiko would return by herself, by sea, and Tekkan would follow in a few months. They were both unhappy. Though Akiko wanted to go, she felt she had failed him. She dreaded being parted from him again. Pulled in both directions, there was no right decision.

On her last evening in Paris, she watched the late summer sun from their window as it sank behind the rooftops. The building across the street glowed for a last golden moment, and the clatter of leaves in trees mingled with voices, the honking of horns, the clink of glasses, the throaty bong of church bells. The sun would continue setting every evening over Rue Victor Massé long after she was gone, just like this. She would grow old, but this street would look mostly the same. For a long time, she stood still at the window.

On September 20, 1912, Akiko departed Marseille aboard the postal carrier *Hirano Maru*. Tekkan watched from the dock as the ship's tall stacks poured black smoke into the sky, its belly heavy with mail and its decks crowded with Japanese citizens returning to a new emperor and a new era.

船ゆれて紅茶の椀の匙鳴ればわがすすり泣聞くここちする
The ship rocks
My teaspoon rings against the side of my cup
Sounding the sadness in my heart

XXVI: GOOD WIFE, WISE MOTHER

1913-1918, Akiko is in her late thirties
Tokyo

One night, in the season of baby chicks, I was imprisoned in a maternity room until I could deliver myself of a baby boy. My doctor would not allow me a brush to write with or a book to read. But since most of the time my life is very busy, to be sequestered away quietly and alone for a while felt almost as though I had gone off by myself to a hot spring resort to relax. I had time to think about things that I don't have time for when I am living my normal life. So, don't tell the doctor, but I wrote down some thoughts ...

—Tales of the Maternity Ward, 1913

Within days of pushing out her ninth baby in April 1913, Akiko was back at her desk in Tokyo, thick cloths between her legs soaking up the blood. One of her first tasks was to pen a letter in tortured French to Monsieur Rodin, announcing the birth of her son Auguste. Of all her memories of Europe, she would treasure meeting the sculptor most of all. Madame Rodin had given her a bunch of blooms from her rose garden, and before leaving Paris, she had pressed them into a book to bring home with her.

A chorus of excited children awaited her at home; they had all changed so much in her absence. Hikaru had shot up like a sapling and Rin was talking fluently.

Her list of pressing problems had grown, too. She was behind on her writing commitments, which included new poetry, children's stories, social essays, and an autobiographical novel.

It was around this time that she delivered something else: the final chapter of her serially published *New Translation Tale of Genji*. The project had required more than six years of work. At a crowded publication party, Kanao presented her with a bouquet of flowers and reminded guests that his star author just back from Paris was the first person to translate the entirety of *Genji* into modern Japanese. Others had managed only partial translations. It was a major achievement and an important contribution to Japan's national literature.

She didn't say so at the time, but Akiko was already dissatisfied with it. She had wanted to revisit earlier chapters, to improve them as her understanding of Murasaki Shikibu's classical language deepened, but there simply hadn't been time. Looking over the published translation, the problems stuck out to her like sores. After press attention to the project tailed off, she approached Kanao with a new proposal. She wanted to write a *Tale of Genji* commentary—a section-by-section analysis, alongside an improved translation.

Kanao lacked the deep pockets to finance another major project, though, so Akiko appealed to Tenmin, whose futon business in Osaka was doing well. Eventually, Tenmin and Kanao agreed jointly to invest. They would pay her monthly advances over the five or six years the project would require. She nicknamed it the *"New-New Translation Tale of Genji"* and started work on it immediately.

Meanwhile, three of the Yosano daughters were growing up in foster homes: Sahoko, Hélène, born in 1915, and Uchiko, the airplane baby's twin. Uchiko had been an infant when she was sent to live with the Sakurais just before Akiko left for Paris. The Sakurai family farmed a small plot and ran a produce market outside city limits near Kichijoji Temple. They had lost an infant in early 1912 and, in their grief, had been eager to take in a baby in exchange for a few yen per year.

Sending the girls away was not a happy thing, but it was necessary. Fostering was not uncommon; after all, as children, Akiko and Tekkan had both lived with foster families. *There's no shame in it*, Tekkan sometimes said, but neither of them liked to talk about it. There was no firm plan for when the daughters would be brought home, and as time went by, it became easier not to think about it. Yatsuo and Nanasé assembled care packages for them; Akiko wrote them letters, and about once a year, they came to visit. Akiko dreaded these awkward interviews. Her daughters hardly knew her. When Uchiko came, it felt as though her sister's ghost had come to cast judgment on her.

"Welcome, Sakurai-san, welcome!" called Tekkan, assuming a *seiza* kneeling position next to Akiko as their two guests, one tall and one very small, entered the study. On this hot September day in 1918, the window was closed and the curtains drawn in a vain attempt to keep the room cool. Akiko was fanning herself, the collar of her cotton kimono pulled open as far as propriety allowed. On her desk were writing projects in various stages of completion—reviews of her essay collection *Love, Reason and Courage*, and another, *To My Young Friends*, which Tekkan was editing. She had several open letters in draft that were part of her escalating argument with *Bluestocking*

editor and self-proclaimed "Thunderbird" Hiratsuka Raichō over government policy toward women.

Thin as a scarecrow in his starched white shirt, Sakurai placed a gift bag of radishes and cabbages on the tatami before him. "Just a bit of produce from our farm. I wish there was more." He couldn't be more than twenty-eight or twenty-nine years old, Akiko thought.

Next to him cringed Uchiko, now seven, her hair cut short in a bob. She had carried in another bag of vegetables, almost as heavy as her. Following her adoptive father's example, she pushed them forward and bowed her head to the floor.

"It's hot, isn't it?" Tekkan said cheerfully and called for cool *mugi-cha* tea. Akiko watched the little girl closely as the men talked. Uchiko kept her head low, like a puppy in a new house.

"How is the farm?" asked Tekkan.

"It's been a difficult year, I'm afraid," Sakurai said as the tea arrived. "Yields are down because of the wet summer." Still cowering close to him, Uchiko was beginning to look around curiously.

"You must be getting a good price for rice, though, with so much sent overseas for the war effort."

Sakurai shook his head. "Yields are so low that it doesn't make up the difference. Now it looks like the war is coming to an end, so government orders will go down. We can only hope that things get better soon."

"Not soon enough, it seems. The protests are getting out of hand."

Labor protests had turned violent over the summer, starting with female dockworkers in a fishing village in Toyama Prefecture. Dockworkers—who loaded rice bales onto ships—were primarily women, and over the past year, conditions had deteriorated as prices climbed. The women were growing resentful as they loaded boats with rice for overseas consumption while their children went hungry at home. When they demanded better conditions, they were ignored. Work walkouts led to arrests and beatings, and now, sympathetic protests and riots were spreading up and down the coast. Osaka, Kobe, and even Tokyo were roiling. "Just this week I saw fires burning down by the docks. Arsonists are burning warehouses filled with rice!"

Sakurai shook his head. "The government brought this on itself. They can't go on treating people like slaves."

Eventually, discussion came around to more mundane matters.

"Uchiko," said Tekkan gently, "are you being a good girl for Mr. Sakurai?"

She nodded, looking at the floor.

"Are you studying hard in school?"

She nodded again, and Sakurai, chuckling, said, "Speak up for your honorable Mother and Father."

Uchiko cleared her throat and said in a tiny voice, "Yes."

Tekkan and Sakurai laughed. "She is going to school near the temple. It's a backwards little country school, I'm afraid. People laugh at it. It has a dirt floor and paper windows, but the teacher is kind." Sakurai looked at Uchiko. "Isn't that right? You like your school?"

She nodded.

"I was sorry to hear about her illness this spring," Akiko said, "but she looks healthy now." On the way home from school in the rain one day, Uchiko had slipped on a wet bridge and toppled into the stream below. A classmate had pulled her out, but she had arrived home drenched and shivering, with a bloody elbow and knee. Within a few days she was running a fever. Sakurai had walked miles to pick up medicines for her and had written to Akiko asking for a few sen to help pay for it.

Sakurai nodded. "She is much better. And on rainy days now, I pick her up from school."

Akiko's frown deepened. "Is that necessary? You must be busy."

"Oh, it doesn't take long. I carry her on my back, so it's quick. There's not much for farmers to do on rainy days anyway."

Tekkan looked at Uchiko, cowering on her cushion. "Don't be a burden to Mr. and Mrs. Sakurai. You must be a big girl, do you understand?"

Uchiko nodded, still looking at the floor. *She looks terrified*, Akiko thought. *What must she think of these two strangers who are supposedly her mother and father?*

"I've been concerned about the bad strain of flu this year," Akiko said, looking back at Sakurai. "I don't know what will happen this fall. You are safer in the countryside, I think; I worry about the crowds downtown."

As the interview ended, they invited Sakurai and Uchiko to stop in the kitchen on the way out; the maid had prepared bowls of tempura rice for them.

"Be a good girl!" called Tekkan after them. Akiko watched mutely as they left.

"She seems to be doing well," said Tekkan, turning back to his editing. Akiko didn't answer, so he looked up. "Don't you think?"

"She shouldn't be a burden on the Sakurais. They are too easy on her. My mother never would have tolerated that kind of behavior." She was fanning herself; beads of sweat stood on her brow. "Imagine, picking her up from school when it's raining and carrying her home! Were you treated like that?"

"Of course not. But she is a girl, after all."

"We do not teach girls to be weak!" Akiko said, with such force that Tekkan did not say more.

It was a sore topic. She was publicly debating this very issue with Hiratsuka Raichō. After the *Bluestocking* magazine debut, Raichō and her followers—budding young feminists—had become some of her most ardent fans, even accompanying her to Yokohama to see her off when she left for Paris in 1912. Their friendship had begun to fray, however, as differences in philosophy emerged in essays published in magazines such as *Ladies' Discussion*. They agreed that official government espousal of "Good Wife, Wise Mother," a concept rooted in Meiji-era reforms, legally and philosophically subordinated women to men. A "Good Wife" obeyed her husband and followed orders, clarifying the chain of property ownership and inheritance. "Wise Mother" was about educating the next generation. Mothers must be able to help their children study.

But Raichō believed that in return for fulfilling such duties, the government should support widows and single mothers, whereas Akiko argued that women must be treated as equals of men in all respects. Akiko believed that singling mothers out for state support retarded progress by encouraging women to think of themselves as dependents.

Raichō's criticism became increasingly personal. She publicly accused "Mrs. Yosano" of setting a poor example by having more children than she could care for, adding that Akiko should not confer her superhuman levels of endeavor and capability on every woman. Akiko argued that children were a mighty gift to family and country. As for working hard, she believed everyone should do it.

For far too long, we women have abdicated the ability to think. Women have been just arms, legs, and mouths. Look at any factory: the ones who are working for the lowest wages, under the most horrific conditions, are women. Moreover, they are looked down upon by men, treated harshly. This is because they are only moving their arms and legs, like machines. They are not moving their brains ... Women must get moving, they must quickly sharpen their wits!

Journalists began referring to Akiko and Raichō as *"new women,"* a popular term for feminists. Akiko didn't like being lumped in the same group with Raichō and felt the term was belittling. *I am not a 'new woman,' nor am I an iconoclast. I am a pragmatist. Men are culpable in creating the current system, but unlike many young women today, I recognize that women bear some responsibility for it, too.*

Akiko was pregnant again. After Hélène, Akiko had delivered two more boys: Takeshi in 1916, and Sun, who died after two days in 1917. She hardly spoke of Sun to anyone, and—perhaps out of sympathy again—hardly anyone spoke of the baby to her. It was as though he had never existed.

If she survived this newest pregnancy, she hoped it would be her last. She could no longer hold the life inside her womb, her back could no longer carry the weight, her heart could no longer pump the blood. As the delivery date approached, she put her affairs in order.

In spring 1919, at the age of forty-one, Akiko gave birth to her sixth daughter, her eleventh and last surviving child. Fujiko was small and thin, with alarmed little eyes and almost no hair. Akiko curled little Fujiko's fist around her pinkie finger and wondered how she would take care of this child, too. She already had a houseful of accident-prone, coughing, sniffling, misbehaving offspring, all of whom needed shoes and underwear, hanten jackets in winter, and rice to eat.

"I may love you the most of all, Fujiko-chan," she whispered. "I am not a very good Mama, but I will try for you. Will you be patient with me?"

It made her sad to think that so much of her life was gone already, and she had hardly seen it go, like an aromatic cigarette smoked too fast, or a book skimmed for lack of time. She had hardly noticed her children shooting up around her or her husband aging at her side, not to mention her sent-away daughters. But they had not forgotten her.

XXVII: THE SCHOOL

1920-22, Akiko is in her early forties

学院のテラスの薔薇の花咲けば
鵠の羽かげにあるここちする

When roses bloom on the school terrace
It feels like we are sheltering under a swan's wing

The Yosanos' financial luck was finally turning. At forty-six, Tekkan landed a lecturing position at Keio University, something he had been seeking for years. Hot spring resorts and hotels in tourist areas hired them to lead poetry seminars and lectures, so Akiko and Tekkan were often on the road. They could finally afford a few non-essential items, like a piano for the girls to play. The sound of Nanase practicing musical scales brought back sweet memories of the Spanish girl downstairs at Rue Victor Massé.

In May 1920, after an event at a hot spring resort in Karuisawa, Akiko and Tekkan continued south to the country home of architect

Nishimura Isaku, an acquaintance from their days in Paris. He had traveled the world, from Singapore to Europe to the United States, absorbing ideas like a curious child at every stop. Recently, he had been pestering Akiko to visit his hometown of Shingu on the southern tip of Kii Peninsula. It was out of their way, but he had an exciting proposition for her, he promised. She had been wanting to see the Western-style house Nishimura had designed and built. Taking the time away felt like an indulgence, but they agreed to go.

Shingu Station was little more than a train platform at the convergence of two dirt roads. The warm May breeze bore the scent of apple and orange blossom as they stepped off the single-gauge train. Everywhere, trees were leafing out in the ecstasy of spring.

Striding across the platform toward them was a young man whose urbanely tailored suit made him stand out like a colt in a field of grass. His thick hair was swept up off his high forehead, revealing a contagious smile.

"Ah! Thank you so much for coming. You look great!" He shook Tekkan's hand energetically in the Western style.

"Not at all," said Tekkan. "It was a beautiful ride along the coast. Refreshing."

"Humph! I don't know about that!" he chuckled, winking at Akiko. He led them down to a dirt road where two rickshaw drivers stood, hoping for customers. Nishimura passed them though, stopping in front of his automobile, parked in the dirt nearby.

"What do you think?" he asked proudly, gesturing at the handsome machine. "It's a Mitsubishi Model A. I wanted one of these in Tokyo, but it makes more sense in the country. My wife thinks I've lost my mind."

Tekkan was more impressed than Akiko: she disliked the noise and gas fumes of automobiles and suspected they were always one bump in the road away from a flat tire.

Nishimura kept up a steady banter over the din of the engine as he drove. "I grew up here, so I built my house on my father's property. It's a kind of experiment. I saw so many lovely houses in the United States. I tried to adapt their design to our way of life here. The light, the space—it will be good for the children's intellectual development."

They bumped along a dirt road that cut a straight line through rice paddies filled with seedlings in perfectly spaced rows, the water reflecting the blue sky. He swerved around an ox cart as Akiko clutched her hat with one hand and the side of the shiny black cabin with the other. "I'm a free thinker, that's what I tell them." He didn't ascribe to any point of view other than his own, which sometimes was a problem. "I got in trouble for saying the Emperor was not so different from a normal person last year. Maybe you heard." He struck the steering wheel happily with his palm. "That's why I like you two! You aren't afraid to speak out either. I'm so glad you've come. And I have another house guest this week."

Akiko nodded, but it was Tekkan who answered. "Hakutei! He wrote to us. Wanted to make sure we came." Ishii Hakutei was another friend from Paris, a painter.

"That's right!" Nishimura said, pleased with himself. "I had to get my free-thinking friends together for something very important."

It wasn't until the next afternoon that Nishimura revealed his big idea. He had brought them into his bright, French-inspired conservatory to show them his amateur paintings and sculpture. "Would you like to make a painting to remember your visit by?"

Akiko had taken painting lessons in Paris, so she and Hakutei—a jowly man with a good-humored growl and shrewd eyes—shrugged on smocks while Tekkan excused himself to walk in the garden. Nishimura set two easels before an earthenware bowl containing tangerines and a single fig. Akiko took up a brush with a determined look.

"The Japanese education system needs an overhaul," Nishimura began, walking back and forth like a lecturing professor as Akiko and Hakutei assessed the fruit bowl. "Particularly for girls. We need to move faster in encouraging our daughters to think for themselves."

He rearranged the tangerines as he spoke. "They need more exercise, fresh air. They need exposure to European art and music. They need to think for themselves."

"Stop moving the fruit," Hakutei growled. He had wrapped a towel around his thick grey hair and was filling his brush with orange paint.

Akiko looked up from her easel and fixed Nishimura with a steady gaze. "Go on."

"I have five daughters, and if I may say so, my eldest, Aya, is quite clever. She is coming to high school age, but there isn't a single school in Japan I would send her to."

Hakutei smiled under his thick mustache, which he waxed and twisted up at the ends. "There is no school in the world good enough for your Aya-chan."

"Ah! I wouldn't say that. But as I was looking for a school for her, I started to think about what exactly I wanted." He swept one arm toward the tall windows that flooded the studio with light and afforded a grand view of his fruit trees. "I would want the school to have windows! Light! Air!"

Hakutei nodded, dotting his canvas with orange circles.

"And art," Akiko said. "It should be a beautiful place. Like this one."

"You're too kind," Nishimura bowed. "Now tell me what you think of this: *No uniforms*."

Akiko's smile grew. "Are you going to found a school?"

"I am."

Hakutei was dabbing bits of white and blue on his orange globes. "What else will you teach them? Sculpture? Music?"

Nishimura had disappeared into a back room; he reappeared with a jar of murky liquid. Something was floating in it. He held it aloft. "Science! Math!"

He placed the jar next to the bowl of fruit. Akiko shuddered. *Were those frogs?*

"And one more thing," Nishimura paused for effect and looked over his shoulder as though police were about to break down the door. He lowered his voice conspiratorially. "*Boys.*"

Akiko was sitting back now, her painting just started, but she was too interested in what Nishimura was saying to focus on it. "Co-education? Bravo! But did you bring us all the way here just to tell us about your plans?" She was hoping he would ask her to teach at his exciting new school.

"Frogs off the table, Nishimura," Hakutei said.

"Well, no," Nishimura removed the jar. "I have something rather special in mind for you two."

"Out with it then," said Hakutei. "The paint will be dry before you get to your point."

Nishimura leaned toward them. "Hakutei, I want you to be the Head of the School. Akiko, you will be Second in Command."

There was a moment of silence. Both looked astonished. Then Akiko spoke.

"You know I don't have the background or credentials for that. I'm sure Hakutei will do very well, but I'm not—"

"Madame, you are precisely the person I am looking for. It must be you."

Akiko turned to Hakutei, who set down his paintbrush and picked up a rag to wipe his hands. "I'm afraid you've taken leave of your senses." He stood up. "I love the concept, but I am not an administrator or a school principal."

It was hard to resist Nishimura's charisma, though, and the more they talked about it, the more excited Akiko became. The school would be staffed by artists, architects, scientists, and scholars. Students would be encouraged to follow their passions, to think independently, even wear Western-style clothes. The campus would be filled with flower plantings and windows flung open to the air. Students would be challenged to study foreign languages and pursue the arts for personal fulfillment. Eventually, even Hakutei came around.

Nishimura bought a former hospital in the Surugadai neighborhood of Tokyo for his school, knocking out walls, widening windows and installing porches. At first the school would enroll girls only, but they planned to bring in boys within a few years. Bunka Gakuin ("Culture Academy") opened its doors in spring 1921, Japan's first co-educational secondary school. At the inaugural ceremony, Akiko read from the podium:

> *Our educational goal is this: For each to express her own creativity, free of outside pressure, according to her individual strengths and wishes, in a place where she can freely apply herself. To date, education has been oriented toward practical pursuits, but we want to provide education that goes above mere practicality. In other words, by avoiding becoming a slave to money or a trade, the individual becomes her own master; she pursues activities that are suitable to herself as an individual. In this way, we can nurture adults who know the joy and pain of making, in even a small way, a contribution to human culture.*
>
> *To say it another way, our sole purpose is to create a 'whole individual'. A whole individual is not someone who does all things at an average level, nor is it a legendary genius who can do no wrong. If an individual can find her own special skill and dig deep into that, it is sufficient. It is more than enough to build a meaningful life.*

Akiko came to love Bunka Gakuin. She cherished walking the hallways that echoed with happy voices and whose walls were crowded with artwork. She worked to make it the school that she would have wanted to attend. She persuaded Nishimura and Hakutei to establish a scholarship for talented girls whose families could not pay full tuition. She built the literature program and trained new teachers, drank tea in the staff room and, when the weather was nice, graded papers on the porch. She was too busy to sit still for long, but she found a deeper satisfaction at Bunka Gakuin than she had felt perhaps anywhere else.

Moreover, the dark clouds that had dogged Tekkan since his return from Paris were lifting. Perhaps his teaching position at Keio had finally dispelled the humiliation he had always felt about his poor education. He lectured in tailored suits; he sported a pinkie ring. At forty-eight, he still turned heads, particularly among his female students, but—for once—Akiko didn't feel jealous. There was someone else on her mind.

火の山もおさへ波をも鎮むべし恋しきことをいかが すべきぞ
I must calm this mountain of fire, I must quiet these waves,
What shall I do with these feelings of love?

One fine spring day, Akiko stepped into the teacher's lounge between classes to pick up a notebook. Arishima Takeo, a Bunka Gakuin instructor, was standing at the window. Akiko had met him ten years earlier, at his wife's funeral. A respected novelist from a former samurai family, he had studied at Harvard in the United States. His wife's death left him with two small children. It had been a vulnerable time for Akiko as well, having just returned from the dream of Paris to a houseful of demanding children, debt, and a depressed husband. He had asked her to critique his eulogy, after which they had struck up a correspondence. When she began searching for literature teachers for Bunka Gakuin, he was a natural choice.

"Good morning, Mrs. Yosano." He had an aristocratic refinement that Tekkan lacked; on this morning, bathed in light from the window where he stood, holding a page in his book with one finger, he looked like a watercolor from the Louvre.

"Do call me Akiko." She bent to search the bookshelf.

"It's a beautiful day," he said. "Did you see? The roses are coming in early. With all this rain, they'll be blooming soon."

Akiko located the notebook and straightened. "Oh, I hope so. The girls planted some new bushes last fall, and I can't wait—" She startled as something brown flashed in front of her. A tiny bird had blundered in from the hallway. It somersaulted toward the window and slammed into the glass.

"Oh!" Akiko cried.

"Poor thing," Arishima said. "Stay still, and it won't be so frightened." He looked around, "I just need a cloth."

Akiko motioned to a folded wash towel on the table.

"Yes, excellent," he picked it up and approached the little sparrow who was flapping about in a daze on the floor.

"All right, sweet one," he crooned, opening the towel and sinking to his knees. "What happened, did you fly in the door, my dear?" He moved with unhurried conviction, lifting the towel and gently laying it over the bird. It stopped struggling immediately and went quiet. He continued his soothing words as he curved his hands tenderly around the lump.

"My dear, schoolhouses are not good places for birds. You should take your reading elsewhere." He looked at Akiko, gesturing with his head toward the window. "Do you think you could unlatch it?"

She had been rooted to her spot but hurried to the window then, pushed back the curtain and unhooked the latch. As she slid the window open, a breeze blew into the lounge, filling her lungs and arms. It carried the sound of girls' laughter from the garden. She felt a thrill as she stepped back. He leaned through the window and opened the towel. She watched as the sparrow, still stunned, wavered for a moment in the breeze.

"Don't let it fly back in," she whispered, and they crowded together to block the way inside. Suddenly, in a flash of speckled breast feathers, the sparrow burst into flight, disappearing in an instant into the trees.

They turned to congratulate each other and as their eyes met, Akiko caught her breath. She flushed, raised her hands to her face. The moment was concussive, a bird striking a window. Undeniable.

She took her notebook and hurried off to her next class, but the moment stayed in her mind. After that, she blushed when she passed him in the hallway. When her concentration wavered, she thought of him; he even visited her dreams. Angry at herself, she tried to push the thoughts away.

On her way home from school one day, as she stood waiting on the Ochanomizu train platform, she looked up from her book to see a group of ladies staring at her. She looked down at herself: she was wearing a flowered dress, red socks, European buckled shoes, and her favorite wide-brimmed French hat. She had cultivated a fondness for Western clothes during her time in Europe—she especially loved loose-fitting dresses with wide collars for her mature, ample body. They showed off more neck and a freer bosom than appropriate, but they were so comfortable. She must be an odd sight, but she cared less than ever what society ladies thought.

She knew something they didn't: she was almost finished with her *"New-New Tale of Genji"* commentary. She had improved her original translation and added detailed comments on sources, interpretations, and word choice. She was proud of the thick manuscript—more than a thousand handwritten pages. She kept it in a big wooden box in her study along with stacks of personal notes and reference books. Sometimes she opened the box simply to look at it. More than motherhood, writing was her life's joy.

It occurred to her then, standing on the train platform, that the precious manuscript was, in fact, alarmingly large. Vulnerable. What would she do if the house caught fire, or there was a flood? The children sometimes played in her study—what if they spilled ink on it or ripped the pages? There was only that one, irreplaceable copy.

For safekeeping, she should move it. Her office at Bunka Gakuin was locked and out of the way of any potential flooding from the Sumida River. The building was built of reinforced concrete, so it was safer from fire. Moreover, having it at school would make it easier for her to nip out to work on it between classes. With it there under lock and key, she would sleep better at night.

It was decided, then. She would move it this weekend.

XXVIII: THE DAY THE MOUNTAINS MOVED

1923, Akiko is forty-five
Tokyo

空にのみ規律残りて日の沈み廃墟の上に月のぼりきぬ

Order prevails only in the sky

The sun sinks into ruins

The moon rises from them

At 11:59 a.m. on September 1, 1923, Tekkan was fidgeting in the front hallway. His new linen suit was perfect for the hot, dry day. He was adjusting his straw boater hat in the mirror as he waited for Akiko, who was taking her time with her makeup. They were about to leave for a poetry event in Yokohama, and except for Hikaru (working in Kanagawa) and Shigeru (who had rented a room at Bunka Gakuin downtown), everyone was home. Four-year-old Fujiko was playing. Yatsuo and Nanasé, now enrolled at Bunka Gakuin, were home for summer break. Even the elementary school-aged children, Rin, Auguste, and Takeshi, were home for lunch, having been released from school early following the new semester ceremony.

There was a sudden crash and the house jerked sideways. For a long second no one moved as they tried to process what had happened. An accident out front? Did something fall from the sky? Then began a cacophonous chaos of swaying and toppling. Nanasé pushed Fujiko under the table and cried, "Earthquake!"

Akiko lurched into the sitting room from one direction and Tekkan, who had fallen hard against the hallway wall, staggered in from the other. Fujiko shrieked and struggled but Nanasé held her tight. A great tansu dresser rocked back and forth, then fell with a mighty crash, just missing the table where several of them were sheltering. Dishes, books, pots, and pans fell like hailstones.

Akiko crouched by the doorway and held onto the door jamb. It seemed for a moment that the shaking might slow, but then several wrenching jerks followed. Rin crawled across the floor toward her with a cushion. He put his arms around her and together they held it over their heads, leaning into the doorway as a light fixture swung crazily above them. Rin's lanky, bare legs jutted out to the side, and Akiko reached out to cover them with a futile hand.

"Mama!" cried Fujiko, and Akiko called for her to stay still. The remnants of lunch—half-filled soup bowls, bits of rice and fish bones, a pot of soy sauce—crashed to the floor. The cacophony of pots, pans, and dishes in the kitchen squawked like a flock of mad birds, accompanied by screams from the children and the maid. The butsudan shrine tipped over, a pot of ashes scattered. A pile of books fell, a ceramic pot toppled and smashed. Someone yelled that the piano in the front entry was moving across the floor.

When the shaking finally slowed, Tekkan barked, "Is everyone all right? Akiko!"

The air was filled with dust, and the ground swayed queasily. Takeshi's cries were shrill.

"Yes! Yes!" Akiko coughed. "Where's Takeshi?"

"Here! We're okay!" Yatsuo called from under the table. He was weeping in her arms.

Rin slowly relaxed his hold, and as he lowered the cushion, Akiko could see blood welling from a gash on his arm. She was trembling all over. Dust was thick in the air. Rin sneezed. Someone else coughed.

Tekkan stood in the doorway, rubbing the side of his head, surveying the damage. "Is anyone hurt?" he said again.

Overturned dishes covered the floor, and pools of tea and soy sauce spread among broken shards. New cracks spidered across the walls, and the ground was still gently swaying, but everyone seemed to be all right.

"Fire!" The maid's voice from the kitchen wrenched them into action.

Tekkan, followed closely by Rin, made for the kitchen, picking through the wreckage in bare feet.

"Everyone outside," Akiko said, her voice shrill. "Go out the front. Put something over your heads. The cushions."

Yatsuo went into the front hallway carrying Takeshi on her back, then turned back. "I can't! The piano!" It was blocking the door.

Smoke was leaking through the kitchen doorway, but Tekkan called, "It's all right." He coughed. "It's out. Come this way."

They followed him through the kitchen to the back door. In single file, they pushed past the maid, who stood frozen in the doorway holding her apron to her mouth. Akiko, who came last, took her arm and pulled her along.

Tekkan leaned down to pick up Fujiko as he emerged into the narrow back alley. He surveyed the chaos for a moment, then wobbled like a drunkard as he forged a path through the detritus. The sky was eerily dark, and the air was dense with dust and voices. Across the alley, a wall had collapsed, partially blocking their way. All that remained of the wall was a bamboo and wood skeleton grid, with clumps of clay and straw clinging to it. Akiko could see a woodstove and a pile of green onions on the packed earth floor, an unexpected glimpse into a neighbor's interrupted lunch.

Chickens squawked around her feet, and when she looked down, she saw the leg of one protruding from the rubble. It was still jerking. She shuddered and looked away, up to the line of her children with cushions on their heads. The older ones were carrying or holding the hands of the younger ones, and part of her was gladdened by it. She put an arm around the maid, who leaned into her.

They made for the embankment of the old castle moat against which their neighborhood was built. People were already gathering there: it had long been an evacuation spot, as it was safe from falling debris and provided visibility and water in case of fire.

Tekkan turned briefly to count faces before leading them up the embankment. Akiko counted, too—there were six children. Twenty-one-year-old Hikaru was probably safe in Kanagawa seventy kilometers to the south. Shigeru was at Bunka Gakuin downtown. Then she thought of her sent-out daughters—Sahoko, Uchiko, and Hélène—in the country outside Tokyo somewhere. She had no way of knowing their fate. *Of eleven children, five are beyond my reach*, she thought, and this time it was the maid who supported her when she stumbled.

Tekkan ordered the children to stay close. Under no circumstances was anyone to go into the house or inside any other building, or to wander off, without permission. Their biggest risk for now was falling debris during an aftershock. And fire.

At the top of the hill, in view of the river, Tekkan dropped his cushion and set down Fujiko, who clung to his leg. For a moment, his eyes met Akiko's. *What is to become of us now?* he seemed to be thinking, standing in his linen suit, his hair ruffling in the hot wind, one hand resting on Fujiko's head.

Akiko looked past him, across the moat, to where columns of smoke and flames climbed in the eastern sky and spread on the hot wind. Figures scuttled along the far embankment like insects; debris floated in great clumps downstream, and as Akiko looked, she saw that some of it was alive. A man floated by, clinging to what looked like part of a roof, then another person, swimming, then a dog, then a dead horse. *We must move from here, we must do something,* she thought, but she did not know where to go.

Think. Food, shelter, water. She eyed the river, hoping it would protect them from fire. There would be no sleeping in the house tonight, clearly.

Soon, she was on her way back to the house with the maid. They took turns standing guard while the other dashed in for necessities—jugs of water, a bag of rice, a pot, a box of eggs, two heads of cabbage, blankets, mosquito nets. On the embankment, Tekkan and Rin set to work creating a makeshift tent with burlap and bamboo poles, overlaid with mosquito netting, while eleven-year-old Auguste gathered kindling for a cook fire. As they worked, they glanced wordlessly at the sky. It grew darker, like a brooding storm. At the horizon orange flames arched from east to south.

The smoke thickened as the sun set, casting everything in an ominous, orange glow. When the wind shifted, floating embers and bits of paper flew in faces, leading to a chorus of coughs. Crows gathered along the river, picking through the debris. At one point, a confused rat went skittering helter-skelter through the crowd and practically across Akiko's lap. Soon everything was coated with ash, making smoke smudges under noses and tear tracks on dirty faces.

Akiko's gaze kept going eastward. Somewhere in that wall of smoke were Shigeru and Bunka Gakuin. And her manuscript. When paper floated down from the sky, she wanted to catch the bits to see if they were hers. Her gut told her that Shigeru was all right. Nothing ever held him down. But her manuscript—under lock and key in her office—had no legs. She imagined the building on fire, her office, and her box of papers in flames.

What kind of monster are you, thinking about your manuscript before your son? The voice inside her head made her skin prickle because she could not deny it.

At that moment, she felt a tiny hand in hers and looked down. It was Fujiko.

"Mama."

Akiko squeezed her hand and looked to the east again. This was divine retribution. Karma. She had never been religious, but today, karma fit. She had spent too much time on her writing and not enough time on her family. She had long known this, but the inferno drove it into her gut with the force of a wooden stake.

"Mama?" Fujiko was pulling her arm.

"Yes, yes," Akiko looked down at her youngest daughter. With a sigh, she knelt to her eye level. "What's wrong?"

"Are you crying?" asked Fujiko, her forehead knitted, eyes wide.

"Am I?" Akiko put her hand to her face and felt her wet, gritty cheeks. She wiped her dirty nose with the back of a sleeve. "It's nothing. I was just thinking that I haven't been a very good mama lately."

Fujiko looked serious. "You're a good mama."

At that moment, a fresh round of shouts pulled Akiko to her feet. Holding Fujiko by the hand, she watched as a wave rolled slowly up the river, dull and deathlike. It moved the river stupidly backwards, carrying a black wave of debris and bodies upstream. Dogs. Rats. Dead horses. Some people on the embankment couldn't look, others couldn't look away. One woman retched.

Fear and coughing kept Akiko awake most of the night. Cookfires dotted the embankment, and the river glowed red, reflecting the burning sky. Unable to sleep, people gathered in twos and threes to whisper and watch the horizon, looking ghoulish in the sickly light. Akiko prickled with worry as she leaned against a bag of rice, one arm over Auguste next to her, Fujiko's head in her lap.

She lost count of the aftershocks. It was like being on the homebound ship in 1912: after a while, the rocking became normal. Sometimes the movements were sharper, though, and periodically an injured building would collapse with a great crash.

The worst of the fires were in the direction of the Sumida River and downtown, still far away, but when the wind shifted partway through the night and blew toward them, Tekkan roused the children and readied them to run. He and a neighbor had worked out an escape plan, west toward Shinjuku and the Kanda River. If they got separated, they would meet at Shinjuku Station.

The Yosanos and their neighbors awoke the next day unscathed, but their eyes burned and their throats were raw. As the sun rose, fires still raged across the city, but the wind had shifted away again, none too soon.

A group of women approached Akiko for help in pooling resources and preparing communal meals, so she found an apron to tie over her travel clothes. They dragged pots from their houses, carried water in buckets from backyard wells, and built cooking fires. They rolled *onigiri* rice balls by the dozen and brewed pots of miso soup and tea for queuing neighbors. Akiko even scrounged enough sweet beans to make a few batches of sticky *o-hagi* rice balls, thinking wryly that her Surugaya training had come in handy after all. Sooty-faced strangers gratefully stood in line to take one ball each.

As she worked, she looked up from time to time at the horizon. She must have sighed because her neighbor Chié, standing next to her on the soup line said, "You have family over there?"

Akiko nodded. "Yes. My son is in college, he's staying in Kanda."

Chié nodded sympathetically, ladling miso soup as Akiko handed her bowls one at a time.

"I teach over there. Bunka Gakuin. My son rents a room on the campus." *My manuscript is there, too. A thousand pages.*

When they ran out of soup, Akiko told Tekkan that she would go with Chié to fetch more miso paste from the warehouse two blocks away. Chié had borrowed a pushcart so they wouldn't have to carry the barrel back.

"Be quick," he said. He was sitting on the embankment sharing a pipe with a neighbor. "Don't stay inside for long."

The two women walked down the slope. Chié was worried about her parents in Yokohama. She had heard that the tsunami had been bad there, and she had no way of knowing if they were safe. The telegraph office had collapsed. She'd gone to the post office, but it was closed, as was the bank. There was no money, and once the food on hand was gone, what would they do?

What, indeed? Akiko had a troop of hungry children. They probably had a day of rice left, and a little cash. Tekkan would wire Tenmin in Osaka as soon as the telegraph office opened and ask him to send Akiko's next Genji advance early. They reckoned they would need enough cash to get them through a week or two.

Chié and her husband, a miso wholesaler, shared what they had, hoping that government relief was on the way. The old stone warehouse on their property had an ice cellar in which rows of miso barrels were stored. Akiko stepped into the darkness of the warehouse behind Chié and, as her eyes adjusted, looked up nervously into the rafters. Was she imagining that the south wall leaned inward? Without comment, she followed Chié down the steps into the cool, dark cellar. Neither spoke. As quickly as they could, they rolled a barrel together up the ramp and out the doorway. They stopped in the entrance while their eyes readjusted to the light and caught their breath. They were both jumpy.

"Yosano-san? Yosano-san!" called a voice.

Akiko whirled around. About a half block away a woman, surrounded by six or seven children, was waving. Akiko stared for a moment, unsure. Then she walked toward them. They looked grubby and tired, covered in soot. The woman's face was streaked with ashy tears.

"Mitsué. Nishimura Mitsué," the woman said. It was Nishimura's wife and children, from Aya and Yuri, whom Akiko knew as students from Bunka Gakuin, down to the youngest, who was Fujiko's age. The two youngest held their mother's hands. Next to them was a wagon piled with belongings.

"Have you seen my son Shigeru?" Akiko blurted. The Nishimuras lived on the grounds of Bunka Gakuin.

"He hasn't come back?"

Akiko's stomach lurched. "No."

"No, we didn't see him, but I'm sure he's all right. There was time to get out before the fires. Please don't worry." *The fires? Don't worry? It has been almost twenty-four hours.*

"Where is your husband?" Akiko asked, fighting to regain her composure.

"He is at our country house in Shingu. But our house here is gone."

Chié came up behind Akiko with the pushcart. Akiko was trying to swallow the lump in her throat. "And the school?"

Mitsué shook her head sadly. "It was burning when we left. I doubt anything is left. But we are all right, at least." She was holding a child's hand, and she lifted it, a gesture of gratitude.

My manuscript must be gone, then. Akiko took a tremulous breath. "Have you anyplace to stay?"

"No," Mitsué whispered.

The shame in her voice gave Akiko a tiny stab of courage, so she grasped at it. "You must stay with us, then." Isaku's wife and children had nothing to be ashamed of. "Our house is safe. Tekkan says after today, we can move back in. We'll manage."

"Oh, we couldn't possibly—"

"Think nothing of it," she said firmly. One step at a time. Focus on what we can do in the moment. "Since we have the cart, why don't we cut through the backstreet to my house? We can pick up more bedding for tonight." She looked at Mitsué and the seven children with a frown. "I'm sorry, it will be tight, but it will have to do."

As they made their way down a side street toward the Yosano house—Akiko in the lead, followed by Chié, Mitsué, and the children—Mitsué said, "I haven't been able to send word to my husband. He must be panicked. I thought he might expect me to contact you, so that's why we came here. I did not expect you to take us in. I wouldn't presume—"

"We walked the whole way," one of her boys piped up as they rounded the corner to the Yosano house's alley entrance. "We were so—"

The ground lurched suddenly. Another aftershock, and a strong one.

"Cover your heads!" They pressed up against a wall as the buildings rattled like old bones, and Akiko pulled one of the children close, covering her head with an arm. Mitsué crouched next to her, pulling two children into her embrace. Roof tiles and bits of wood rained onto the ground around them. *Amazing, that there are still things left to fall.* Then there was a tremendous crash nearby, quite large, enough to make the ground shake. A building must have collapsed, but they could not see where it was. Dust and debris rose around them, and they covered their faces with their sleeves. They stumbled the rest of the way to the Yosano house, and after looking it over from the outside for signs of obvious damage, Akiko decided it was safe to dash in.

She came out seconds later with two blankets in her arms. "This is all we have," she said, setting them in the cart. "Let's get back; the others will be worried."

As the ragtag group climbed the embankment, with two carts now to push and pull, Akiko saw several things at once. She saw Shigeru standing with the other children, covered in ash. He looked all right, yet instinctively she knew something was wrong. They were all looking away from her, down the hill. Tekkan was missing.

"Shigeru!" Akiko cried, running toward them.

"*Mama!*" They all whirled at once. "*Mama!*" They ran toward her.

"What's wrong?!" she demanded, looking from face to face. "Where's Papa? Are you all right?"

"He went looking for you!" one of them said. "To the warehouse! It fell, just now, we saw it from here!" She had been in there only minutes ago. That's what collapsed, making the terrible sound. *He probably thinks I'm trapped.*

Akiko touched Shigeru's dirty face. "Stay here. I'll be right back," and she dashed off. She pushed past people, trying to run in her geta sandals over the uneven ground. She was still wearing her travel dress from the day before, but her legs and sockless feet were filthy.

Down the embankment she plunged, trying not to trip, around the corner to the road in front of Chié's warehouse. It had fallen forward into the street, blocking the way with stones, timbers, and broken masonry. Several people were gathered before it, and one or two of them were climbing on the collapsed roof. Then she heard Tekkan's hoarse voice. "Akiko!" He was on the roof, splayed on all fours on the slippery roof tiles, grabbing pieces of debris and casting them aside, digging downward. *Looking for her.* "Akiko!"

"I'm here!" Akiko called from below. "I'm here!"

Tekkan spun around, lost his balance, and slid several feet on his back before stopping. He sat up and stared at her for a moment, as though confirming. Then he pulled his knees up to his chin and hid his face in his hands.

"I'm all right!"

He didn't move, his head bowed, his hair white with dust. A man standing next to Akiko said, "Poor bastard. He thought he lost you."

XXIX: LIFE GOES ON

1923, Akiko is forty-five

十余年わが書きためし草稿の跡あるべしや学院の灰

Of ten-plus years' writing

You'd think something would remain

In the ashes of the school

They moved back inside on the third night. The old house absorbed eight Nishimuras, ten Yosanos, and two maids without complaint. They slept like eels in a box, in ragged lines, alternating head to toe and side to side, some in the hallway and some in the tiny back courtyard under the stars. They told their stories, again and again.

Shigeru's journey home from Bunka Gakuin had been an adventure. On a normal day, the walk home would have taken an hour, but with the chaos and confusion of impassable or unrecognizable streets, it had taken twenty-four. He had walked for a while, but as the fire grew, he had run. When night fell, he made his way under the orange-glowing sky, staying north and west of the advancing flames, going far out of his way and adding to his confusion. He had eventually found the house, but finding it empty, made his way to the embankment, where he recognized the piano. Someone had dragged it outside, and though it was tilting at an odd angle on the hill, he would have known it anywhere.

Mitsué and Akiko were working in the kitchen on the morning of the fourth day when they heard a voice calling outside. "Mitsué! Aya-chan!"

There was a scramble as the children tumbled over each other toward the door. "Papa!"

Mitsué and Akiko ran out with their aprons and dish towels to find a man standing at the door in a dirty cotton shirt and trousers. With several days of beard, Akiko might not have recognized him but for his familiar grin. It was Nishimura Isaku, looking dead tired but relieved.

In the crowded sitting room, with a cup of soup and crackers before him, he told them about his ordeal. Some of the children hung on their father's shoulders before going back to their play; the older ones lingered to listen.

As soon as news of the earthquake had reached him, he said, he had headed for Tokyo, but trains took him only as far as Yokohama. Railroad tracks were damaged; phones and telegraph lines were down. From there, he had hired a horse-drawn cart, fretting as it plodded slowly toward downtown Tokyo.

The driver would take him only to the edge of the fire perimeter at Iidabashi Bridge. Bunka Gakuin was another half-hour walk from there, deep in a moonscape of smoking ruins, dead horses, and ash-covered people, shuffling like wraiths.

"All I could recognize of Bunka Gakuin was the gate and the skeletons of trees from the garden," he said. "Our house was gone. I didn't know where you were," he said, looking at his wife. "I didn't know if you were alive or dead. There were bulletin boards with names on them, but yours weren't there. I looked under piles of rubble at the school. I looked everywhere. I called your name. Then, I made a sign." Everyone was looking at him now; even the little ones were silent. Three children stood in the doorway.

"I walked around with your names written on the sign. I asked people if they had seen you. There were so many other people doing the same thing, it was terrible." He ran a hand through his dusty hair. "Then I saw Hirano-san," meaning the poet Hirano Banri, a friend and *Myōjo* contributor. "He had seen you. He thought you were going to the Yosanos."

Mitsué nodded, her eyes lighting up. "Yes, we saw him! He lost his house, too."

Then he looked at Akiko. "The building with your office ..." he began. He knew about her manuscript.

She looked at him, waiting for confirmation. She could hear her pulse in her ears.

"I'm sorry," he said. "There is nothing left."

Akiko managed a smile and shook her head. She did not trust herself to speak, and anyway, what was there to say? She could not imagine starting over again. She would pay Tenmin back for his years of advances, God only knew how. She could work for free for Kanao, perhaps. What mattered was that the people had escaped, wasn't that right?

Tekkan shifted in his seat. She could feel him looking at her, but she couldn't look back. Isaku continued.

"It was fire, more than the earthquake, that destroyed downtown. An announcement on the board said that more than one hundred thousand people are probably dead; no one knows for sure. Half a million homes burnt to the ground. Three million people homeless. Most of Tokyo is a smoking pile of ashes. You are lucky here."

Lucky. It was true. Their house was habitable. There were no serious injuries. It had taken several nervous days, but she had heard from all her children: Hélène and Sahoko's families were safe; Sakurai had driven a wagon of vegetables through the ruins to share with them and other friends, and to assure them that Uchiko was unharmed. Hikaru visited from Kanagawa, making the trip by bus, bicycle, and on foot.

As was her way, Akiko spoke little of the lost manuscript. Instead, she rebuilt other parts of her life, leaving that one where it had fallen. *Tokyo Shimbun* approached her for poems to help others grieve, so she obliged. Writing was still easy.

焦げはてしピアノの骨の幾つをば見ん日なんども誰おもふべき

> *Someone loved this,*
> *I say to myself again and again,*
> *As I gaze at the bones of a charred piano*

Life went on. Twenty people, more than half of them children, living in a seven-room house, required patience and flexibility. "It's like living in a hive," said Tekkan, "everyone crawling over everyone else." There was beauty in it, though: the tumble and scrape of little bodies, giggles, arms, and heads of soft hair survived in a dark world that had swallowed up other, less important things.

Grandmothers blamed the earthquake on Onamazu, the giant catfish that thrashed in the mud deep underground to warn people when they had lost track of their priorities. Akiko did not believe such nonsense, but for weeks the black, whiskered fish stubbornly slimed in the back of her mind. *You are the monster,* it whispered, *not I. You think of yourself and leave your children to fend for themselves.*

I will do better, Akiko promised Onamazu as she wrote articles, mended clothes, washed dishes, and boiled rice. *I have wasted too much time in my Genji fantasies, ignoring my duties. I will be a better mama. I will make amends.*

Bunka Gakuin was rebuilt, and she was soon teaching again. Into the big trunk of grief and guilt she dragged behind her, along with the airplane baby, the infant Sun, memories of Tomiko, her sister Hana, and the dream of Arishima, she hid away the lost *Genji* manuscript. She wrote almost nothing about these things that were, even for a poet, too sad for words.

XXX: THE BETTER MAMA

1927-1930, Akiko turns fifty

母もまたしかく云ひけりその昔ななめに聞きし教の中に

All those things my mother told me

And me, only half-listening

It was time to bring the daughters home. This was Akiko's first decision as a "better mama," but she needed a larger house. Their rental in Kojimachi had been conveniently close to Bunka Gakuin, but it was too small. The front of the house was slightly below street level, so it never got much light, and a musician neighbor practiced for hours every day while Akiko was trying to concentrate.

Even before the earthquake, the influenza pandemic of 1918 had left Akiko pining for natural light and fresh air for the children. The flu had torn through Japan as it had the rest of the world—infecting millions and killing hundreds of thousands. The earthquake was the last straw.

She told Tekkan she wanted to live closer to farms where food could be had in an emergency. Tokyo was expanding rapidly, meaning that farms one year would be suburbs a decade later and downtown a decade after that. They seemed to be always moving outward, but the train lines kept pace, going faster and reaching farther every year. A new train station opened near the rebuilt Bunka Gakuin, making the prospect of life in a quiet suburb more practical. A friend told her about Ogikubo, a neighborhood on the western edge of town. They could finally afford to build a house big enough for everyone.

Akiko designed it with Isaku's help—roomy, two-stories, Western-style. A second, one-story building in back in the traditional style provided more bedrooms. A ladder leaned against the main house, leading to a wooden fire deck on the roof, patterned after the one Akiko remembered from her childhood. A small wooden teahouse, a fiftieth birthday present from her students, was erected in the garden.

She and Tekkan recklessly filled the remaining garden space with every flowering thing under the sun: cherries, plums, bougainvillea, maple, forsythia, dogwood, azalea, and hydrangea, and soon it was a chaotic, homey tangle. In the very back, a household garbage heap attracted crows, tanukis, cats, wild turkeys, and rats. A low stone fence encircled it all, and a wrought iron gate marked the front.

Akiko called Sahoko, Hélène, and Uchiko home in 1927 when construction was complete. At seventeen, Sahoko was not interested in starting over with the family that had rejected her. After a short stay, she officially changed her name to that of her foster family and said they needn't trouble themselves with her any further.

Twelve-year-old Hélène, quiet and sweet, adjusted to her new life at Ogikubo. It was sixteen-year-old Uchiko—smart and stubborn like her mother—who struggled.

"Yatsuo!" Akiko stood in the front parlor, one hand on her hip and another on her forehead as she thought through her to-do list.

"*Hai*!" Tall and slim in an A-line skirt and thick socks, Yatsuo appeared from the back. With her striking good looks, she reminded Akiko of Hana.

"Your sister Uchiko is coming today after school. Tell her whatever you think she needs to know, then bring her upstairs to me. I'll show her to her room."

"She's staying?"

"She's staying," Akiko answered, without further elaboration.

"Understood," said Yatsuo, and disappeared again. Her children knew not to express personal opinions or ask unnecessary questions.

Akiko wondered what Uchiko would think of this house. Like the garden outside, it was a sprawling, tangled mess. The entry was crowded with boxes of magazines and books, a line of shoes in varying sizes, a stand bristling with umbrellas, and a mirror on the wall. She had managed to keep the parlor nice—with framed Parisian prints, a sofa, two stuffed chairs with doilies on their backs, and the piano against a wall. Further into the house, rooms degenerated into disorder. Akiko had imagined Nishimura's stately French-style country house when she designed the Ogikubo house, but she had neither time nor temperament for decorating.

Still, it was home. The steamy aroma of cooking rice came from the kitchen, schoolbooks sat on the front table, and Tekkan's voice sounded from upstairs.

She dropped her hands to her side with an audible slap and climbed the stairs to join him.

About an hour later, the front door creaked open.

"Hello?" a soft voice called. Akiko froze, listening. She heard Yatsuo's voice answer downstairs.

"Uchiko? I'm Yatsuo. Mother told me to look for you."

"Yes, I remember you."

Yatsuo's briefing floated up from the hallway to Akiko's ears: *Get yourself up in the morning. Breakfast is laid out in the sitting room. We have daily chores; ask the maid. Mother and Father are working upstairs; Mother will show you to your bedroom. Do your homework. See that your clothes are clean and your futon is stowed away each morning. Mother and Father do not like noise, and they work late, so keep things quiet. Be on time for dinner because food disappears fast. My brothers are always hungry,* she added.

A moment later, Akiko heard stockinged feet on the stairs, then a tentative knock on the door. Tekkan took off his glasses and smiled as Uchiko came in. She was wearing her school uniform, but at sixteen, she was a young woman. She had Akiko's sturdy body and thick hair. Her eyes were dark and—it seemed to Akiko—brooding.

"I'm back," Uchiko said, as though she had only left for school that morning, then she blushed.

Akiko felt her blood pulse in her temples. The airplane baby kicked somewhere deep inside as she looked upon the colicky monster who had screamed and struggled in the hard months before Akiko sent her away. The twin who survived. *What would her sister have been like? Would we have gotten on?*

With few words, Akiko led Uchiko downstairs and across the wild garden, explaining that she would share a six-tatami-mat room with Reiko, a friend of Yatsuo's from school who was boarding with them. There were futons in the closet.

In the bedroom, Akiko turned to face her.

She blames me. I blame her. But really, no one is to blame.

They had not been alone together since Uchiko was a baby. There seemed to be no possibility of kindness or softness between them in this moment, though. Akiko could feel a protective shield rising around her, in case Uchiko started stabbing.

But Uchiko stood quietly, as though expecting something more. An explanation, perhaps. An apology. She crossed her arms in her school uniform, then uncrossed them. She took a step backward and kept her face hard.

"Where are your bags?" Akiko asked.

"I left one at the door. And my Ma—Mrs. Sakurai—is sending more."

Akiko flinched. "You've been living in the countryside a long time."

"All my life," Uchiko answered pointedly.

"I can hear it in your accent. Don't teach Fujiko to talk like a hick."

The girl's chin quivered.

"The maid will call you to dinner," Akiko said as she left the room.

Why am I so angry? Why does the sight of her fill me with despair?

One might think that a mother with many children would be all right if one child caused her pain. But one child can break a mother's heart forever.

Weeks went by, and Akiko—with a tight *Mainichi News* deadline, a trip to Kyushu, and the unexpected departure of a teacher from Bunka Gakuin—left Hélène and Uchiko to fend for themselves. They got themselves to and from school every day and showed up at the dinner table each night. If they had questions, they must have sought answers from their siblings because they did not come to her. Other than at dinner, she hardly saw them.

One afternoon at the end of the winter semester, Akiko noticed that the door to Uchiko and Reiko's room had been left open. She rarely went into the children's rooms, but the house was momentarily quiet. The children were at school. Reiko had probably left the door open as she carried her bags out on her way home for the spring holidays. Akiko hesitated, then went inside.

Futons were folded neatly against one wall, and under the window next to a cold hibachi and a pile of *zabuton* cushions was a low homework table stacked with books, folders, and notebooks. A first-place ribbon for a math contest lay next to a kanji dictionary and a historical atlas, a gift from Tsuné to Hikaru many years ago. She ran her hand along the atlas's embossed cover, then opened it, the binding crackling softly. There, tucked inside, was a folded piece of paper.

Akiko opened it. It was a half-finished letter from Uchiko to her foster parents. She looked once over her shoulder to ensure no one was around. Then she began to read.

... This is such a strange place, it feels like a boarding school, run by a headmistress. It does not feel like a home.

My parents work long hours and often travel or attend evening events, so sometimes a week will go by without me seeing them. No one talks much; it's quiet as a library most of the time.

When I get home in the afternoon, I take a snack from the shelf in the kitchen and go up to my room. We lock our doors, and Mother speaks through the door if she has something to discuss. Can you imagine?

My parents, if they are home, are often late for dinner. At such times I have witnessed a furtive feeding frenzy. Entire plates of food silently devoured by my brothers and sisters, then replenished by someone dashing into the kitchen. When our parents enter the room, they are greeted with full dishes and a row of innocent faces.

Akiko turned the thin sheet over, thinking, *we are not so oblivious as you think.*

I rather like Father; he speaks to us at dinner. To avoid trouble, my brothers and sisters excuse themselves from the table as soon as possible, but at least he smiles. The other day he made me laugh when Rin excused himself early; he said, 'Only barbarians don't drink tea after dinner!'

Mother barely speaks. If I pass her in the hallway, she looks away. The other day I saw her leaning against a pillar by herself, gazing out at the garden. I tiptoed past her. I suppose she inhabits a different world ...

Akiko put the letter back in the atlas. *Yes, I "inhabit a different world." It pays for your food. It holds this house together.*

At one time *The Tale of Genji* had peopled that world; it had nourished and comforted and kept her sane. *Genji* still lived inside her, of course; like a taproot, she reached subconsciously for him in her dreams. In her waking hours, though, she had shut that part of herself away. It had been a costly failure. A disastrous indulgence.

So, Uchiko liked her father better because he smiled? Akiko went out to the garden, thinking, *smiles were never mine to give.*

If she was silent much of the time, it was because speaking sapped her energy. Those of her children who had grown up with her understood this, and at the risk of further alienating Uchiko, she would not change for the sake of dinner conversation.

Akiko and Tekkan were now traveling regularly, leading poetry events and lecturing all around Japan and as far as Manchuria, courtesy of the South Manchuria Railway Company. Tekkan even ran for a Diet seat in a rural Kyoto district. Akiko begged him not to, but—hardly in a position to argue against acting on whims—accompanied him dutifully when he stumped in his district. He lost by a large margin, and though he wanted to run again, she and his friends talked him out of it.

They were both feeling their age. Tekkan's knees and lungs gave him trouble and she had a weak heart and high blood pressure. Yet they were as content as they had ever been. They were grandparents now. Tekkan had mellowed, and they were growing together over time, rather than apart. Sometimes he looked at her in a way that struck her dumb with sadness: a premonition of loss, a reminder that all things end.

She missed working on *Genji*. Sometimes she lectured on its chapters and poems, but when students asked whether she would reattempt a second translation, she recoiled. That was a pot better left with the lid on.

Hikaru had married Tenmin's daughter, knitting their families even closer together. Nanasé married Arishima Takeo's nephew, although Takeo did not live to see it. At nine years old, Fujiko, their youngest, was old enough to understand that Mother and Father had busy lives.

Uchiko was still a problem. Her simmering anger was a cookfire that spat and popped. A sense of entitlement burned in her that the other children did not share. She wanted to go to college, but money was hard earned and hard spent in the Yosano household. She would need to live on inner toughness and intelligence, not French literature.

Akiko recalled something her mother had said to her many years ago, when she was about Uchiko's age. After Tsuné's stroke, Akiko had spent many hours helping her mother eat and bathe, reading to her, sitting with her. It was, she realized now, the best time they ever had.

Tsuné had been sitting up that day next to the glowing hibachi, wrapped neck to toe in blankets. Akiko had been sitting nearby, reading aloud an article about kimono dyeing and weaving from *Ladies' Picture Book*.

The old woman spoke. One side of her mouth did not move, and as she tried to form words, spittle formed at the corner of her mouth. One eye drooped, and every now and then Akiko wiped the tear that welled up in it.

"That *Asanoha* pattern ... kimono beautiful on your sist—," she said slowly. "Your g-andmother ... bought the fab-ic ... for her."

"Yes ..." Akiko looked at the pretty geometric pattern in the magazine. She would have loved to have worn something like that as a child. "Why—" she hesitated, "why didn't you let me wear pretty things when I was a girl?"

"What?" Tsuné said, looking confused. "You did."

Akiko paused, unsure. "I did—?"

"You did wear p-etty things."

Akiko leaned forward to blot her mouth. "No, Mother, you made me wear boys' kimono and cut my hair short. Don't you remember?"

Tsuné shook her head. "Daughter. Too ... p-ide..ful. You ..." she gestured, "a-ways ... think of ... yo-self."

Akiko flushed. "I don't think it was prideful. I just wanted to be a *girl.*"

The old woman's speech faltered, but her eyes were clear. "Like air ... girls ... should be." She waved her hand as though clearing clouds. "Don't see her ... don't hear her ... but she—" She touched her head. "She *know.*" Then she reached out to tap Akiko on the knee, and held up her index finger, her eyes like bright beads in her dried persimmon face. "You, Sho ... do not ... know ... yo- place."

Looking back, Akiko knew that moments like these had made it possible for her to run away. Unlocked the box. If she had not met Tekkan, she would have found another reason to leave. She had not forgiven her mother, but she understood her better now. A girl was safer in obscurity, locked away; that is what her mother had believed.

Now Akiko had her own daughters. She had come to think that dressing like a plaything, tottering on tall geta like a geisha, was a kind of self-sabotage. If men found feminine weakness sexy, then girls would aspire to it. Why be self-sufficient when it was difficult and unfeminine? Her daughters should be able to take care of themselves. Uchiko should work so she did not have to rely on a man or the government for support. Akiko may have made a career of poetry, but she did not recommend it. She had foolishly spent more than a decade trying to create a *Tale of Genji* commentary. With her eighth-grade education, and as a woman, it had been folly—hubris—to think it would be accepted by the literary establishment, even if it had not been destroyed by fire.

As Akiko worried about Uchiko, Tsuné had worried about Akiko. She had suspected that her daughter's precociousness and pridefulness would spell trouble. She hadn't been wrong.

XXXI: DON'T SAY HER NAME

1935, Akiko is fifty-seven

わが命に百合からす羽の色にさきぬ 指さすところ星は消ぬべし

My lilies bloom the color of crows' wings
And where I point in the sky, stars go dark

The winter of 1935 hunched like a crow over Tokyo. Coal soot settled in bones and lungs. Freezing rain fell on wet snow, ice crusted the streets, and at night, telegraph wires sparkled in the lamplight. Belching taxicabs and buses—replacing rickshaws as the primary modes of city transport—roared by at all hours. The house in Ogikubo rang with coughs and sneezes.

Tekkan was fighting a head cold when he took a trip to meet former students at the Funabara hot spring resort in February. He drank until late with friends and hoped that the mineral waters would revive him but returned home sicker than before.

A week later, against Akiko's advice, he went hiking in the mountains with a poetry group. Akiko went along to keep an eye on him;

as they headed down the mountain in the drizzle, he leaned on her, flushed and feverish.

Over the next week, his cough began to sound like mud mixed with gravel, and his fever pitched and rolled like a long, hot wave. He lay on his mattress and moaned.

"This could be the death of me."

"Don't be silly," Akiko snapped, but that afternoon she called Hikaru from the telephone in the parlor.

"It sounds like pneumonia," said Hikaru, who was a medical assistant with the police department.

"He hates the hospital," Akiko said in a low voice. "He won't go."

"I'll call someone to look in on him," he said. "Don't worry, he'll be all right."

But she was worried. Pneumonia was a killer. As she hung the earpiece back on the wall, she leaned for a moment against it, remembering the emptiness when Tekkan had left her for Paris. And another time, when he had stormed out after an argument and not come home for a week. The memories chilled her, like descending into a cold cellar and feeling the spiderwebs and mold creep into her bones. For thirty-five years she had been knitted so tightly to him that separating now might kill her.

When Tekkan went to Paris—when she sent him away—she had learned she could not survive alone after all. To replenish her soul with new wine, she had to come out of her study sometimes. Tekkan understood this, but somehow, she had not learned the lesson. The earthquake had opened a crack in the ground at her feet into which Genji had fallen. She had wanted to follow him into the darkness, but Tekkan had pulled her back. Together, they had covered over the crack, tamped it down, and turned to other things: she had focused on being a good mama, a good wife, and in her writing, on social commentary, essays, and lectures. That was ten years ago. Wasn't she happier now?

Once, when they were sitting together in their teahouse, Tekkan brought up *The Tale of Genji* translation with her. It was time for her to get back to it, he said. It would go faster this time. It was all still in her head, and she had more time to work, with the children growing up and moving out.

No, she had said with daggers and shields. *Maybe later.*

But suddenly, time felt short.

Tekkan was combative when a doctor pulled up his undershirt to reveal his bony, feverish back and listened to his breathing.

Akiko saw the doctor to the door, where he quietly confirmed the pneumonia diagnosis and recommended that Tekkan be moved to the hospital. "Keio University Hospital is excellent. Sensei will feel at home there," he said, handing Akiko a prescription for aspirin, sulfonamides, and mercury.

A loud voice rasped from the bedroom. "I will not go. I want to die here. I want my wife to give me my last water."

"Your *last water*?" Akiko scolded him after the doctor had gone. "Don't get excited. You will be fine. Being in the hospital is better. I am no nurse."

When the taxi came the next morning for Tekkan, he had to be carried out on a litter.

For the next two weeks, Akiko stayed with him, dozing in a chair next to his hospital bed, one of a dozen in the Men's Infectious Disease Ward. She washed herself in the basement washroom and read aloud to him when his fever eased. Neither of them ate much, and there was little to talk about. The doctor was upbeat, but Tekkan's symptoms persisted.

He was needy. If she tiptoed away when he was dozing, his eyes would fly open. He pestered the nurse when Akiko was in the washroom. She held his hand, brittle and thin as a dead branch, and talked about relaunching *Myōjō*, planting more plum trees, and adding another room to the teahouse.

His skin took on the color of watery tea and his eyes sank deep into their sockets. He talked about his mother, memories of playing in the mountains with his brothers as a child, cutting his head after falling off the temple roof. He remembered his adventures in Korea, the mushrooms at Tsujino Inn, and the piano on the embankment after the earthquake. Akiko feared such stories. Long-suppressed secrets might come out in his feverish state, and there were things she did not want to hear.

One morning, as light changed the room from charcoal to speck-led *konnyaku* grey and Akiko dozed in a chair, he called to her.

"Are you awake?" It was a whisper; in the half-lit ward she could hear other whispers from other beds. There were coughs, too, and occasional moans. At the far end of the room near the door, the nurse was nodding off.

Akiko struggled to sit up.

"No, don't get up. I'm just thinking."

Akiko was already out of her chair though, so she took his hand.

He spoke quietly. "You must start Genji again."

Akiko let go and turned to the window, which looked across a narrow courtyard to a row of dingy windows in the next wing. It was foggy, and rust stains streaked the walls outside, running into patches of black mold close to the ground.

"No," she said.

"It's been more than ten years. And—" He strained to prop himself on his elbows. "Still, no one has translated it, only you. Others have done only parts of it! You're the only one who can do it again, and you're better. Write your commentary. People are *waiting* for it.

People would *buy* it." The sales instinct lurked inside him even now. She almost chuckled.

"No. I put you all through too much. And it came to nothing, while I ignored other things. I've been a poor mother. I couldn't even pay Tenmin and Kanao back."

They refused to take any money from her, and seeing them only brought the debacle back to mind. "It's too late to start again."

"You never used to talk like that," he said.

Tekkan's periods of wakefulness became less frequent. Half-asleep, his energy was spent breathing. Sometimes he rocked his head back and forth, dreamlike, or lifted a hand, then dropped it to his side as he fought for air. At times, he was delirious.

"You were hard on her!" he burst out once.

"Who?" asked Akiko. *I was hard on many people.*

A moment later, he was weeping. "I hit the children. I frightened them."

"There is nothing to forgive," Akiko said, and she meant it. He had always been mercurial, quick to lose his temper, but he also forgave quickly. Akiko was more even-tempered, but she held grudges.

There were many telegrams and visits from former students, *Myōjo* contributors, Bunka Gakuin staff, poets, and friends. Masako and Chino came, as did Tekkan's brother and sister; so did Kato-san, from *Mainichi Shimbun*. Several members of the Nishimura family stopped by; Tenmin came all the way from Osaka and visited with Kanao. Matsuoka Shoson, friend from their days in Paris, brought flowers.

Except for Sahoko, all the children came. Hikaru visited from Kanagawa. Yatsuo brought food. Nanasé came with the baby. On the day he graduated from Tokyo University School of Engineering, Auguste (who had changed his difficult name to Iku) brought his new diploma. Tekkan did not attempt to hide his pride: it was like a dream for a dying man, he said.

Then, late one evening, when the ward was quiet and the overhead lights were turned down, a secret found its way out.

Akiko was reading aloud; it was a new novel with a complicated plot that was hard to follow. The light from the tiny electric reading lamp was dim, and her eyes were tired. When she looked up from her reading, Tekkan was looking back at her like he had something to say, so she closed the book.

"I want to get better," he murmured, his lips cracked and dry.

She set the book on the nightstand. "You will. It's just taking a little longer. You're not as young as you used to be."

"I shouldn't have gone hiking." A smile hinted at the corners of his mouth.

Akiko pursed her lips. "I told you."

"If I don't get well—" he began.

"You will." A sudden spark of fear pushed her back in her seat. She took up the book again and looked for her page.

"Listen to me," he said. "If I don't get well—" he paused to breathe. "I want you to know—that—you are my wife. My only wife."

She tried to clear the lump in her throat. "Shall we read again?"

"I—" He began to cough, so she helped him turn on his side and blotted the phlegm that came from his mouth. It was flecked with blood. For a moment, he panted while she rubbed his shoulders and back. She hoped he would lose his train of thought.

He didn't. "I want to tell you. About her," he said when his breathing steadied.

"I don't want to know." After all these years, in this of all places, she didn't want to hear her name.

"Tomiko. I did love her. She loved me. You should know."

There it was. It could not be unsaid. Akiko's throat constricted further. *Second choice, after all.* She had betrayed her family, failed as daughter, writer, and mother, and now, it would seem, she had failed as a woman, too.

"But." He wasn't finished. "*You* are my wife. Mother of my children. Forgive me. I am weak."

Forgive you? In this moment? He had voiced the thing that had not been said for thirty years. What did he expect her to say? Suddenly, she wanted to hurt him back.

"I want you to know something, too," she blurted.

His face froze.

"I loved another man," Akiko said, and tears sprang to her eyes. *A husband can take a lover, but not a wife.*

"Arishima," he accused, and as she nodded, the tears started down her cheeks. She had been holding it for so long. Like breath, the pressure had become unbearable.

One day, not long after the incident with the sparrow, Akiko had been going over her notes in the staff lounge when Arishima appeared. He had a leatherbound notebook under one arm and a white flower in his lapel.

"Arishima-san, there you are," she said, brightening. "I need your help. Will there be time to go over my speech before the assembly? It's at ten-thirty."

He bowed, and with a lovely smile, came to look over her shoulder. "It sounds like a poem I just read. '*There will be time, there will be time* ...' Have you heard that one?" he sat next to her, and she felt warm. "It's rather new, by a chap named T.S. Eliot. He's at Oxford. American, I think. It's called 'The Love Song of J. Alfred Prufrock.' I saw it in a poetry magazine." He searched over the mess of papers and books on the table. "It was just here. May I read it to you?"

"I want to hear it, you know, but we don't have much—"

"Here it is," he said, finding the English language magazine and paging through it as she fidgeted. "Just a bit of it, not the whole thing, mind you, it's long." And he read in English:

Time for you and time for me
And time yet for a hundred indecisions
And for a hundred visions and revisions,
Before the taking of toast and tea

Hearing Arishima speak in English was like listening to music. She didn't understand the words, but she *felt* them.

And indeed, there will be time to wonder
"Do I dare?" and "Do I dare?"

She forgot about the school assembly. "What does it mean?"

"Do I dare?" he went on softly, "Do I dare disturb the universe?"

He was sitting so close to her that she could smell him—pipe tobacco, leather, and lavender water. He began translating for her, pointing at the English words on the page as he went.

When two other teachers came into the lounge, they set aside the poem and turned to her speech, but she was still trembling when she stood to address the student body an hour later. *Time for you and time for me? Do we dare?*

When Arishima's teaching contract ended later that year, he and Akiko resumed their old correspondence. During the day, Akiko thought about what she would write to him that night. Since they often discussed literature, it helped her prepare for lessons—or so she told herself. This was before the earthquake, and she had been busy with *Genji*, so she tested ideas on him.

Letter writing was an escape for her, and it seemed to ease his lone-
liness, too. He softened things about her that being married to Tekkan
had calloused. Even when she knew their friendship had crossed a
boundary, Akiko let her heart guide her pen, lacking the strength to
resist. He tucked a forget-me-not into a letter, and she sent him back
a pressed yellow *yamabuki* flower sprig.

They planned a summer trip to the beach—he would bring his
children, and she would bring Tekkan and her brood. There was
nothing wrong about it, Akiko told herself, no sneaking around.
They would walk on the sand and talk while the children played; they
would watch the sun go down and read aloud. He looked forward to
talking to her and Tekkan about philosophy, Christianity, human
rights, labor movements, and poetry. Her feelings would stay locked
in her heart. His passion was palpable, his ideas were new wine, and
she would drink.

But Tekkan snarled at the blue-blooded, college-educated dandy.
He must have suspected. When he made her cancel the beach plan and
declared that they would go to the mountains instead, she didn't speak
to him for a week. Alone in the mountain hotel bath in the evening,
she wept as though her heart would break.

She had been just over twenty years old when she met Tekkan, and
she had never given herself time—her circumstances hadn't allowed
it—to meet anyone else before committing to him. She knew herself
better now. Arishima appealed to her more mature, sophisticated side.
Her married life was gritty and tough, but she sometimes longed for
finer things. In Arishima, perhaps she saw something of her father.

He was a volatile man, though. When it became clear that she
would not leave Tekkan, he broke off his correspondence and began
an affair with another married woman. Less than a year before the
earthquake, he and his lover hanged themselves. The "love suicide" was
covered gratuitously in newspapers and magazines. As usual, Akiko

grieved privately—not for him, perhaps, but for that part of herself that loving him had nourished.

XXXII: A MAN IS LIKE A NAIL

1935, Akiko is fifty-seven

男をも灰の中より拾ひつる釘のたぐひに思ひなすこと

I have made up my mind:
A man is like a nail picked out of the ashes

Uchiko visited the hospital ward one day. She was dressed in her school uniform and carried a book bag. A bandage was wrapped around her head, a vestige of an injury she had suffered two months earlier when she fell down a staircase at her school. The injury had been serious enough that doctors had been unsure whether she would fully recover. She was made of the same sturdy stuff as her mother, though: she suffered from headaches and double vision; she wore glasses now, but she had returned to classes.

As she looked around the room, she wrinkled her nose and made a face—what did she smell? Cold miso soup, alcohol, and illness? Her eyes met Akiko's in silent acknowledgement, then she pulled up a chair next to her father, careful not to scrape it on the floor.

Uchiko and Tekkan had come to share a bond that Akiko envied. They had similar personalities—quick to anger, quick to laugh. Tekkan had once said that Uchiko had his mother's eyes. Was that why he doted on her? If she caught a cold, he brought her hot, sweet sake, and if she left for school without her scarf, he called after her with it. She always looked startled at such times, as though she did not expect warmth from her birth family. From Akiko's perspective, the last thing this coddled child needed was more coddling, but there it was.

As though sitting on opposite ends of a seesaw, Akiko stood up as Uchiko sat down. She retreated to the far side of a vacant bed, her leg brushing against something. She looked down and recoiled: this must be what Uchiko smelled. Visitors earlier that day had brought a fresh carp—its blood was a folk remedy for pneumonia—but the doctor had prohibited blood drinking. The fish was hanging by its tail now in a bloody bucket, forgotten, pushed partway under an empty bed.

Uchiko was looking intently at her father, who had opened his eyes. His breathing was shallow, but he stirred. She began to tell him about her day. When she paused, he said suddenly, "Uchiko, you must go to college."

Her eyes opened wide. She glanced sideways at Akiko, who quickly looked down at the floor. "I want to," she said softly. Other than Japan Women's University, higher education options for women were limited, but there were a few private post-secondary institutions. She wanted to study literature, but Akiko had resisted, and she controlled the family purse. Everyone in the household understood this.

He is saying this now, in front of us, so there can be no question what his wishes were, thought Akiko. *Damn him.* After almost thirty-five years of marriage, these were the man's tools. He wanted for his children what he had missed—a real education—but Akiko wasn't so sure. She had come to regard college as a privilege for rich girls with questionable value. She suspected that college would not have taught her more than life had, and though Yatsuo and Nanasé had attended post-secondary colleges, she was not convinced it was the right choice for Uchiko.

"You must go to college," Tekkan said again.

"I will, without fail," Uchiko whispered.

His eyes went to the bandage on her head. "You are smart, like your Mama."

"You've always been kind to me," she said as she got up to leave. She glanced pointedly at Akiko, then down at her father. "I'll be back soon."

A few evenings later, Shigeru and Hikaru urged Akiko to go home. *Sleep in your own bed tonight*, they said. *We'll stay with him.*

She hesitated. He was not so feverish tonight; there was color in his face. He was breathing easier. She did not want him to wake with her not there, but it *had* been a fortnight since she had slept at home or had a proper bath. Reluctantly, she gathered her things, and giving his hand a gentle squeeze, left with Fujiko.

A chilly wind was blowing as they walked home from the train station that March evening. Akiko pulled the collar of her jacket tight around her throat, lost in thought. Fujiko walked next to her, carrying a laundry-filled overnight bag. They were both quiet as they wove through the maze of narrow backstreets. Shops were closed for the evening, and except for the occasional electric streetlight, the roadway was dark. Akiko guided Fujiko by the elbow toward the side of the street instinctively, even though nothing more than the occasional bicycle passed them.

"Mama, what are you thinking about?" asked Fujiko. She was a lanky sixteen-year-old now, fast becoming a perceptive young woman and one of Akiko's trusted confidantes.

"Oh ... just thinking about something your father said."

"What was that?" Fujiko asked. "You know, he isn't making a lot of sense these days, so if he said something harsh—"

"No, it's not that. He said something like, '*you are my wife, my only wife, the mother of my children.*'"

"That doesn't sound so bad."

"Well, we were talking about the old days. I'm just trying to understand what he was getting at." This was going to be hard to explain without mentioning *her*. Fujiko knew nothing of Tomiko, and Akiko preferred to keep it that way. That was all long before she was born.

"Maybe," Fujiko slowed down, thinking hard. "Maybe he meant that you were always the most important person for him."

"I don't know. I try to make myself useful."

They were almost home. Down one more street and to the right, the metal gate protesting loudly as they cranked it open, then through the dark, overgrown garden, trying not to trip on the stones.

Because she had always feared that his heart did not belong to her, Akiko had ensured that Tekkan *needed* her. She made herself indispensable. She wrote beautiful poetry. Gave birth to his children. Earned money. Cleaned house. Managed the books. And when he reached for her at night, she gave herself to him.

"Mama! You know Papa cares for you. I don't think it's because you're *useful*." Fujiko followed her up the path to the door and waited on the step while she unlocked it. It was cold and dark inside. They slipped out of their shoes and hurried into the sitting room, flipping on the overhead light. The maid was out for the night.

Fujiko went into the kitchen to start hot water for tea. "Remember when you got sick last year at the *onsen*?"

Akiko was on her knees lighting the gas heater. Of course, she remembered. She had been lecturing at a hotel in Tochigi Prefecture. Fujiko had been in the audience—a lucky thing, it turned out. Akiko had been feeling ill; an odd pressure, like heartburn, had spread through her chest, into her shoulder, expanding outward. She remembered breaking into a sweat, leaning into the lectern and thinking that she needed to sit down.

Then she was on the floor with unfamiliar faces pressed over her. Someone put something vile under her nose. A buzzing in her ears made it hard to understand what people were saying, and no one would listen to her when she tried to speak. When she struggled to get up, hands pushed her back down. Even Fujiko wouldn't listen.

Her next memory was waking up in her hotel room with Fujiko and two nurses nearby. It must have been some hours later.

A heart attack, the doctor said. He ordered her to stay in bed for at least a week to recuperate. Akiko had been mortified. She wanted to get up, but she was not allowed.

"If we have to, we'll tie you down," the nurse had warned. They would not even let her get up to make a cup of tea, or have a smoke, or fold her clothes. Tekkan had rushed in on the next train, accompanied by Nanasé. Tenmin and a host of others sent telegrams, letters, flowers, and gifts in the following days. The incident was even written up in newspapers, to her horror.

Fujiko came in with two cups of tea and some rice crackers. She set them on the table and sat down, pulling the kotatsu quilt up to her armpits. "Mama, when that happened, you weren't useful at all, but Papa cared for you anyway."

Akiko was not in the mood for a teenager's lecture.

"Do you love Papa less because he is ill?" Fujiko pressed.

"Don't be ridiculous," Akiko snapped. Idleness was anathema to her. She thought of Tekkan's illness years ago when Tomiko was still alive. His fragility had made her want to protect him. Women carried the world on their shoulders, cleaned up the messes, protected their babies, got on with things. Others were loved in frailty, but not them.

Branches skittered along the roof that night as Akiko lay awake. She watched shadows move up the wall, buoyant in the color-drained night. Sleep was anywhere but in the room with her.

Eventually, she sat up and looked around at the familiar outline of boxes, books, magazines, receipts, and unopened mail that filled the room. Some of the piles were Tekkan's, including disorganized decades of poems, articles, and journals. A collection of unused ceramic pots sat in a corner. In the shadows she could make out dead flowers in a vase, teacups, ashtrays, a pile of cushions, and Tekkan's folded mattress. As a young child, Fujiko had been afraid to play in here because monsters had too many places to hide.

"You still have things to say, my love, don't you?" she said aloud, softly.

On an impulse, she leaned over to a pile of his notebooks and took the one on top. She knew vaguely what she was looking for: a letter from Tomiko, perhaps, or a journal entry that mentioned her. Instead, she found two poems in his hand that were not about Tomiko at all.

妻病めば我れ代わらんと思ふこそ 彼女も知らぬ心なりけれ
When my wife is ill,
I think it better if it were me;
She doesn't know this

人の屑われ代わり得ば 今死なん天の才なる妻の命に
My genius wife lies close to death;
Take my wretched life, not hers

The sound of the wind was closer now, like it had come into the room to look over her shoulder. She checked the notebook's date: he had written these poems last year when she was ill.

"*Genius wife*"? It sounded alien, like something that would be said about someone else. Would he really trade places with her? She remembered the look on his face when he arrived in her hotel room after the heart attack. When dinner had been brought to her on a tray, he had acted like a maid, making sure she had water, chopsticks, soy sauce. Where was the old Tiger Tekkan?

Stop fussing, she had said.

The soft breathing of the wind continued, and she looked up, half expecting to see him, but no one was there.

He wanted her to restart *The Tale of Genji*. She had been saying no for years; why change now? They didn't need the money anymore. It would be an emotionally exhausting endeavor. It would require years. It would take her away from other important things—like her children. They had been toddlers, then youths. Fujiko, her baby, was a young woman. She had grandchildren now, and she didn't want to miss their blossoming.

A *Genji* commentary, if she managed to complete it, would be picked apart mercilessly by so-called experts. They would remind her that she was an uneducated woman. There would be problems, mistakes, and academic disagreements. She frankly didn't need the grief.

She didn't need to do it for Kanao or Tenmin, or for her students, or even for Tekkan. Why *do* it? Who was it *for*?

She thought of the two babies she had lost. No one would ever have the chance to know them. How different each of her living children had turned out to be—Hikaru, with his quiet loyalty and work ethic, Shigeru, with his reckless charm, Fujiko, with her empathy. Even Uchiko, stubborn and smart. She had released each of them like fireflies, unique and flawed, to make their way in the world. Two had *almost* lived but now only she remembered them.

Akiko convulsed suddenly and made a strangled, stricken sound. She put her hand over her mouth, hoping she hadn't woken Fujiko in the next room, but grief came suddenly hard, as though it had broken loose after pounding unheeded inside her for years. *Those beautiful babies.* She moaned. She hiccoughed. She didn't remember their faces—in fact, she hadn't even *looked* at Uchiko's sister. Or named her. Liquid leaked from her nose onto her hands. So many mistakes, so much regret. She leaned her head on the table and let it come, dark as bilge, a viscous storm.

> *My genius wife lies close to death;*
> *Take my wretched life, not hers*

Do I dare? Do I dare disturb the universe?

If she didn't dare, someone else would translate Genji. They probably wouldn't do as well as her, because no one else knew it as she did. No one else loved it or dreamed about it as she had. No one else had put in the hours translating and interpreting it. No one else had lost it in an inferno.

Her first version was not her final word; she had learned so much since then. Could she yet pull it like a nail out of the ashes, was there time? Her name was Hō, after all: the Firebird, the Phoenix. If she *could* do it, after she was gone, people would say, *Yosano Akiko was the first person to translate the entirety of The Tale of Genji into modern Japanese. She was a woman, did you know? Like the author, Murasaki Shikibu, a thousand years ago.*

Only excuses remained. How many times had she chided her children: *If there is no dinner, do you care why? Of course not. You only care that you're hungry. You can't eat excuses.* Likewise, no one would miss what she didn't do. No one can use a thing that never gets made.

There was still time. She was quicker now. But time was not limitless. Some doors close, and do not reopen.

All right, then. She would bring it up with Tekkan in the morning.

It was barely seven a.m. when the telephone rang. It was the nurse. *His pulse is racing, about 120. You should come.* Akiko woke Fujiko and ordered her to dress quickly. She paced in the parlor as she waited, her hand cupped over her mouth, the clock ticking loudly in the hall. Silently, she scolded herself for leaving him. Then the phone rang again. It was Hikaru.

"Come quickly! His heart. Come now!"

Akiko slammed down the telephone. "Fujiko! Fujiko, now!"

She would never forget the long cab ride to the hospital that cold morning with Fujiko silent and pale next to her. It might have been faster to take the train, she fretted as the minutes ticked by and the cab pushed its way through the traffic, but she could not imagine walking to the station and waiting on a train platform.

They arrived in the ward at a half-run. Hikaru and Shigeru were standing by their father's bed, their faces white. His eyes were closed but his mouth was open slightly, and she could see his shallow panting.

"Just a few minutes ago he asked for you," Hikaru said, his eyes filled with fear.

"I'm here, Papa," Akiko said, touching his arm.

The others stood close, unable to look away as he struggled for air. She spoke to him and ran her hand up and down his arm. "You are wise and strong, you are a good man, a good man." She said anything that came to mind, because speaking to him would keep him here, on this side of death. "You are a father, a husband, a son, a poet ... we are here with you ... you have more to do. Please try for us. For me."

Shigeru grasped his ankle, thin under the sheet, and everyone breathed with him, in and out, in and out.

"Isn't there anything you can do?" Akiko asked, turning frantically to the nurse, who stood silent behind them. She shook her head. Akiko turned back again, and this time it was a command: "Stay here, old man. I have something to tell you."

But his breaths were coming less frequently. He was leaving her, leaving them all, and she couldn't stop him.

"Papa." Hikaru said. Someone else joined the group at the bedside. Akiko sensed it was Uchiko but did not look up, because at that moment Tekkan let out a long sigh.

Breathe, Akiko thought. She held her breath with him until she couldn't hold it anymore. Eventually, she had to breathe in, but he didn't.

For a long time, no one spoke; they kept waiting long after there was no more hope. Fujiko quietly put her face in her kerchief and turned away. The nurse noted on her clipboard: *Yosano "Tekkan" Hiroshi. Time of Death: 8:30 am, March 23, 1935. Cause: Heart failure. Age: 63.*

XXXIII: ONE POET

1935, At fifty-seven, Akiko is alone

筆硯煙草を子等は棺に入る名乗りがたかりわれを愛できと

The children put his inkstone and tobacco in his coffin

But it was me he loved

So, this is what it feels like. Thirty-five years of marriage extinguished like a guttering candle. Her children were there, but her partner was gone. As she stepped away from the hospital bed, she felt arms around her, guiding her to a chair.

When he had sailed away to Paris, he had come back. Now his ship had gone over the horizon, beyond all recall, and she was the sole custodian of their memories.

When she went home to Ogikubo, her children spoke quietly and touched her carefully, like unexploded ordinance. She was prohibited again from doing anything for herself—no getting up for cups of tea, no washing, no tidying. For the moment, she couldn't bear to write.

"Don't treat me like a temple relic," she grumbled as Fujiko helped her move aside piles of papers so she could sit down.

They let her walk about the house and garden by herself, but she could feel their eyes, watching her. *This is what it feels like to have outlived one's usefulness.*

She was standing with her garden clippers in her hand one day when Fujiko walked out and quietly asked her if she would like some lunch.

"If you think I am going to fall apart now that Papa is gone, you are mistaken."

Fujiko smiled. "I would never think that. I just wondered if you were hungry."

Akiko gazed beyond Fujiko's shoulder to the big old house she and Tekkan had built together. With just three children and a maid still living there, it felt too big, as though her marriage had taken up space.

The friendship they had nurtured was different from the passion of their early days. The star children would not recognize the homely pair they had become. As youths they had been striking and fragile as forget-me-nots; the old couple was beautiful and scarred, like old trees.

She missed their secret language and quips, things that no one else would understand, like his feet. They were always cold. She knitted thick socks for him, and on winter mornings he would wind a muffler around his neck, tuck his hands under his armpits and put his feet in her lap. She missed the way he babied his plum trees, digging around their roots every spring, trimming the branches, putting on his spectacles to examine the blossoms, never letting anyone else touch them.

She even missed his temper, which flared and then quickly burned itself out. Once, he had punched the kitchen door and broken a hole clear through it. Rin noticed that the hole was owl-shaped, and that you could look through it without being seen—a very handy thing. They never got around to fixing that owl hole; she had been furious at the time, but it made her smile when she looked at it now.

She missed his vanity—he dropped clothes all around the house and left his shoes in a mess by the doorway, but when he went outside, he always looked smart. He flirted with girls. His boxes of Cherry Brand cigarettes and unopened bottles of Sho-Chiku-Bai saké now sat untouched in the teahouse.

君を見し夢の話も自らに語る外なき朝つづくかな
Will mornings go on like this
Telling myself about the dream in which I saw you
Because there is no one else to tell

A tsunami of sympathy letters, flowers, and gifts washed over the Ogikubo house. More than fifteen hundred mourners turned out for the funeral, forming a line that stretched from the newly rebuilt assembly hall at Bunka Gakuin, through the gates, and down the street. Akiko, flanked by her children, received them with gratitude. Even Kōno, looking more like an old monk now than the hungry poet she remembered, made the trip from Sakai to honor his childhood friend. So many people had loved him. After all the years of overshadowing him, she was deeply grateful.

Death generates paperwork. Akiko filed forms at city hall, wrote hundreds of thank-you notes, and made dozens of decisions. Dispensing quickly with one particularly unpleasant task, she called Uchiko into her study.

"Papa is dead now," she said, looking up from her work.

Uchiko's face was pale, as though she had been dreading this moment.

Akiko got right to the point. "You must forget about college and find a job. You will make an excellent math teacher."

Uchiko waited for Akiko to say more. They stared each other down, waiting for the other to blink, like that day in the bedroom when Uchiko moved home. Akiko felt weary as she regarded her troublesome girl. The ghost of her twin sister hovered somewhere between them but Uchiko, with her mother's body and her grandmother's eyes, stood solid and alive.

"Understood," Uchiko said finally, when it became clear that there was no explanation coming. She turned and left, and a moment later a loud crash came from the hallway—something toppled with a swift kick.

Someday you'll understand, Akiko thought, but knew it wasn't true.

As soon as she could, Akiko started her last great project: a full *Tale of Genji* translation. She told others it was for Tekkan, or something to "get on with," to occupy her mind. But pulling out her Genji reference volumes and notes from long-unopened boxes, touching the pages, reading her old handwriting, she fell swiftly back in the arms of her lover the Shining Prince, drinking old wine that tasted new.

She tried working in the teahouse as she and Tekkan had done for years, but his memory was everywhere in it, so Fujiko and Rin made room in the main house and moved her books and writing desk there. The room had good light and a view of the garden and teahouse. It was on the main floor, as going up and down stairs had become difficult for her old heart. They put her favorite books on the shelves and chose a hanging scroll for the alcove. Rin moved the butsudan there too, and they set a photograph of Tekkan before it, with incense and a hand bell so she could call for him and he could watch over her.

She knew this was her last chance. The temple of human endeavor had been built mostly by men, but her pen was her hammer, ink was

her box of nails. She opened a new notebook, dipped her pen, and
started to write.

古ゆちからなしとしあやまちし乙女の末に今日われを置く

Today I take my place
among women,
daughter
of those who
from ancient ages
have stumbled,
believing they are powerless

(translated by Janine Beichman)

XXXIV: THE TODDLER'S GHOSTS

1937, Akiko is fifty-nine

筆とりて木枯らしの夜も向ひ居き木枯らしの秋も今一人書く

We worked at the same desk, brushes scribbling as the
autumn wind blew
Now the wind blows, but I write alone

"What wild grasses flower in spring, in the mountains up north in, say, Sendai or Niigata?" Akiko called from her study one afternoon about two years later. Uchiko, to whom the question was directed, came into the room holding a broom. She had finished a contract as a math teacher at a girls' school in Osaka recently and moved back to Tokyo. Akiko, looking to make amends, had found her a teaching position and invited her to move back into the Ogikubo house. Mostly for financial reasons, Uchiko had complied.

Akiko was kneeling at her writing table, facing the garden, head shrouded in smoke. Her notebook and a half-empty box of Shikishima cigarettes sat before her. "I've got a book on the shelf, *Flowers and*

Grasses of Japan. Get that down for me, would you?" Akiko's eyesight was poor these days, so she often called on her children for help—her two youngest, Takeshi and Fujiko, were still at home, and now Uchiko was, too.

Since her head injury, Uchiko's eyesight was not much better than her mother's. She retrieved the heavy book from the glass-fronted case and opened it, balancing it on one arm and adjusting her glasses.

"Well, yamabuki is a good one, those little yellow flowers," she said after a moment, turning the pages.

"Any purple ones? I'd like to use purple or blue."

"Lupine is lavender," Uchiko said, tracing her finger down the page, "Wisteria is blue, but it doesn't bloom in the mountains ... same with hydrangea; they aren't grasses anyways ... Oh! How about this: '*the* katakuri *is an 'ephemeral flower' because it blooms soft purple early in spring in the mountains, before the forest turns green, for a short time, and then dies back.*'"

"Katakuri," said Akiko. "I had forgotten about that. Well done."

Uchiko put the open book on the table in front of her mother and pointed to the illustration, then moved the ashtray under Akiko's hand, "Look out, ash is going to fall."

"Oh!" Akiko said. "Sorry."

"There are burn holes all over this table," Uchiko complained. "And in your clothes, too. I see them when I'm washing."

"I know. I know," Akiko flicked the long stub of ashes from her cigarette. "I must get through *Genji*. I'm getting there. Chapter twenty-three now, '*First Warbler.*' Almost halfway."

Uchiko walked to the door. "Was that it, then?"

"One more thing. I'm going to a poetry seminar at a resort in Izu next week, but Fujiko has other plans. Can you come with me?" Akiko did not like to travel alone since her heart attack.

Uchiko hesitated. When Fujiko was busy with exams or sports, Akiko expected Uchiko to step in, edit her work, escort her to lectures, and sleep by her side in hotel rooms.

"It would be a favor to me," Akiko offered. The fabric of their relationship had always been full of tears and snags, but she hoped it was not beyond repair.

Uchiko pursed her lips. "Of course."

The ocean breeze felt warm on their faces as mother and daughter stepped off the train in Atami, a seaside town on the Izu Peninsula. Akiko adored onsen spas, as they soothed her arthritic joints and loosened the muscles in her aching back. She hoped that Uchiko might enjoy the beach and a dip in the hot springs as well, and not see the trip as entirely onerous.

Their room had a veranda overlooking the ocean, and when they slid open the door, the air was noisy with squawking gulls and the rhythm of waves breaking on the rocks below. Uchiko made two cups of tea and brought them out to the veranda, where Akiko stood with a cigarette.

"Your father loved Atami," said Akiko, taking the cup from Uchiko. "We came here once when the kids were small—" She stopped.

"When was that?"

"Oh, I think I was pregnant with Hélène, so Yatsuo and Nanasé would have been eight or nine."

Pause. "So, I would have been about four."

"That's right," Akiko said. "I must get my hat. It's so bright." She went inside to fetch it, and Uchiko waited, tapping her fingers on the railing.

"You shouldn't smoke so much," Uchiko said as Akiko reemerged. They watched the waves, and Akiko sat down in the wooden patio chair.

Uchiko stood with her back to her mother, looking toward the ocean. "I would have been four when you were here. Living on the farm."

"The Sakurais were kind to you, we were fortunate." Mr. Sakurai was dead now, a victim of stomach cancer. He had been only thirty-six.

"They were. I was loved," Uchiko replied, an edge to her voice.

She knew what Uchiko meant. "We tried to provide for you." Akiko set down her teacup.

"You sent me magazines."

"We sent Sakurai-san money for years. We paid for your clothes and medicines."

"You wouldn't pay for my bicycle."

"Your what?"

"I needed a bicycle to get to school, remember?"

"Do you know how many bills we had to pay? We did our best."

"I was always an afterthought."

"That's not true," Akiko said. "When you got your concussion, I—"

"You visited me in the hospital. How selfless." Uchiko was staring so hard at a seagull that Akiko thought she might knock it from its perch on the telegraph wire.

This wasn't how Akiko wanted today to go. "When I saw you in the hospital, do you remember what I said to you?"

"No. I was barely conscious. I don't think I remembered my name."

Akiko nodded, taking a final puff before stubbing out her cigarette. "I suppose you're right. I told you about why I didn't want to redo the *Genji* translation. When I lost my manuscript in the earthquake, I thought it was—I don't know—divine retribution, for not taking better care of you and the others. For being selfish."

Uchiko was listening now.

"I know I haven't been a good mother to you."

"No," Uchiko said evenly, and turned around to face her mother. "Are you trying to apologize?"

"I'm trying to do better. I have more time now. It was hard before. I don't know if you can imagine what it was like for me."

Uchiko's hair, cut short in a bob, ruffled in the breeze, and the black tie on her sailor-style dress flapped as she regarded her mother, emotions competing on her face.

"You have always been prideful, Uchiko, if you could only—"

"So have you!" Her eyes filled with tears.

"We sent you away because we believed it was best for you." Akiko could feel her face flush. "I hope there is still time for us to—"

"I don't need a mother anymore," Uchiko said, her voice rising in pitch.

Akiko took a breath. "I don't know what I owe you. You're welcome to stay at Ogikubo as long as you want."

"I never felt wanted," Uchiko's voice was choked. "I didn't deserve how you treated me. It isn't my fault that—"

At that moment, a knock on the door announced their host, who had come to escort them to dinner. Uchiko hastily wiped her eyes, and Akiko got to her feet with a sigh.

At dawn the next morning, a breeze carried the thrum of ocean waves through the open veranda door to Akiko's ears. She opened her eyes and raised herself on one elbow. The sky was turning pink. Uchiko slept soundly next to her. She took her notebook and pencil and padded out to the veranda, twisting her greying hair around one wrist and laying it across her shoulder.

The air was warm, so she took a seat to wait for the sun, feeling like she had stepped into a theater as the curtain was about to rise. She had assigned overnight writing homework to her poetry retreat participants, so she herself could not arrive empty-handed.

It was hard to concentrate, though. *I never felt like you wanted me*, Uchiko had said. She thought of that old saying, *the toddler's ghosts linger one hundred years*. And what Akiko realized then, as the gulls wheeled dark against the waves tipped with pink and yellow, was that the wounds of childhood, like the slope of a nose or the brown of an eye, are written on our souls almost before we are born. She had unknowingly passed on what she had inherited from Tsuné, and what Tsuné had probably inherited from her mother before. Even if you want to stop the cycle, sometimes you can't.

XXXV: KINTSUGI

1939, Akiko is sixty-one

劫初より作りいとなむ殿堂にわれも黄金の釘一つ打つ

Long ago,

When the Great Hall was built,

I, too, drove a single, golden nail

The taxi inched through Tokyo traffic. Following the earthquake, rubble had been cleared and buildings hastily rebuilt, leaving little time for civic planners to widen thoroughfares for the thousands of automobiles and street cars that now shared them with pedestrians, horses, rickshaws, and bicycles. The noise was deafening, but Akiko did not hear it. Her plum-colored dress matched her plumed straw hat; she wore her silk stockings and leather shoes with straps— her best outfit. It was an important day: the publisher Kanao Bunendo was holding a reception to celebrate the publication of her *New-New-Translation Tale of Genji*.

It was not the press event that had accompanied her first translation in 1912. Times were hard, inflation was high, and Kanao had a limited advertising budget. Moreover, celebrity author Tanizaki Jun'ichiro had scooped them—*Chuo Koron* magazine had just started serial publication of his *Tale of Genji* translation.

Still, Akiko was feeling pleased, and happy to have Fujiko next to her. They were a great team, and Akiko was already thinking ahead to her next project. Some people had asked her to write a memoir, but that didn't interest her. *Only old people who have stopped living write memoirs*, she said. Rather, she wanted to write about *Tale of Genji* authorship. She was convinced that the last third of *Genji*, the final fifteen or so chapters, had been written not by Lady Murasaki Shikibu, but by Shikibu's daughter. The writing styles were different, down to the tanka poetry woven throughout the text. Shikibu could write better poetry, but her daughter wrote better prose.

She looked over at her own daughter, dressed in her best silk kimono, hair pulled back prettily against her head. She had Tekkan's long, thin face, and Chūsaburo's warmth.

Feeling her gaze, Fujiko turned to smile at her.

"These cab rides take forever, don't they?" Akiko complained pleasantly, shifting in her seat. "I'm not good at sitting for long periods anymore." She shook her head. "I'm not good at standing, for that matter. Everything hurts."

Fujiko patted her hand. "You're like one of those old *kintsugi* pots," she said. Kintsugi was the traditional method of mending cracked ceramics using gold or silver. "The beauty is in the mends, isn't that what they say?"

"Oh! I don't know about *that*," Akiko laughed. "I've looked in the mirror. My mends are not so beautiful."

"They aren't? I wonder," Fujiko replied as a streetcar clattered past. Akiko looked up at the faces in the windows. Some of them looked back: men in fedoras, school children, grandmothers. There were fifty stories in that one car.

"I wish your Papa was here," Akiko said softly.

"He would be proud of you," Fujiko answered, and Akiko hoped it was true.

They passed a temple whose old wooden gate loomed gaping. People streamed up the stone stairs and past the glaring *niō* statues like bees bringing pollen to a hive. Schoolgirls sat on the steps eating rice balls, and rickshaw drivers milled about, waiting for fares.

"Writing is harder than raising children," Akiko mused.

Fujiko snorted. "I doubt that!"

"No, I mean it. Children mostly raise themselves. But writing—" She shrugged. "You set your pen down and everything stops. Every word must be made. Even when you're finished and send the book off to the publisher, something always goes wrong. It's like sending a child to kindergarten. You don't know what will happen." Readers were always finding meaning in her poems she hadn't intended. Like her children, her poems were never really hers, fireflies in her hands.

The taxi was close to the venue now, and Akiko squeezed the purse in her lap which held her speech, her spectacles, a few yen, and a handkerchief.

"Would you have done anything differently, do you think?" Fujiko mused.

"What do you mean?"

"I don't know. I'm just wondering. Like, having eleven children?"

Thirteen, thought Akiko.

"Or running away from home like you did? Marrying Papa. Or other things ..."

"Other things?" Akiko felt the familiar clench in her stomach. She thought of the awkward child she had been, with close-cropped hair and dingy hanten jacket. She had grown into a naïve, passion-crazed girl who broke out of her box and betrayed her family. She had run away a second time in a fit of whimsy across the Siberian steppe to Europe. And she had run away a third time, from Genji, for a whole precious decade.

Twenty years she had spent in childbirth, doubled up, biting pillows as midwives pulled human beings from between her legs. She had lost some of them through exhaustion, illness, or neglect. She had bled enough to fill a house with chapped elbows and dirty laundry. She had launched them, sometimes before they were ready. Some perished, but most survived.

The queue of commitments and problems had never let her sleep. Somehow, she had kept her heart open. How else could she have written new poems day after day, year after year, that made her readers sigh? *For God's sake, what 'other things' must I atone for?*

"Oh, I don't know," said Fujiko, tracing the patterns on her kimono with a finger. "What you expected of all those 'new women'... like Hiratsuka Raichō?"

That privileged woman! thought Akiko. *She thought she understood better than me what it meant to be a woman.* Would she have said anything different to her? Not a word.

"You wrote that women aren't ready for the vote. Did you mean that?"

"Of course, I meant it. They are too stupid right now. They have been sleeping too long; they can't be self-righteous after just waking up. They've been coddled. First, they must learn."

"They need education?"

"Yes, Fujiko," Akiko said, momentarily exasperated, "but not just in school. It will take time." Everything she had ever created or tried to shape: her children, her students, her poems, flowers in her garden, and this new generation of women—she had to let them all go. Uchiko did not belong to her, as she had never belonged to her own mother.

They were pulling through the gates of Keio University. The vine-covered buildings were cluttered with bicycles and students—all men, of course; pedestrians pushed across the street before the cab and pressed in behind it. They lounged on the steps in hakama and Western clothes, some bent over books, others cavorting like children. Bulletin boards and walls were plastered with hand-painted political slogans. A premonition of trouble filled the air. If there was war, these boys would be sent to fight, and so would her own sons, to discard the lives she had suffered to give them, or to take them from other mothers' sons.

"No, I don't think I had a choice," she said finally. "I don't know what I could have done differently. I leave my writing and my children to the world."

Fujiko nodded, but she looked disappointed.

Akiko sighed. "Yes, Fujiko, I could have done better. I must have seemed unkind at times, but I—" She felt in her purse for her handkerchief.

"I'm sorry, I didn't mean—"

"I had to fight for every inch. I tried so hard." Her hand shook as she dabbed at her eyes. The cab stopped in front of the World Literature Building, but the driver sat motionless, giving them time.

"I know you did, Mama," Fujiko reached over and squeezed her hand. Now there were tears in her eyes, too. "You did well. I'm proud of you."

They looked at each other and, sniffling, tried to laugh, so the cab driver got out and opened the door for them. Stepping onto the crowded street filled with bicycles, cars, and people, Akiko looked up to see a young woman waiting for them on the sidewalk, a bouquet of flowers in her arms. She had a sturdy body and a strong chin, and her hair was pulled back in a neat bun. She was dressed in her best kimono.

"Congratulations," Uchiko said, stepping forward with a tentative smile, and Akiko reached out to take her arm, tears starting again. Together, the three women walked into the lecture hall.

PHOTO GALLERY

Akiko at about three, dressed as a boy, with her half-sisters Teru and Hana.
(Courtesy of Museum of Modern Japanese Literature)

Sakai Surugaya Confectionery on right with thread-making shop on left. Note
Western-style clock and shutters, acquired by Akiko's father Sōshichi.
(Courtesy of Sakai City Central Library Archive)

Yosano Tekkan circa 1900 (public domain image)

The Meiji-Era Hamadera Station building still stands. (Photo by the author)

Tomiko, kneeling, and Akiko (Courtesy of Yamakawa Tomiko Kinenkan)

The Sanmon Gate at Nanzenji Temple in Kyoto. Originally built in the 13th century, the current structure dates to 1628. (Photo by the author)

Tekkan and Akiko wedding portrait, October 1901
(Courtesy of the Museum of Modern Japanese Literature)

Tangled Hair cover (reprint) (courtesy of Yosano Akiko Club)

Akiko's personal copy of Tale of Genji (Courtesy of Kurama Temple, Kyoto)

Akiko in Western dress and wearing one of her beloved sun hats
(Courtesy of Bunka Gakuin Archive)

Tekkan and Akiko at their Ogikubo house, circa 1933
(Courtesy of Kurama Temple Archive)

REFERENCES

I wish to acknowledge the following direct quotations:

Chapter I: Firebird
Excerpt of Akiko's letter to Kōno Tetsunan is by Meredith McKinney, translator of Seiko Tanabe's *Thousand Strands of Black Hair* (*Sentsuji no Kurogami*), Thames River Press, 2012.

Chapter V: Poets on the Beach
"Waiting for you/My heart is filled with longing" is taken from *The Manyōshu, Nippon Gakujyutsu Shinkōkai translation*, Columbia University Press, 1965, p. 11-12.

Chapter VIII: Forget-Me-Nots
The Tale of Genji, by Murasaki Shikibu, translated by Edward Seidensticker, Charles E. Tuttle Company, 1976, vol. 1, p.58.

Chapter X: The Secret
This version of Ono no Komachi (c.825 – c.900)'s poem is a variation of the Jane Hirshfield and Mariko Aratani translation "Did he appear" on p. 3 of *The Ink Dark Moon: Love Poems by Ono no Komachi and Izumi Shikibu, Women of the Ancient Japanese Court* (NY: Vintage Classics, 1990).

Chapter XI: The First Escape
'Winter is best when it's fearfully cold', from *The Pillow Book* by Sei Shōnagon (966 – 1017 AD), translated by Meredith McKinney, Penguin Random House 2006.

Chapter XX: One Long Day and Two Decisions
The Tale of Genji, Seidensticker translation, Vol. 1, p.84.

Chapter XXIV: The City of Light
Letter from Vincent Van Gogh to his brother Theo, dated 23 or 24 September 1888, excerpted from the Van Gogh Letters online archive with permission of the Van Gogh Museum (https://vangoghletters.org/vg/letters/let686/letter.html).

Chapter XXXV: Kintsugi
"Today I take my place among women...", translated by Dr. Janine Beichman, "Yosano Akiko's Princess Saho and its Multiple Speakers" Waseda Rilas Journal No. 8, October 2020.

Note on Translations
In her writing, Akiko drew heavily from classical literature, particularly *The Tale of Genji*. As a result, her poetry can be challenging even for native speakers of Japanese. I could not hope to translate her words without considerable help. In most cases, I started with the original tanka and a modern Japanese language interpretation. I drew inspiration from English translations of her poems where I could find them. An exhaustive list of English and Japanese language sources would be too long to include here, but the bibliography below includes the most important ones. Detailed notes as well as other anecdotes for the truly curious can be found on my website at www.jeangordonkocienda.com.

BIBLIOGRAPHY

Works in English

Beichman, Janine. *Embracing the Firebird: Yosano Akiko and the Birth of the Female Voice in Modern Japanese Poetry*. Honolulu: University of Hawaii Press, 2002.

Hirshfield, Jane, trans., with Aratani, Mariko, *The Ink Dark Moon: Love Poems by Ono no Komachi and Izumi Shikibu, Women of the Ancient Court of Japan*, New York: Vintage Books, 1986.

Keene, Donald, ed. *Modern Japanese Literature*, New York: Grove Press, 1956.

Moers, Ellen. *Literary Women: The Great Writers*. New York: Anchor Press/Doubleday, 1977.

Murasaki Shikibu, *The Tale of Genji*. Trans. Edward G. Seidensticker. New York: Charles E. Tuttle Company, 1976.

Rowley, G. G., *Yosano Akiko and the Tale of Genji*. Ann Arbor: The University of Michigan, 2000.

Seiko, Tanabe. *A Thousand Strands of Black Hair*, translated by Meredith McKinney. London: Thames River Press, 2012.

Works in Japanese

Mori Fujiko, *Midaregami* [Tangled Hair], Rukkusha, 1967.

Mori Fujiko, *Yosano Hiroshi, Akiko no Sue Musume ga Tsumugu Chichi Haha no Omoide* [Yosano Hiroshi and Akiko's Last Child Weaves Memories of Her Mother and Father], Sakai City Museum, 2018.

Nagahata Michiko, *Hana no Ran* [A Chaos of Flowers], Bunshun Bunko 1992.

Naoki Kōjirō, *Yamakawa Tomiko to Yosano Akiko* [Yamakawa Tomiko and Yosano Akiko], Hanawa Shobō, 1996.

Ōta Noboru, *Yosano Hiroshi Akiko Ronkō* [Essays on Yosano Hiroshi and Akiko], Yagi Shoten 2013.

Tawara Machi, *Tawara Machi Yaku Midaregami* [Tangled Hair - Tawara Machi Translation] Kawade Shobo Shinsha 2018.

Ueda Hiroshi and Tomimura Shunzō, ed., *Yosano Akiko wo Manabu Hito no Tame ni* [For Those Who Study Yosano Akiko], Sekai Shisōsha 1995.

Watanabe Jun'ichi, *Kimi mo Kokuriko Ware mo Kokuriko: Yosano Tekkan Akiko Fusai no Shōgai* [You are a Coquelicot, I am a Coquelicot Too: The Lives of Yosano Tekkan and Akiko], Vols. 1 and 2, Bunshun Bunkō 1999.

Yosano Akiko, *Midaregami* [Tangled Hair].

-----------------. *Kokyo to Fubo* [My Hometown and My Parents], *Fujin Kōron* magazine, Vol.21 Issue 1, January 1936.

-----------------. *Watakushi no Oitachi* [My Upbringing], Iwanami Shoten, 2018.

----------------., Murasaki Shikibu, *Teihon Yosano Akiko Zenshū* [Yosano Akiko Complete Works (Japanese Edition)], Kodansha 1981.

----------------., Murasaki Shikibu, *Yosano Akiko Zenshū 138 Sakuhin 1 Satsu*, Yosano Akiko Zenshū Shuppan Iinkai, 2015 (Kindle Digital).

Yosano Hikaru, *Akiko to Hiroshi no Omoide* [Memories of Akiko and Tekkan], Shibunkaku Publishing 1991.

Yosano Uchiko, *Murasakigusa* [Purple Grass], Shintōsha 1967.

I would also like to acknowledge the Japanese language website Merry Diary. I have been unable to track down the author or website owner (https://merry1109.exblog.jp/i0/). Thank you, Merry, whoever you are!

GLOSSARY OF JAPANESE WORDS

adzuki (あずき): small, red beans boiled into a sweet paste, often used in Japanese confections

butsudan (仏壇): Buddhist altar which can be found in Japanese homes, used to pay respects to departed family members

chirimen (ちりめん): delicate, woven silk crepe characterized by its wrinkled texture

eboshi (烏帽子): black lacquered tall cap worn by court officials and royalty starting in the Heian Period (794-1185 AD)

fusuma (襖): sliding room divider covered with thick paper

furoshiki (風呂敷): square cloth for carrying personal items such as bathing items, books, or gifts

geta (下駄): wooden sandals; ubiquitous everyday footwear in pre-twentieth century Japan

haiku (俳句): 17-syllable poem with 5-7-5 syllable structure; a descendent of the 31-syllable *tanka*; popularized in the 17th century

hakama (袴): traditional trousers worn over special kimono, worn originally only by men, esp. in martial arts, but also in the Meiji Period (1868-1924) by female students *hanten* (半纏): quilted unisex jackets worn over kimono in cold weather

hi no yōjin (火の用心): literally, 'fire awareness'; chanted by neighborhood volunteers esp. in winter, to remind people to extinguish fires and turn off gas heaters before bed

irori (囲炉裏): open hearth in center of many Japanese farmhouses; common through the end of the Meiji Period (1868-1924)

*irasshaimase (*いらっしゃいませ): a welcoming salutation; also: *irasshaimase dōzo.*

itte kimasu, itte irrashai (A: 行ってきます ・ *B:* 行ってらっしゃ い): Polite salutation when one person leaves home. Departing person says, "I'm leaving but will be back," and person staying behind replies, "Go but come back."

kamado (釜戸): stove, heated with wood or coal fire, with a moveable pot; often used for cooking rice

kimono (着物): traditional Japanese garment

konnyaku (蒟蒻): grey-speckled, almost tasteless jelly-like food made from Asian yams; used in noodles and a plethora of other dishes

kotatsu (こたつ): low table with a heater underneath and covered with a quilt

koto (琴): thirteen-stringed zither-like musical instrument

manjū (まんじゅう) : sweet, dense, flour-based confection, often accompanied by bitter green tea; *usukawa manju* is a thin-skinned, softer variant

mochi (餅): sticky rice that has been pounded into a paste, used in confections and savory dishes

Myōjo (明星): literary magazine published by Tekkan's New Poetry Society between 1900 and 1908; *Myōjō* means 'bright star', or Venus

niō (仁王): wooden carved statues of muscular, glaring guardians positioned at the entrance to many Buddhist temples

Nōh (能): classical Japanese dramatic theater

obi (帯): wide fabric sashes worn over kimono

onigiri (おにぎり): triangular rice balls usually wrapped with nori seaweed

onsen (温泉): hot mineral spring resort

osenbei (お煎餅): savory rice crackers

seiza (正座): formal sitting posture; pelvis rests on knees and heels, back straight

sen (銭): A unit of Japanese currency. One sen was worth one-hundredth of a yen.

sensei (先生): teacher, master, or doctor; a respectful title

shakuhachi: a long, bamboo flute

shoji (障子) : sliding room dividers of wooden lattice covered with translucent rice-paper

takuan (たくあん): pickles made from giant daikon radishes

Taka Shimada (高島田) : traditional women's hairstyle with full bun and rounded sides

tanka (短歌): 31-syllable poem with 5-7-5-7-7 syllable structure; ancestor of the 17-syllable *haiku*; originating in Heian Period (794-1185 AD) royal courts

tansu (箪笥): wooden chest or cabinet

tanuki (狸): raccoon dog, common in Japan

tatami (畳): woven rice floor mats

ukiyo-e (浮世絵): woodblock prints and paintings popular in the seventeenth through twentieth centuries; literally, 'floating world pictures'

uta awase (歌合): poetry-composing contests popularized in the Heian Period, around the time that *The Tale of Genji* was written (eleventh century)

wasabi (山葵): a spicy condiment similar to strong horseradish, made from the root of the wasabi plant *washi* (和紙): rice paper, fibrous and often hand-made

yakimochi (やき餅): 1) glutinous mochi rice, grilled with sweet sauce; 2) jealousy

yōkan (羊羹): sweet confection of adzuki bean paste, gelatin, and sugar, often served in bars

yukata (浴衣): light cotton kimono for summer, worn by men and women especially after bathing

yūzen (友禅): dying technique used in washi paper and kimono fabric

zōri (草履): formal sandals worn with kimono, made of straw or fabric

YOSANO AKIKO FAMILY TREE

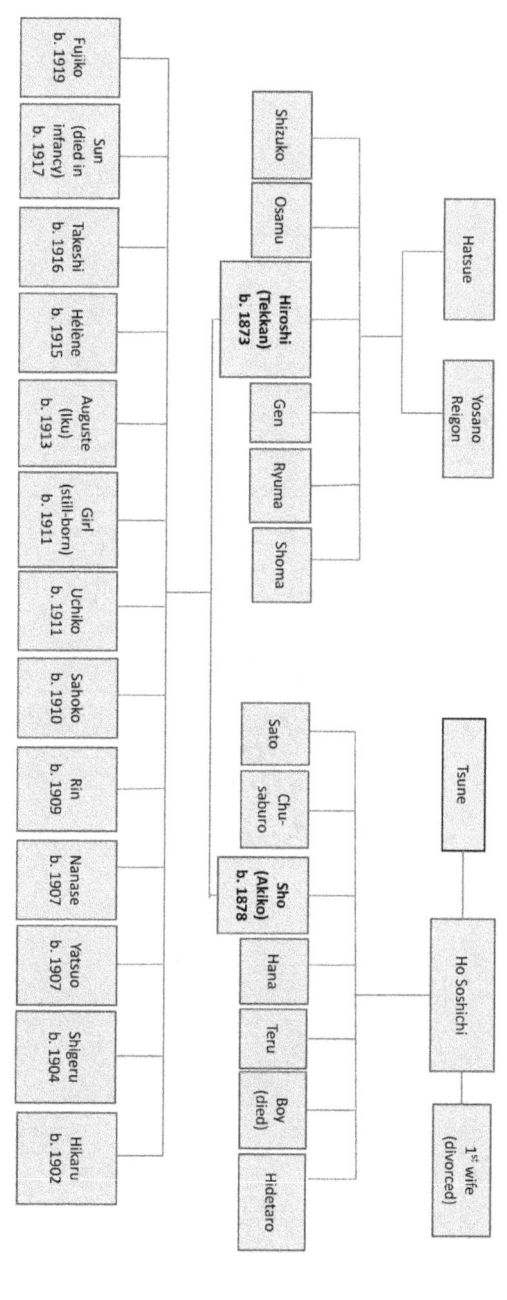

Enjoy more about
Girl in a Box: A Novel

Meet the Author
Check out author appearances
Explore special features

Photo by Halyna Astapova

ABOUT THE AUTHOR

JEAN GORDON KOCIENDA is a former Silicon Valley geopolitical risk analyst and intelligence officer. She holds a B.A. from Colgate University in English Literature and a M.A. from George Washington University in International Affairs. She taught English and studied Japanese language in Japan in the late 1980s and early 1990s, attending Kyoto University for one year as an auditing student.

She and her husband Ken live in Marin County, California, where they are supervised by Siamese cats Miso and Wasabi. She teaches English to refugees and recent immigrants and serves as President of the California Writers Club of Marin.

www.jeangordonkocienda.com

ACKNOWLEDGMENTS

It is a pleasure to thank the friends, experts, family members and unnecessarily-kind-people who helped bring this book to life. Here is an incomplete list:

For introducing me to Akiko back in 1994, George Washington University Professor Jonathan Chaves. For friendship, inspiration, and early thoughts on this book, Yoko Kato. Insight into Japanese culture and history, emotional support, walking tours of Akiko's old haunts, boxes of books during the pandemic, and translating help, Noriyo Tokuchi, Chizuru Shimizu, Hinako Hidaka Suurd, Mark Davis, Masayo Baillet, Kate Mashiko, and especially Makiko Hiraoka (who knows, as I do, that Suzuki-san is smiling down from heaven). For beautiful illustrations, Azusa Smith-Uchida and Mio Tanikawa.

Jess Elliott, Genevieve Kocienda, and Marie Craft were beta readers. Professional editors include Pamela Feinsilber, Laraine Herring, Liz Dee, and Suzy Vitello.

I received invaluable advice and encouragement from the Yosano Akiko Club of Sakai, particularly Tenri University Prof. Emeritus Noboru Ota, and Sakai City Cultural Representative Yukihiko Kotani. At Waseda University, thanks to Prof. G.G. Rowley for her generosity and kindness. Thank you April Eberhardt for introducing me to Sibylline Press. I was in good hands there.

Thanks to family and friends who cheered for me and 'liked' my social media posts, especially my son Calvin. Let me know if there is a greater feeling than having your child tell you he's proud of you. The California Writers Club of Marin was my local community of friends and cheerleaders.

Above all, thanks to my husband, Ken. He told me many times that the only way to become a writer is by writing. When my confidence wavered, his never did.

STUDY GUIDE QUESTIONS

1. Was Akiko a 'good mother'? How do you define one? Do you think mothers are under more pressure today than they were in Akiko's day?

2. Why do you think Akiko had so many children? Did she want them all? She didn't have access to modern birth control, but what other options did she have?

3. Do you think Uchiko forgave her mother in the end? Did Akiko deserve forgiveness? What was her greatest 'sin' with regard to Uchiko? What surprised you about Akiko's treatment of her daughters?

4. To bring Akiko's story to life, the author created fictional scenarios, dialogue, and setting. What do you think of historical novels that fictionalize a real person's life? What are the advantages and disadvantages of it?

5. Do you like 31-syllable tanka poetry, and why or why not? How is it different from haiku? How is it different from Western long-form poetry?

6. Akiko opposed government support for single mothers. What do you think of that?

7. Was Akiko a feminist? How do you define feminism?

Three Marys: A Wild Horses Mystery
BY ROBIN SOMERS

MYSTERY
400 Pages • Trade Paper • $21

ISBN: 9798897400102
Also available as an ebook and audiobook

When a serial killer strikes amid wildfires in Gold Country, crime reporter Eleanor Wooley races to uncover the truth before the Rodeo Queen becomes the next victim. Joined by Anishinaabe guide Leonard Parker, she faces danger, loss, and renewal in a community where the wild land and its people are bound by fire, fear, and hope.

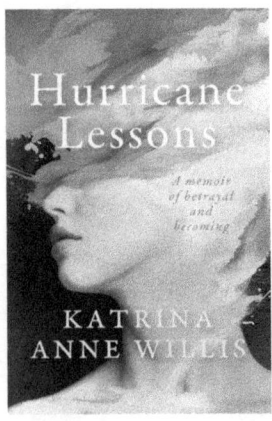

Hurricane Lessons: A Memoir
BY KATRINA WILLIS

MEMOIR
256 Pages • Trade Paper • $19
ISBN: 9798897400140
Also available as an ebook and audiobook

When 46-year-old Katrina falls for her female Pilates instructor, she's forced to confront the truth about her sexuality and the cracks in her decades-long marriage. As lies, manipulation, and abuse spiral out of control, she must decide whether surviving the storm means saving her marriage—or herself.

Griftopia: A Novel
By Suzy Vitello

FICTION

394 Pages • Trade Paper • $21
ISBN: 9798897400164
Also available as an ebook and audiobook

Orphaned sisters Pearl and Scarlett
Freischin, each reeling from scandal and
loss, must find a way to survive as their
fractured family teeters on the edge of ruin.
Desperate and nearly destitute, they turn to
a string of dubious online schemes, expos-
ing the darkly comic underbelly of modern
hustle culture.

Last Summer at Feather River: A Novel
By Karen Nelson

FICTION

304 Pages • Trade Paper • $20
ISBN: 9798897400188
Also available as an ebook and audiobook

Ten years after a tragic accident closed
her family's beloved Camp Feather River,
Brooke returns to care for her grandfather
and confront the past she's long avoided. As
buried secrets surface, she begins to suspect
that the so-called accident was something
far more sinister.

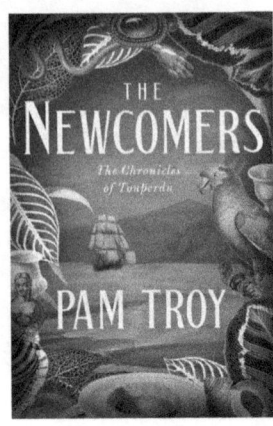

The Newcomers: The Chronicles of Touperdu, Book I

By Pam Troy

FANTASY

472 Pages • Trade Paper • $22

ISBN: 9798897400089

Also available as an ebook and audiobook

In 1880, two immigrant families—a Creole chef seeking peace and a matriarch of witches craving freedom—journey to the mysterious Isle of Touperdu, hoping for a fresh start. But as they soon discover, the island's promise of refuge may be an illusion, forcing them to confront what they're willing to sacrifice to belong.

Sibylline Press is proud to publish the brilliant work of women authors over 50. We are a woman-owned publishing company and, like our authors, represent women of a certain age.